SUMMER REIGN

C.D. BUSHROE

PublishAmerica
Baltimore

ISBN: 1-60836-640-5
PUBLISHED BY PUBLISHAMERICA, LLLP
www.publishamerica.com
Baltimore

Printed in the United States of America

Terror is not a byproduct
Of the infliction of pain.
Rather, it is born in those
Moments anticipating pain.

C.D. Bushroe

ONE

Judge Martin Abraham Gregg slowly opened his eyes and surveyed his surroundings. He was in serious trouble and he knew it. The last thing he'd remembered before losing consciousness was a rag clamped over his mouth and nose, the smell of chloroform, and a voice that was ice on his spine, whispering,

"Soon you will be bathed in the purifying waters of terror and agony. You *will* know the depths of anguish in that moment when sanity takes flight and then, as the last breath flees your shattered body, the Lord of Hell will come to claim your soul. Sleep now. When you awake, *we begin.*"

Now, as he lay on a small cot in the dimly lit room he assumed was his prison, clad only in his underwear, a polo shirt, and chino pants, Gregg was recalling those words and fighting off the tsunami of fear that was washing over him. It was abundantly clear that he was in the clutches of a madman; a madman who intended to brutalize and murder him. The reasons for this animus were not, however, so clear and were it not for the urgency of his situation, he would have attempted to determine why this person wanted to harm him. But, the simple fact was that contemplating his predicament was pointless because he would very soon be dead and the reasons why would be academic.

A bone chilling terror spread through him at the realization that even sooner he would very likely be subjected to pain so visceral as to literally wrench the screams from his tortured body. Sheer panic threatened to send Gregg over the edge, causing him to abruptly sit up and grasp his legs in an effort to steady the tremors that owned him. His captor would be coming for him and Gregg had to be in control when the s.o.b. did.

I have to remain calm. Have to be ready in case I get a shot at this bastard.

Taking stock of his surroundings, Gregg noticed that the room was about 10' square and 9' high. Save for the cot there was no furniture. In fact there was nothing in the windowless room that could be utilized as a weapon. No place to hide and take his adversary by surprise when he entered the cell door. The steel door was securely locked. The ceiling bulb was covered with a heavy wire grate, not that he could reach it anyway. The cot was bolted to the concrete floor and was bare except for a dirty, thin mattress. No help there. Lifting up the mattress he felt a momentary surge of hopefulness at the sight of several long steel wires forming the bed of the cot.

Yes! A weapon. Make a hell of a garrote.

But getting one off was easier said than done. They were thin and sharp and they were firmly anchored to the cot. Gregg pulled the mattress onto the floor, sat down beside the frame, grabbed onto one of the wires with both hands, and began to work it rapidly in a back and forth motion. After slicing his fingers open in two places, he took off his undershirt and tore it into strips, wrapped his hands and went back to work. He could feel the wire heating up as the friction weakened it. When the wire finally broke he went to work in an area about three feet away from the break. Five minutes later he had his garrote. He placed the mattress back on the cot, stuffed the remainder of his undershirt under the mattress, put his polo shirt back on, and curled up on the cot, feigning sleep. Now he was as ready as he could be for whatever was to come. He was feeling a bit stronger. He thanked God for giving him the time to prepare a defense against the attack that was sure to come, but fear still clawed at him due, in part, to the fact that he was out of his depth here and he knew it. He was 55 years old, a shade under 5'10" tall, and 186 lbs of muscle going to fat since he quit working out six months ago. He hadn't the slightest idea what fighting for your life entailed. He'd never been a fighter, not in school or afterward, and the idea of being in a fight that would decide if he lived or died scared the hell out of him. The simple truth was he would soon be tested as he had never been before, and he didn't have a clue as to how to meet that challenge. Worse, he feared he wouldn't have the courage for whatever he would be called on to do to survive.

As he had thought, the wait was not long. Fifteen minutes had passed when Gregg heard the metallic click of a key being inserted in the door He stiffened in anticipation. The door swung slowly open. Through narrowed eyelids Gregg saw a figure move into the room and stop just inside the doorway.

His heart nearly blew through his chest. The guy was huge! Framed in the backlit doorway he was the supreme predator. The garrote in Gregg's hands suddenly seemed ridiculous, a shoestring with no shoe to tie. A groan of despair fought to escape from within him. As the figure moved forward into the room, his head tilted slightly up and began slowly swiveling. A thrill of horror passed through Gregg.

What the hell? He's sniffing the air. Sweet Jesus! Son of a bitch is trying to pick up my scent, like I'm some animal.

A sudden fury welled up within Gregg and the urge to spring from the cot at his tormentor was overpowering. But he suppressed it and smiled inwardly.

Just let him get a little closer. I'll wrap this around your neck you sick schmuck, and then we'll see whose stink we smell when I cut off your freaking head. A little bit closer, a little more...NOW!

With a roar intended to bolster his courage as much as to surprise and freeze his adversary, Gregg came off of the cot with an energy he didn't know he possessed, looping the garrote in the air towards his enemy. He could see that he had surprised the bastard. As Gregg brought the noose down to encircle the man's head his attacker did indeed freeze in confusion as he had hoped.

I did it. He's in sho...

A searing pain speared Gregg's side! He was catapulted backwards and up into the air, then crashed to the floor, writhing in agony and completely incapacitated.

Then the Empire State building fell on him. Just before he blacked out from the blow to his head, a memory buried in his subconscious surfaced and jolted him to a startling realization.

This is the second time tonight I've been electrocuted!

Gregg's hands still grasped the garrote, its superheated metal smoking and burning the flesh on his hands.

The man stood there looking down at the body quizzically, a small cattle prod in one hand, a sap in the other.

"Well, now." He mused aloud. "That was a silly thing to do. It does make my job a bit more difficult though. Too bad. I'll just have to wake you again later, though I'm sure you'll wish I hadn't when you see what

I've arranged for you. Ah well, I would like to oblige you, really I would, but it just wouldn't do for you to miss the evening's events. This has been arranged just for *you* after all, and one *should* be awake for one's own trial, especially when it's a capital case. After all, a person who is about to be executed *should* know why.

Two

Detective Lieutenant Morgan Jeffords stepped off the curb and angled across Vine Street, heading for the police station on Second Avenue. He was smiling and it was clear that he was observing his surroundings with pleasure as he walked along. It was a warm, cloudless May morning. The pavement was still splotched with the remnants of the rain that had fallen the night before. The full sunlight lit up the droplets of rain, bejeweling the buildings and grounds of the city's business district.

This was his home, the only home he'd ever known and it had grown up as he was growing up. In 1926, when he was four, Deliverance was a small, rural Oregon town of 850 people, 30 miles southwest of Portland. The community consisted mostly of fruit farmers, as his father had been before dying of pancreatic cancer that year. A year later, Donnelly Pharmaceuticals, a major agricultural chemical corporation, built a huge research and development complex right next to the town and everything changed. Over the next 35 years the population skyrocketed to 55,000, and the economy shifted from agricultural blue collar to mostly scientific white collar. Now, in 1961, Deliverance had become the model for other cities in the state; boasting excellent schools, a relatively low crime rate for a city that size, and abundant economic opportunity. The low crime rate was due, in part, to Morgan's joining the police force in 1952.

He had gone into the police academy in Portland right after completing high school in 1940 and had become a street cop there a year later, having been declared 4F for the military because of flat feet. It took him a total of six months to work his way into Portland's homicide division as a fledgling detective.

After a 10 year stint in homicide in Portland, during which time he'd been promoted to the rank of Detective Sergeant and received two Combat Crosses and a Medal of Honor, he decided in 1952 to take a position with the Deliverance Police Department. He longed to be back in Deliverance and the frail health of Agnes, his mother, was the clincher that convinced him to make the move. As an only child, he knew the care of his mother rested solely with him.

He was welcomed with open arms, started at his Portland rank, complete with gold shield, and was placed in Homicide, a request that was part of the deal to come to Deliverance.

Now, 9 years later, he was proud to be considered by the city's law enforcement officials as its best detective; an honor he justly deserved.

Standing 6' tall, Morgan had jet black hair flecked with gray that bespoke his 39 years. He weighed 195 lbs. athletically distributed on a wiry, muscular frame. Magnetic indigo eyes set deep in a weathered, rugged face, and a full, neatly trimmed moustache the color of smoke completed the picture of a man who certainly cut an imposing figure. The Levi Strauss button fly jeans, Woolrich charcoal chamois shirt, and Browning bison hide hiking boots he was now wearing only added to his charismatic appearance.

Over the past 9 years he had compiled an impressive arrest record and a reputation for running to ground and taking down the most elusive of criminals. That record had earned Morgan the title "Bulldog" from his fellow officers. Once he took on a case and sunk his teeth into it, he gnawed on it like a dog with a bone, worrying at the progress of the investigation until he'd secured all that was needed to collar the perp and sew up a conviction for the D.A. He was without a doubt a highly intelligent, competent, and successful police officer. The citizens of Deliverance were aware of this from articles printed about him in the local newspaper, *The Centurion.*

However, the furthest thing from Morgan's mind on this beautiful morning was being a good cop. He was heading to the station for the sole purpose of confirming with Captain Harold Byrd, the commander of the Deliverance Police Department, his plan to take some leave time. Morgan had made it known that he would be heading to Jackson Hole, Wyoming for a week of hiking, cycling, and fishing. That his destination was a place he'd not visited in the nearly six years since his wife had died, raised eyebrows around town and brought hopeful looks from the people closest to him.

Within two years of coming to Deliverance Morgan had met, courted, and married Senna Ireland, a beautiful raven haired, cobalt blue eyed college professor. She had transferred to Judson College in Deliverance from the University of Wisconsin in Madison a year after Morgan had returned to Deliverance. It was obvious to friends and family alike that it was love at first sight for both of them. A year after the marriage Senna was pregnant and Morgan was ecstatic.

Then, only days before Christmas of 1955, Senna was shot and killed in the course of a robbery at a bank where she had gone to cash a check. She was about to enter the bank when a man burst through the door wildly firing a .357 magnum revolver. A stray bullet crashed into her, entering her stomach and causing a massive hemorrhage. Both Senna and the baby died. It was later discovered that the bank robber had panicked when a security guard inside the bank came out of a restroom and surprised him. A gun battle had then ensued, culminating with the robber attempting to flee. Senna was only 29 at the time of her death.

The horrific death of his wife and unborn child crushed Morgan. For weeks he was little better than comatose, refusing to eat and unable to sleep. He sat in their apartment all day, staring at the walls, his countenance gaunt and sallow, all the while refusing to communicate with anyone, even his mother. At one point, noticing the febrile glow on his face, his mother, fearing for her son's sanity, broke down and began sobbing inconsolably. Morgan's reaction was immediate. He came out of his stupor, went to her, put his arms around her, and began to whisper softly in her ear.

"It's alright Momma, I'll be okay. I just need to find a light at the end of this black hole I've been dropped into. You be strong for me now and I'll be okay."

Slowly, with the help of her love and caring ways he began to come back to all the people who loved him and by summer he was back on the job. He never talked about the murders after that and he never talked about Senna or the child. The man responsible for their deaths was convicted of double homicide and sentenced to two consecutive life sentences without the possibility of parole. As time went by Morgan went back to being his old self but the people around him were acutely aware that he had not gotten over Senna's death. He never dated and seemed uncomfortable around women. Even three years later it was apparent that Morgan Jeffords would never love again.

Then, in 1959, Dr. Jennifer Lime came to Deliverance to become the city's ME. She was a thirty year old, emerald green-eyed, auburn haired beauty, originally from London, England, who also happened to be bright and enchanting. An athletic 120 lbs on a perfectly proportioned 5'6" figure, she drew several glances from a number of the men in Deliverance—married and single.

At first, Morgan's reaction to her was the same as with other women—businesslike, cool, and seemingly interested only in how she could help him solve cases. But people began to be aware of him looking at her and he would occasionally ask questions about her, questions that weren't just professional in nature.

Finally, nine months after she moved to Deliverance, he asked her out, she accepted, and the women of Deliverance, most notably Morgan's mother, smiled and hoped.

Nothing was carved in stone of course, but now Morgan was returning to Jackson Hole, where he and Senna had spent so many happy hours together, and he was dating again. That had to be a good sign.

THREE

"S.T. in, Dusty?' Morgan asked Fran Hull, Byrd's secretary, as he entered the police station. Fran was the glue that held the second floor of the station together. She was single, 45 years old, 5'5" tall, 130 lbs packed into buxom, beautiful frame. Her shapely figure was complemented by liquid, chocolate brown eyes and shoulder length, lustrous chestnut colored hair. Morgan had given her a nickname, just as he gave most everyone in the department a nickname. In Fran's case, the name referred to her habit of always cleaning Byrd's office, even when no one except Fran thought it was dirty.

In Byrd's case, S.T. stood for Short Timer because Byrd was always threatening to quit the force and open up a gun shop. He was always complaining that his people didn't appreciate him or show any gratitude for his patience with their bungling ways. The truth was Byrd loved his people but he wasn't going to appear soft in front of them lest they take that as a sign of weakness and take advantage of him. So, it was rare for a week to go by without the Captain threatening to retire and leave them all up a creek without a paddle.

"It's only nine, what do *you* think?" Fran replied, sliding a look down her nose, the sarcasm in her voice close behind. "Actually, he just called in five minutes ago. We got a call to check the toll way overpass out on Gunther Street. Evan drove over there and found a ripe one lying underneath it. Apparently it was bad enough that he called Byrd at home. Byrd was still in bed of course, so he wasn't exactly thrilled when he picked up the phone, but he sat up and took notice when Evan told him why he was calling. Byrd called here as soon as he arrived on the scene and said to get hold of you ASAP. He said that we had a bad homicide on our hands. He wanted you at the crime scene *yesterday,* and said not to spare the siren on your car. He also said you could forget about that vacation. Morgan, he sounded badly shaken and you know the Captain doesn't rattle easily."

"Great! I should've just headed out this morning and called in from Jackson Hole when I got there. Okay, I'm outta here. Call Evan and tell him I'm on my horse."

"Before you saddle up pardner," Fran said, "Jennifer called to remind you that you owe her a lunch for the work she did for you on the Rhymer murder case. My impression was that this was not negotiable."

"I hear you. More to the point, I hear *her.*" Morgan threw over his shoulder as he walked out the door.

On the drive to Gunther Street Morgan mulled over what Fran had said. First, he agreed with her that whatever Evan had found under that bridge must have been pretty brutal to cause Byrd's reaction. Secondly, if the Captain felt it necessary to go to the crime scene himself instead of just instructing Morgan to go, it was something *big.* But what really concerned Morgan was that Evan had felt the need to call Byrd instead of him. Whatever Evan had found must have upset him so much that he felt he needed the Captain to be in on it.

*This isn't a routine homicide. Something outrageous has happened. I just **know** this is gonna ruin my day. Evan may be young but he's gut* *tough and smart. Four years as his partner has taught me to trust his instincts. If he's this spooked we've got big trouble.*

As Morgan accelerated, a brief chill passed through him, an uninvited passenger riding shotgun to a grim destination. He fervently hoped Evan had somehow misread the seriousness of this, but he knew that when he arrived at the scene Evan would be there looking like he'd stepped in what this case was likely to become.

FOUR

Detective Sergeant Evan Flack was 27 years old. He had perennially tousled brown hair, stood 6'3" tall, weighed 215 lbs on a heavily muscled frame, and had the most beautiful sea green eyes ever, at least according to Fran. He'd been on the force for five years and had been hand picked by Morgan to be his partner. Morgan would have trusted him with his life and, on one occasion, had.

Evan had come to Deliverance as a street cop in the fall of 1956, having completed a Bachelor of Science Degree in Criminology at UCLA. His grades at that prestigious university, together with his having graduated third in his class, led to his being named the youngest detective in the city's history in October of the following year. Morgan's partner, Doyle Oslen, who'd also come over from the 7th, retired shortly afterwards. A few days before he left the 2nd for the last time, Doyle and Morgan were having lunch at a local cop's pub called *The Steakout.*

"Bud, who should I pick to replace you?"

Morgan had started calling Doyle "Bud" within the first few weeks of their being assigned together. Every day he bought a small blush tea rose from the flower lady in the train station across from the 2nd. He would then place it in a bud vase on his desk. When their shift was over

Doyle would gently wrap the flower in moistened paper towels and take it home with him to give to his wife. The nickname seemed natural to Morgan.

"Evan Flack." Bud replied immediately, knuckling a morsel of food from the corner of his mouth. "He's the smartest young cop on the force, he's dedicated to putting the bad guys away, *and* he listens when you tell him something."

That was all Bud needed to say. The next day Morgan asked the Captain to give him the "new kid" and a partnership made in heaven was born.

***

Just as Morgan had predicted, Evan was waiting for him at the base of the bridge.

"You are not gonna believe what's been dumped over there, Morg." Evan said, approaching Morgan and pointing back to a concrete support. "Somebody has seriously lost their sense of humor."

As they walked, Evan filled Morgan in as Morgan put on surgical gloves.

"Fran took the call about seven this morning. It seems some kids were walking to the park when they found a body under the overpass. They freaked and flew out of there and across the street, screaming like they'd been scalded. Damn near knocked down the front door of a man named Ed Franklin. Franklin opened the door, tried as best he could to make sense out of the gibberish the boys were spewing and, when he heard 'body', immediately called here. Fran flagged me down at home and I got here at 7:22. Almost lost my breakfast when I saw the vic.

He's pretty messed up. One of the uniforms recognized him. This guy's a high roller Morg, I've seen him before; a circuit court judge out of Portland named Martin Gregg. V*ery* prominent…"

"Did you say Martin Gregg?" Morgan blinked in surprise. "Damn! He's only the governor's brother-in-law. S.T. must be swallowing his tongue right about now."

"Yep. When he heard the guy's name, he forgot all about nailing my privates on the bulletin board for waking him up. Yelled at me to freeze everything until he got here; at which time he started bouncing around like a jackrabbit in heat giving orders and swearing the whole time. I think he's scared the press will get hold of this and panic the public.

Anyway, the area's been secured; the lab boys from forensics and the crime scene photographer are all here, and we're keeping the press back. The ME, er Jennifer was here too. She walked the grid, processed the body and took off about five minutes before you got here. I tried to get you on the phone but no luck."

Morgan nodded his head. He admired Jennifer's thoroughness in dealing with a crime scene. By "walking the grid" Morgan understood that Jennifer had set up an eight-by-eight grid over the crime scene, using yellow cotton string. She then carefully and methodically inspected each of the resulting 64 squares for forensic evidence. She was joined in this by two of her assistants whom she always brought with her on these occasions.

Then Jennifer would personally process the body, making sure to bag the head, hands, and feet and, remove and bag all articles of jewelry. She did this, even though the physical evidence technicians usually did most of the evidence recovery, because she didn't want anyone touching *her* body until she'd had a chance to examine it herself. Jennifer had established this procedure with the Deliverance Forensic Department when she'd first taken the job, pointing out that she was not trying to trod on someone else's turf. Rather she was anticipating those times when the lab guys got to the crime scene before she did.

"Said she'd send the autopsy report in early tomorrow. Well, here we are. Hold your nose, man."

"Sweet Jesus!" Morgan recoiled from the sight spread out on the ground before him, as he fought against the bile rising in his throat like a runaway locomotive. He knew from newspaper photos that the judge had cut a fairly distinguished figure when he was alive. Now, what lay on the ground before him looked surreal; a Picasso gone horribly wrong.

Gregg had been crucified naked on a cross using three, seven foot long, 6"x2" boards. The beams met in a point just behind Gregg's head and each one extended another eight inches above the head. His hands, and feet had been secured to the beams with large hex bolts, the head was strapped to a beam with a dog's spiked collar, and the entire abomination was lying on the ground near one of the bridge supports, body up.

"Looks like the Vitruvian Man." Evan observed, drawing a quizzical look from Morgan. "You know the DaVinci drawing depicting two superimposed positions of a naked man. The figures are inscribed inside the intersection of a circle and a square. It was Leonardo's exemplification of the blend of art and science during the Renaissance and…"

CD6
CD BUSHROEgment>

I know what The Vitruvian Man is, Evan. What's it got to do with this?"

"I dunno, maybe the head case that did this has a thing for DaVinci. The cross was upright against that support when we got here but Jen needed it down so she could process the body."

"Maybe. File it in that computer brain of yours for now."

As Morgan leaned closer to the body he could see that the eyes were covered with what appeared to be two gold coins. Looking closer he was horrified to see that the coins were plastic, had melted, and were fused to the eyelids.

"Awww. The sick creep *heated* these things and then placed them on his eyes. I'll bet the vic was alive and conscious when he did it too. Eyeballs probably boiled when the plastic touched the lids. That had to hurt big time. Look here."

Morgan was pointing at something protruding from Gregg's mouth. It was a wad of money rolled lengthwise that had been forced into the mouth and down the throat with great force. The denomination of one of the bills was visible.

"Can you believe it?" Evan exclaimed in disbelief. "He rammed a wad of hundred dollar bills down Gregg's throat!"

"That's not all, partner." Morgan sighed, indicating an area beneath and between Gregg's legs.

Spreading Gregg's knees, they discovered that a second roll of hundreds had been inserted deep into Gregg's rectum.

"Bastard's got an interesting technique for throwing away his money." Evan declared in a clipped voice dripping with sarcasm, while recording the grisly discovery in his notebook. "What's that?"

Evan was pointing to a large elliptical bruise on Gregg's right bicep.

22

"Looks like he was hit with some hard, flat object." Morgan conjectured. "But why only in the one place?"

Inspecting the body further led to the discovery something else. The letters TLOMITROAE had been etched the length of his right shoulder.

"Now *that's* interesting!" Morgan reached down and ran his fingers over the letters, as if he were blind and reading Braille. "Whattaya make of this, partner; these letters have been *branded* into his skin."

"The freak fries 'em for fun." Evan's reply was direct and blunt. "Oh, I found this on the ground by the body." Evan removed an 8mm film canister from his jacket pocket and handed it to Morgan. Inside was a reel of film. "It's been printed so you can handle it."

"The question is where it came from and to whom does it belong? Morgan said, turning the film over in his hand slowly. "There are no identifying marks anywhere on the film or the canister. I think we'd better find out what's on this as soon as we get back to the squad room."

Finally, the detectives noted several burn marks on Gregg's hands, as if he had tried to defend himself against an attack from something that was very hot.

"Any guesses as to what made these?"

"Don't know," Evan said inspecting Gregg's hands through the plastic bags. "But they don't look the same as the other burn marks. Forensics will figure it out though."

Pointing to the trunk of his car, Evan said cryptically:

"Look over here; I've saved the best for last."

Next to a small red velvet sack were a miniature, plastic replica of a Chevrolet Corvette, a small, plastic container of brown liquid, and a portrait of a woman in medieval armor.

"What the hell is this?" Morgan exclaimed.

"Great minds *do* think alike. That was my question, too. The sack was lying on the ground 20 feet behind Gregg's body and those items were in it. I was hoping you'd have an idea as to what they mean."

"Lovely. And right after I tell you, I'll predict this year's World Series winner. Maybe some kid left it there. Then again, maybe the perp is playing a game and these mean something. If that's the case he'll leave more the next time he kills and believe me, this fruitcake will kill again. We'll add them to the evidence and hope we can figure out what they mean later."

After double checking the crime scene to make sure nothing in the way of evidence had been missed, Morgan dismissed the two patrol officers who'd been keeping the crowd and the press back. He issued a terse "No comment." for all of the press to hear. Then he and Evan conferred with Captain Byrd for a few moments before climbing back in their car and heading to the 2nd.

"Byrd couldn't have made it clearer." Morgan remarked as they drove along. "He wants this solved quickly and with as little publicity as possible."

"I heard it slightly different." Evan ventured. "We solve the case quick or all vestiges of our manhood will disappear. S.T. can do it too."

Morgan shot Evan a look, and a slow nod of agreement joined the smile that had formed on his mouth. One thing was sure. Time *was* critical. The amount and nature of the cruelty inflicted on Gregg told Morgan that this killer *liked* inflicting pain. That led to the inescapable conclusion that he would seek out another victim soon.

"There goes my vacation." Morgan complained gloomily, his face a neon sign flashing 'aggravated' for all to see. "Unless, of course, we catch this loose screw today, which we both know ain't gonna happen.

"You're right about one thing though, old buddy. Byrd's probably in need of a change of shorts by now thinking of what the press could do with this."

"I'm not so worried about the *Centurion* Ev. Miles Benton, the editor, is a friend of mine. He plays it square and won't undercut us. He'll simply print the facts and stay away from the sensationalism.

I play poker with him. He plays it tight and smart and his running of the *Centurion* is the same.

The *Portland Crier* is another story, though. It's a yellow rag at best, little better than a tabloid. They'll eat the juicy parts of this scene like rock candy and churn out a story that focuses on the lurid details, neglecting what responsible journalists do; answer the five basic questions of any news story—what, where, when, how, and who."

That's especially true if Emmet Murray writes the story. It'll be a front page, full color, manipulation of the facts so as to be the most sensationalized copy in town.

Unfortunately, it sells papers, mores' the pity.

FIVE

The Deliverance police station was a red brick and concrete three storied building that looked like many of the government buildings of the 1950's. It had been named simply the 2nd or "Deuce" as the cops called it. It housed eighty uniformed policemen (referred to as beat cops by most), twenty-one detectives, ten office staff, and Captain Byrd. The uniformed policemen and detectives had their locker rooms and showers on the second floor. The cafeteria, mailroom, and uniform's day room were also located on the second floor. Their squad room was on the first floor. Most of the beat cops alternated their duty time between their squad cars, the squad room where they got their daily assignments, and the day room where they could relax with a game of pool or watch T.V. The cafeteria was seldom frequented by the uniforms because they usually ate in the field.

The entire third floor of the 2nd was the domain of the detectives and the Captain. It had been tagged by the men as the *Aerie*, a subtle reference to the fact that they had to climb two flights of stairs each day and were not happy about it. The sarcasm was not lost on Byrd who responded by nailing up a cartoon on the squad room bulletin board, depicting a bald eagle with a set of captain's bars, one each pinned to the left and right shoulder blades. Beneath the eagle twenty-one smaller cartoon figures of turkeys were seen scurrying around, running into one another, with perplexed looks on their faces. Beneath all of this was the caption:

How can you soar with eagles when you work with turkeys?

The poster got laughs all around, especially when someone added a postscript to the caption that read:

The only "soar" around here is the "sore" feet the turkeys get from all the unpaid extra work the eagle thinks up for them.

The detectives were evenly divided between the homicide, robbery, and vice divisions; and they worked in pairs. Morgan and Evan had their desks situated in the rear of the detective's squad room, close to the interrogation room where suspects and witnesses could be interviewed, while being viewed via a one-way mirror/window. Their desks were also close to the room air conditioner in Byrd's office. Being in close proximity to the Captain had its pluses and minuses, depending on whether or not he was in good humor and whether or not he was mad at either one of *them*. The only buffer afforded them on a bad day was Fran's desk and Morgan and Evan were not too proud to hide behind her skirts (figuratively speaking) on those days. Nobody wanted to lock horns with Byrd when he was on a jag, and with good reason. The Captain stood 5'10" tall, and weighed 215 lbs. on a thick-set frame that had taken on little fat in his 63 years. His salt and pepper gray hair belied the youth and vigor he possessed, but the piercing granite gray eyes that bored through you when you were the target of his wrath made it abundantly clear that this man did *not* suffer fools easily.

"Set up the screen and projector in the interrogation room." Morgan said. "I gotta hit the head."

"Grab two coffees for us." Evan called out as he headed for the equipment room. "I'll get sandwiches from the fridge."

Ten minutes later the two men were seated in the interrogation room watching the movie found at the crime scene while eating their lunch. The movie depicted a room full of people enjoying themselves at what appeared to be a banquet. At one point a man who was obviously the host of the ceremony approached the dais and launched into a long-winded speech praising Martin Gregg for his invaluable support of The Big Brothers of Portland, the organization who, it seemed, was putting on this shindig. Upon finishing his speech the host introduced Gregg and sat down. Gregg got up from his seat, walked to the dais, and spent several minutes thanking everybody in the metropolitan area of Portland, or so it seemed to the two detectives. The remainder of the film showed Gregg shaking hands with several people, including some very influential people from Portland and Deliverance; people with impressive financial and political clout.

"So, what was that all about?" Evan said, finishing his coffee.

"You got me. Could be Gregg's film, could be the killer's."

"One thing." Evan cut in. "The film looks kinda amateurish."

"Yeah, I noticed the camera shake and inconsistent lighting. It's like whoever made the film, didn't know what they were doing."

"Or they were doing it on the sly, trying not to get caught." Evan ventured.

"Either way, since Gregg was found naked, the film was left by the killer." Morgan concluded. "The question is *why*. Why don't you stay here and call all the photo shops, camera stores, and anywhere else you can think of. See if you can find out where the canister came from and, if possible, the film. Maybe we can trace it back to someone who could lead us to the killer. I'll go see Mrs. Gregg."

Before they left the squad room, Morgan and Evan met with Captain Byrd in his office and filled him in on what they already knew and where they were going.

"If anything comes in from Jennifer or the lab, I'll have Dusty call me on the mobile radio in the car and come back." Morgan informed Byrd who nodded. "Otherwise, when I get through breaking the bad news to Mrs. Gregg, I'm off to the Big Brothers of Portland headquarters in downtown Portland. They're over on Vincent Ave. I'll see what I can dig up about Gregg and that organization. If that's the original film it might be theirs. If it's a copy maybe they'll know about it."

"Okay, Morg." Byrd replied, looking at his watch and noting that it was 12:30. "I'll reassign a couple of the vice cops to nose around Gregg's past. Maybe they can find something to link the judge to possible suspects. Anything goes on this one. Tom Koenig called me thirty minutes ago. His wife is a wreck and he wants fast action on this. Now, maybe pleasing the governor doesn't rank high on your list, but his wife is Gregg's sister and when he said he wants this mess cleared up quick or else, well—. Let's just say I was listening real hard and the words *hell on earth* flashed into my mind at the thought of not giving him what he wants. And, if hell on earth is *my* plight then the flames from that hell will certainly fan out to others. Get my drift? Remember, I'm not due to retire for at least five more years."

"Yeah, yeah. Looks like two of the turkeys are gonna have sore feet again." Morgan declared. "Have your guys start with fellow judges and judicial connections, neighbors, and friends, *and* his background from the time he was a baby. I'd like to find out if somebody with one helluva grudge against him did this or if it's just a nut. Maybe it's both."

Morgan stopped by Fran's desk on his way out and told her what he'd discussed with Captain Byrd. He asked her to have a couple of the maintenance staff set up two 6' by 4' corkboards and two 6' by 4' marker boards in the incident room, along with plenty of magic markers and thumb tacks. Then he picked up his and Evan's unmarked police cruiser and headed towards Brentwood Estates, a gated community on the affluent west side of town. In fifteen minutes he would be inside the Gregg home, telling a woman her husband was never coming home to her. It was one of the more unpleasant aspects of his job; mostly because he knew that no matter how he put the news it would do nothing to comfort the person to whom he was giving it. Rather, it usually left them confused, grief stricken and angry; emotions Morgan didn't care to witness, let alone have to deal with.

Six

Evan spent an hour making calls to various shops in the hope of tracing the film left at the murder scene. The sum total of his efforts was the discovery that the can had a serial number on the inside of the rim of the lid. The manager of Carson's Photographic and Filmmaking Supplies, a large camera shop in downtown Portland, instructed Evan to look there. Using a magnifying glass he found SF2687 inscribed inside one of the threads in the screw-on top.

"The SF means the can was manufactured in San Francisco." The manager, Ron Reed, said. "That serial number will allow you to trace the can to the store that purchased it from the manufacturer. That will tell you where the film came from, *if* the film in the can now is the same film that was placed in the can by the store that originally bought it, and *if* you can find the camera store where the film was developed. You'll be really lucky if it was the same store. Actually, I can tell you where the can was manufactured right now. What was the number again?"

Evan read the number off the can and five minutes later the manager returned to the phone.

"According to my indexing system the can was manufactured at the Harvard Photographic Packaging Company located at 237 E. Broadview in San Francisco. I don't have their phone number, though."

"Thanks Mr. Reed, I'll take it from here. You've just saved me a major headache and I really appreciate it."

A quick call to the packaging company got Evan a somewhat irritated man with a heavy accent that cloaked his words.

"Excuse me sir, could you please repeat that. We seem to have a bad connection." Evan's fingertips excavated frustration trenches in his forehead as he struggled to understand what the man was saying.

"Ah said! The cahyn was shipped to Im—ah—ges Cam—rawh stoh in Pohtland. Ah don't have a ahddress or phone numbah."

"Uh, that's Images Camera Shop in Portland, right."

"STOH! Camrawh STOH!"

"Yes sir. Thank you for your help." Evan hung up the phone and leaned back in his chair.

"Jeez! That was like pulling teeth. Come to think of it that's probably what's wrong with the guy."

"Now you know what days around here are like for me." Fran called over to him from her desk, chuckling.

"Less B.S. and more work out there." Byrd chucked the command out of his office like a live grenade, but there was no real bite in his words. He just liked to let his people know he was there and listening.

"I'm going over to Images Camera Store." Evan announced getting up from his chair and slinging his dark charcoal sport jacket over his shoulder. Like Morgan, Evan was a sharp dresser and today he was wearing butterscotch chinos and buckskin colored calf hide cowboy boots to go with the jacket. His sky blue oxford shirt completed the ensemble.

"If Morg calls in or returns, tell him I'm hot on the trail of that film. Maybe we'll get lucky."

Evan walked out to the parking lot, hopped into his snow white 1958 Chevy Impala convertible and headed towards the I-5 turnpike to Portland. If the people at Images could locate the person who bought the film in can SF2687, Evan might have a direct connection to the killer, especially if that film had been the one that was used to record the honors banquet he and Morgan had watched.

SEVEN

The Gregg home was pretty much what Morgan had expected—luxurious and expensive. A French colonial set on a couple of wooded acres in Deliverance's prestigious Rosewood community. As he strolled up the red brick walk Morgan wondered what Gregg could have done to cause someone to hate him so much. Well, if Mrs. Gregg didn't go completely to pieces after hearing that her husband was dead, he might be able to interview her and, with luck, get a little closer to answering that question.

"I'm truly sorry for your loss, Mrs. Gregg." Morgan offered sympathetically, though she didn't seem all that grief-stricken. They were sitting in the living room, he on the sofa, and she in an upholstered wingback chair. Minutes before Morgan had been admitted to the house by Mrs. Gregg, and escorted to the living room where, after identifying himself, Morgan had given her the bad news.

"I just can't understand why this happened. Martin has no enemies. He's liked and respected by everyone we know."

Virginia Gregg was a remarkably attractive woman of 47. She stood 5'9" tall, weighed a trim 130 lbs. with shoulder length dishwater blonde hair and deep caramel brown eyes. She was wearing a sleeveless, knee length lime green dress that fit her like a glove. Three inch, black patent leather heels completed the picture.

Morgan was drawn to the quality of her voice. It was raw and husky, made that way, Morgan guessed, from years of whiskey baths and cigarette saunas; a voice that was deeply arousing but also, alas, cold and unfeeling.

Morgan noted that she'd twice referred to her husband in the present tense, as if he were still living. That could mean one of two things. Either she hadn't yet made the mental adjustment to his demise or; she'd *already* known he was dead and was making an attempt to convince Morgan she hadn't.

"I suppose somebody he put in jail might've held a grudge against him, but he's never said anything to me and he hasn't seemed *that* upset about anything in particular lately. Except…"

"Except what?" Morgan prodded.

"Well, Martin said something odd at the dinner table two nights ago. He said he hoped his zeal for insuring justice in his court wasn't affecting his common sense. When I asked him what he meant by that he said he couldn't comment on a case he was presently presiding over. I got the message and dropped the matter."

Morgan jotted this revelation down in his notebook.

"I know this is a bad time, Mrs. Gregg, but if you're up to it I'd like to ask you a few questions. I need all the help I can get. You might remember something that turns out to be important to the case. Just for purposes of elimination, where were you between say ten last night and one this morning?"

"Spouse always the first suspect in a murder case, right detective? Well, I was at a friend's home from eight p.m. last night to about 1:30 a.m. It took me approximately fifteen minutes to drive home and I've been here ever since."

"Thank you, ma'am. I assure you I'm just trying to establish where everyone who knew Martin Gregg was at the time of the murder. By eliminating people as suspects we save time and effort, which makes us more efficient."

The rest of the interview took less than an hour and revealed two further points of interest. Virginia believed her husband had been bothered by something for a long time.

"Starting four years ago he began sitting up late at night in the den, staring off into space and drinking. Sometimes I would hear him carrying on a conversation. At first I thought he was on the phone, but when I looked in on him one night he was talking to himself. On one occasion I heard him ranting about not having the time to pay his debt. I have no idea what he meant by that and if you knew Martin you'd know that I wasn't about to ask him."

The other interesting piece of information was the fact that Martin had six months ago purchased a .44 magnum revolver which was odd considering that he was the chairman of a committee to outlaw handguns in the state of Oregon. I had no idea why he'd bought the gun but I wasn't surprised considering his recent state of mind."

"One other thing Mrs. Gregg." Morgan said, after ascertaining where and when Martin Gregg had purchased the gun. "We need you to come down to the morgue and identify the body. I'm sorry to have to ask you but it's necessary. Can I have an officer drive you there now?"

"No!" She said it too fast. Her eyes warily fixed on Morgan for just a moment, asking if he'd noticed the slip.

He had.

"Uh, how does tomorrow morning around eleven sound? That way I can keep an 11:30 luncheon date with a friend."

"Certainly Mrs. Gregg. I'll make a point of being there with you."

Not too eager to view the remains are we lady.

No love lost here. I wonder why.

She's a real possibility for this.

Leaving the house, Morgan turned the interview over in his mind. First, Virginia Gregg was one cool customer. She hadn't as much as batted an eyelash when he'd hit her with the news that her husband had been savagely murdered—no tears, no crying, *nothing.* She did express sorrow that her husband was dead but it seemed almost perfunctory to Morgan. Still, she'd gone white when he'd told her she needed to identify her husband's body but that could've just been revulsion at having to look at a dead, mutilated body. Second, Judge Gregg's cryptic comment at the dinner table piqued Morgan's interest. How did his zeal for justice conflict with his common sense? Had he allowed the letter of the law convict a person who was innocent according to the spirit of the law? What debt was he so anxious to pay and why was he concerned about having the time to pay it? Why would a man who hated guns buy the most powerful handgun sold? So many questions with no answers. The only thing Morgan *was* sure of was that he didn't trust Virginia Gregg.

*Talk about the merry widow. Bet she's the beneficiary on a big, fat life insurance policy. Smart too. Gotta check out her alibi but I'll bet the bank she was where she said she was at the times she stated. Doesn't mean she didn't hire someone to do it. Thing is, hitters aren't usually this messy. In any case it means a lot of footwork. One thing for sure, this is the **last** time I check in before taking vacation time.*

Eight

Images Camera Store was a large stone block building located at the corner of Burnside St. and East Grand Ave. in downtown Portland, just east of the Williamette River. Evan had considered phoning the store before he went there but had decided to show up unannounced. He had found that he often gained a distinct advantage in interviews when the interviewee was not given time to prepare for it. He entered the store, took out his notebook, and walked up to the counter.

"Can I please speak to the manager?" Evan noticed that he and the man behind the counter were the only people in the store.

"My name is Ben Price. I own Images. Can I help you?"

"Detective Evan Flack, sir." Evan replied, showing Price his shield and laying the film canister on the countertop. "I'd like to ask you a few questions regarding this 8mm film canister you sold. I'd like to know who you sold it to and when."

Price studied the can for a few moments.

"This was part of a shipment that came in about a year ago." He replied, pointing to a small number written on the canister's label. "I'll have to check my records in the back."

Five minutes later, Price was back.

"We sold this canister and a blank film to the Big Brothers of Portland on March 7th, 1960."

"Thank you, Mr. Price. Was the film developed here?"

"Yes. I checked on that too, in case you wanted to know. It was returned on October 25th of 1960 and picked up a week later."

"Well, thank you, Mr. Price. You've been a great help. I'll need a copy of your records showing the sale. "

"Can you tell me what this is all about, Detective Flack? Is there a problem?"

"No, sir. My visit here is part of an ongoing investigation and I'm not at liberty to say anything further. It has nothing to do with you or your business. Again, I thank you for your help."

After securing copies of the sale, Evan left the store and headed back to the 2nd. The revelation that the film belonged to the Big Brothers of Portland did little to brighten his mood. He and Morgan knew that if the film didn't belong to the killer, it had most likely been given to Gregg by them as a memento of his being honored at the dinner shown on the film, which posed a new question. Was Gregg carrying the film, at the time he was assaulted, or was the killer in possession of it? Evan hoped the answer to that question would help to find Gregg's killer. Of course, the film might not have anything to do with the murder and thus be of little value. But the question was still there and Evan's detective mind would not let it go until he knew why the film was lying next to Gregg's body.

NINE

"Any luck with the film?" Morgan slid into the booth, opened a menu and signaled for the waitress who began walking over to them. "I've had a hell of an afternoon. Tell me you've got good news."

"Yeah, well I'm not *already* sucking on my second beer because *my* day was a roaring success." Evan countered. "The film and the canister were bought by the Big Brothers of Portland, no surprise there. No help either. Hope you or the lab rats come up with something 'cuz I drew a blank."

The two friends were having a working supper at *The Steakout.* Dave Ways, the owner and bartender, had been a detective in Portland and Deliverance for twenty-five years until he'd retired in 1955. He had then opened a pub, tailoring it to the likes of the cops with whom he'd worked.

A magnificent oak and mahogany bar was the centerpiece of the pub, literally. It was a twenty-five foot oval sitting diagonally as an island in the middle of the huge 50' by 40' foot dining room. The top of the bar was deep green granite flecked with gold. Twenty red oak bar stools ringed the bar, mute witnesses to the flow of bitching and commiserating that pervaded the atmosphere of the place. An eight foot pool table, foosball game, and dart board provided relaxing entertainment. This pub had been built for men, as Dave had intended.

Cops came to Dave's because it was a place where they could unwind and unload. *The Steakout* provided them with good food, good liquor, fellow cops to talk with, and privacy if privacy was what they wanted. Beside the booths and tables placed around the main room, Dave had thought to furnish the pub with a back room where the men could sit in private booths and discuss matters pertaining to cases they were working on. Morgan and Evan were sitting in one of these booths now.

Everything about *The Steakout* was designed for cops, even the cook. Linda Ways, Dave's wife and co-owner, was a great cook and, more importantly, a cop's wife. She was perfect for the job, as the men often pointed out to Dave. They also reminded him that Linda was a hell of a lot easier on the eyes than he was and that it was always pleasant to see her face at their table.

Over the past six years the Deliverance community had come to understand that this pub catered exclusively to policemen. It had cost Dave some business but he and Linda didn't really care because they liked cops, were most comfortable around cops, and enjoyed the cop talk that filled the pub. Besides, word had gotten around and now the pub was drawing policeman and their families from all the surrounding communities, including Portland. (Tuesdays and Sundays were designated family night and the men were expected to conduct themselves accordingly on those nights so that the wives and children could come and not be offended by rough language).

"I had an interesting *chat* with Mrs. Gregg but I too drew a blank with the Big Brothers of Portland except that Gregg was a big shot in the organization. It seems he was responsible for most of the money raised because he was intimately acquainted with the prominent people who gave the lion's share of that money." Morgan sighed.

"Well, I did call them when I learned the film was theirs." Evan said. "They had one of their members shoot that film in June of last year. As far as everybody at their main office knows, the film was in a file cabinet and had never left the office. Martin Gregg never asked for a copy nor was he given one. Anyway, let's order. We can talk while we're waiting for the food to come."

"I'd like the twelve ounce New York Strip steak medium well done." Morgan said to the waitress who'd just arrived at the table. "Also, a baked potato, steamed vegetables, and a small dinner salad with ranch dressing."

"What would you like to drink, sir?"

"Uh, water's fine as long as somebody refills my glass once in awhile."

The waitress finished writing Morgan's order on her pad, then turned to Evan. It was immediately obvious to Morgan that Evan was getting the once over by this very pretty young woman as evidenced by the arched eyebrow, fleeting smile and slightly long stare. Morgan smiled inwardly. His partner's boyish good looks never failed to attract the attention of women wherever they went. Women were drawn to Evan like flies to honey. What amused and touched Morgan was that Evan was genuinely unaware of the mesmerizing effect he had on women. He was one of the most selfless, well-adjusted young men Morgan had ever met, and when anyone complimented him he often blushed. That quality enchanted women all the more. Whatever Evan had, Morgan wished he could bottle it—he'd make millions selling it.

"When you're ready, partner," Morgan said, attempting to get

Evan's attention. Evan was buried in his notebook and oblivious to the waitress's presence.

"Huh! Oh, sorry." Evan said, barely looking up. "Uh, just give me a Cobb salad, cup of minestrone soup, and black coffee."

"Yes sir. What dressing would you like with your salad?"

"Ranch please."

Evan did not look up at all this time, so focused was he on his notes.

"Would you like me to bring you a glass of water also, sir?"

"What? Oh, uh sure. Thanks."

Evan was still focused on his notes, still not looking up. Morgan just smiled and shook his head from side to side.

"Would you like the salad dressing on the side or on your salad, sir?"

"Hmmm. I guess on the side. That way I can decide how much I want."

Evan had looked up slightly, as if considering his choices, then answered without making eye contact with the waitress.

"You did say a *cup* of soup didn't you sir. A bowl is only twenty cents more."

"No, a cup is plenty for me, Thank you."

Again, no eye contact.

It took all of Morgan's self control not to burst out laughing. This very pretty young lady was flirting with Evan and he didn't have a clue.

"Earth to Evan." Morgan had decided to save his partner from himself. Evan looked up and blinked at Morgan quizzically.

"It's customary to look at someone who's speaking to you, buddy. Good manners and all that, old chap."

Evan's brow furrowed in confusion. His eyes followed Morgan's outstretched hand and came to rest on the waitress. He blinked again;

then his eyes got as big as saucers and his mouth slowly opened wide.

"Oh! Uh, I'm, uh, *really* sorry, miss, er, Ellen." Evan stammered, noticing the name tag on her uniform. His face was flame red, and his eyes fled from her, foraging for a hole to crawl into.

"Sometimes I get too caught up in my work." He explained, imploring her forgiveness with the most contrite, engaging smile Morgan had ever seen. "I gotta be the dumbest guy on the planet not to notice a beautiful girl standing right next to me. Blind too."

With a smile emitting the incandescence of a thousand suns, Ellen nodded her acceptance of Evan's apology, whirled, and glided across the room as if on an invisible magic carpet. Evan went back to his notebook and Morgan looked at him thoughtfully.

Most amazing thing I've ever seen. I'd have sworn the kid was gonna get his head handed to him. But, just when she was about to go off in huff, the puppy dog look bailed him out. Figures, though. Evan is blindingly honest and sincere, and women are uncanny when it comes to sensing that. She immediately forgave his rudeness because he was truly unaware of it and, because he instantly and genuinely regretted his insensitivity when it was called to his attention. What a guy!

Over the next hour, the two men discussed the day's events while eating their meals. Evan took copious notes on everything they talked about.

"So, whatta we got?" Morgan said, finishing the last of his steak. "Besides the mother of all murders, and a hunch this head case will do it again. That's on one side of the ledger, what's on the other."

"We've got the usual suspects. The wife and the people connected with Big Brothers of Portland, which probably includes half of Portland." Evan started, referring to his notebook. "We have a lead on a piece of evidence that *could* link to the killer—the film, and I think I can safely assume that it was left at the murder scene by him. But who is that person and why did he or she leave the film there? Maybe one of the folks at Big Brothers of Portland wasn't such a big brother to Judge Martin. We've got the body which Jennifer will process, money and plastic coins to trace, not too mention whatever other evidence the lab boys dig up. We've got friends, relatives, and associates of Gregg's to interview, plus those kids who found Gregg's body. I'd say we've got more than enough on our plates to keep us busy. I just hope it's not so much that we run out of time before our boy gets lonely again."

"Yeah, well if he does I hope I get to be his next date. I'll give him all the love he'll ever need, starting with a .357 caliber Cupid's arrow through his black heart."

The look on Morgan's face told Evan his partner was only half kidding.

"Yeah, I know, partner." Evan concurred. "Crap like this reminds me of ancient Rome's direct method for handing out justice—quick, severe, and in like kind. An eye for an eye kind of thing. Then again, what do I know?

"Anyway, let's figure out tomorrow. I want to be at the morgue at eleven when Virginia Gregg I.D.'s her husband's body. I wanna see the look on her face when they pull back that sheet. We should have the lab report back by nine. Let's see what shakes out from that before we divide the work. Jeff Levine and George Peters are doing the initial interviews with everyone except the kids that found Gregg under the bridge and Gregg's family. They're also going to check out why Gregg bought the gun. If you take the kids I'll see his family. He had an older brother, a younger sister, and a daughter, in addition to his wife. By the way, Fran did some checking around and it appears little Miss Sunshine is the beneficiary of a cool million bucks from a life insurance policy her husband took out just six months ago. Wanna bet she knew it before her husband died?"

"I don't make sucker bets, partner." Evan smiled. "What about Gregg's parents? Who interviews them?"

"They're both dead. Not to put too fine a point on it, but it does make our job easier. Okay partner, any questions? No. Let's get outta here and get some down time. We're gonna need it tomorrow.

"Right." Evan agreed. "My turn to catch the check."

Ellen came over, cleared away their dishes, and then gave them the check. She waited patiently while Evan pulled some bills out of his wallet. She watched as he laid down two ten dollar bills for a twelve dollar tab.

"I'll get your change, sir?"

"None necessary." Evan replied. "It's the least I can do for you putting up with a jerk like me. I'll let Dave know how great the service was and how patient you were. He's an ex-cop. He'll understand. By the way; I'm Evan and he's Morgan for when we come back. Thanks again for your patience."

The young woman smiled broadly, thanked them both, and left. True to his word, Evan talked to Dave and the two men left. Evan got into his Impala, Morgan climbed into their squad car and they went their separate ways.

TEN

The lab results showed up the next morning at 8:30, ten minutes ahead of the ME's report, speeded up by Morgan's insistence that this was priority one, and Jen's concurrence. Morgan had arrived at the 2nd at 8:00 on the off chance that the reports would come in early and he could get a head start on a day he knew would be long, tiring, and probably frustrating. Morgan was not surprised, therefore, when Evan walked into the squad room as he was preparing to take the new evidence into the incident room.

"Great minds think alike, partner." Morgan called out as he opened the door to the incident room. "Grab some coffee and come in here."

"Way ahead of you, partner. I got us some decent coffee from the bakery across the street—a dozen blackberry jelly buns too. Can't put in a hard day's work with no fuel to run the engine."

"Did you have breakfast?"

Evan nodded sheepishly and Morgan rolled his eyes, a look of disbelief etched on his face.

"You must have the metabolism of a shrew. You eat like a horse and look like chiseled stone."

"The lab rats did a good job." Evan said, ignoring Morgan's jibe and spreading the forensic evidence on the table.

The "lab rats" were the forensic experts from the pathology laboratory located on the other side of town. A large, modern glass and steel structure, it housed the various forensic rooms and equipment necessary to the solving of crimes scientifically, and the offices of the ME, complete with a state of the art autopsy room. The city morgue was located in the basement of the facility.

"We got blood workups from the forensic serologist, fiber tracings, fingerprint results, the plastic coins and money rolls have been tested, tox reports; hell, they've even figured out what those burn marks on Gregg's back are." Morgan pointed out. "The burn guy says the letters on Gregg's back were definitely done with a *branding iron,* and here's the kicker. He figures this guy took the time to make an iron for *each* letter because there were no lines on the body indicating that the letters were connected to one another by metal strips.

Then, this fruit cake had to heat and apply each brand individually which, of course, extended the time and intensity of the torture Gregg suffered. Can you believe this guy, Evan?

Anyway, let's see if we can get a profile of our boy started. Maybe we'll get lucky. Lord knows if we don't, the next poor bastard this guy gets hold of will have run out of any luck *he* ever had. I'll take the blood, fiber, and fingerprint stuff. You work on the tox reports, coin and money findings, and the burn marks. Then we can go over the ME's report together. Make sure you take detailed notes."

For the next ninety minutes Morgan and Evan pored over the materials in front of them, trying to extract every scrap of information possible from the lab reports. Each piece of evidence was minutely studied from several aspects and the detectives recorded the inferences made from this careful inspection. Notations were made in the margins of the reports and findings, notations that would later be collated and formalized in the report they wrote up. Then Jennifer's report was gone over in great detail and each man's interpretation of the facts contained in the report was discussed and debated.

"Okay, here's what we've got so far." Evan, referring to the notes he'd taken, began listing what they now knew, based on the evidence they'd just studied. As he read, Morgan compiled an itemized the list for the purpose of writing up the report he'd turn in to Byrd. The Captain would review the report and his conclusions, together with Morgan's and Evan's gut feelings would decide the next series of steps in the investigation. When Evan was through, Morgan handed him the list for his confirmation.

1. Two blood types found at the scene—A+ belonging to the victim, and B- belonging to another person as yet unidentified. The unidentified blood sample was collected from the roll of bills stuffed in Gregg's mouth. It is noted by the serologist that the unidentified blood sample was rare. Only 2 people in 100 have this blood type.

2. A blue fiber consistent with carpet fibers. Collected from the outside of the victim's calf.

3. No identifiable fingerprints found at the crime scene. The one clear print found was not in F.B.I. fingerprint identification system.

4. Tox report found trace amounts of chloroform in the victim's blood. Most likely this means Gregg was anesthetized at some point.

5. The coins on the victim's eyes found to be replicas of ancient Roman coins, a Tiberian tribute penny, approximately 2,000 years old. Refer to Dr. Marvin Greenberg, consulting archaeologist for the Portland police department.

6. The rolls of currency found at the crime scene were cleverly made play money. The bills were not of high quality, but could not have been easily detected by the naked eye to be counterfeit.

7. The burns on the victim's hands appear to be the result of an electric shock being administered while holding something metallic in nature. This may be the method used to initially subdue the victim and is supported by the bruise found on the bicep. A cattle prod may have been used.

8. It can be concluded from an examination of the contusions, abrasions, and minor cuts on the body that the victim was alive, probably conscious, and struggling when many of the insults to the body were inflicted. Bruises and scrapes on the victim's nose, chin and lips indicate the mouth had been pried open and clamped with an unknown metal device.

9. The ME's autopsy report shows that the victim had consumed a chicken salad sandwich and a cup of coffee about 9 p.m. the night of his death. Marks on his forehead, chin, neck, wrists, forearms, knees, ankles and torso indicate that he was securely restrained, most likely during the periods of torture he endured. COD was asphyxiation as evidenced by victim's cyanotic condition, petechial hemorrhages in the eyelids, swollen airway, and severely depressed blood oxygen level. These conditions were due to an obstruction inserted into the victim's trachea. TOD set at approximately at 11p.m. on May 30th.

10. Each of the rolls of currency that was inserted into the victim's trachea and rectum were found to have been singed and blackened on the insertion end. Furthermore, the trachea, and rectum were severely burned.

11. The letters on Gregg's brand appear to represent some form of

coded message, which needs to be analyzed by a professional in languages and cryptography.

12. Holes had been drilled into the hands, and feet to allow for the bolts.

13. An "I" had been sculpted into the hair on the back of the head near the base of the neck.

14. The toy automobile, the portrait, and the brown liquid had been processed. The report revealed that the car was a 1960 Matchbox miniature of a Chevrolet Corvette. The portrait was of Joan of Arc, the 15th century French girl who became a legend and a saint primarily because of her heroism in the Hundred Years War between England and France. The brown liquid was a cola beverage.

"Sarah Ellison can handle #11." Morgan said. "She's the cryptanalyst with the Portland F.B.I. we worked with on the Aaron Myers case. I'll get the letters over to her today."

"So, he lit the money on fire before he shoved it up Gregg's backside." Evan had just realized the significance of what he was reading.

"Did the same thing with the wad he stuffed down the poor guy's throat after prying his mouth open." Morgan grimaced and shook his head. "I don't know what Gregg did to tick this guy off but he didn't deserve this. This goes beyond rage killing or revenge. Maybe he had a sane reason for doing this when he started out, but somewhere between the plan and carrying it out he went off the rails. Our luck is he probably got a paper cut from the money as he was shoving it in Gregg's mouth and bingo, we got his blood. Poetic justice. And what's up with the "I"?"

When Evan merely shrugged his shoulders, Morgan continued.

"Maybe it's some kind of signature. Thing is, it's a sure bet he's gonna do this again—he likes it. I think inflicting pain gets him off; he's hooked on it. And, like any addiction, he has to increase the amount and frequency of his fix.

I'm telling you Evan this thing has me a little spooked. We need to get back to S.T. with this stuff. *Everything* else is going on the back burner. I want the Captain to take us out of the loop. This is the only case we're going work and we'd better work it damn fast!"

Evan's head snapped up at Morgan's last statement and the look on his partner's face chilled him to the bone. He had never before seen fear in Morgan's eyes and seeing it there now shook Evan.

A madman had come to Deliverance, bent on slaughtering people. What Evan saw in Morgan's eyes was based on the realization that they were dealing with the worst kind of homicide. This murder, and the ones Morgan and Evan were sure would follow, had been committed by a person compelled to destroy human beings with an uncontrollable, mindless savagery.

Furthermore, it was likely the motive for the crime was not rational, making catching him doubly difficult. So, unless the killer made a big mistake, they would be looking for a maniac whose irrationality made him invisible and who would, because of his insatiability, kill with increasing frequency and brutality.

No wonder the look in Morgan's eyes; this was a cop's worst nightmare. Unfortunately, it was a nightmare from which he and Evan might not soon awake. Worse, it was a nightmare from which some poor souls would never awake.

ELEVEN

"Hey, d'ya see the *Centurion* this morning, Bulldog?" Don Cairn, the morgue attendant, knew Morgan was an avid New York Yankee fan. "Mantle and Maris are on a tear. Mick got his 14th and Roger his 12th yesterday."

"Yeah, Evan was crowing about it this morning. Thinks Mickey is gonna break Ruth's record of 60 homers in a season this year. He just might too, guy hit 52 in 1956. But I've a hunch. Maris hits 3rd in the lineup, Mickey hits 4th. If they walk Roger intentionally then they have to pitch to the man who's been considered the most dangerous long ball hitter in baseball for the past ten years. So they're gonna pitch to Maris every time, but they might give Mantle an intentional pass if they can get Roger *and* the situation calls for it. That means Roger will have more chances to hit a home run than Mickey. Anyway, that's my theory. Hope I'm right because I bet Evan ten bucks that Maris will hit more home runs than Mantle.

More to the point is Emmet Murray's article in this morning's *Portland Crier.* He managed to twist the facts of the Gregg murder just enough to avoid a libel suit and still splash the front page with enough unmitigated crap to fill Yankee Stadium."

Morgan was waiting for Mrs. Gregg to show up to identify the body of her husband. It was 11:45 and he was getting impatient. He had a noon luncheon date with Jen, and this woman was going to mess it up if she didn't come soon. He'd promised Jen he'd take her out to lunch after she'd provided him with the key piece of evidence in closing a murder case three months ago. Since he'd already put her off twice, he knew he'd better show up today, and on time.

"If she doesn't show up in five minutes I'm outta here." Morgan said disgustedly. "She's only gonna take a quick look, say it's him and leave. Still, I'd like to see her react…"

The door to the viewing room opened and Virginia Gregg walked in. Morgan looked at Don with a "Can you believe it?" expression on his face. Gregg was wearing a burnt red leather mini skirt, an electric blue, sequined halter top, and calf high suede boots the color of snow. Don's response was to cast his eyes to the floor and sigh.

"Okay, what do I do?" Virginia was clearly annoyed and impatient, which was interesting because it was she who'd made *them* wait.

"Just step up to this window, Mrs. Gregg." Don instructed. "I'll go around and bring your husband out for you."

Don then left and headed for the cold room where the bodies were stored until such time as they were claimed by family members. Morgan got the feeling that he couldn't get out of there fast enough, which was understandable. This woman was creepy. She was wearing clothes thirty years too young for her at a time when she should have been wearing black in keeping with the fact that she was a widow. On top of that she was clearly put out, not the reaction one would expect of a woman who was emotionally distraught over the loss of a loved one.

"Okay, Mrs. Gregg." Don said rolling the stainless steel gurney her husband's body was resting on to the viewing window. "I'll pull back the sheet and all you have to do is nod your head."

Morgan fixed on Virginia's face as Don pulled back the sheet, exposing Judge Gregg's body from the head down to the stomach. This was the moment Morgan had come for. He stiffened slightly in anticipation of her reaction and he was not disappointed.

"Oh God! His *eyes*! What's wrong with his *eyes,* and his *mouth?*" Virginia violently recoiled from the window, staggering back as tears welled up in her eyes and flowed in rivulets down her cheeks. She flailed her arms about, grasping for something to keep her from falling. What she found was Morgan's arm and he winced from the force with which she gripped him. In that moment Morgan felt pity for her. She had been severely shocked by what she'd seen; shocked and deeply moved. The emotions were raw and visceral, he was sure of that. Maybe he had been wrong about her. Maybe she really was saddened by her husband's death and had been merely trying to bear up when he'd visited her yesterday.

Morgan tried to clam her down without success. Then suddenly, it was as if a curtain had come down over her features.

"I'm going now." She bit off each word in a voice that could have frozen a volcano. "If you have anything further to discuss with me, please contact my lawyer. His name is Jason Blaine and his number is in the phone book."

With that she turned and marched out the door, nearly colliding with Don, who was coming back in.

"What's the matter, didn't I clean her hubby up enough?" Don's attempt at humor was lost on Morgan.

"Gotta go, Don. Jennnifer's waiting at Dave's place. I do *not* want to be late again."

"You better start treating that girl better my friend or she'll find someone who will. Ya know what they say; a bird in the hand is worth…keeping. Don't let this bird fly away."

"I'm working on it, my man."

TWELVE

By the time Morgan arrived at the restaurant, it was 12:15. He grinned sheepishly when Jennifer, already seated and looking at her wrist watch, greeted him with:

"I *must* have this watch looked at.

It runs fast at the strangest times. What do *you* think could be wrong with it, Detective?"

"Uh, must be my *magnetic* personality." Morgan had noticed the smile in her eyes and took a shot at some mild sarcasm. "Seriously, Jen, I'd have made it but for this woman at the morgue."

"Picking them kind of dead lately, aren't we? Well, at least she'll make a great date; won't eat much and *definitely* won't monopolize the conversation."

"You win. Can you *possibly* cut me some slack if I say I'm *really* sorry? The lady at the morgue was Virginia Gregg and she was there to identify her husband's body. She was supposed to show up at eleven, but didn't get there until 11:45. I'd say something about women and time but I figure I've already pushed the envelope with the personality crack."

"Well, I guess so, *if* you pay for lunch and *if* you help me plan the party at my house Saturday night."

"Done. Let's eat. I have to interview Gregg's family this afternoon. For once Lady Luck didn't dump on me. The brother and sister are in town for the funeral and the daughter lived with Gregg and his wife, who just happens to be Governor Koenig's sister. They're coming down to the Deuce at two. I'm hoping they'll be cooperative so I won't have to get them together again for a second interview. Of course Lady Luck made up for it by having Virginia Gregg's alibi for the time of the murder check out. Now I'll have to find me another prime. Unless, of course Lady Luck decides she loves me again and we find out Virginia hired someone to kill her husband."

For the next hour Morgan and Jennifer ate while discussing the Gregg murder and Jennifer's Saturday evening party.

"To sum up, the victim was immobilized, possibly with electric shock, chloroformed, bound and gagged, removed to wherever the perp tortured, mutilated, and killed him, and then transported, most likely in a truck or station wagon, to the underpass. Clean, surgical, and precise. Morgan, you should know that this person was consummate in what he did to Gregg. I'm pretty sure he maximized the pain he inflicted on the victim. The pain involved here was not as severe or enduring as to cause the victim to pass out much. But I assure you that Judge Gregg suffered horribly. I know this because the perp chose parts of the body that are especially sensitive to pain. You're right. This person is addicted to other people's agony. He likes what he's doing but he's not just a garden variety sadist. He's inventive and proud of it. To him these murders are works of art. Regardless of any other motives, his prime directive is to keep on doing this until he's created his masterpiece."

The words fell from Jennifer's mouth devoid of any emotion, crisp and succinct. Morgan often wondered at the cold clinical manner in which this warm, wonderful woman approached the most heinous of acts. He understood the need to distance herself from the horror with which she came in contact, he dealt with it himself. Still, seeing it in Jennifer was a little scary.

"I've been thinking, Morg. The burns on Gregg's hands, they remind me of something I've seen before, but I can't remember where or when. It's like he grabbed something hot and couldn't let go. But they weren't that type of burn. It's why I think he was electrocuted somehow as a means to subdue him. I just can't pin it down."

"Don't worry Jen; it'll come to you… Just relax and let it. As for Gregg's killer, whatever he is, he's human. We'll get him. By the way, on another subject, Evan wants to know if he can bring a friend Saturday night."

"Evan got a new girl friend? My, that boy *does* get around."

"No, it's a guy he met a couple of weeks ago at the chess club Evan belongs to at his church. He challenged Evan to a game; they struck up a conversation and discovered they had a lot in common. Evan says he's a lot of fun and really smart which, coming from my genius partner, is saying something. I guess the guy owns a company that makes party games so I thought I'd ask Evan to get him to bring one. Who knows, it might be fun. Anyway, it'd be a break from charades and pinochle."

"Sure. Tell Evan to bring him along. Uh, right now I've got a date with one of my cold friends back at the morgue. Could you grab the check while I visit the little girl's room?"

"Sure. I've gotta run anyway. See you Saturday night at seven."

Morgan quickly picked up the check, paid the cashier, and left to make his appointment at the 2nd.

THIRTEEN

Gillou Junior High School was a two story brick and stone building that had been built in 1951. It had been named for Mrs. Grace Gillou, an exceedingly rich woman who had made her money in real estate in the 30's and 40's. She was a generous woman who had, over the years, donated many times the cost of the school. In 1957, she had given a million dollars to help erect a sports complex and cultural arts center for the high school.

"Good morning Dr. Levine." Evan greeted the principal while seating himself in her office. "I'm here regarding the murder that took place yesterday. Unfortunately, two of your fourth grade students, Eddie Pearson and Connor Dabney, discovered the body and I need to interview them. I called their parents and they agreed that bringing the boys down to the police station for the interview might be intimidating so they authorized me to interview Connor and Eddie here, with your permission."

"I spoke to the parents this morning, Detective Flack." Judy Levine replied. "I've arranged for you to interview the boys in the main conference room. It's near the end of the school year so there are no more conferences being scheduled. It's soundproofed for privacy and the windows have shades. If you'll wait in the room, I'll get the boys."

Evan sat down at the far end of the conference room, facing the door. He wanted to see the boy's faces when they walked in and he wanted to be seated where they would both be in front of him at all times. This way one couldn't sit on one side of him and one sit on the other. Then when he posed questions, he could see their reactions without having to swivel his head from one boy to the other. He had thought of interviewing the boys separately, but had decided that might be too intimidating.

"Good afternoon, boys." Evan said as the boys entered, making sure his badge showed on his belt. "I'd like to ask you a few questions about what you saw yesterday. This won't take long and I'd appreciate your help."

The boys sat down, looking nervous and a bit frightened. Evan knew he had to ease their anxiety if he was going to get anything useful out of them.

"This is no big deal, boys. I just need to know if you saw or heard *anything* before you came across the body. Take a few minutes to think; did you see *anyone* near the bridge? Maybe in a car on the bridge? How about sounds? Anything that seemed out of the ordinary. Take your time, there's no rush. You guys could be a really big help."

Eddie and Connor looked at each other. Then they simultaneously cradled their heads in their hands and Evan had to stifle a laugh. These were obviously two great kids. They were trying their best to do what Evan had asked of them, racking their little brains to come up with something Evan could use.

"Are you gonna make us deputies, mister?" Connor gazed at Evan with awe. He had relaxed considerably since entering the room, as had Eddie.

"Yeah, do we get badges and guns?" Eddie asked, his eyes twin dinner plates.

"Just call me Detective Flack, boys. Well, I don't know about the guns but I'll see what I can do about honorary badges and a tour of the police station." This time Evan couldn't suppress a chuckle.

Nice kids. Bright too.

"I might even get you guys a commendation for community service. Now, how you doing? Anything come to mind?"

"No, sir. We were going to the park to play ball because we didn't have school yesterday and we saw something under the bridge. When we went over to see what it was…uh, man it was bad. Eddie screamed and we ran to that guy's house."

"I *didn't* scream."

"Did too."

"Did not."

"You peed your pants."

"No way. You're a fraidy cat."

"You're…"

"Whoa! Hold on guys. Nobody's a fraidy cat. You're both very brave. You saw something terrible and you ran and told someone. That's brave *and* responsible. I'll tell you something. I saw what was under that bridge and *I* was afraid. Anyway, if you're both *sure* you didn't see or hear anything out of the ordinary I'll let you get back to class."

From the pained expressions on their faces, it was apparent that neither boy was anxious to go back to class. However, having nothing further to add, they got up and slowly headed for the door. Then, one of the boys turned back towards Evan.

"That man said he saw a car." Eddie's statement was simple and electrifying.

"Man?" Evan motioned to the boys and they returned to their seats.

"Now, what are you talking about?"

"He's right, Detective Flack." Connor concurred. "The guy said he saw a car." Connor knew he had important information and was obviously feeling proud.

"What man?"

"The man who lives next door to the man whose house we ran to." Eddie had sensed Connor's excitement. "He came out of his house 'cuz we were yelling this morning."

"He said he wasn't surprised the body was there because he'd heard a sound outside his home last night. When he looked through the blinds on his front window he saw a car parked across the street. Five minutes later he looked again and the car was gone."

"Did the man say what the car looked like?"

"No sir." Eddie replied. "He went back in his house before the police came."

"Okay boys. You've been a big help. You go back to class now."

"Do we get badges now?" Connor looked anxiously at Evan.

"You bet, and everything else I promised you. Thanks again, boys."

Before leaving, Evan looked in on Principal Levine and thanked her again for her help. He wrote a note to himself to see if any of the police at Gregg's crime scene had interviewed the witness who'd seen the car. He assumed that one of the officers had but if that hadn't happened then somebody would have to go see him.

This man may have seen the killer, or at least the car the killer had used to transport the body. If he could describe the car or, a prayer passed through Evan's mind, if he'd managed to get the license plate number, then the car could be identified and, hopefully, found. Once the car was located it was only a matter of time until the vehicle's owner was found. Then the process of determining whether or not the vehicle was involved in Martin Gregg's murder would begin. Evan left the school hurriedly, anxious to give Morgan and Captain Byrd the news.

It can't be this easy, can it? Gregg's body was discovered a little over 24 hours ago and we get a lead that could break the case wide open. God, I'm afraid to breathe.

FOURTEEN

The interview with Gregg's brother, sister, and daughter took longer than Morgan had expected, partly because he had chosen to interview them separately, and partly because none of the three knew anything or rather, were aware that they knew anything. Thus, it took a lot of digging to get the few scraps of information he felt might be useful. Boiled downed to the bare bones Morgan's notes read:

1. Gregg's brother, Jeremy Gregg, remembered that Gregg was concerned about a drug bust case he was presiding over. Martin had told Jeremy two days before he was murdered that he suspected there had been jury tampering and he was going to find out who was involved.

"The D.A. came to me a week ago, Jer." Gregg had told his brother. "He said he'd gotten an anonymous phone call stating that juror number four had been approached and offered a bribe. The D.A. and I called the juror in but he denied the allegation. But I wasn't satisfied. It's been bothering me ever since. I think I've got a lead though. If it pans out I'll let you know."

Jeremy never heard from his brother again.

2. Gregg's daughter, Sara, knew nothing specific but she did say her father had been "kinda jumpy" lately, like he was expecting something bad to happen.

3. The Governor's wife, Julia, was of no help. She hadn't seen her brother for six months. She was so upset Morgan decided not to push her, figuring he could always interview her at a later date if it became necessary, which he hoped he wouldn't have to because it would upset the governor and *that* would upset Byrd.

Truth be told, Morgan was surprised that the woman had even deigned to show up. Governor's wives usually weren't too cooperative when it came to the police, and Morgan had a hunch he'd be the subject of her dinner conversation with the Governor that evening. That meant another call to Byrd. Morgan could feel the flames from *hell on earth* starting to lick at his legs, which were uncomfortably close to a more sensitive area of his anatomy.

After escorting the three people out of the building, Morgan went back to the incident room and added Jeremy Gregg's and Sara Gregg's statements to one of the marker boards. Cradling a cup of coffee in one hand, he pulled up a chair, sat down and stared at the boards reflectively.

On the face of it, this was nothing more than a simple homicide, complicated somewhat by the manner in which it had been committed. There was no real reason to suspect anything more than revenge as a motive. Profit was out, too much sadistic violence for a mere greed killing. No, everything pointed to someone who had a grudge against Gregg. Probably a person Gregg had sentenced.

It just doesn't feel right, though. This level of sadism screams full blown psycho, and those cracker factory residents don't stop at one. Whoever this creature is he's had everything human scooped out of him. Dead mind, dead heart, dead soul. Uh, uh. If this is a grudge killing, it's not going to be limited to just Gregg. Somewhere out there is a driven madman, obsessed with righting some wrong; and if we don't get him he's going to kill a slew of people trying to satisfy that obsession.

FIFTEEN

"How was your day, partner?" Evan entered the incident room, coffee in hand, and seated himself beside Morgan. "Anything with Gregg's family?"

"A couple of nibbles. First, the brother said Gregg told him three days ago that the judge was concerned there was jury tampering on a case he was presiding over. Interesting, but it didn't really set off any alarms.

But then Gregg's brother said something interesting. According to the brother, Gregg said he thought he had a lead on the identity of the person responsible for the tampering. *That* could mean something so I put it on the board. We'll check it out just to be sure.

Second, Gregg's daughter said her father had been very nervous lately. Her exact words were 'like he was expecting something bad to happen'.

Finally, Gregg's sister. Governor's wife, nothing to add, end of story. Be glad you didn't have to interview her. Once she talks to her husband and he calls S.T., you might be looking for a new partner."

"Well, I may have just the tonic your tired mind needs." Evan said noticing Morgan's clouded brow and worn expression. "One of the kids I interviewed said an onlooker at the crime scene saw a car the night Gregg was killed. He lives next door to the Franklin guy, the guy whose house the kids ran to. I called the Franklin right after leaving the school and he gave me the guy's name and phone number. The guy's name is John Swanson and he said he glanced out his front window around midnight last night and saw a white or cream colored Chevy station wagon, maybe a '57 or '58. Didn't know the model. Said all station wagons look the same to him. He said it was too dark to see the license plate because the street light was out. I checked it out myself and the bulb *was* burned out.

But, this could be a break, Morg. If we can locate the car it might lead us right to the killer."

Evan went to the marker board and wrote down everything he'd told Morgan.

"Good work, partner. We'll get DMV to run a list of all of the white or cream 1957 and 1958 Chevrolet station wagons in and around Deliverance. If we don't get a million hits we might just run this lead down quickly. I'll have the Captain tell one of his boys to interview Swanson again. He might get the guy to remember something else. One thing for sure, the killer had to get that cross to the murder scene and a station wagon would have done the trick."

"What say we call it a day? I'm bushed." Evan was using his best hang dog look, trying to get Morgan to agree.

"Okay, old man." Morgan smiled. "I keep forgetting you're in your declining years. What with the loss of hearing, heart palpitations, and enlarged prostate, you're up way past your bed time. Let's get you home to a glass of warm milk, and a hot water bottle for those blocked arteries. Maybe you'll be rested enough by noon tomorrow to be able to drag yourself out of bed. And, if you're still too exhausted to make it here on your own we'll send a police car for you, siren and all."

"Funny! Seriously Morg, I've got a lady waiting for me to pick her up at eight-thirty and its seven-thirty now. If I leave like, ten minutes ago, I can get home and cleaned up in time to get to her house on time. I promise to get an early start tomorrow on tracing Gregg's 'mad money'. And…"

"Deal!" Morgan bit off the word a bit too quick and Evan knew his friend had out foxed him again. "I assume you mean the money our madman stuffed in two of Gregg's orifices. I've been trying to figure a clever way to unload that headache on you and now you've done it for me. Thanks, partner. By the way, Jen says to bring your friend to the party tomorrow night. She asked you to get him to bring one of his party games. We both think it could be a lot of fun. Just show up at 6:30 and bring some beer with you. Say, what's the guy's name?"

"William Kane. He's a really decent guy, Morg. Plays chess like a grand master. What I like about him is he never takes himself seriously, is brilliant and rich, has a beautiful Cape Cod over in Burning Oaks Estates and a cabin in the woods, and drives a 1960 Aston Martin Zagato. The guy looks like a Greek god too; taller than me on a huge frame made of granite, so you'd better keep him away from Jen, or she'll swoon for sure. But he doesn't seem to be aware of any of it. As far as William is concerned, he's just an average guy who's had a few lucky breaks and is grateful for everything that's come his way. His kind is few and far between. He's a lot like you, Morg; that's probably why I like him.

That and he sings in the choir at my church. "

Evan likes William because William sounds like he could be Evan's twin. Morgan reflected. *Only Evan would never realize that because he's too selfless to thinks he's that nice. That's why **I** like Evan.*

"Sounds almost too good to be true, buddy. I hope he has *some* flaws? I'm sure Jen and I will like him though."

"None that I know of. He does read true crime mags as research for the murder mystery games his company manufactures."

Morgan spent another three hours in the incident room, studying the evidence on the two boards, and racking his brain to make *any* sense of the disconnected pieces. Finally, realizing he'd need more information, or a better explanation of the information he already had, Morgan switched off the lights and headed for home. Driving along in the quiet dark, he let his mind float freely.

Life sure is weird. It's like being on a train ride, a one way trip with several side stops along the way. You see other trains passing you all the time. Different tracks, different passengers, different trips.

*Then one day, you see one coming down the line toward you, just like all the others; and only at the last moment do you realize, with horror, that **this** train is on **your** track! And, in the time it takes to draw your last breath, it's over. No more trip, no more **life**.*

My gut tells me this guy was on a collision course with Judge Gregg long before he killed him. Maybe Gregg had actually seen him, had maybe even been his presence for minutes or hours before the guy took him down.

*So how come Gregg's radar didn't lock onto this nut as a threat in time to save his life. It wasn't as though Gregg hadn't dealt with people like this before. He was a lawyer who'd been used to dealing with the dregs of society; He **should** have smelled rotten eggs on this guy.*

I don't know, maybe I'm tired, but it just seems weird to me. What creeps me out though is if Gregg couldn't sense this guy, what chance do ordinary citizens have?

Sixteen

Jennifer Lime mentally assessed how prepared she was for the guests who were arriving in little over an hour. The three steaming crock pots were filled with chili, four cheese broccoli soup, and beef stew, all home made. Fives large loaves of French bread had been wrapped in large white napkins and placed on a warming tray. Another, sliced, was sitting on the breadboard. Slices of roast beef, country ham, chicken breast, and turkey breast were sitting on a large oval platter, surrounded by slices of various cheeses together with condiments. All of these food items had been arranged on the large island in the center of her kitchen, along with condiments, utensils, stoneware bowls and plates, glasses, and napkins. Opening the refrigerator, she noted with pleasure that pitchers of lemonade and iced tea were ready to be placed on the island. She had already checked the small refrigerator in her great room to see that there were bottles of Coca Cola, 7-UP, and Nehi Orange drink. Beer and wine rounded out the beverage choices.

Oops! The coffee. Got to set that up now so I can turn it on when people begin showing up.

It looked like everything was ready for the party. All she needed to do now was to make sure the card tables in the great room had coasters and decks of cards.

Now my only problem is getting Morgan and Evan away from the pool table long enough to socialize with the other guests. Maybe Evan's friend will bring one of his games. I just hope it's the kind of game that everybody will like.

If everything went as Jennifer had planned the guests would all arrive between six-thirty and seven. Everything was set up for the people to come into the kitchen, take what food and drink they wanted, then mill around the kitchen, the 30' by 30' great room, and living room until everyone had shown up. Then, after eating supper in various groups throughout the house, Jennifer planned to call everyone into the great room for game playing and conversation.

In addition to an eight foot custom made red oak pool table, the great room contained an area with a boar's hair dart board encased in a red oak cabinet with hinged saloon type doors, and two octagonal red oak card tables, the playing surfaces of which were covered with pine green felt that matched the pool table. The eight chairs around each card table were also red oak and were upholstered in a black, red, and pine green fabric that displayed chess pieces, dice, playing cards, and pool balls.

Guests would be encouraged to participate in any game they wanted to until about ten when everybody would gather in the spacious living room for coffee and dessert, and more conversation.

Jennifer figured the evening would end around midnight.

Dessert! Oh my God! I forgot dessert! Uh, think Jen, think! There is absolutely nothing in the house that would even remotely pass for a dessert.

On the verge of panic she suddenly remembered Morgan and made a quick call to his home.

"Morg. Can you pick up some vanilla ice cream, hot fudge sauce, and whip cream at the store before you come? I forgot dessert for tonight." Jennifer asked and then, preempting what she knew he was thinking, added, "Any sarcasm right now, however well intended, would *not* be appreciated. I've been slaving around here for hours and I'm not in the mood for unwanted humor."

"One gallon of vanilla ice cream, a bottle of hot fudge sauce and a can of whipping cream coming up, Massah Lime. Jus' don't beats me." Morgan knew he'd pay for the "massah" comment but he just couldn't resist.

"Make that order two gallons of ice cream and two bottles of hot fudge sauce, please." The brittleness in her voiced coupled with the clipped way she bit off each word told Morgan he'd be paying sooner rather than later.

It was a tone of voice reminiscent of that which his mother had used when, as a child, he had irritated her; a memory now bittersweet because of her passing in 1960.

Okay, that covers everything, I think. Now if Morgan just remembers.

Jen need not have worried. At six-twenty Morgan, Evan, and William were walking up her flagstone walk and Morgan had a grocery sack containing everything Jennifer had asked him to get.

"Nice digs." William remarked, noting Jennifer's home.

Jennifer's home *was* remarkable to look at. A sprawling four bedroom, red brick ranch with an attached three car garage, it was set back on two wooded acres and fronted by two massive sugar maple trees that were each approximately seventy-five feet tall and four feet in diameter. A functioning weather vane depicting a rooster in silhouette sat atop the garage roof.

"I wasn't aware ME's were paid so well." William said.

"They aren't. Jen inherited a ton of money from her mother." Evan explained. "She doesn't like to talk about it though, so don't mention it."

"Talk about what?" The tone in William' voice and the smile on his face said he understood.

"You hurt your leg?" Morgan inquired, noticing William' slight limp.

"Auto accident when I was a kid." William explained. "It just never mended right. No big deal. I was lucky, considering the car was totaled."

Morgan pressed the doorbell and the three men were greeted with strains from the theme music for the 1949 movie *The Third Man.* The significance of this, which was lost on William, was that one of the characters in the movie was named Harry Lime, and he was a thoroughly *bad* guy.

"Coming!" Jennifer opened the door and invited the three men into her home. "Evan, why don't you introduce me to your handsome friend so we can get the cordialities out of the way."

"William Kane, This is Jennifer Lime, our ME."

"Ahh! Hence the musical doorbell. Clever." William said, admiration written in his blue eyes. "But, I suspect, Harry was as different from you as darkness is to light. Justice did catch up with him though. It's nice to make your acquaintance, Miss Lime."

"Jennifer, please. Thank you. You're pretty clever yourself, William. Evan's the only other person to make that connection and Evan's the smartest man I've ever met."

"Well, if the local chapter of the Mensa organization is through, there is a man with just an average I.Q. standing here with a very simple observation. The ice cream is melting." Morgan's grin offset the sarcasm in his remark and everybody laughed good-naturedly.

"Oh, Morgan! Just put it in the refrigerator. I swear William, sometimes he's just impossible!" Jennifer rolled her eyes and gently pushed Morgan toward the kitchen.

Over the next half hour Morgan, Evan, and William helped themselves to food and drink and began playing pool in the great room. Jennifer, after spending some time watching the men play, returned to the kitchen to make sure everything was ready for the guests yet to arrive and to look at the party game William had brought.

By seven, all four of the remaining guests had shown up. Kevin and Sara Wenger, friends of Jennifer had driven with Jennifer's younger sister, Ruth Verble, and her husband, Seth. By seven-thirty the group had been introduced to William, had been fed, and was gathered in the great room.

"All right, gang, we've got cards, darts, pool or a new party game that William thoughtfully brought with him."

"Maybe not so thoughtful, Jen. I own the company that makes these games and I shamelessly promote them whenever I can." William' smile was as charming as was his suggestion as to why he'd brought the game. "Why don't I give a short explanation of the game and then we can decide if everyone would like to play."

Murder Weekend, was a boxed game intended for at least six people. The rules were simple. A heinous murder had been committed, and the object of the game was to identify the killer through a series of investigative techniques.

The game began with one person passing out sealed packets

containing instructions to each guest. One packet was intended for the person who would be designated as the killer. The instructions in this packet detailed how this person was to act for the rest of the game. It included a list of things the person was to say and do in response to the other participant's questions or comments. The other packets described, in detail, the murder that had been committed, assigned roles for each guest, and gave a list of suggestions for proceeding with the investigation. Only the person getting the "murderer's" packet knew they had been chosen as the killer, and they were also assigned a role so as not to give away their true identity.

Then a cardboard cutout of a dead body was placed on the floor of the great room as a means of getting the players in the proper "mood". Around the body were placed pieces of "evidence", such as "forensic clues", to be processed by the would-be detectives. Players would then began asking questions of each other and examining evidence until a reasonable period of time had elapsed, when each player would secretly write his candidate for "killer" on a piece of paper.

If the game went as it had been designed to go, the combination of clues, evidence, and suggestions for questioning various players, together with the instructions given to the killer, would result in at least one of the players correctly identifying the murderer.

One variance on the rules that William had included just before the game went into production was that people could choose to work in groups instead of going it alone.

Of course, success hinged on the "killer" playing the game fairly. Otherwise it was not always possible to link that person to the crime as it had been described.

Once William had explained the game, it was decided that this was just the thing to liven up the evening. Jennifer, having reviewed the game earlier while waiting for the rest of the guests to arrive, knew it would spark a lot of conversation and was excited at the prospect of playing. And, with the exception of Evan and Morgan, everyone was excited at the opportunity to play detective.

The game began with Jennifer (unknown to anyone else) drawing the murderer's packet. The clues and evidence were numerous and had been cleverly created, lending a sense of authenticity to the game. The group plunged in with enthusiasm, with Morgan and Evan having to admit the game was fun and intriguing.

Early on, the motive was established as greed. A great deal of money had been stolen from the dead man's safe. Some of it was still clutched in the dead man's hand. It appeared he'd caught the person in the act; a struggle had ensued, and he'd been shot because he'd been in the wrong place at the wrong time.

In the end, two pieces of evidence tripped Jennifer up and she played her role masterfully. To begin with, Jennifer's alibi for the time of the murder hinged on her assertion that she was in a park photographing trees. But, the shadows cast by the sun in the photos she had supposedly taken were in the wrong position for the time of day she'd claimed to be there. The clincher came when Jennifer mentioned that she'd only been in the victim's home once and that had been a month before he'd died. He'd given her a drink as she sat in a leather recliner discussing a tax sheltered annuity her company was selling. Unfortunately for Jennifer, the recliner had not been delivered to the victim's house until the day before he was murdered.

The evening was a huge success, partly because William had constructed the game so that most people would get at least a piece of the solution to the crime. Later, as the group sat in the living room eating dessert and talking, he was asked if there were any more games like the one they'd just played and how he got started in the business.

"So far, there are ten different *Murder Weekend* scenarios for sale in various department and discount stores in Portland. Ingram's department store is the only place in Deliverance that carries the line.

I've been fortunate that the series has met with success.

It started as a lark when I was younger. I got the seed money from an insurance company as the result of an injury settlement.

"The neat part is that it's given me the financial freedom and time to pursue my hobby of digging into the past—literally."

"Well, I for one plan to check the list out." Ruth declared, taking a sip from her cup of coffee. "This has been as much fun as I've had in a long time."

"Yeah, it *was* fun, more than I expected." Evan said almost grudgingly. "I was somewhat surprised at how close the game is to real police investigation procedures. Good job William."

"Thanks, Evan. Does that mean I can pick your brains from time to time in creating new scenarios for my brain child?"

"You may want to rethink picking *Evan's* brain, William. You never know what might fall out." Morgan teased.

"*Very* droll." Evan replied curtly. "My partner's been in this game so long most of his methods for crime solving are outdated. So, he's had to rely on me more and more lately. Tends to make him a bit peevish when others look to me for expert advice. Not to mention…"

"Oh for Pete's sake, you two. Enough of the Abbot and Costello act." Jennifer's mock exasperation only made the moment more comical, resulting in peals of laughter on the part of the other guests.

"Well, I don't know about the rest of you people," Kevin said as the laughter died down and the moment passed. "But it's going on midnight and I've got to be up by seven tomorrow morning. This has been a lot of fun."

"Yeah, and when he gets up he's like a bull in a china shop, stumbling around." Sara teased. "Thank you Jen, for having us over."

Jennifer saw the Wengers and the Verbles to the door then came back into the living room where Morgan, Evan, and William were talking.

"Alright, you guys. It's time to go home."

"We get the message. Thanks again Jen for a great evening." William said as he opened the front door to leave. The other men followed him expressing their appreciation as they went.

SEVENTEEN

Wednesday looked to be a busy day for Evan and Morgan. At the top of their list was tracing the car seen outside John Swanson's home the night of the murder. Plus, Evan wanted to be sure that Eddie and Connor got citations from the mayor, honorary badges, and a tour of the 2nd. All of that plus they'd scheduled meetings with George Peters and Jeff Levine in the morning and Sarah Ellison in the afternoon.

"George and Jeff will be up in a few minutes," Morgan said as Evan sat down at his desk with a cup of coffee. "How long is the list from DMV?"

"Don't ask. There are a total of two hundred thirty-seven white or cream colored Chevy station wagons in this county. It's gonna take at least forever to run through them all; and that's if I don't run into any snags, which you *know* I will."

"Don't sweat the car too much partner. It's a long shot at best. Maybe it had nothing to do with the murder. Trouble is we can't afford not to take it seriously."

"Yeah, I know. Say, after George and Jeff give us what they've dug up, I'm heading over to the mayor's office to pick up the citations for Eddie and Connor."

"Sure. I'll start making calls on the station wagons until Sarah shows up this afternoon. She said about two but the traffic out of Portland is murder in the afternoon so I don't have a clue as to when we'll see her."

"That's the problem with you guys. *Neither* of you has a clue." George Peters strode into the room, talking around the cigar anchored firmly in the corner of his mouth. He and Jeff Levine walked over to where Morgan and Evan were seated.

Friendly needling between the men in the detective division was a part of life that all the detectives understood and accepted, though tempers had been known to flare.

"*That* must be George?" Morgan sighed, without turning around.

"How*ever* did you know, O Great One?" Evan's smiling eyes were married to Morgan's.

"Easy. The smell of cheap cigar smoke in competition with world class body odor."

"Sounds like the wonder boys here have been digging into a sack of cow dung for their comebacks to our brilliant sarcasms, Jeff."

"Yeah, and if you keep sucking on that cigar, your lungs are gonna *look* like sacks of cow dung." Evan observed, pushing an ash tray toward George. "But enough of the light banter, Pete. What did you and Repeat here find out?"

"For openers, the people who hobnob with circuit court justices do *not* take kindly to being questioned by cops." Jeff's face darkened at Evan's remark but the mood passed quickly, a cloud passing in front of the sun. "*And*, they have the clout to bring the wrath of God down on anybody that puts the squeeze on them."

"That sounds like you got squat for your troubles." Morgan's disappointment hung in the air uncomfortably, like a relative that comes to visit for a week and stays for six months.

"Not quite." George replied. "Several of the people who worked with Gregg at the courthouse said that he's not been himself lately. He's been irritable and jumpy for the past week. The bailiff that works in Gregg's little throne room noticed Gregg talking to the D.A. and a defense attorney last week, and he was *not* asking them to fill his dance card. The bailiff overheard part of the conversation; or rather he couldn't help *but* overhear the conversation. He said that Gregg was ranting about not allowing some jackass to make a circus out of *his* courtroom. Gregg claimed he had an informant who was going to tell him who had tried to bribe a juror and he was making it a priority to nail the bastard. Furthermore, if he found out that either of the attorneys was in anyway connected, they had better give their souls to God because the rest of their misbegotten carcasses belonged to him.

That's pretty much it. Oh, Virginia Gregg was with her husband when he took out the life insurance policy that left her a rich woman. Not a lot to go on, but a few crumbs worth considering."

"We didn't come up with anything on the gun Gregg bought, other than what you already know. But, considering he verged on the psychopathic when it came to outlawing handguns in this state we figure he had to have had a powerful reason for bringing the mother of all handguns into his home." Jeff suggested. "I believe he was either afraid for his safety or, and this is out in left field, he was contemplating suicide."

"I don't know Jeff." Evan said. "It seems a bit of a stretch. We don't have any leads pointing in that direction. I'd hate to waste time chasing my backside."

"Hold on, Evan" Morgan interrupted. "What are you getting at, Jeff?"

"It's just a gut feeling, but here's the thing. First, the guy said he was worried about a debt he might not have enough time to settle. That statement says two things to me. Something had a stranglehold on the judge, and he had serious doubt that he was going to be around much longer. I mean a guy that's only 55, rich, healthy, and has a prestigious job doesn't worry too much about having enough years left to do things, unless he's got a crystal ball into his future.

Then, he was running around like some cloak and dagger nut looking for a jury tampering suspect. Why's that? Some cop should be running that down, not the judge. The guy could've got himself hurt or worse, killed. It's like he felt morally obligated to set this wrong right to the point of endangering his life, or looking for a quick way to take a bullet.

Anyhow, why should he have felt *that* responsible about this case in particular, and why *wasn't* he more concerned with his own safety?

I don't know, I just think it's possible that he was feeling guilty about something and it was affecting his behavior."

Then there's this. Gregg hated guns, which means he probably didn't have clue one how to handle them. So why would a guy like that buy a .44 magnum, presumably for protection? Wouldn't he buy something a little easier to handle, like a .38 revolver or a .25 automatic? I mean Jeez, Morg. A .44 has a helluva kick.

I'm just saying that maybe the reason he bought a .44 is because he knew that when he ate it, his head would come clean off. No chance of screwing things up and winding up a vegetable. Also, no chance of an *attempted* suicide triggering an investigation into his past, and turning up something he might have to face if he were still alive. Oh, and if there *was* something dirty in his past, *that* could be the debt he was worried about, *and* a reason for suicide if he thought it was going to come out. "

"That's really good, Jeff." Evan said. "When did you have the time to think all that out, and why?"

"You guys know I've been harping on these gun control nuts popping up all over the country. So, the late Martin Abraham Gregg had been on *my* radar for some time.

If he had his way we'd have a Sullivan Law on the books in Portland, which means the idiots at City Hall here would be pushing to get the same thing passed in Deliverance.

You know what *that* would mean. The bad guys would have all the guns and the poor schmuck citizen would be left defenseless against burglars and wackos who could then break into homes armed because they'd *know* the law abiding home owner wasn't packing. So much for the Second Amendment.

Anyway, Gregg buys the farm and in the process of helping you two, I find out he'd actually *bought* a gun, and a cannon at that. So naturally my antennae go up 'cuz that does *not* compute.

So, last Friday, Pete and I dig into the stuff you and Byrd asked us to, and I think long and hard over the weekend about what we've dug up. What I just told you is the result, which *I* think should be considered a theory and should be followed up."

"Sounds possible to me." Morgan agreed, smiling at Jeff's reference to The Sullivan Law.

The law was the result of a 1911 New York State Senate bill, introduced by Senator Timothy Sullivan. The intent of the law was to eliminate handguns in the city, which would then decrease homicides, or so Senator Sullivan promised the citizens. Unfortunately, it simply took a means of defense out of the hands of law abiding citizens who were trying to protect themselves against the violent criminals that ran rampant in the city, especially in the Red Hook District of Brooklyn, the district Senator Sullivan represented when he was in the State Assembly.

The law essentially allowed only people with police permission (licenses) to carry handguns legally within the city limits.

But what Senator Sullivan forgot to allow for was the fact that criminals seldom concern themselves with the legality of what they're doing. And, as anyone who's ever lived through or read about Prohibition knows, when governments make something that is highly attractive, illegal, a vacuum opens up. That vacuum is then filled by people who are only too willing to find a way around the law in order to make money and, bingo, the criminal element in society has access to *illegal* handguns. Hence, Jeff's comment that "the bad guys would have all the guns".

"That still doesn't tell us who killed him, unless you think he did all that to himself just before deciding *not* to blow his brains out with the .44." Morgan said, and the men laughed.

"Look, why don't you and Pete follow up on your hunch. See if you can come up with something *prior* to Gregg becoming a judge that might be a reason for committing suicide that could also be connected to his being murdered. Evan and I will take it from there. And while you're at it, do us a favor and see if you can find the car that was spotted at the murder scene the night Gregg was dumped there. Evan's got the list of possible vehicles and I've got the address where Gregg bought the gun."

"Okay, but you clowns belong to us if we end up collaring your perp for you." George threw back as he and Jeff headed out of the room. "Jeez, I wish Byrd would hire at lest *one* more *decent* detective, so we wouldn't always have to clean up your messes."

A thrown glasses case just missing George's head was Evan's reply to the detective's parting shot.

EIGHTEEN

Twenty-four year old Sarah Ellison was shown into the incident room by Fran at two p.m. on the dot. She was dressed in a lemon colored silk blouse with tan cotton slacks and brown leather penny loafers, which complimented the pulled back long blonde hair the color of straw and her jade eyes. A thin, angular face, highlighted by prominent cheekbones and a slim nose that turned up at the tip, gave her an austere, reserved beauty.

A trim 5'6", she looked like a cross between a college professor and a spinster librarian. But Morgan and Evan both knew that she was 115 lbs. of human dynamo.

"Sarah has the best damn brain in the country!" Evan had once exclaimed enviously. "It's like working with a cyborg, though. I sometimes wonder if she was secretly engineered in a laboratory, considering that coldly precise, razor sharp, analytical mind and single-minded fixation with whatever she's working on.

She'd be a raving beauty if she'd let her hair down and dress a bit different. As it is, she's not exactly hard on the eyes, not that it would do me any good. She doesn't know I'm alive."

At the time Morgan was mildly surprised by Evan's candid admission of his interest in Sarah. Evan usually kept to himself when it came to feelings concerning women, save for an occasional remark, and then only when prompted by Morgan's curiosity.

But upon reflection, Morgan realized that Evan was captivated by the very thing he was complaining about—Sarah's mind. It was that simple. She was a brilliant thinker and that drew him to her like a moth to a flame. Unfortunately, Sarah showed no interest in Evan, so what could have been the pairing of two superior minds ended before it ever had a chance to start.

"Good to see you, Sarah." Morgan said, holding out his hand. "I hope you've got something for us."

"That would depend on your idea of *something*." Sarah replied, sitting down at the large rectangular table where conferences took place when the room wasn't being used as an incident room. "I'm still attempting to clarify exactly what it is we're dealing with here. What I can tell you at this early stage is that this is, most likely, either a cipher aimed at conveying a message through a series of words, or an acronym for a series of words. Unfortunately, I can't ascertain which situation we're dealing with for two reasons.

If it's the former, either the author either chose to eliminate the word spacing in order to increase the difficulty, or one of the letters is in itself a space." Sarah got up and wrote the letters TLOMITROAE on the marker board. "Notice that only two of the letters are repeated, the 'T' and the 'O'. We can eliminate the 'T' because you don't have a space at the beginning of a message. That leaves the 'O'. If the 'O' is intended as a space we have three words—a two letter word, followed by a four letter word, followed by a second two letter word. That would represent the easiest scenario for me to work with though I've been without any success thus far.

On the other hand, if the 'O' does not represent a space between words, any of the other letters could be the space and we have a two words in the message, each of which will be of indeterminate length because we don't know which letter represents the space.

If the message is an acronym for a series of words, then the difficulty lies in my inability to do much with a single sample. I can run several single modality computer scans in hope of achieving a recognizable pattern that would allow us to decipher the acronym. However, the probability of success is less than one in over ten thousand. Of course, if the acronym is well known, the odds of getting a match using computer scans increases exponentially the more well known the acronym is. Any questions?"

Morgan looked over at Evan and almost laughed out loud. His partner was sitting across from Sarah, leaning forward, chin on his hands; completely mesmerized by what the young woman was telling them. Even more amusing to Morgan was the look of adoration in Evan's eyes. If it would have been possible, Morgan would have cast a love spell on Sarah for his obviously smitten friend.

"Well, I don't know about the cop-in-a-trance here, but *I* don't understand enough of what you just said to know if I *should* have a question, let alone *what* it should be." Morgan was not exactly telling the truth. He understood Sarah perfectly, but he thought he'd play Dr. Watson to Evan's Sherlock Holmes on the off chance Sarah might take notice when Evan explained to him what Sarah had just related, thereby demonstrating *his* intelligence for her.

"Morgan!" Evan ejaculated, coming out of the trance to which Morgan had called attention. "What she said could not have been more logically framed or clear-cut. We're looking at two relatively equal cipher forms here, neither of which is going to be easy to deal with due to limited data. Determining *which* form we're dealing with only exacerbates the problem. As to questions, I have a couple.

What happens if this particular cipher hasn't been constructed using the English language?

Worse, what if the language used requires transliteration; that is, taking these English alphabet letters and changing them into the alphabet of the language the message is in, such as Russian or Greek, or vice versa?

Also, is it possible that the author of this message, and I'm assuming for the moment that it *is* a message, was actually using letters to represent *numbers* and the message is an address or the combination to a safe or locker, or something like that?"

Sarah looked at Evan as if seeing him for the very first time. She blinked, scooted her chair closer to the table, and seemed momentarily at a loss as to what to say in reply to Evan's questions.

That was revealing! Morgan thought. *She just scooted her chair closer to the table which, interestingly enough brings her closer to Evan who is directly across from her. Maybe this is the beginning of a beautiful thing. Or maybe I'm nuts.*

"That's quite insightful, detective Flack." Sarah acknowledged. A new appreciation of Evan was evident in her eyes. "If the message needs transliteration prior to deciphering it, it would represent a major roadblock. If it's merely a matter of translating a language that uses the Standard English alphabet, the rules are the same and translation can occur after the deciphering process. I admit that would further complicate the analysis, but not nearly as much as the need to transliterate would.

As to your other conjecture, I considered that to be a possibility from the beginning. I've since written a simple alphanumeric computer program that will generate the entire list of combinations and permutations of letter to number exchanges within the cipher. That will, however, take some time to run. Fortunately, I've got access through a friend to a brand new IBM 7090 mainframe computer at the IBM Data center here in Portland.

I think that pretty much covers it unless either of you have any more questions. I'll get back to you when I have something more or, God forbid, if you come across further samples. If so, please forward them to me.

Oh, I have one further observation. It is possible that the series of letters represent gibberish and were left merely to confuse and mislead the police, but I see that as an unlikely possibility because this type of killer likes to boast or preach—sometimes both."

"Well, thank you Sarah." Morgan said, extending his hand as the three rose to leave. "We'll let you know if we come across any other messages. In the meantime, please call us right away if you uncover anything."

"Here, take my card." Evan said, reaching into his wallet. "Call me *anytime.* My home number's on the card too. Your input could be vital to the case.

Oh, before we let you get away, do you have any idea as to what the capital letter 'I' shaved into his hair means?"

"Only that it's probably the killer's way of marking his victim." Sarah replied, taking the card from Evan's outstretched hand. "But as to its significance, I'm in the dark. Maybe he's telling us he's got his 'eye' on wrongdoers."

Morgan noticed the teasing smile on Sarah's face as she took Evan's card and the caring way in which she tucked it into her wallet.

Not so nuts, maybe.

"I'm outta here, partner." Morgan said, putting on his jacket and picking up the empty coffee cups. "You comin' to the poker party at Bud's home tonight?"

"Yeah, I'll be about a half hour late, though. I'm picking Dusty up from her sister's place at five so by the time I get her home and get back to Bud's place it'll be about five-thirty."

"Then we'll see you when we see you. I'll save you one of JoAnne's Stromboli sandwiches for as long as I can but too don't be too long."

Every month Bud hosted a poker party for his cop friends. The game was limited to draw poker, five card stud, and seven card stud. No wild cards were allowed and there was a three raise limit. The ante was a quarter and raises limited to fifty cents. As Bud had once said, it was poker in its purest form.

The men played in Bud's oak paneled den on a beautifully refurbished mahogany poker table he'd found in a saloon in Deadwood, South Dakota. Bud said the table was a genuine antique from the late 1800's and proved it by showing the other players old photographs of the table in which they could see Wild Bill Hickok seated at the table.

The owner was closing the saloon and was selling everything so he let Bud have what was then a dilapidated old table for fifty dollars. The man intimated that the table was the very one Hickok was sitting at when he was shot in the back by Jack McCall in 1876.

What made that particular shooting so interesting was that Hickok was a famous gunfighter who always sat in a corner to keep from being shot in the back by cowards who didn't have the guts to face him. But on the occasion of his death he couldn't find a corner seat and sure enough he was shot in the back and killed. The poker hand that Hickok was holding when he was shot was a pair of aces and a pair of eights. Ever since the shooting that hand had been called the "dead man's" hand.

Morgan and Evan were regulars along with Captain Byrd. Three men, who were friends of Bud from the 7th over in Portland, rounded out the seven man game. They had been on the force with him and were also retired. Occasionally, George Peters or Jeff Leavine would sit in when one of the other seven couldn't make it.

The men had been meeting every month for four years, and the game had been canceled only twice during that period. On one occasion Bud and JoAnne's oldest granddaughter had gone into labor an hour before the game was to start, and once JoAnne had the flu with a temperature of 104.5 on the day of the game and had been taken to the hospital.

The game was kept friendly with small stakes, good food and drink, and a lot of cop talk which included good-natured ribbing of one another.

***

Morgan walked outside to an angry sky the color of worn pewter, stained with dabs of dirty green and wisps of white smoke.

Great! One hell of a thunderstorm is about to unload on me. I hope I can get home before it gets too bad.

He was headed home to get ready for the game, and he was feeling relaxed and happy. This monthly escape from the routine of his job and life was a breath of fresh air and he looked forward to it with great anticipation. Not even the summer storm that was coming could dampen his spirits.

Unfortunately, another storm was brewing at that very moment; a storm that would alter Deliverance and its people forever, plunging them into an abyss of fear, horror, and rage.

The beast was coming! Teeth bared and breathing fire; an abomination born out of wrath and madness, and ripped from Hell's womb.

NINETEEN

"Crap!" The word shot from Evan's mouth, as he launched his cards into the air, frustration distorting his features. "*Nobody* draws to an inside straight."

"They do when the pot odds are good enough, son." Bud said with a slow grin, and Evan felt the needle go in ever so smoothly. "Next time kick in a raise big enough to force me out."

"Looks like your night, Bud." Morgan observed. "That's five pots you've picked up in the first nine hands."

"Maybe. We'll see who's got bragging rights at the end of the evening." Bud, always the gentleman, said politely. "Anyway, Evan took me for a bundle last month so I'll probably just break even at best."

By "bundle" Bud meant ten or twenty dollars over the course of an evening, an amount any man could lose and not feel bad.

Around midnight JoAnne came into the den.

"Morgan, Ron Kopple's on the phone. He says it's important."

Morgan went into the living room and picked up the phone.

"Ron, what's up?

"Sorry, Bulldog. I know it's your poker night but you're going to want to know what I've got over here." Detective First Grade Ron Kopple was one of the seven detectives working homicide for the

Deliverance police department. He and his partner, George Dunston, had been working the murder of a woman for the past three months. Only recently had they closed the case when they got the woman's husband to confess to the crime.

"I'm not going to like this, am I?" Morgan knew Ron well, and he knew that if Ron was calling him, it was serious.

"I'm out at St. Catherine's cemetery." Ron continued, ignoring Morgan's remark. "George and I were on duty this evening. John Fredrich, the night duty officer, took a call at 11:25 p.m. and relayed it to the squad room where we were playing cribbage. A guy, who wouldn't give his name, said there was a dead body in the cemetery. He said he and his girl friend had gone in the cemetery for a little necking when they stumbled on it and got the devil scared out of them. He said they bolted out of there and ran to a phone booth.

I didn't necessarily believe this joker's story because he sounded a few eggs short of a dozen, but I figured we'd better check it out anyway.

So, George and I high tailed it over here and damned if the guy wasn't right. There's a body propped up on one of the gravestones.

Morgan, you will *not* believe what some really screwed up degenerate did to this poor guy. Based on what I've heard about your case I think it's the same guy. I've notified the ME's office and the forensic guys are on their way, along with the police photographer."

"Evan and I are out the door now. We'll be there in ten minutes. Thanks for the heads up, Ron."

"Sorry again, Morg." Ron had heard the dejection in Morgan's voice. "I wish it wasn't what I think it is, but I'm afraid this one is connected to yours; which means we may have a spree killer on our hands here in Deliverance."

Morgan sighed and returned to the den to tell Bud that he and Evan had to go.

"Ron Kopple and his partner caught a sloppy one over at St. Catherine's cemetery and they think it's connected to the Gregg case. Sorry about the game, guys. We'll catch you next month."

"I'm down eleven bucks, partner." Evan moaned. "If this *is* our boy, I am personally going to take those eleven dollars out of his hide when we catch him."

The drive to the cemetery gave Morgan little time to tell Evan what he'd learned from Ron.

"When we reach the crime scene I'll check in with Ron and the forensic people. You take a look at the body. Mark down any similarities to the Gregg murder in your notebook. If we're gonna tell Byrd we got one killer here we need to be sure, and we need the facts to convince him."

St. Catherine's was the largest cemetery in Deliverance, taking up three square city blocks. It had been built in 1932, the same year as the church of the same name had been erected. The gravestone the two detectives were looking for was located in the center of the cemetery about a hundred yards from the front entrance. Considering there were over a thousand people buried in St. Catherine's, it would have taken them some time to find it if Ron hadn't been waiting at the front gate.

"I've seen some stuff in my time that would curdle your blood, Morgan." Ron said as they approached the body. "But this goes beyond anything in terms of sheer savagery. The poor devil looks like he walked into a propeller and that's not the worst of it.

I don't know guys. I think I'm getting too old for this job."

When the three men reached the crime scene Morgan went off to talk to the forensic officials and make sure the crime scene had been sealed off properly. Evan went over to the body, notebook in hand, looking for similarities to the Gregg murder.

Eddington Carr, as he was later identified by a check on his fingerprints, was propped up against the gravestone, completely naked, his arms at his side and his legs straight out and spread wide—clearly posed by whoever had done this.

At first Evan thought his face was contorted, an obvious result of great suffering. But upon closer inspection he discovered something far more disturbing. The man's entire nose had been removed and crammed in the gaping hole left by this was a large amount of white powder. In addition to this horror, the reason for Carr's legs being spread was all too apparent. The victim's genitals were blackened and charred, so severely had they been burned, and the positioning of the body left no doubt that the killer wanted to display this atrocity. Finally, as had been the case with Martin Gregg, the victim had been branded with a series of letters; DCOYNTSYF emblazoned on his forehead. A "V" had been sculpted into the hair at the base of the neck and a half dollar sized bruise had been found on Carr's inner left thigh.

Evan put all of this in his notebook, shaking his head the whole time. When he'd finished he walked over to Morgan who was talking to Jennifer.

"It's him, Morg." Evan stated flatly. "The letters, the burning, the mutilation, the whole enchilada. I can feel it Morg, it is *definitely* him."

"Yeah, my gut says so too, only this time it's a 'V'." Morgan agreed, then turned and walked over to where Ron and George Dunston were making sure the area had been properly sealed off. "Ron, George. I know you're the first responders but I'd appreciate it if you'd give this to Evan and me."

"That was the idea when Ron called you, Morgan." George said. "When we realized what we had, Ron and I agreed that if you guys concurred we'd give it to you. Too many cooks spoil the broth and all that. Besides, you two are going to have your hands full until you get this crud. This way Ron and I are free to take anything else that comes up in homicide and, considering our plates are not likely to be full, we can still help out when you need some leg work done."

Morgan smiled, patted the two men on the shoulder and thanked them.

"Before we take off we found these near the body." Ron said, handing Morgan a film canister and a bundle. It was another red velvet sack that had been tied up at the corners and it was apparent that something was inside.

"Yeah, we found one of these at the first murder. Our boy likes to leave goodies for us. Let's see what Santa Claus left us this time.

Say, that's what we ought to call him." Evan said, raking the air with his hand in imitation of a bear's paw. "As in Santa *Claws.* He leaves gifts, some of which the vics would rather not have gotten."

Spontaneous groans from everyone present erupted. Cops liked nothing better than hanging a tag on perps, especially when the perp was a psycho and the tag was appropriately macabre.

"How about *Vindicator*?" Morgan offered. From the looks of the first two crime scenes I'd say this guy is looking for some *serious* revenge."

Nods of approval followed.

Morgan opened the package and removed a Valentine's Day card, a toy stethoscope, and a small coffee can.

"What the Hell is this stuff, Morg? Some kind of message?" George asked.

"Don't know, man. We'll have to work it out as we go."

After touching base with the techs, Morgan caught Evan's eye and signaled him over to where Jennifer was tending to the body.

"Evan, first thing tomorrow call the cemetery director and get a list of every employee that was on duty for the last…what's your best guess for when the vic died, Jen?"

"Well, based on the postmortem lividity, and the body's postmortem core temperature, together with the fact that we had a heavy rain this afternoon and mild temperatures, I'd say sometime between nine p.m. and midnight."

"So, let's say anybody who was working in this cemetery after eight o'clock tonight. Maybe somebody saw something but I doubt it.

Let's get out of here. Seven o'clock is going to come awful fast."

As Evan turned to leave, Jennifer caught Morgan by the sleeve.

"I thought you'd like to know that one of my guys found a set of footprints in the wet grass near the body. The storm this afternoon left the soil soft enough that we got two clear impressions. We've cast them and should be able to get the shoe size and approximate height and weight of the individual who left them. It doesn't mean they belong to the killer, but until we know different we can assume the possibility they do and treat this information as evidence."

"Good work. Uh, Evan." Morgan called out to Evan who was making his way out of the cemetery. "Check with the cemetery director and find out who's buried in that grave and the graves immediately surrounding it, along with their friends and relatives. I want to eliminate the footprints of anyone who had a legitimate reason for visiting one of these graves."

Evan waved back to Morgan, signaling that he'd heard and understood.

Satisfied that nothing further needed be done until morning, Morgan bid Jennifer goodnight and headed for home. A deep sense of fatigue suffused him; a fatigue he knew was not attributable to physical exertion, or lack of sleep.

This fatigue could not be alleviated through rest. Only the capture of Carr's and Gregg's killer, which would bring this nightmare to an end, could pull Morgan out of the blue funk he'd fallen into. Unhappily, the track record on this kind of murderer said that a quick capture was unlikely.

I should've listened to my father all those years ago and been a farmer. At least I wouldn't have to worry about sadistic strawberries and psychopathic pears.

Twenty

Three weeks had gone by since the body of Eddington Carr had been found in St. Catherine's cemetery early on Thursday morning, and during that time several developments had occurred, which Morgan dutifully entered on the marker boards as they came in. He'd also had a large street map of Deliverance tacked up on a second cork board and had placed it in the incident room. On it he'd marked where Martin Gregg's and Eddington Carr's bodies had been found with red pins.

1. One of the lab rats, Dennis Rickey, had come up with a brilliant theory as to what had caused the burns on Gregg's hands and had called Morgan at the 2nd immediately.

"Jen believes he was electrocuted so, if he was holding something metallic when he was electrocuted that would account for the burns. Now, the fact that the burn lines were so thin and long on each hand, and that they formed a band around the bottom joints of each hand, suggests to me that he was holding a long wire wrapped around each hand. What does that mean to you, Morg?"

"A garrote?"

"Right on, my man. Now what the hell was a judge doing with a garrote and where did he get it?"

"Oh, thanks. Answer one question and leave me with two more.

Interesting though. What was the wire made of?"

"Common steel."

"Well, I can guess who the garrote was meant for, Dennis, but as to *how* Gregg got hold of it…"

"Yeah, I know. It's doubtful Gregg was carrying it around with him on the off chance that someone would attack him. I couldn't prove it, but I'd bet that he came by it *after* he was abducted.

But that doesn't tell us where he got it or what transpired that made him feel he needed it. It also doesn't tell us where he got the wire in the first place, although Jen did find some superficial cuts on his hands which could be construed to mean that he injured himself in the process of procuring the wire."

"In any case, thanks Dennis. Every question we clear up puts another piece into the puzzle."

2. Two days after Eddington Carr was found another break surfaced. One of the detectives interviewing colleagues of Martin Gregg had talked to a cleaning lady who was working in the courthouse the night Gregg was murdered.

She remembered asking the judge when he would be leaving because she wanted to clean Gregg's chambers. The judge told her not to bother because he was meeting with a person at 10 p.m. who had information concerning misconduct in connection with a case that Gregg was hearing.

The significance of that revelation was that it opened up the possibility that the person who was going to meet Gregg that evening was, in fact, Gregg's killer.

It also meant that the detectives were going to have to retrace their steps and re-interview everybody who had been in and around the courthouse that night; a discouraging thought, but very necessary.

Evan observed that this meeting, being late at night with someone Gregg presumably didn't know, may have been the reason he made the statement earlier about his zeal compromising his common sense.

"Maybe the judge finally realized the dangerous the game he was playing. I find it interesting he told a cleaning lady why he was meeting this person."

3. It was determined by a consensus of the four homicide detectives that Virginia Gregg had not hired someone to kill her husband because if that were true, she would have been one unlucky woman, picking the one hit man in the world who was also an out of control, full-blown homicidal maniac; something hit men *definitely* were not, at least not *successful* hit men.

4. The forensic department and Jennifer had sent over their workups on Eddington Carr the day after he'd been found. Evan transferred the pertinent information to the marker board:

a. A razor sharp knife made from animal bone, found at the scene of the crime, was the instrument used to remove Carr's nose. The removal of the nose would have required considerable strength as the knife would have been required to cut through bone and cartilage. The age of the knife was placed at somewhere around 2,900 years.

b. The powder found in the cavity that had once been Carr's nose was identified as common talcum powder.

c. A pair of old bronze tongs, along with several pieces of charcoal, were also found at the crime scene and are believed to have been the instruments used to barbecue Carr's genitals. Age of tongs around 2500 years.

d. A film of the victim had been found near the body. It shows the victim in several short scenes talking to young people on street corners.

e. A round, flat brass disk was found at the scene. The profile of a horse's head and neck on the disk. Possibly part of a cufflink.

f. No fingerprints or any trace evidence were found.

g. M.E. determined COD to be asphyxiation and TOD around 11:30 p.m. on June 6th.

h. Trace amounts of chloroform had been found in vic's blood.

i. The bruise on Carr's neck was most likely caused by a cattle prod.

j. The "V" shaved into Carr's hair was different than the "I" shaved into Gregg's hair. No one had any idea as to the meaning of *these* letters.

5. Sarah Ellison had called to say that she had received the new cryptogram and had two things to report.

First, she had pretty much eliminated the possibility that the messages would require transliteration. She had called Evan at home, and after brainstorming various theories concerning the cryptograms, agreed that Vindicator *wanted* the message or messages to be deciphered. Therefore he wouldn't make that process too difficult.

Secondly, based on the feedback from her computer runs, she had eliminated the possibility that the letters represented numbers.

Sarah said she would call when she had anything further.

6. Eddington Carr was one sleazy street thug, dealing in drugs and prostitution in Portland, a fact that did not escape Morgan's and Evan's attention. Their guess was that his profession was the most likely motive for his murder. The film left at the crime scene only strengthened that. Carr lived in an affluent part of Deliverance. None of his neighbors had a clue as to his means of income.

7. The grave sites near the one Carr had been propped up on had not

been visited for more than a week, ending a possible lead.

8. The articles found in the velvet sack were common, sold in many stores and untraceable.

9. Victim was 5'9" tall, 155 lbs., stocky, sandy brown hair, blue eyes, and ruddy complexion.

10. Burns on the body and an open wound on the right bicep indicate victim suffered an electrical shock.

11. A ticket stub for the Portland Symphony Orchestra found at crime scene.

TWENTY-ONE

Evan sat at the large table in the conference room, sipping on a cup of coffee and waiting for Morgan. It had been a long day and his feet were tired from all the legwork. He hoped Morgan would get back soon so they could wrap this day up before Evan fell asleep on the job.

"Hey, partner. What's shaking?" Morgan strode into the room. He'd spent the last two hours in a meeting with the mayor, the police commissioner, and Captain Byrd.

"Well, for starters, Morg, Sarah called an hour ago. She says she isn't getting anywhere with the cryptograms and has an idea. She'd like for us to get her a list of everything we've got in the way of workups, crime scene reports, etc. She now believes Vindicator *is* sending us messages, and she wants to compare the cryptograms to the write-ups. If she can pull out the message he was sending based on what he did to the victim, then she's hopeful that she can decipher each cryptogram into a message mirroring those feelings."

"Makes sense. I'll have Dusty Xerox the files and get them over to Sarah right away."

"Uh, actually I'm heading right past Sarah's place later this evening. I could take the copies with me and save the postage." Evan offered, a little too quickly.

"Well, I don't know. I mean this *is* official business and sending the copies by mail will give us an official record of the transfer of confidential material in a murder investigation." Morgan struggled to keep a straight face and an official tone in his voice.

"You're not gonna make this easy for me are you?" Evan looked like he'd sucked on a lemon. "Okay, taking the copies gives me an excuse to see Sarah."

"Just teasing, partner." Morgan didn't want to carry his needling too far. "Actually, I'm glad to see you taking an interest in her. She's one of the nicest people I've met and you deserve someone who's as nice as you are. Besides, it's a relief to see someone who can intellectually run circles around my genius partner."

"Right. I love you too. How'd the meeting with the brass go?"

"How does it always go? Bureaucrats running around trying to cover their backsides and looking for someone to feed to the wolves if things don't go the way the press and the public expect them to, or as soon as they expect them to.

Bottom line, we got seventy-two hours to come up with something they can give to the press or they'll reassign the case to Dunston and Kopple.

I'll say one thing; S.T. defended us, but they weren't listening, especially the mayor."

"Then I guess we'd better get to it." Evan got up and walked to the marker board, picking up a magic marker as he went. "I'd like to compare what we have on Gregg to what we have on Carr. Maybe we can see a connection that goes beyond the obvious ones. "

"That's as good an idea as any I've got. Use numbers and put the same number next to items that match. Don't forget the bulletin board.

Use pins, one pin for match number one, two pins for match number two, etc. I'll compile a separate list on paper that we can show to Byrd, *if* we come up with something."

For the next two hours Morgan and Evan dissected the information that had been written on and pinned to the four large boards commanding the front half of the room. They studied, discussed, theorized, and questioned every aspect of the information before them. They compared and contrasted pieces of evidence, searching for similarities.

In all of this work the ultimate goal was to somehow gain insight into the deranged mind responsible for these two heinous murders.

"That's it, partner." Morgan leaned back in his chair, washed his face and neck with his hand, and sighed deeply. "Now, what have we got that the Captain or, more importantly, Mayor Raines will accept as proof that we're making progress."

Evan took the list Morgan had compiled as the final draft. It was the result of an additional forty-five minutes of arguing, compromising, scratching out, writing in, and revisiting ideas they'd already accepted in the first draft. He moved around the table to sit beside Morgan, placed the final draft between them and together the two men once again scanned through the list to see if there was anything else that needed to be changed or added.

SIMILARITIES

1. Both men were found naked.
2. Both men had been subjected to extreme heat as a form of torture.
3. In each case a film of the victim had been left by the killer.
4. Both men had had something inserted into bodily orifices.

5. Both men's work had negative physical ramifications on the people they dealt with.

6. Both men were electrocuted, possibly as a means of incapacitating them.

7. Both men had been branded with coded messages.

8. Both men had had their genitals assaulted.

9. Traces of chloroform found in both victim's blood—method of sedating victim?

10. Both murders involved the use of novelistic weapons and instruments of torture.

11. Both victims were male.

12. Both victims around 50 years old.

13. Both victims were subjected to extreme torture beyond anything imaginable.

14. The bodies of both victims were posed.

15. Both bodies found outdoors.

16. Both victims subdued in a way that did not require much strength on part of the killer.

17. Both men were Caucasian—any connection to the killer's race.

18.Both men had capital letters cut into their hair.

QUESTIONS

1. Were the crime scene locations part of what the killer was trying to say?

2 Any messages in the way the victims were killed?

3. What role is the killer playing and what is his mission?

4. What is significance of films?

5. Is there a sexual connection because genitals mutilated and both men naked?

6. Considering #16 in SIMILARITIES and #5 in QUESTIONS, could the killer be a female?

7. Who does the brass disk belong to?

LEADS

1. A white or cream colored, 1957 or 1958 Chevrolet station wagon, possibly with blue carpet, observed at the Gregg murder scene the night he was killed. Trying to trace.

2. Two plastic coins left by the killer at Gregg murder scene. Will try to trace.

3. Bone knife left at Carr murder scene. Will try to trace.

4. Brass disk found at Carr murder scene. Will try to trace.

5. Footprints found at Carr murder scene. Will try to trace.

6. Tongs found at Carr murder scene. Will try to trace.

7. Carpet fiber deemed to be consistent with automobile carpet. Will try to trace.

8. Killer has B- blood?

SUSPECTS

1. Unsub who was to meet Gregg the night he died.

2. Driver of station wagon.

TENTATIVE THEORIES

1. Killer believes he is meting out justice for the wrongs the victims have committed.

2. The tortures are symbolic of rituals.

3. The strange weapons used necessary to making murders fit the ritual.

4. The films are a means of showing why the victims were targeted.

5. Killer takes on role of judge, jury, and executioner God's Avenger?

6. The murders are not for sane reasons such as greed, revenge, etc. These are irrational and rage driven murders. Therefore, these murders won't stop until the killer is stopped.

7. The coded messages are his way of stating something he wants the world to know.

8. The victims were killed someplace other than where they were found as determined by an examination of the crime scene, lack of blood, and the materials required to commit the murders in the way they were committed.

"If I look at this stuff much longer I'm gonna toss my lunch." Evan complained gloomily. "I'm telling you, Morg, I don't see jack to give Byrd. It's all smoke and mirrors."

"Well, it is and it isn't, Evan." "The simple truth is we don't have anything here that will let us get in the car and drive directly to where Vindicator's holed up. So, we can't tell Byrd that he can assure Raines we'll have a collar in the next 24 hours.

On the other hand, we *do* have a couple of things in our favor. All those similarities pretty much confirm that we have one killer here. Plus, we have a *bunch* of material evidence and some of it, like the tongs and the knife, are going to be slam dunk case breakers if we can trace them back to somebody.

So, we show the Captain this write-up and assure him that we are in the process of tracing some fairly unique items back to their owner and *when* we do, we got our perp. Now, we both know that Byrd is too smart to buy that story. But he's also smart enough to know there's a grain of truth in it and if we're given a little time we might just pull it off.

I think he'll take this list and our theory, and decide the mayor will be only too glad to have something concrete to give the press."

"Yeah, the press." Evan spat in disgust. " Mostly they gather like leeches around a tragedy, looking for the nearest information meal. Not my favorite night creature."

"They're not all bad, Evan. The *Centurion* is a good paper and even Emmet Murray's handled the Carr murder reasonably accurate. We have to remember that, for the most part, newspapermen are just like us, trying to do their job the best they can and having to deal with bosses who need to please the fickle public.

"That's why you get the big bucks, O Great One." Evan's mood had suddenly brightened. "Let's go into the Captain's office and get this over so I can get outta here."

"Whoa, big fella! We need to edit this list first. I don't want everything we know getting back to the press. Now, what do we take off of the list?"

It took only five minutes for Evan and Morgan to take the tongs, blood type, coins, and station wagon off of the list and put the edited write-up on the Captain's desk. Byrd looked it over while Morgan and Evan watched him, hoping he'd give them the thumbs up.

When Byrd looked up, they knew they were in.

"You clowns don't fool me. This is a list is little more than wishful thinking. I know it. But, it'll keep Raines happy for now so it works for me—for *now!*

Morgan and Evan didn't need to be hit over the head. They got out of Byrd's office as fast as they could, grabbed their jackets off of their desks and split. The day was over and they were only too happy to go home.

Twenty-Two

Morgan and Evan pulled into the downtown Portland courthouse parking lot and parked next to a side entrance. Parking there was for courthouse personnel, so Evan slapped a permit on the dash that proclaimed the car to be a police vehicle.

Once inside the building the two men headed straight for the courthouse records room. They had decided to spend as much of the morning as was needed looking through transcripts of all the trials Martin Gregg had presided over. Morgan had put this task on the front burner when Georg and Jeff reported back regarding Gregg's past prior to his becoming a judge.

"There's not much there, Morg." Jeff had said. "The guy was basically a cipher until he was 22. He came from your average family, went to public school where he showed little motivation to learn, although he got decent grades and never got in trouble. He then spent four years in the Army from 1924-1927. Nothing outstanding there either. He served honorably, if unremarkably, achieving the rank of staff sergeant. Again, not much fire in the belly.

"But then something must have jump started him because by the time he was 27, he had graduated from law school and landed a job as an attorney in the D.A.'s office in New York City." George continued.

"He spent the next fifteen years as a fair prosecutor, but there were no wrinkles in any of the cases he tried that raised any flags with me or George. Not one case where he put someone away who might have been looking for a little 'get even' when he got out of the joint, or where Gregg might have done something unethical that could come back later to bite him in the ass. It was like he went out of his way to avoid anything that might jeopardize his future in any way.

Anyway, in 1948 he moved to Portland where he was elected to the bench, and that's where we left it."

"Bottom line?" Jeff chimed back in. "Martin Gregg led the most boring, cautious life imaginable, at least for the time frame we investigated. So, if there's something in his life that led to his contemplating suicide, or that caused someone to want his death, it happened after he became a judge."

Upon hearing all of this Morgan resolved to focus on Gregg's tenure as a judge in Portland, which is why he and Evan were at the courthouse now, preparing to search the transcripts of all of Gregg's trials. If they could find what he felt he'd needed to make amends for, or what someone had decided he needed killing over, the road to catching his and, most likely, Carr's killer would be made considerably easier to travel.

"You take his cases from '48 to '54 and I'll run through '55 to this year." Morgan said as the two detectives sat down in one of the document examination rooms set aside for the scrutinizing of court records.

"Sounds like a plan, partner." Evan replied, taking half of the large stack of records sitting in front of Morgan.

At one o'clock Evan looked at his watch and nudged Morgan.

"What say we check out the records we haven't gone through yet, haul them to the *Steakout* and finish the job there over some food?"

"Exactly how are you going to get the records clerk to let us do that, my friend? These records aren't allowed to leave the building."

"How many cases do you still have left, Morg? I've got three files I haven't taken notes on."

"Well, if you give me five minutes I'll be down to two. That still doesn't answer my question."

"Watch me." Evan reached over, put the two files Morgan hadn't as yet touched with his three, got up from his seat, and walked over to the records clerk's desk.

"Excuse me, Emily." Evan purred, catching the young woman's attention. "My partner and I are Deliverance detectives working on the brutal murder of Judge Martin Gregg; perhaps you've heard about it. I'd like to ask a favor of you.

The judge's sister is the wife of Oregon's governor and she, through the office of the governor, has put tremendous pressure on our Captain to solve this case ASAP. He, in turn, has made it clear to us that our lives depend on doing so.

Unfortunately, leads are scarce but we've gotten hold of a *very* solid lead concerning a defendant in one of the cases that the judge presided over. We're trying to trace a defendant who blamed the judge for the harsh sentence he received. We need to identify him, and find the case he was the defendant in.

So, here's the problem. We need to search all the transcripts of the trials the judge presided over and we need to do it by early this afternoon. We've been at it all morning and I'm about to pass out if I don't get food soon, but we don't have time to run out, grab a meal and come back here to finish before a meeting with the mayor and our boss at three. Could we *please* check out the five remaining files to work on while we eat?

I know it's against policy, but we're really in a bind and I'm hoping you've been in a similar situation before and can look the other way for about an hour."

I don't believe it! Morgan thought, shaking his head and rolling his eyes. *He's trying to sweet talk that girl into giving him those records. It looks as if my partner isn't as naïve about his effect on women as I thought he was.*

"I'm sorry sir; we can't let the records out of the office." It was clear from her face that the young woman was conflicted.

"Yeah, I understand." Evan replied and, as his shoulders visibly sagged and his voice registered deep disappointment, he placed a hand to his forehead and slowly turned to go.

"Sorry, partner, we're outta luck." Evan called over to Morg in a mournful voice that was tinged with frustration. "Boy, I hope the Captain doesn't get *too* mad. After that robbery case I messed up last month, he's liable to suspend me."

There's no way he's going to get away with this load of bull. Morgan was looking at Evan as if his partner had lost his mind. *It's so transparent a blind man could see through it.*

"Uh, Detective Flack. I suppose it would be alright since you're policemen and these records directly relate to a murder investigation. But I need for you to have them back by 2:30 when I go off duty, and only for the five you've shown me."

"You have my word, Emily. The files will be on your desk by then. Thank you so much." Evan scooped up the file folders and started back towards Morgan who was getting up from his chair. "Could you please do us one more favor? Could you please re-file the records we've finished with?"

"Sure, Detective Flack."

"Thank you again, you're an angel.

TWENTY-THREE

Morgan was still shaking his head when he and Evan seated themselves in the rear of the *Steakout.*

"Whaaat?' Evan's mask of incredulity evoked a chuckle from his partner.

"You really are the living end, my friend." Morgan picked up a menu and studied it. "That was a shameful thing you did back there, manipulating that girl with those baby greens and that smooth as churned butter voice. Talk about a con job. I mean really! Have you no shame?"

"Honest Morg. That was no con job. We really are under the gun and it *is* true that those records are a genuine lead. Besides, this a *major* murder case so I'm allowed a *little* slack."

"Yeah, but I doubt you'd have used your 'aren't I just too adorable to resist' approach if *Emily* had been 65 years old, gray haired, and wrinkled. Then again you probably would have."

"Aw, c'mon Morg. It didn't have anything to do with her age or how she looked. Most women are more compassionate than men. I was counting on her realizing how important this was to us and give us a break."

"What about those little white lies you told her? You haven't fouled

120

up any burglary investigation, you're not about to be suspended, and we *don't* have a three o'clock appointment with the mayor."

"I *did* get a little carried away, didn't I? Okay, that was wrong, but the rest of it was legit. I just embellished the facts a bit. You aren't really mad at me, are you?"

"No, of course not. And I don't doubt your honesty or sincerity. I just couldn't resist putting a little salt on your tail and, at the same time, reminding you that we need to be careful in what we say to the public if we're to expect them to trust us.

Now, let's get some food and tackle these records."

Evan's thoughtful nod told Morgan that his young friend understood and was acknowledging the older man's insight and wisdom.

Over Reuben sandwiches and German potato salad washed down with steins of Heinekens beer the two men finished their work on the files and compared notes.

"There are only two cases in his thirteen years on the bench that set off any bells for me." Evan said. "The Faulkner murder trial in 1958 and the Morrison rape case in 1955 both of which occurred when he was on Portland's third district court."

"I'd add one more to that list, partner. The Jacobson murder trial in 1950. Let's get out of here, get these files back to the courthouse then head on to the Deuce. It's going on two and I'd like to spend the rest of the day on the three cases we've selected."

Twenty-Four

By five-thirty Morgan and Evan had thoroughly dissected the three cases and had drawn up a synopsis of why they felt each case was worth considering as the reason for Gregg's anxiety and/or the motivation for his murder.

1. The 1950 Jacobsen murder trial had featured a unique defense tactic. Carl Mason, the defendant's attorney, argued that his client, Denham Jacobsen, was not guilty of murdering Sharon Wolff because at the time he was plunging an eight inch knife into her chest 73 times, he was sleepwalking and was therefore not responsible for his actions. When Mason presented this theory to the jury there was a stunned silence in the courtroom for fully fifteen seconds before prosecutor Avril Payne leaped from her seat and cried foul with a vigorous objection. A heated exchange between the prosecutor and defense attorney then followed.

Finally, Gregg intervened, calling for a two hour recess and instructing the two attorneys to meet with him in his chambers, where he chastised them both for conduct unbecoming members of the bar. He then assured them that any further outbursts in *his* courtroom would result in contempt citations and a vacation in the county jail.

However, when the trial resumed, the atmosphere in the courtroom had changed and a number of people, most notably three jurors, later declared that the incident had affected how they viewed the rest of the trial.

Up to that point the jurors felt that the prosecution was at least keeping up with the defense and they were still on the fence with respect to the verdict. But when Mason and Payne were allowed to trade jabs for almost thirty seconds before Gregg put a halt to their sparring match, these three jurors began to more critically view the prosecution's presentation of evidence.

They claimed this was due to a couple of comments Mason had made obliquely criticizing Payne's legal acumen and Payne's "caught in the headlights" expression in response to those comments. The jurors also noted that the confrontation seemed to take the wind out of Payne's sails, and for much of the rest of the trial she did not exhibit the confidence she had prior to the exchange.

In fact, when the case finally went to the jury much of the discussion centered on Payne's credibility and therefore the credibility of her case. Several of the jurors wondered why it took her so long to react to Mason's "sleepwalking" defense and concluded she'd been caught flatfooted.

That, coupled with her loss of confidence, led the jury to question whether or not she believed in her case and therefore in the veracity of some of the witnesses she'd called, especially with respect to circumstantial evidence. They looked closely at the crucial testimony of the psychiatrist who'd refuted Mason's "sleepwalking defense" and concluded that his testimony did not convince them beyond a reasonable doubt that Jacobsen had known what he was doing at the time he killed Sharon Wolff.

The foreman of the jury summed it up nicely.

"We thought in our hearts he was guilty but the law doesn't let you decide based on your heart. So, we found him not guilty because the prosecution failed to convince us that he *was* guilty. If the lady had presented a stronger case or had been more convincing in her presentation, the verdict might have been different."

Ultimately, Jacobsen was acquitted and the newspapers went wild, claiming another vicious murderer had escaped justice. The media did not mention Gregg's possible complicity in the outcome of the trial, choosing instead to focus solely on the sensational defense strategy that blew the prosecution's case clean out of the water.

However, that was hardly necessary as far as Sharon Wolff's family was concerned, especially her fiancé who was outraged at him.

"If I were Sharon's fiancé I'd be mad too." Evan observed. "It's clear to me that the prosecution lost the jury when Gregg didn't stop Mason and Payne from bashing each other.

I'd go so far as to say that Mason used his set-to with Payne to open the door for considering that nutty defense to be plausible. Then it was a short leap from plausible to beyond a reasonable doubt."

"I think the jury forgot why they were there." Morgan said. "I believe that because of what happened in those thirty seconds between Mason and Payne, bolstered by Payne's subsequent loss of confidence, which probably occurred precisely because of those thirty seconds, the jury did exactly what the foreman said they didn't do; decided the case on emotion instead of on the facts.

So, I agree with you. Sharon Wolff's fiancé had a good motive for wanting revenge and so did the other members of her family. The question now is if one of them killed Gregg, what led that person to kill

Carr and how do we get from a revenge killing to the murder of unrelated victims by the same perp."

2. The 1955 Bremer rape case drew the detective's attention primarily because of the sentence Gregg had handed out to Emlyn Morrison. Morrison, a 16 year old Portland High School dropout, had, on July 15th of that year, savagely beaten and raped his 15 year old girl friend, Nancy Bremer. The attack was so brutal that Miss Bremer was in the hospital for three weeks and needed facial reconstruction. Morrison was convicted on all counts, including aggravated battery and first degree rape. It was expected that Morrison would be sent away for several years.

But Gregg decided otherwise. He sentenced Morrison to one year in a minimum security facility which was equipped to provide him with the therapy Gregg felt he needed, citing the young man's clean record, drug addiction and youthfulness as mitigating circumstances.

"Emlyn is a highly intelligent young man who has no previous record of violent behavior. At the time of the assault, he was under the influence of amphetamines, a powerful drug that has been shown to cause anger, panic, and paranoia. I believe the state would be best served by attempting to rehabilitate this young man; and I am confident that with time and the proper care he will be returned to society and go on to be the productive individual he's capable of being."

"You know, when I first read through this case I didn't see much possibility in it." Morgan said. "I mean Gregg's sentence *was* within reason, even if the rest of the state thought the guy should've been fried. And, there was nothing else about the case that raised any alarms.

But then I remembered something from the newspaper accounts of the trial. Emlyn's father is William Morrison, one of the most influential men in Portland at the time, as he is now. Nancy Bremer's parents accused Gregg of letting Emlyn off because his father was powerful. Their claim didn't get much play in the newspapers or on T.V. though people in the Portland area seemed to support the family's contention that the media was afraid to go up against Morrison.

I don't know that any of that was true, but it doesn't matter. If one of Nancy's family members believed it, then we have to consider the possibility that the frustration that person must have felt festered over time and may have led him or her to kill Gregg."

3. The final case, the 1958 Faulkner murder trial was in the running for one simple reason.

The defendant, Madeline Faulkner, was accused of murdering her husband, James. The trial seemed straight forward. Madeline confessed to the crime, her fingerprints were found on the murder weapon, and she was found at the scene of the crime sitting in a chair, her husband spread out on the floor at her feet.

It was a dream case for any D.A. and a surefire win. As predicted, Madeline was convicted and sentenced to life and that should have been the end of it.

But when the case was appealed to the Oregon Fifth Circuit Court of Appeals, the verdict was overturned on the grounds that Madeline did not receive an adequate defense from the public defender who had been assigned to her case. And the reason it was overturned was reflected in the majority opinion written by newcomer Justice Martin Gregg who convinced enough of his colleagues to nullify the conviction.

"What makes this case interesting is that as a result of the appellate court decision, Madeline walked free. That allowed her to retain the rights to the book she had written about the murder, the trial, and the abusive husband she'd finally been forced to kill because no one, including the police, would stop him from beating her."

"And, *that* prevented her brother, Dominic, from collecting the royalties on the book which Madeline had willed to him when she thought she was going to be electrocuted, her having no other living relative." Evan continued, reading Morgan's mind. "I read the papers too, Morg."

"My, aren't we the cynic." Morgan chuckled. "You wouldn't by any chance be suggesting that the brother was interested more in the half million clams that book made than in the welfare of his sister?"

"What I know is there are 500,000 green reasons for Madeline's brother to hate Gregg.

What I also know is if Gregg had a drop of conscience, these three cases alone might have given him a reason to contemplate suicide."

"My thoughts too. Well, that gives us three new suspects. The sore foot index just went up.

"Sore feet and long hours." Evan added, glumly. "Oh well. I guess when I see Sarah tonight we'd better make it special 'cuz it could be awhile before we see each other again except in connection with this case."

"Yeah, I owe Jennifer a good time too. Hey, you think they'd like to double date at that new restaurant over in Leesburg."

"I think that's a great idea. Those two would definitely like one another. Besides, Sarah doesn't really have any girl friends; this might be a chance for her to find a buddy. I'll call her now and you call Jen. How does seven p.m. sound if the girls are up for it?"

"Fine. Why don't we meet at the restaurant? I'll make reservations for seven."

Both women agreed and the two detectives headed home to get cleaned up, praying that the evening wouldn't be interrupted by.

TWENTY-FIVE

"How's the case going?" Jen opened the conversation when they were seated in the restaurant at seven that evening.

"Not as good as Evan's bet with me on the home run race." Morgan said evasively. "Mickey hit number 27 today, but Roger got his 28th."

"There's plenty of time, Morg. Mickey Mantle is the greatest ball player I've ever seen. In fact, he'll not only hit more than Maris, but break Babe Ruth's record of 60 to boot.

Now, can we please get away from cop talk and eat? This is supposed to be the finest Italian food in the county."

Fantastico was reputed to have excellent food and the ambience added to the feeling that one was sitting in an Old World Italian bistro.

The couples ordered the restaurant's signature salad for four with garlic breadsticks to begin the meal, and a bottle of Cabernet Sauvignon to go with the main course of lasagna. Green beans sprinkled with smoked almonds were also ordered by all.

"Seriously, Morgan, are you making any headway?"

"I'd like to know too." Sarah cut in. "I've put a lot of time into those coded messages and I'd like to think it's been with good reason."

"Well, we've got three new suspects based on the cases Gregg adjudicated during the thirteen years he sat on the bench." Morgan explained, realizing he and Evan were outnumbered. "We also know from the Portland PD that Eddington Carr had competition for the prostitution game in Portland, one Joey Cordova. This guy Cordova is bad news with a mean streak a mile long. The Portland boys think it's quite possible he put out the hit on Carr, or that he made it himself. Other than that you two got an unedited copy of the report we gave S.T. to give to the mayor, so you already know everything we do."

"Yeah." Morgan interrupted. "I remember Cordova from my days in Portland. Bad hombre."

The food arrived and it was agreed that shoptalk would cease until the meal was finished. Instead, the conversation turned to a discussion of vacations, partly because none of the four had taken one in a long time.

"You know, I was headed for Jackson Hole when this hit the fan." Morgan said. "If the rest of you can get a week off when this case is over I suggest we all take a break and head there."

"That's where the Tetons are, isn't it Morg?"

"Yes, and a prettier mountain range you'll never see. Trust me; it's a vacation you won't forget."

"Sounds like fun, whatta you say Sarah?" Evan asked. "That is if you wouldn't mind being stuck with me for a week."

"I've got a month's vacation time coming to me and I can't think of a better way to spend a week of it.

Jen? I'll need a roommate and someone intelligent to talk to>"

"Count me in." Jen laughed at Sarah's oblique jibe at Evan and Morgan. Morgan owes me a good time and I'm not about to pass up a chance to collect."

"Then it's a go, just as soon as we catch this creep." Morgan declared and three heads nodded vigorously.

"Speaking of that report you gave to Byrd, why do you feel that the victims weren't murdered at the crime scene?" The dinner dishes had been cleared and the couples were enjoying coffee, and Jen was steering the conversation back to the case.

"Well." Morgan began. "Considering the things that were done to the bodies, there had to have been a massive amount of physical evidence, none of which was found at the crime scene."

"Except for what the perp wanted us to find." Evan broke in. "We know Vindicator left certain pieces of evidence as messages to us. We need to figure out what those messages are trying to tell us."

"We found no blood at the Carr crime scene, and there should have been plenty, considering his nose had been removed." Morgan continued. "Then there's the fact that a considerable amount of equipment must have been used to restrain and torture those men, not the least of which was Gregg's cross. No, they were definitely killed somewhere else."

"Well, I've got something to add to that list of yours." Sarah exclaimed. "I've been working on those cryptograms and, together with my read on that report you sent me, I believe we can eliminate the idea of messages utilizing words or sentences.

I think we're dealing with acronyms intended to say *something* about the person on whom they've been branded. I think it's this killer's signature.

Now that I'm aware of this I'm focusing my efforts to decipher them with that in mind."

"As long as we're on the subject I've got something too." Jennifer said. "The cast of the footprint found at the Carr's murder scene has been examined and our conclusion is that the person who made that impression is about 6'3" tall, weighs approximately 220 lbs. and has a shoe size of eleven.

That should be helpful when you begin to bring individual suspects in for questioning, not to mention allowing you to eliminate or continue to regard as suspect people you've already got in the headlights."

"That's really good news, Jen." Morgan said. "When we finally collar this animal you and Sarah can be proud that you played a major part in the arrest."

The couples spent the rest of the evening at Jennifer's home playing cards and putting the events of the past weeks out of their minds for a few hours, unmindful of the malevolent force slowly enveloping the city, bent on consuming all that it hated.

TWENTY-SIX

Vindicator stood outside the home, staring up at the second floor bedroom window, looking past the window, the house, the lights from the Fourth of July fireworks, beyond even the stars that shone so bright on the clear, warm July evening. Anyone noticing his transfixed demeanor would have been surprised to discover that he was actually looking at a point in the future, and waiting patiently for that point in time to come into the present; waiting and anticipating it with relish.

Glancing around, he checked the immediate area to verify that no one was there to witness what he was about to do, then silently and swiftly moved to the rear of the home, melting into the shadows as he did.

The lock on the sliding glass door leading from the patio to the kitchen was off, as he had known it would be. People like Brenda Hart never saw themselves as possible victims. Crime was for the poor schleps trapped in a world that floated somewhere outside and below the universe populated by the chosen people, of which Brenda Hart was a card carrying member.

Vindicator gingerly opened the door and slipped into the kitchen, listening for sounds that would herald the presence of someone else in the house. He knew Brenda Hart was upstairs because he'd seen her in the second floor bedroom window only moments before. *His* concern was that someone else was with her, someone capable of staying the Sword of Justice about to descend upon her head.

But the darkened home was deafeningly silent, as if it had been sucked into a black hole.

Carefully Vindicator hefted the small, black, leather physician's bag, transferring it from his left hand to his right as he rounded the island counter, headed for the front hallway, and the staircase to the second floor.

Dressed all in black and wearing crepe soled shoes, he was a specter gliding silently up toward the door he knew led to her bedroom. The light from the bottom of the door spilled out onto the landing, dimly illuminating it and, as he neared the door, clothing Vindicator in an eerie luminescence.

He paused, once again listening intently for sounds that would indicate Brenda was near the door. The light meant she was probably not yet asleep but he needed to know where she was before committing to his next move.

A wicked smile sculpted Vindicator's features, the result of the sound of running water.

She's in the bathroom!

Cautiously and methodically Vindicator turned the doorknob, easing the door open, and peering into the room as he did. He edged through the opening, crossed over to the bathroom, and his eyes narrowed as he realized that Brenda was taking a shower.

*You cannot rid yourself of the filth of your sins with water, daughter of Gomorrah. Your soul is damned and **nothing** can save you!*

Vindicator removed a cattle prod from the black bag and stood, back against the wall, just to the right of the bathroom door; a malignant spider patiently awaiting its prey.

Brenda Hart stepped out of the shower, toweled off, blow-dried her hair, and walked into the bedroom where she'd laid out a pair of satin pajamas on her four-poster. She was particularly happy this day, due primarily to the award she'd received earlier in the evening at an AMA banquet. She'd been honored with the Medical Executive Meritorious Achievement Award for leading a landmark campaign in Oregon to cap contingency fees for attorneys, ensuring that patients would receive at least 70% of medical liability awards.

She was especially proud of the fact that she was the first woman in the state to receive this award, and that knowledge supported the belief that her career had been completely restored after suffering a devastating blow several years back.

So immersed in her reverie was she that she failed to detect the presence of mortal danger until it was too late.

Vindicator closed the distance separating him from Brenda in the space of a heartbeat, the cattle prod pointed outward.

At the last moment she turned slightly, a sixth sense alerting her to some impending calamity, and stepped straight into Hell.

The cattle prod touched her and the reaction was immediate and massive. Her eyes shot up into her head, she began to convulse violently while screaming wildly, and within seconds had collapsed on the floor in a quivering heap.

Vindicator pounced on the stricken woman, covering her mouth and nose with a cloth soaked in chloroform.

Before sinking into unconsciousness, she got a look at her attacker and inwardly recoiled at what she saw.

The face above her was stone, completely devoid of emotion. There was no pity in that face, not a shred of human compassion.

And the eyes—ah, God, the eyes! Cold, lifeless black points—shark's eyes! They bore into her like twin lasers, emitting a palpable malevolence made all the more terrifying for the souless evil she knew lay behind them.

The message in those eyes was clear. Brenda Hart was going to die and the manner of that death would take her sanity long before it took her life.

In her final moment of awareness Brenda Hart *knew* her time on earth had come to an end. She then succumbed gratefully to the abyss that summoned her because she did not *want* to be conscious for what the hideous beast above had in store for her.

***

Vindicator placed the limp body in the station wagon and drove out of town. Ten minutes later he was ensconced in his cabin in the woods some miles west of Deliverance. It served as his sanctuary. He carried the body down to the basement, secured the head, arms, torso, and legs to the table that had obviously been made solely for the purpose of securely restraining humans, and stepped back to survey his handiwork.

He slowly circled the table, checking to see that all of the restraints were securely fastened and sufficiently tight so as to allow no movement. Then he walked over to a large workbench and selected a bronze surgeon's scalpel, a small iron chisel and an iron hammer, plus a large iron C-clamp from the numerous tools that were neatly stored there.

Placing the tools on a cart next to the table, he reached down and took a bottle of water and a small container of ammonium carbonate crystals from the bottom shelf of the cart.

Awaken, spawn of Hell! Lucifer hungers for your soul!

Vindicator mixed the crystals with water in a glass bowl and held the mixture up to Brenda's nose. Her eyelids fluttered and opened, and she attempted to shake her head as consciousness slowly returned. At first she was disoriented and confused, but then her eyes opened wide as she became aware of her surroundings, the restraints that bound her, and saw again with horror the cruel, black eyes of her tormentor.

She began to laugh, softly at first, and then wildly and uncontrollably as her mind snapped under the crushing realization that she was not to be spared the unbearable pain those demented eyes were promising her.

TWENTY-SEVEN

"I hope this isn't just a wild goose chase." Evan pulled out of the station parking lot and headed toward the I5 interstate. He and Morgan were on their way to Portland where they were meeting with Christopher Verble, a criminalist with the Portland FBI. "How can someone lead us right to our perp just from "reading" the crime scenes, whatever *that* means, going through the evidence we've collected, and constructing the behavior patterns of the victim and the offender. What *is* a criminalist anyway?"

"Chris applies scientific techniques in collecting and analyzing physical evidence in criminal cases, and he's *not* going to lead us to the perp, Evan." Morgan replied patiently. "Sarah said he'd help us to create a picture of the killer's personality and that, in turn, will make it easier for us to predict what he's going to do next. That will allow us to anticipate his movements, and if we can do that we'll increase our likelihood of catching him."

Sarah had mentioned Chris during a phone call to Morgan a week back.

"Chris is the best criminalist on the West Coast." She'd stated admiringly. "He's smart, dedicated, and passionate when it comes to trying to understand the criminal mind. He's also pioneering a new scientific crime solving technique. He calls it portraiting and it focuses on the behavior patterns of the victim and the perp, together with the evidence uncovered in crimes involving violence. I think he can help us to catch our guy."

"Exactly what is this *portraiting?*" Evan asked. "I don't think portraiting is even a word."

"That's why we're going to Portland to see this guy, partner." Morgan was trying to get Evan in the mood to listen to Chris, something Evan was clearly resisting.

"Yeah, well I'll believe it when I see it. Cripes Morg! I spent four years learning all the best techniques for catching bad guys and *never* was I told that a personality picture of the perp would nail him.

Working the case through miles of legwork and grinding the evidence is how you catch the bad guys. It's always been that way and it always will be.

Of course, all our hard work doesn't mean justice is always served, because we can't guarantee some slick lawyer won't get the perp off once we collar him, or some bleeding heart judge won't give him a slap on the wrist even if he *is* convicted."

"Even if all of that is true, would it hurt to listen to the guy?" Morgan asked. "He might be able to help us and if he does we get a new crime busting tool for free. If not, all we've lost is a little time and gasoline."

"Okay, but I think we're wasting our time." Evan was determined to have the last word and Morgan wisely let him have it.

The trip to Portland took another hour, primarily due to a stranded motorist the detectives came across and stopped to help.

By the time they arrived at The Bureau's offices in downtown Portland it was coming up on noon. After being shown to Chris' office and introducing themselves, Morgan suggested that the three men have a working lunch.

"I imagine you know where to get a good meal and some privacy around here." He said. "You can outline your program over lunch."

"Sounds like a plan to me. Working for The Bureau I've learned to eat and talk at the same time." Chris concurred. "There's a small pub right around the corner from here. The owner is a friend of mine and he'll set us up with a private booth."

TWENTY-EIGHT

"Basically, my job is to aid law enforcement officials in understanding the psychological makeup of violent offenders." Chris began after the three men had been seated in the pub. "If we can get 'inside' their minds, see through their eyes so to speak, we can begin to understand what makes them tick. We limit our studies to violent crimes involving great bodily injury or death because the personalities that commit those crimes are well wide of the norm and therefore more difficult to portrait.

We believe that an offender's behavior with respect to the crime he has committed is a reflection of his personality and vice versa. By analyzing the evidence in a crime and the way in which it was perpetrated, a psychological portrait of the criminal begins to emerge. Hopefully, that portrait can help in identifying him.

From this beginning we extrapolate a number of the aspects of his personality based on the choices he's made before, during and after the crime. Then we combine that with the relevant details of the physical evidence and the behavior patterns of the victim.

Finally, we compare all of this information with the characteristics of known criminal personality files and psychological abnormalities to construct a working description of the subject.

And, that's about it."

"So how do we use this portrait?" Morgan asked, mindful that Evan was taking notes and still looking skeptical.

"I've developed a little tool I like to use with the detectives investigating a crime. I would like to emphasize that this is just a tool to get you started, something to guide you in your investigation. It is by no means a panacea and should not be used as such.

It's still going to take a lot of hard work and considerable luck to nail this guy. At the end of the day you'll probably get him because of some dumb mistake he makes and you're fortunate enough to stumble over.

Don't misunderstand me gentlemen; I'm not demeaning your skills as investigators. It's just that with this much carnage, the mind behind that carnage is almost always comprised of a deadly combination of unpredictability, ruthlessness, and a high degree of intelligence. The major obstacle to his apprehension is that he can strike *anywhere* and *anytime.*

Your best hope is for a person so deranged he begins to behave in a manner disorganized enough that he will make that dumb mistake you're hoping for *and* hoping to recognize when it *does* come your way.

I, and some of my colleagues, have developed the portraiting technology to increase the chances that you *will* recognize that mistake when it occurs. I am also convinced that if it's used correctly, you will come to know the perp, begin to predict his moves and finally anticipate his next move which will allow you to capture him."

"Tool?" Evan interjected. "What tool?"

"It's a mind set really; four series of questions that you constantly ask yourself as you proceed through your investigation. These four questions, coupled with the portrait a trained professional will develop, should give you a decided advantage.

First, ask yourself what fantasies was this person operating under before he committed the crime. In the particular case now on your plate, you need to be proactive in determining what caused this person to act on some days but not on others. Does he seem to have a plan or were the acts spontaneous? Once you get the portrait started you might want to revisit each crime scene and view them from the perspective of the killer. How did he access the areas where the murders took place and, more importantly, how did he exit those areas?

Second, what sorts of victims were chosen? What links them? What method was used to commit the murder? Shooting? Stabbing? Strangulation? It's important to make the link between the victim and the perp, and between the vics. Those links are the landing lights that will lead you straight to the person responsible for these crimes. Sometimes the only link to the killing method is simply the sheer savagery of it. But even then there is almost always a more subtle connection between the method and the reason *why* the offender is killing in that manner.

Third, how was the body disposed? At the murder scene? Somewhere else? Was the body just dumped or was it staged and if so, why?

Finally, and this can be critical, what is the killer's behavior *after* the murder. I've found that many criminals are curious as to what is going on with the investigation. They will go so far as to contact the investigators or the media, especially if they think they're not being given enough attention. They've even been known to hang around police stations because their frustrated cop wannabes. Be watchful for someone who asks questions or offers theories to investigators out in the community. What may at first seem to be a nosy neighbor may, in fact, be your unsub.

"Unsub?" Evan had begun to furiously take notes and Morgan was relieved to see that his young partner was at last exhibiting a real interest in what Chris was saying.

"Sorry. It's a tag I made up to hang on any perp that is as yet unidentified. It stands for *un*known *sub*ject. By the way, be careful when using a portrait. If a possible suspect fits the portrait early on, be careful not to close down or neglect following up other leads.

Well, that's pretty much it. Now if you'll supply me with what you've gathered so far I'll start working on a portrait. I'll need to see the crime scenes and collate all the evidence. Figure three days because I've got a job here too and I doubt your captain will sign off on paying my salary out of your city's coffers.

If portraiting works well on this case we could set up classes at Lucerne Community College in Deliverance to train some of your detectives to be able to portrait.

I've got a three o'clock class at the FBI Academy here in Portland, gentlemen so I'll take my leave now. Send me copies of everything you've got. And, I'll call you in a few days and let you know what I've come up with."

"*That* was informative." Evan exclaimed as he and Morgan drove back to the 2nd. "I think this could work. I should've known the guy was the real thing. Sarah's smart, she knows moxie when she sees it."

"I agree. I think we'll take his four questions and start using them now. Wouldn't it be just too crazy if this technique resulted in our catching the guy?"

The rest of the trip back was made in silence. Both men were digesting what they'd just heard and considering how they could use it to their advantage.

One thing was certain. They'd regard anything that even remotely promised to end this nightmare sooner as a gift from heaven.

"Beggars can't be choosers." Was the quote that came to Morgan's mind noting that he and Evan would be the ones on the street with tin cups and pencils if something didn't break soon.

Twenty-Nine

July in Portland is usually near perfect, weather wise. Days are generally filled with sunshine with highs around 80. The nights are clear and cool with temperatures dipping into the middle 50's.

But today was different. A cold, raw wind knifed through Morgan's light cotton jacket, causing him to draw it more closely around him, though he was unaware of the movement. The sky was a patchwork of subtly different hues of grey broken with slivers of ice crystal blue. The noon temperature was a frigid 47 degrees; a November day dropped into the middle of summer.

Though he was walking through a cemetery, Morgan was far away from it, in a time and place long since past. Reaching a familiar headstone he stopped and glanced down, his eyes coming to rest on the woman's name neatly chiseled in the polished marble. He stooped and inched closer to the headstone, as if by doing so he could reach out and touch her.

Caressing the letters of the name etched in the stone he began to weep softly.

"Hi, Senna, it's me. I miss you honey." His voice was low and rough. "I'm really up against it right now and I need you. I remember how you used to tell me that I worried too much, like when I couldn't get my head around a case. You said to just step back and let God take over for awhile, that life had a way of working out for the best. Then you'd take my head in your hands and pull it close to your chest.

It was so safe there, sweetheart. All the pain would just melt away and all the worries that were pressing down on me ceased to matter. I need to be there now, Senna, only I can't find the way. I try to keep my mind off of the gun I carry every day; I'm working hard and staying in touch with my friends, but it's hard and getting harder. Everyone thinks I've gotten over losing you; it's what I let them think. But the truth is, a day doesn't go by that I don't put that .45 in my mouth and try to pull the trigger. I know that isn't what you want me to do—that it's a coward's way out, but I'm dying anyway; the only difference is the gun would be quicker.

If it weren't for Evan and Bud, I'd probably have eaten a bullet by now. That and the work. The work gives me a reason to live. I'm needed by the people who'd otherwise become victims like you. The work demands from me what I wouldn't demand of myself—placing others first."

"So, what do I do, Senna? I know what you'd tell me but the pain is so great sometimes I don't think even God can take it away. I'm trying really hard, honey. I just don't know how much longer I can hold on.

I guess for now I'll keep coming here when it gets bad."

Rising slowly, Morgan gazed longingly one more time at the headstone that bore Senna's name in large Copper Plate Gothic letters. His eyes clouded over as they moved lower on the stone and took in the smaller Century Gothic letters that spelled out Lauren Agnes Jeffords and the dates 1956-1956.

Tears spilled out of Morgan's eyes, cascading down his cheeks, and spilling onto the stone he was looking at.

Racking sobs followed, doubling the man up with pain and despair. Morgan dropped to his knees and wrapped his arms around him tightly, as if to keep the overwhelming anguish from exploding inside of him. He remained that way until the energy from his grief was finally spent.

THIRTY

"Joey's come on some hard times since you were on the force here, Morg." Max Herrick informed Morgan. "His days as a number one pimp are over. The poor sod's stable's been reduced to three girls he must have recruited from a geriatric ward, and his drug trafficking is zilch. You had a lot to do with that Morg, so he's not gonna be too thrilled to see your ugly kisser."

Max Herrick was a Detective Sergeant in the Narcotics division at the 7th Precinct in Portland. He had worked at the 7th with Morgan during the time Morgan was in Portland and they had struck up a friendship as a result.

A beefy red-faced man, some 5'8" tall, with thinning gray hair, Max was definitely a cop's cop; a no-nonsense, black and white, nuts and bolts kind of detective. And, he was damned good at what he did, which was to take down bad guys on a regular basis.

Morgan had called him a few days ago and asked if Max could accompany him Thursday morning when Morgan went into Portland to run down Cordova for questioning concerning the Eddington Carr murder. Morgan, ever mindful of stepping on fellow cop's toes when it came to jurisdiction, had wanted a Portland cop with him when he caught up with Cordova.

"*Really*? Well I'm real sorry to hear that, Max." Morgan declared, his voice weighed down by sarcasm. "Such a *nice* man too. Pray tell, how did such *terrible* misfortune come his way?

"You remember the heroin deal that went down on the south side of the city back in '57? The one at the warehouse on Saimon St., just across the Willamette River?"

"Yeah, we busted up a Mob deal that day. Got us both commendations from the mayor as I recall. So?"

"Well, it turns out that Joey engineered that little deal. It was a sort of initiation to see if he could pass muster with the wise guys, and thus get an in for himself with an organization that could do him a lot of good and extend his power in the drug trafficking and prostitution business in Portland.

But when that deal went south, not only did Cordova spend time at "The Rock" on Alcatraz Island in San Francisco Bay, but the botched venture also got him in hot water with the Mob boys; something one does not do if one values one's health.

When he got out of stir seven years later he had nothing, and the Mob made it clear to him he was persona non gratis.

In the last four years he's been on the streets, hustling prosti's mostly. He stays away from drugs because the Mob made it clear that if they heard he was dealing again, he would shortly be inducted into the Portland Hall of Dead."

"But why does he have a grudge against me? There were sixteen guys in on that bust."

"But none of the other fifteen spent six months running the deal down, and none of the others put Joey into the driver's seat when it came to who planned the whole thing, which led the cops straight to the doors of the Organization.

Joey spent considerable time convincing the Mob the plan could work and when it blew up in everybody's faces not only did they lose money, one of their own got collared and spent time in the slammer. You can imagine how that endeared him to the Dons. The only reason he ain't dead is 'cause his uncle is a Don in New York.

Trust me Morg, he hates you.

Here's his hangout now. Oh look. Isn't it thoughtful of him to be here just waiting to spend some quality time with us?"

Yeah, I'm all choked up." Morgan replied.

Joey Cordova was sitting on a bench near a pair of basketball courts where six men were engaged in serious battle. Pounding up and down the court, they drove one another relentlessly, but the peals of laughter said the game was still fun.

Joey was intently watching the game, really into it. Turning his head he noticed the two detectives approaching him and his expression immediately changed, his face an Etch-a-Sketch that someone had suddenly shaken.

Oh, No! Bulldog! Of all the faces I'd least like to see, his ugly kisser is at the top of my list.

Bastard ain't human. **Nobody** *spends six months, 24/7, doggin' someone's footsteps for a lousy two bricks of smack. But this creep did, and when he finally ran me down he slapped the cuffs on me without so much as a blip registering on his radar. It was like he was making a peanut butter sandwich for lunch. Cold as ice—it ain't human and I* **don't** *care what anybody says.*

It took Cordova all of ten seconds to note this and another ten to decide whether or not to try to run. By that time Morgan and Evan were nearly on him.

He bolted off the bench and hit the ground running towards a group of abandoned and rundown buildings two blocks down the street.

"Oh, crap." Max ejaculated and took off after Cordova at a dead run. Morgan was right behind him.

"You go right, I'll go left." Max shouted back and veered left around the corner of a dilapidated building that looked as if it had once been a donut shop. "There's a chain link fence at the end of that alley he just went in to. I'll go around and keep him from climbing over it; you go down the alley and keep him from doubling back.'

Morgan ran into the alley, drawing his weapon. He'd seen the look in Cordova's eyes. Either the guy was on something or he was crazy with fear.

The way ahead was littered with debris—boxes, bottles, wooden crates, and the like. Morgan advanced slowly, wary of each crate large enough to hide behind.

A cat shot out of a doorway and darted back towards the entrance to the alley, causing Morgan to jump and stumble against a brick wall.

He could see a fence some one hundred feet ahead and correctly assumed it was the fence Max had mentioned; only there was no Max behind it and, worse yet, no sign of Joey.

Morgan stopped, scanning the remaining distance to the fence.

Can't see anything. Where the hell is he? There's nobody ahead so where the hell is he? Max must have been wrong. Cordova didn't come in here or he got to the fence before Max did and climbed over. Unless...

Morgan whirled around looking back from where he'd come.

*Son of a bitch didn't hide **behind** a crate; he hid **inside** one of them.*

Morgan began to retrace his steps, being careful to check each box he passed. Half way back he came upon an old mattress lying on the ground.

A slight movement caught his eye. He smiled as he walked up to the mattress, flipped it over and leveled the .45 at the prone figure beneath it.

"Good day, Joey. Lovely weather we're having." Morgan said in a voice seasoned with a light touch of mockery that Cordova probably didn't detect. The salutation was *not* intended as a friendly greeting.

"Go to hell, Copper." Joey bit off acidly, rising to his feet. "You and I ain't got nothing to say to one another."

"That's right scumbag, you're gonna do all the listening and we'll *tell* you when to open your greasy mouth." Max came up from behind Morgan and stepped right into Cordova's face, burrowing into the man with twin orbs of fire. "Capiche?"

"Yeah, okay. Whatch you guys want from me? I ain't done nothin'." Joey's eyes betrayed his bravado. He was clearly on the verge of wetting his pants.

"Well, for starters where were you from 9 p.m. May 30th to 1 a.m. on May 31st, and for the same time frame on June 10th and 11th." Morgan locked eyes with Cordova waiting for his reply.

"How the hell do I know? That late at night I'm usually at my club on Burnside Street, but I couldn't say for sure." Joey's voice rang scared. He began to chew on his lower lip as if he was worrying over a disturbing thought and both detectives picked up on it. Morgan decided it was fear he'd seen in the man's eyes back by the basketball courts.

"You look worried, Joey." Max said. "You playin' us? Hiding something? You better tell us 'cause we're gonna find out and if we have to do it the hard way we're for sure gonna drop on you like a stone wall. Better for you to spill your guts now."

"I'm tellin' ya I ain't done nothin! Why you guys bustin' my chops? I know why you're here—Eddie. I didn't have nothin to do with that."

"Well, Gee Joey." Max said. "We'd like to take your word and all but we didn't take our silly pills this morning, so here's how it's going down. You are going to dig into that cesspool you use for a brain and think of at least two reliable witnesses who will place you *anywhere* but the crime scenes for the times and dates we've laid out for you.

We're giving you a pass for now but you've got just 48 short hours to button down an alibi and come down to the Twelfth Precinct with it. Otherwise I'm personally going to harpoon your sorry ass and book you. Do I make myself clear? Do you even *know* what a harpoon is?"

"You should take that routine on the road copper.

Reliable witnesses huh. You're gonna have to cut me a little slack on that one. I don't exactly rub up against high society ya know. And keep Bulldog off my case, will ya? He's not normal."

"Watch your mouth scumbag! Just get the alibi." Morgan's voice was tempered steel. "And, while we're at it we'd like a blood sample from you. We've already got your fingerprints. Whatta ya say? I've got the kit right here."

Cordova reluctantly agreed and Morgan took a vial of his blood.

"Okay, my man, you're free to go." Max said. "Just remember to come see me. Don't make me come get you."

"I hear you man. I'll be there."

With that he turned and walked away, looking back once.

"He's trying to convince himself he got out of here with no harm done. What d'ya think?

"I'm not sure." Morgan replied, shaking his head. "He's mean enough to have done it but then why kill Gregg? Besides, you'd have to see the bodies to even begin to understand the sick mind behind these murders. I don't think even Joey is *that* crazy."

"Unless he was on something at the time when he offed those two."

"That *is* a possibility. Let me run his blood to see if it matches the sample we got at the Gregg murder scene. If it does I'll be back."

Looking at his watch, Morgan shook hands with Max and moved to his car.

"I gotta get back to the Deuce. I left Evan to track down the few leads we've got. It's after two and I'm pretty sure he's waiting for me at *The Steakout.*"

"Well don't be such a stranger old man." Max called out. "Friday afternoon at the Twelfth we cut out early and meet around six at Frank's Pub for beer and supper. Drop by some time and we'll swap war stories. If you can make it, we're meeting tonight."

"It's a deal, just as soon as I clear the boards on this one. It's as bad as they come, Max. We've got to get the sicko that killed these people before he does it again. Until then I can't focus on anything else."

THIRTY-ONE

Morgan stopped at a pay phone and called the 2nd before heading over to *The Steakout.* To his surprise Evan was still there.

"Hey buddy, I thought you'd be scarfing down some appetizers right about now. What's up?"

"Nothing, I just got tied up checking out a few of the leads we put on that report we gave S.T. to feed to the mayor. I'm free now though. You want to meet at the restaurant in twenty minutes."

"Actually, I've got a better idea. Why don't I pick up some burgers and fries and come back to the Deuce. We can discuss what we learned today over a late lunch, enter any new info on the boards and call it a day."

"Sounds fine to me." Evan replied. "I'm kinda tired and that'll save my running out for food."

"Okay. I'll be there in ten minutes. Say, are you free this evening? A few of the guys I used to work with are getting together tonight around six for a bull session at a pub up in Portland. You wanna go? I was thinking we could bring copies of that report with us and the bunch of us could brainstorm it. They're seasoned cops and their input would be invaluable. Besides, they'd love to chew on a case as interesting as this one. What say? It's Friday and neither of us has to get up early tomorrow unless something breaks on the case."

"Yeah, that works for me as long as we get out of the Deuce by four so I can grab a little shuteye before we go. I'll pick you up at 5:30, okay?"

"Right. See you in ten."

By three-thirty Morgan and Evan had pretty much reviewed everything new they'd discovered and the net results were interesting.

1. Evan had run down the origin of the coins left on Gregg's eyes. They were sold by a chain of novelty stores located in Portland and Deliverance. All told there were fourteen such stores who sold the coins in bags of fifty for a dollar. They were made in Chicago, pretty common and hard to trace.

2. Evan had visited several jewelry stores to see if he could trace the brass disk found at the Carr's murder scene. No one could recall any cufflinks that looked like that but each salesman said he would attempt to locate a set.

3. Two of the station wagons on the list of possible vehicles seen at the Gregg murder scene had blue carpeting and samples from those vehicles had been taken for purposes of comparison.

4. Morgan entered the blood sample obtained from Joey Cordova into the evidence column on the board and then had it taken over to the forensics lab to be typed.

5. The bone knife and the bronze tongs could not be traced for the moment. Evan conjectured that they might be archaeological artifacts because they were old; especially the bronze tongs, and Morgan agreed they should work from that premise for the time being. It was agreed to send the knife and tongs to Dr. Greenberg.

It's been a long day, what say we close up shop." Morgan suggested, leaning back in his chair and stretching;

"Makes sense. We've gleaned all we're going to out of this stuff, at least for today."

"I'll see you at 5:30 then.

Thirty-Two

Frank's Pub was Portland's answer to *The Steakout*. The similarity between the two restaurants was not a coincidence. Dave and Linda Ways owned both of these establishments.

Frank's had been named after Frank Harbin. A uniformed veteran on the Portland P.D., Frank had been the one who brought Dave and Linda together and had been very close to both of them.

The standing joke was that Frank, a sworn lifelong bachelor, had sacrificed a brother officer just to keep his cousin's big sister from ending up a spinster, as if Linda, a stunning blonde, needed *anyone* to help her find a mate.

In 1953, at the age of 29, he was killed in the line of duty, taking a bullet meant for another cop. When Dave and Linda opened their second restaurant in 1959 they decided to name it after Frank.

"This is the kind of place Frank would have loved." Linda had said, her voice thready with emotion. "I'd like to think he's here in spirit, kind of like he's still with us."

The motif was essentially identical to *The Steakout* except that a large mahogany framed shadow box picturing Frank Harbin in his patrolman's uniform was prominently displayed over the bar. Pinned to the right breast of the picture was the Medal of Honor he'd received posthumously.

"Morgan, Evan, glad you guys could make it." Max Herrick waved and signaled the two men over to where he and three other men were seated at a large, rough-hewn oak table situated in the rear of the pub. There were three large pitchers of beer sitting on the table, along with wooden bowls of peanuts, pretzels, and barbecued pork rinds. It was evident that the men were relaxing after a long work week, and the isolation afforded them by the location looked inviting to Morgan and Evan who joined the group, eager to unwind.

"Jimmy, Ray, Mike, this is Morgan Jeffords." Max said to his three comrades. "Morg is one of the best detectives Portland's ever had. And this is his partner, Evan Fleck."

"I'm Mike Raines; this is Jimmy Oakes, our resident newbie in homicide." The man sitting to the left of Max said, offering his right hand to Morgan. The guy with the mile long cigar is Ray Banks."

Evan noted with a smile that Ray was a dead ringer for Humphrey Bogart and that Mike could have been a stand-in for Peter Lorre.

Handshakes all around signaled for Morg and Evan to pull up a couple of chairs and get comfortable.

"So, you're the legendary "Bulldog' Jeffords." Jimmy, a youthful, thin, tall, blond haired man said, initiating the conversation. "I've heard a lot about you. To hear Max tell it, you pretty much owned the streets around the 7th when you were here. The bad guys either stayed out of the precinct or risked locking horns with you. If I've learned anything in the year I've been here it's that when Max is impressed, I'm impressed."

Morgan just sat there, completely caught off guard by the young man's ebullience. It was a full ten seconds before he could recover enough to respond.

"I appreciate your respect, Jimmy." Morgan said; his face scarlet. "The fact is I do the best I can just like you and the rest of the guys on the force. If I've been successful in helping to keep the streets safe, its due in large part because of guys like Max, Mike, and Ray here showing me what the job's like when it's done right."

"But Morg; weren't you saying just the other day that you were lucky you got out of the Portland PD? Something about the detectives there not being able to put one foot in front of the other?" The angelic look on Evan's face belied the pure devilry behind what had apparently been an otherwise innocent, though unwise, comment.

Morgan closed his eyes and grimaced then opened them and looked heavenward, muttering something under his breath that, while unintelligible, was clearly intended to condemn his young partner to an immediate and painful demise. All that actually happened was that the other four men burst out laughing at Morgan's embarrassment. The moment served to completely break the ice and soon the five policemen were talking shop and discussing cases they were presently working as well as interesting ones they'd worked on in the past.

"Did Morgan ever tell you about the famous, or maybe I should say *infamous,* Symington murder case? Max said at one point early in the evening.

"Oh, no!" Morgan exclaimed dolefully, prompting another round of laughter.

"Max, *please* don't tell that old story again."

"No, I'd like to hear it." Evan chimed in. "Is it possible that the great 'Bulldog' has a chink in his armor."

"Well?" Max looked at Morgan.

"Go ahead. This clown will drive me crazy nagging about it if you don't."

"It happened in the summer, about 5 years after Morgan got his shield." Max began, taking a swig of his beer to wash down a bite of the hamburger he was laboriously working his way through. "Morgan was partnered with Bud Oslen by then and good thing too because Morgan was green as a frog.

Bud later transferred to Deliverance and Morgan followed soon after, we think because Morgan was afraid we'd find out Bud did all the work when they were partners in Portland."

More laughter and Morgan's blush deepened.

"Anyway, Bud took Morg under his wing which, by the way, is the real reason your partner is as good a cop as he is today.

One day, they caught a murder/suicide over on the southwest side of the 7th, one of the richer areas in Portland. When they arrived at the crime scene Bud told Morg to see to the bodies and take notes on what he found.

Now, you have to understand the scene. There was an old woman of about eighty stone cold in her bed, an I.V. hooked up to her arm. At the foot of her bed the body of a young woman had been found, curled up on the floor in a fetal position and equally as croaked. A Cocker Spaniel was sitting off in a corner watching everything that was going on.

Neither of the bodies showed any exterior signs of foul play, and the whole thing was a mystery that would hopefully be cleared up by the coroner. Morgan had cleverly observed two small punctures in the old woman's I.V. and deduced that something nasty had been injected into her, possibly by the unfortunate soul lying on the floor. He also noticed a hypodermic needle on the floor by the young woman.

Two days later, the autopsy report came in and its findings were not a surprise. A large concentration of strychnine had been found in the blood of both vics. A broken cup found a few feet from the body on the floor also contained traces of coffee and strychnine. The old woman had been identified as one Marian Symington, a wealthy member of Portland high society who was renowned for her charitable work.

It was also discovered that the young woman's name was Emma Colfax. She was the old woman's niece, lived with and took care of Marian, and was the only heir to her aunt's very large fortune.

Morg felt the case was open and shut. The young woman had injected the strychnine into the old woman's I.V. and then, in a moment of morbid regret, had drunk the coffee laced with the same poison. Hence, murder followed by suicide.

Bud wasn't so sure. He wondered why Colfax had *injected* her aunt and then *drunk* the poison. For that matter Bud wondered why she'd committed suicide so soon after killing her aunt. The whole thing didn't seem right to him and he'd said so.

But Morgan figured that Colfax had done that because she was afraid of needles. As to *why* she'd committed suicide, Morg believed she'd either freaked out when she'd seen the horrible, convulsive way her aunt had died, or she suddenly realized she couldn't get away with such a stupid stunt and decided not to hang around and wait to be electrocuted.

Bud gave in and said okay, but Morg was to cross all the t's and dot all the i's before he turned their report in to the D.A. Marian Symington was a pillar of the community and the powers that be would want her case handled with kid gloves.

Which is exactly what Morgan did, or so he thought.

He went back over the crime scene and reexamined the body, reread the coroner's report and the notes he'd taken at the scene of the crime; and he concluded that Emma Colfax murdered her aunt, and then killed herself. That was how he wrote it up and that was how it went to the D.A."

"So that's it?" Evan said. "Sounds like Morg did just fine."

Max looked at Morgan who just threw his hands up in resignation and nodded for Max to continue.

"Oh he did fine alright, except for two minor points." Max was trying hard to keep from laughing. "First, the mortician responsible for preparing Marian Symington's body was taking great pains to see that she would look her best for the wake. In the course of his ministrations to her he noticed what appeared to be a small pin prick on her right arm. He immediately called the coroner who hot footed it over to the funeral parlor. Upon closer examination, the coroner decided that the pin prick was in fact a needle mark and proceeded to call a halt to the funeral until he could investigate further.

Needless to say that did not please the D.A., the Chief of Police, or anybody else connected with a case everybody thought was closed.

And, things got worse. The forensic boys had to go over all of the evidence again and they found that the I.V. previously thought to have been the conduit for the strychnine found in Marian Symington's body had traces of some dried substance on and near the area where the syringe had supposedly been inserted.

Which leads us to the second oversight.

It turned out that the substance was saliva."

"Are you telling us that somebody *bit* into the I.V.? " Ray interrupted.

"Not exactly." Max continued. "More like some*thing*. It was *dog* saliva! Pursuant to a thorough investigation it turned out that Marian Symington had killed her niece by putting strychnine in her coffee after which she injected herself with the same poison, flung the needle by her niece's prostrate body, and lay back in her bed waiting to die."

"But what about the I.V.?" Mike cut in.

"That's the strange part. Apparently Marian's puppy sensed something wrong with her mistress and tried to rouse her by tugging on the I.V. Its needle sharp puppy teeth made the holes in the tube and its mouth left the saliva.

"So *why* did she kill her niece." Evan asked.

"Because she found out that Emma was going to leave her and run off with some drummer in a rock band. The old girl couldn't bear the thought of being left alone so, in a rage, she killed Emma. Then, horrified at what she'd done, she took her own life. At least Morgan got that part right, sort of."

"How did you escape being hung out to dry, Morg?" Ray asked, grabbing a handful of pork rinds.

"Dumb luck and a guardian angel." Was the reply. "The brass down at city hall actually preferred my version of what happened. It kept Marian's image as a humanitarian and philanthropist intact. Plus, since she was dead and her niece had no living family, the mayor saw no reason to drag Marian's name through the mud for a single insane, murderous act born out of a terrible fear. My report was altered somewhat to read that *both* women had met their fate at the hands of person or persons unknown and the entire affair was laid to rest.

Actually, I came out of the mess without a scratch. No letter of reprimand placed in my jacket, no suspension, nothing. In fact, I was given a ribbon for initiative—go figure. Of course, I know why all this took place. Bud called in a few favors from the mayor and the police commissioner. Bud was my guardian angel. I think he felt guilty for letting me issue that report without checking it over, especially since he had doubts about my theory in the first place.

Now, if we're finished with humiliate Morgan time, could we switch gears? Evan and I would like your thoughts on this crazy murder case we're working on. I've brought copies of everything we've collected so far in the way of evidence. Take a few minutes to read through them and we can start brainstorming."

***

For a full twenty minutes the only sound coming from the table where the six men sat was the chewing and swallowing of food and drink. Each of the four men sitting with Morg and Evan were concentrating on the papers in front of them. Occasionally, one of the four would pause to ask a question then return to the lists and reports.

When it was apparent that Max, Mike, Ray, and Jimmy were ready, Morg and Evan sat and waited to hear what they had to say.

"For starters, I've seen something similar to those trinkets you've found at the murder scenes." Mike said, breaking the silence. "Back in '57 we had a series of murders in the Bowery.

At each of the four scenes a small wooden letter was left by the killer; an L, an S, a K, and a C. We damn near went crazy trying to figure out what they meant until a hotshot rookie pointed out that each letter in the collection could refer to the word that its pronunciation suggested.

As a result we caught the guy; one Ellis Casey. Get this. He was trying to tell us who he was because he *wanted* to get caught. Go figure.

Maybe the items your guy is leaving are similar in that they're symbols for something other than what they are. For example, the picture of Joan of Arc found at the first murder scene could be Vindicator as he sees himself—a hero and a champion."

"Maybe Vindicator's a woman." Jimmy offered. "I mean wouldn't this nut choose a picture of a *male* hero if he was a man."

"Possibly, or maybe that's a red herring thrown in just to confuse the police." Ray pointed out. "Besides, Mike's theory is just that—theory. We really don't know what those items signify."

"I agree." Evan said. "The value in Mike's observation is not in the details; it's that the items that were left at the murder scenes are symbolic and right now only Vindicator knows what they mean. Now what?"

"That's where Chris comes in, partner." Morg cut in. "I think the way this killer slaughters his victims and the films he leaves are him trying to tell us, or more accurately the world, why he's killing.

And, I'm on the same page with Mike in thinking that the articles left in the red velvet sack are symbolic ways of telling us something.

Any other observations?"

"What if the films are Vindicator's way of exposing a side of each victim we don't know about that he *wants* us to?" Max, who'd been silent for a long time, said quietly.

"Pardon?" Evan remarked, pushing his dinner plate aside and leaning forward, clearly interested.

"What if the films are meant to convey to us *why* the vic is being singled.

For whatever reason, this nut may be bent on punishing people who've escaped retribution for crimes he believes they've committed.

Granted, these people may not actually be guilty of anything. But, if I'm right about this, our head case *thinks* they are and that's the name of that tune.

Hell, for all we know, only *one* of these people may have wronged him, which set him off, and now he sees himself as some half-ass crusader.

Either way, if I'm right, Morg and Evan are quite possibly in for a long, frustrating ride."

Over the next few hours, the discussion ebbed and flowed, each man expressing his observations while the others listened. At eleven, Dave rang the time bell, signaling that the place was closing in 30 minutes.

"It's been a blast, fellows." Morgan said, laying a twenty dollar bill on the table. "Evan and I seldom get to mix business with pleasure. Thanks for the beers, food, fun, and especially the help."

"Yeah." Evan agreed. "Let's do it again—soon."

"We're here pretty much every Friday night." Jimmy said, smiling.

"Check." Morgan replied.

Thirty-Three

Sunday morning started off cool and clear. It had rained the night before, the result of a front pushing through, and Canadian high pressure had settled into the area. Morgan and Evan were on the road by ten, having agreed the night before to drive over to Raleigh Hills, a small village halfway between Deliverance and Portland. They'd received a call from Raleigh Hills Police Department late on Friday afternoon, informing them that a 1958 Chevy Nomad station wagon had been towed to the police department's vehicle compound. It was cream colored and had blue carpeting.

One of the men at the compound had remembered a story in the Portland Tribune that included a description of a vehicle sighted at the scene of the Gregg murder. He called the Portland P.D. and they in turn called Deliverance.

The two detectives had decided to go on the chance they'd score a hit on the vehicle. They were bringing a sample of the blue carpeting they'd found at Gregg's murder scene, hoping to match it to the wagon's carpet.

"I've been chewing on what the guys said last night." Morgan remarked, turning onto Interstate 5. It was forty minutes to Raleigh Hills and Morgan figured they could make good use of the drive time.

"Me too, partner." Evan said. "They had some pretty good ideas."

"Yes. I especially liked Max's take on the films. If we can use the films to figure out what Gregg's and Carr's sins were, maybe we can determine why nut boy hated them so much. Then, if we're lucky, that information will lead us to the perp."

"Oh, crap!" Evan exclaimed. "That means we're gonna have to see the damn things for the third time."

"I know, but it has to be done. What did you think of Mike's suggestion that the things in the sack are symbolic and represent messages of some sort?"

"It's possible." Evan replied, taking out his notebook. "Let's see what we've got. At the Gregg crime scene Vindicator left a toy Corvette, some Coke in a small bottle, and a picture of Joan of Arc. With Eddington Carr it was another toy, this time a plastic doctor's stethoscope; an empty coffee can, and a Valentine's Day card. Care to make a stab at what they mean?"

"No. Granted, a toy was left at each scene. And, I suppose you could say that the Coca Cola and the coffee can are both connected to brown liquids but I don't see the significance of that. You?"

""Naw, I played around with the list while I was eating breakfast but the only thing I came up with was a headache. How are we supposed to figure out what this guy's up to when we both know he's a nut and doesn't think rationally?"

"We might not, but if those things *are* clues I've got a hunch his twisted mind will likely insist on playing fair and make it so we can decipher them *if* we're clever enough. So, we keep on trying."

"Right, except *his* idea of playing fair is likely as twisted as his mind which leaves us at square one again.

Say there's the compound." Evan pointed towards a gray stone building.

Once inside the building, Morgan and Evan made their way to the office where a rotund, uniformed police officer named Harry Stone met them and escorted them to a car sitting just outside the office.

"I had it brought up when I learned you guys were coming to look at it. It was parked in front of 235 North Anther Street. Belongs to Mr. Thomas Simpson who, by the way, does *not* live at 235 North Anther St.

Long story short, Mr. Simpson reported his vehicle missing over two months ago. He'd pretty much given up on getting it back when one of our uniforms spotted it, checked it out and had it towed here. I called Mr. Simpson to notify him that his vehicle was at the compound. I also informed Mr. Simpson that we would be holding on to his vehicle until a formal investigation can be conducted.

That woulda been it but for my remembering your case. I couldn't remember the name of the car you were looking for so I checked out the outstanding warrants board and called Central."

"Thanks, Harry." Morgan said, shaking the man's hand. "We'll take it from here."

The two detectives spent the next ninety minutes giving the interior of the station wagon a thorough going over, checking for possible forensic evidence. Morgan took the cargo area while Evan focused on the front and middle seats. At the end of that time they slowly walked around the vehicle, inspecting its exterior for possible evidence.

"Nothing!" Evan spat out disgustedly. "Even the carpeting is a darker shade of blue."

"That difference could be the result of a number of things. Our sample might have been subjected to sunlight or have been stained and cleaned with a chemical that lightened it. To be sure we have to cut a sample from this carpeting and give it to the physical evidence boys.

As for any other forensic hits, there are some stains behind the rear seat that I want looked at by forensics. However, I think you're probably right."

Morg and Evan cut the samples from the station wagon they wanted for testing, washed up in the compound's restroom, and thanked Harry again for all his help.

"If all the P.D.'s in the state were as alert and cooperative as you guys in Raleigh Hills our closed case rate would be a lot higher."

"One hand washes the other, Morg." Harry said, simply and succinctly.

"Yeah, well we really appreciate it." Evan added as he and Morgan headed towards their car. "Any time we can do you a favor just call."

Just as Morgan opened the door to climb in, Harry came running out from his office.

"Hold on!" He exclaimed. "Got a call for you Morg from your captain. He says it's urgent.

Morgan sighed and headed back inside, leaving Evan to wait with the car.

"Get over to the Burning Oaks Estates subdivision on the double!" Byrd bellowed into the phone, causing Morgan to wince. "The sonofabitch has done it again!"

After taking time to calm the captain down and to assure him that he and Evan were on the way, Morgan had Byrd put the day clerk on the line in order to get the particulars as to where the homicide had taken place. Then he ran to the car and sped away from Raleigh Hills.

"You want the long version or the short?" Morgan glanced at Evan whose set features told him the young detective knew what had happened.

"Makes no difference, it's all bad." Was the terse reply.

THIRTY-FOUR

Burning Oaks was spectacular, befitting the extraordinary wealth that had built it. Each of the twelve homes comprising the subdivision sat on an acre of land, surrounded by fifty to one hundred foot tall Oregon White Oak trees. Each of the homes was easily worth more than a half million dollars.

The entrance to the exclusive community was gated and a burly guard was seated in the guard house, looking properly menacing.

"May I see some identification sir?" The guard said his voice flat and uninviting. "It's a madhouse around here today. Cops all over the place. Medical vehicles coming and going. No one who doesn't belong here is getting through."

Morgan flashed his badge about two seconds ahead of Evan and waited for the man to raise the wooden arm that blocked their way.

"Excuse me detective Jeffords, I need to know why all of these policemen are being allowed into this compound." The guard said stubbornly. "The Covenant is quite specific about allowing non-association members access to the grounds."

"Let's get something straight, Cochise." Evan called out from the passenger side. "We don't *need* to give you a reason! These are police badges and they pretty much let us go where we want. We are here in an official capacity and that's *all* you need to know. Now open the gate!"

Begrudgingly, the guard pushed a button, the arm slowly came up, and Morgan drove on.

"Jeez, these rent-a-cops!" Evan exclaimed loudly enough for the guard to hear as they drove through the gate. "Give 'em a toy badge and a costume rental uniform and the clowns think they're Jack Webb."

"That must be the place." Morgan cut in.

Evan looked to where Morgan was pointing and saw five vehicles sporting flashing red lights. They were parked in front of a palatial stucco and stone house.

Morgan pulled into the driveway, noting that the Boston Celtics could have played their games on it with enough room left over for a hundred fans.

All this wealth didn't mean a damn thing when the Pale Rider came for this poor soul. Morgan reflected as he surveyed the home and grounds, drinking in the opulence and excess.

"Where's the body?" Evan asked a uniform standing just outside the front door.

"Upstairs, first bedroom on the left." The officer replied, noting Evan's badge. "There's a detective Ron Kopple up there now."

"Has the place been nailed down?" Morgan asked, flashing his shield.

"Yes sir. We've sealed off the grounds. Nobody gets in without police authorization. That includes the press."

"Okay, thanks" Morgan said, moving past the policeman and heading into the house. "By the way, who's the vic?"

"Name's Brenda Hart. She's a doctor."

"This is some house!" Evan exclaimed as they made their way up the beautiful red oak spiral staircase to the second floor of the home. "With the kind of money it took to build this monster you can bet we won't hurt for motive."

"In here!" Ron called out from a doorway just to the right of the top of the stairs. "Grab a pair of gloves and watch where you step. Jen is on the way over and she'll have my hide tanned and stretched if I let her crime scene get screwed up."

The sight that greeted Morgan and Evan as they entered the bedroom was grotesque beyond description. A woman was lying on the bed, spread-eagled, on her back; her hands and feet securely tied to the bed posts. She was fully clothed, a fact that seemed strangely out of sync with the rest of the gothic horror show that lay before them.

Were it not for the outline of breasts beneath a sleeveless blouse covered in caked, dried blood, it would have been difficult to make out that the victim was a woman. Her face had been horribly savaged; the mouth a mangled, crimson chasm. Where her eyes should have been, gouged, empty sockets bespoke the madness that had descended upon this poor soul.

The nightmare didn't end there. Her head had been shaved clean and *two* groups of letters had been branded into her scalp, one across her forehead and a second just above the first. AEFAE on top and ATFAT below it.

Both of her hands had been severely burned.

Morgan and Evan stood mutely, biting back the profanities on their lips and trying to comprehend what they were seeing.

"Pinch me, Morg." Evan said disbelief a winter coat for his voice. "I swear we've been dropped into an Edgar Allen Poe story. Have you *ever* seen *anything* like this?"

Easy, Ev." Morgan's face was stone. "Let's just button things up here and get the hell out. Making this day stay down is going to require some company with my friend Jack. And no, I have *never* seen *anything* like this."

"Yeah. Well, if your friend Jack comes in a bottle, I think he's gonna be my friend too."

As with the other murders, a film had been left, and the instruments that had most likely been used to commit the atrocities perpetrated on the victim were lying on the floor next to the bed. There was a scalpel, a chisel, a hammer, and a small, portable vise.

Burn marks on her forearm indicated she'd probably been hit with a cattle prod.

"Well, at least he didn't shave a letter into her hair." Morgan noted.

"Small comfort there." Evan observed sarcastically. "What's with the second branding? You think he's escalating?

"Your guess is as good as mine, partner. It's a change in the pattern though, and definitely worth noting."

The red velvet sack contained a miniature Catholic Bible, a small plastic replica of what appeared to be an aborigine, and a picture of what appeared to be a conference room.

"Okay. I think we've dealt with our end of this." Morgan said forty minutes later. "Jen and the lab rats can take care of the phys ev. Let's go back to the Deuce and transfer our notes to the incident boards. Then I suggest we relocate to Dave and Linda's place. It's two-fifteen now and it will be three before we get back to the precinct. I say we treat ourselves to an early day considering it *is* Sunday.

If you want, we can talk briefly about this mess at the pub, but only for a little while. I'm going to need a break from this case for a bit and the sooner the better."

"I hear you, partner. Sounds like a plan. William and I are going to an open air concert under the stars in Portland tonight. I can give him a call when we get back to the Deuce and plan to meet at the band shell around 6:30 instead of 7:30."

"It's all set." Evan said, sitting down at the backroom table where Linda Ways had seated them. "William just got back from New York an hour ago and he'll have time to change clothes and meet me at 6:30. Said he'd bring some deli sandwiches and drinks so we can flop on a blanket and eat while we listen to the music. Pretty nice guy, huh?"

"That he is, partner. Does William have an outlet for his games in New York?"

"Yeah, it's where he got started. He grew up around The Finger Lakes in New York State. Seneca Lake, I think.

At five o'clock that evening the two men parted company, having spent a couple of hours unwinding at *The Steakout*. Not much had been said concerning what they'd seen that afternoon, both men needing a few hours away from the case.

Morg suggested they meet at the precinct at nine Monday morning and Evan agreed.

"We'll play around with what we got today until the forensics comes in. "

"Get to bed early tomorrow." Evan suggested. "I think Monday's gonna be a long one."

THIRTY-FIVE

A bombshell was waiting for Morgan when he walked into his home at six-thirty. The phone was ringing and Morgan toyed with the idea of not answering it as he walked to the refrigerator and pulled a T.V. dinner out of the freezer compartment. He allowed it to keep ringing while he set the oven to preheat and carried a beer to the living room where he flopped into his recliner.

"I *hope* this isn't going to ruin the rest of my evening." He said aloud to no one and picked up the receiver.

"This better be damned good!" He growled into the mouthpiece, assuming it was either Evan or Captain Byrd.

"It is but I'm not going to tell you if your manners don't improve."

"Oh, Jen. Uh, I'm sorry. I thought it was Evan or Byrd about to tell me my day wasn't over and it's been already been a bear."

"No, what I have to say doesn't require anything from you. I just thought you'd like to know what I discovered when I started the autopsy on Brenda Hart."

"You still working?"

"I know you need this ASAP. Anyway, guess what I found."

"I'm not so sure I *want* to know."

"When I pulled the sheet off of her body to begin the autopsy I noticed an "X" had been shaved into her pubic hair."

"Ah! Evan and I wondered about that. It was one of the differences from the other two murders. We figured he couldn't because he'd shaved her head to make room for the two sets of letters he branded there. We should have known the sick schmuck would find another place to *sign* his work, which is what we've decided he's doing."

"But that's not why I called you. When I looked closer I noticed something unusual. Small pieces of some white material were imbedded in the skin where the 'X' had been shaved. I extracted them and ran them under a microscope.

Morg, they're tooth fragments. I think they're Brenda's teeth. "

"Oh, great, just great!" The frustration in his voice ground into her ears and Jen regretted bothering him when he was so tired. "The hits just keep on coming."

"I should have waited until tomorrow to dump this on you" Jen said. "It's just that it was *so* weird. I'll know for sure tomorrow when I get her dental records."

"No. Actually, it's good you did call. It *is* weird. I think there's something significant about this mutilation, something the nut didn't do with the other victims. Evan and I will note it on the boards and give it an asterisk. Thanks."

Later, as he sipped his beer, Morg reflected on the past several days.

A madman had descended on Deliverance. He or she was determined to destroy an unknown number of people in the grisliest ways possible. That the driving energy behind that unbalanced mind was immeasurable rage was obvious.

But Morgan also sensed a twisted logic behind the fury. Discovering how this killer's mind worked was the key to understanding his actions and, hopefully, to anticipating his moves. If he and Evan were to catch him they had to learn to interpret the clues he was leaving at each scene and use that knowledge to unmask and collar him.

Easier said than done! Morgan sighed, pulled himself out of his chair and headed for the sanctuary of his bed.

Thirty-Six

Evan knew it was going to be a long day. He'd checked in at the Deuce at 9 a.m. to find Morgan writing Jen's new evidence on one of the marker boards. He paused to fill Evan in and then continued.

"Hey, partner, ready to go solo today?"

"Huh?" Evan's reply was as brief as the level of understanding plainly evident in his tone.

"I think we should split up today." Morgan explained. "You take the possible suspects list we worked up from Gregg's cases as a judge and check them out. I have to call Max and let him know that Joey Cordova's blood didn't match the sample we found at the Gregg murder scene.

After that I'll take Chris Verble with me to the three crime scenes and then back to the Deuce for a brainstorming session.

I started thinking after Jen called last night and, when she called me again this morning to confirm that those *were* pieces of Brenda Hart's teeth imbedded in her flesh, I realized that we have to *somehow* get into this man's mind now.

And, to do that we need to decipher all the bizarre clues he's left behind. So, I called Chris and Sarah half an hour ago and set up a meeting in the incident room at the Deuce at two this afternoon.

Hopefully, you can finish up and be there too."

"Good thinking, Morg. I don't see why not. Of the seven people we felt might have wanted Gregg to come to harm only three of them are still in the running.

Sharon Wolff's fiancé moved to Seattle shortly after the trial, then moved back to Hillsboro, last year. Fortunately, Hillsboro is only twenty minutes from here.

Sharon's parents, broken by the death of their daughter, died a few years ago. I do need to see Nancy Bremer's parents. They still live in Portland. As to the Faulkner murder trial, her brother was pretty ticked off at Gregg for setting her free, but he was in an auto accident in 1959 and has been completely paralyzed ever since.

But I gotta ask. If *you* were out for revenge, would *you* be able to wait this long to get it?

I mean, *cripes* Morg, revenge is a hot-blooded act. People don't wait *years* to get back at someone, not this viciously anyway."

"There's an old saying, Ev. Revenge is a dish best served cold. Some people savor the planning as much or more as the actual deed."

"Maybe so, but I've got a bright, shiny dime that says we find someone who had a recent axe to grind with one of these victims we find our boy.

Okay, I'm gonna make like a tree and leave. See you here about two."

"Oh, before you go, the forensics lab called to say the stuff we got from that station wagon didn't match with anything they already had. Plus none of the trace evidence they got from the carpeting sample belonged to any of the victims."

"Looks like another dead end." Evan sighed.

Morgan finished at the board, noted a memo attached to Jen's report stating that the forensic boys hadn't garnered anything useful from the stuff Morgan had sent them regarding the 1958 Chevy Nomad, gathered some papers and a notebook, and headed out the door to his meeting with Chris Verble.

Thirty-Seven

The drive to Charlotte and Edgar Bremer's home in Portland gave Evan time to consider what he was going to say to them. It had been six years since Nancy had been brutally raped and savagely beaten but Evan was fairly sure that the wounds inflicted on these parents as a result of that assault had not completely healed.

Thus, he would have to navigate this interview carefully.

On the one hand he did not want to put these people through any more pain. At the same time he needed to determine whether or not Charlotte and/or Edgar were in any way responsible for Martin Gregg's death.

Therefore, he had to be prepared to ask questions which would reopen those wounds; a thought which unsettled him no end.

*God! I **hate** this freaking job sometimes.*

Two hours later, Evan drove away from the Bremer home, sure of two things. Neither Charlotte nor Edgar had anything to do with Martin Gregg's murder or any other murder, and today he detested his job more than he ever had before.

The interview had started out pleasantly enough. The Bremers, an elderly couple, warmly welcomed Evan into their home. Introductions were made and everyone was seated comfortably in the small living room.

They both looked old and worn out, and Evan couldn't help wondering how much of that aging had been directly linked to the nightmare they'd gone through.

A bit of small talk ensued and a few preliminary questions were asked and answered.

"Can I offer you something to drink? Charlotte said sweetly, after a time.

"Uh, a glass of lemonade would be nice, ma'am." Evan replied, adding hastily, "That's if it's not too much trouble."

"Good choice, son." Edgar agreed. "Hot day. I need to wet my whistle. Why don't you make some fresh raspberry lemonade and bring in some of your oatmeal raisin cookies, dear?"

"Oh, please don't make a fuss Mrs. Bremer. A glass of water would be fine."

"Nonsense! It won't take me more than a few minutes. You two sit there and chat and I'll be back before you know I've gone."

*Just my luck! I come here hoping to find Jack the Ripper and Lizzie Borden, which would have made this easy. Instead I get Ma and Pa Kettle which means I'll probably leave here hating myself. Why can't **anything** be simple just once?*

Charlotte left the living room to mix up a pitcher of homemade lemonade, leaving Evan and Edgar to sit and stare at one another.

"Do you know about my daughter's case, Detective Flack?"

"Well sir, I've read the police files and the medical reports that were included in the transcripts of the trial, so, yes, I guess you could say I knew her case pretty well."

"Then I'd like for you to tell me exactly what happened to my Nancy, and don't leave out any of the details. Please, I need to know."

The request caught Evan by surprise and he felt air fill his lungs,

What the hell! Why does this old guy want to drag this mess up again after six years?

"Surely all the evidence came out at the trial, sir. I mean you must have seen your daughter right after the attack and the reports, you know, uh, they were made public at the trial. And you must have gone with her to the hospital, talked to her doctors, uh…" He was rambling he knew but his brain refused to work, and Edgar just sat there staring at him expectantly.

"I'm sorry young man." Edgar said softly, his eyes locking onto Evan's with a mixture of sadness and sympathy. "I should have explained."

He leaned forward in his chair, as if by closing the distance between them he could more easily make Evan understand.

"When Nancy was attacked, I was in the hospital recuperating from a rather bad bout of pneumonia.

I never saw her and when I was told she'd been raped and beaten, the shock, together with my weakened condition, brought on a massive stroke.

Fortunately, I survived and have pretty much recovered, though I frequently wonder if it wouldn't have been better in the long run if I'd just bought the farm that day in the hospital."

That's why he looks so beaten up.

"Anyway, I never saw my daughter until she'd recovered from her physical injuries. I was obviously unable to attend the trial, and nobody has ever been willing to tell me what happened for fear I'd have another stroke. So, now I'm asking you."

"I don't think rehashing it now would serve any useful purpose, sir." Evan's eyes were pleading with the old man not to do this. He could see how frail Edgar was and he was afraid what hearing of the horror his daughter had endured would do to him.

"I mean you got Nancy back and I'm sure with time and the love of you and your wife she's well on the road to a full recovery."

"You don't understand, Evan."

The sound of his Christian name dropping too quietly from the lips of this stranger brought Evan up short. He knew in his heart he was about to be told something he most definitely did not want to hear.

"Three weeks after the trial and before I ever had a chance to talk to her about the incident, my daughter hanged herself in the basement. Nancy went through the fires of Perdition and I wasn't there to protect her or even to comfort her.

Do you understand what that knowledge does to a father, Detective Flack? When my Nancy needed me most *I wasn't able to help her!*

She not only had to bear the unimaginable pain of the assault, she then had to suffer through the trial and aftermath in a small town not known for its understanding or pity. And, she had to do that without her father beside her.

So, you see I need to know what happened because I need to know why a beautiful, intelligent young girl who, before all this was the liveliest person I'd ever known, found life unbearable to the point that she damned her soul to Hell in one final, desperate act.

I need to know to keep from going mad!"

Evan sat there frozen. Question buzzed in his head, insects nagging at him.

Where is Charlotte? It's been at least ten minutes.

Why wasn't Nancy's suicide recorded anywhere in the records we searched?

But the answers were obvious. Charlotte wasn't coming back any time soon.

She'd be listening though, hoping to find answers too.

And, Nancy's suicide hadn't been recorded because all the records he and Morgan had searched were from the trial which was prior to the suicide.

Damn!

Evan's purpose in coming here no longer had any meaning.

There were no murderers living in this house; just two broken shells, searching for a way out of the darkness that had devoured them, and looking for understanding and peace of mind where there was none.

The loving, vibrant human beings that had once inhabited those shells had long ago departed, and organisms of a far different ilk had taken up residence; mimicking the Charlotte and Edgar Bremer Nancy had known but lacking their uniquely human qualities.

Evan was reminded of a movie he'd seen a few years back entitled *Invasion of the Body Snatchers.*

It was science fiction and in it people were being taken over by giant seed pods from outer space. They looked and acted the same as they had before the transformation, but their loved ones noticed a singular difference—they were devoid of *any* true emotion.

Well, Evan couldn't guarantee them understanding or piece of mind but he could at least give them the knowledge they sought, for what it was be worth.

With great difficulty and eyes lowered to avoid having to see the pain in the man's eyes, he then related what had befallen Nancy Bremer on the night of June 15th, 1955.

When he'd finished he looked at Edgar and had to choke back a gasp.

Edgar's weathered, weary face had corrugated deeply as the realization of what Evan had just told him set in.

It was the cruelest thing Evan had ever had to do; Edgar had aged ten years in moments, years he didn't have.

No father should have to hear what I just told this poor man. I've brutalized him.

Evan would have softened the details but for the fact that those piercing, granite, gray eyes were demanding to know it all, demanding to be supplied with the fuel Evan knew would sustain the rage and hatred that would ultimately destroy his soul.

He had been wrong. There *was* emotion behind those eyes, hatred so malevolent it momentarily alarmed Evan.

Evan knew that he was doing Edgar no favor here because, while Charlotte may have been searching for understanding and peace of mind, Edgar merely wanted to hate. Evan could see it in his eyes.

But he understood and empathized with Edgar's state of mind and reluctantly, even begrudgingly, gave Edgar what he needed.

He was not concerned that Edgar had acted out of hatred to kill Gregg or the others. The man was completely broken, his energy to physically extract revenge diverted to the psychological hatred that would soon consume him.

No, Edgar Bremer would spend his remaining time on earth hating from the chair he was sitting in and Evan shuddered at the thought of that shattered old man wasting away.

When we do catch this sick freak I'll almost be sorry that he might be tried for Martin Gregg's murder.

After all, Gregg murdered three people the day he sentenced that punk to one crummy year. All this guy did was to carry out an execution long overdue.

Charlotte returned and Evan questioned her for a brief period but he was pretty much going through the motions. Neither of these people had murdered anyone and his discomfort increased the longer he remained in the home.

Both Edgar and Charlotte were extremely kind; they didn't need him raking this up all over again.

He quickly finished the lemonade and cookies, apologized for disturbing them and made his exit as quickly as was reasonably possible.

The drive back to the Deuce gave Evan time to review the conversation with the Bremers, too much time.

I think it's time to consider another profession. When you find yourself doing what I just did you have to wonder what kind of person you've become. I've got a degree in criminology, I've always liked the law, and I think a teaching position at some small college would be a perfect change for me.

Yeah, I think when this case is over I'm gonna move on, after I give Morg time to find a new partner.

THIRTY-EIGHT

Revisiting each of the three crime scenes was not high on Morgan's list of things to do for fun, but he knew he'd eventually have done so just to be sure all the t's were crossed and the i's dotted. Besides, Chris had pointed out that by visiting each site, he could determine Vindicator's avenue of access and egress.

"How he gets into and out of each dump site or, as in the case of Brenda Hart, murder scene *and* dump site, may be as important as the forensic evidence gathered." Chris explained, picking his way through the cemetery. The early morning light sifted through the light fog, bathing the gravestones in an eerie glow.

Morgan shuddered involuntarily.

Creepy as hell! It looks like there are spirits hovering just above each grave. Good thing I didn't send Evan with Chris. He'd have freaked for sure.

"Pardon?" Morgan replied, inviting a response.

"Well. If I can determine the path our killer took to enter the cemetery and then to leave when he'd finished with Mr. Carr, we open a window into his thought processes that could prove useful later on.

For example, I believe he entered from the gate on the east side."

"Yes, we found footprints matching those found near the grave Carr was propped up against just inside that gate. But how did you know?"

"Simple, really. You'll notice that there are only three entrances into the cemetery. The north side gate, the east side gate and the west side gate.

The north entrance is out because it parallels Levington Boulevard, a four lane, well lit street. Only an idiot would try to sneak in there, especially if he were carrying a body.

I temporarily ruled out the west entrance for two reasons.

First, if he came through that entrance he'd have to pass right by the main entrance to the office. I called the office yesterday and found out that they keep a caretaker on duty at night who's always in the office.

Second, there's a street lamp right over the office that illuminates the whole area.

Still, it's possible Vindicator didn't know of the caretaker, so I didn't rule out the west entrance completely.

That leaves the east side gate. No lights, opens onto a darkened sidewalk. And, it's not too far from where the body was dumped. That made it my choice, assuming he was reasonably intelligent.

Of course, I intended to inspect each entrance for signs that our boy had been there but it looks like you've done my work for me. Did you find anything at the other gates?"

"Nothing." Morgan replied, impressed. Now, what does that get us?"

"A couple of things. One, this guy is pretty smart. It's clear he's scoped these places out before using them. Remember I said the first dump site was in a darkened area off of a side road? The busy overpass was chosen to mask any sounds he might have made getting that cross and body out of the station wagon and onto the ground.

But the most significant thing was the light bulb in the street lamp. I thought it was pretty convenient that it burned out in time for Vindicator to go about his business in the dark. So I checked with the city and sure enough they recorded a power outage to that lamp the day before the murder. When they got around to fixing it a week later they found that the electrical box that powers the lamp had shorted out. It was put down to rain water leaking in because the gasket that sealed the cover was worn through. Again, pretty convenient.

Now I can't prove it but I'd bet a week's pay that our boy somehow jimmied that cover open a bit and poured water in the opening which shorted the light out. Pretty brazen considering he'd have to have done it in daylight to avoid the risk of shorting out the light at night when it was more likely to be noticed.

Now, what does all of this tell you?"

"That we're in a lot more trouble than I thought." Morgan lamented. "Just my luck to run into a homicidal nut case who's also brilliant."

"Sadly, madness is the darker twin of genius." Was Chris' sage observation. "Let's look around here a bit longer in case we might have missed any signs of his coming and going."

Morgan noted Chris' diplomatic use of the pronoun "we".

He could have said you. Nice to be working with a real professional. No finger pointing, just evidence gathering and working of the case.

"Fine with me, only the sooner we get out of here the better." Morgan suggested a bit warily, his eyes darting around. "I'm none too comfortable in cemeteries on the brightest of days, let alone when there's a fog that chills my bones and makes me think I'm seeing and hearing things I know shouldn't be there."

"I hear you brother. I regard going into cemeteries as a way of tempting fate. You know—like when you were a kid and someone dared you to go up and knock on the door of that old house on your block. The one where we all thought a maniac lived and that every kid in the neighborhood *knew* was just waiting for some dumb kid to come too close.

Well, I don't like cemeteries for the same reason I never knocked on that door. I don't want the Grim Reaper thinking I'm daring him to take me just like I didn't want that maniac thinking I was daring him to catch me.

I know it's silly for a grown, educated man to talk like that, but its how I feel. I just don't tell too many people I do.

We'll be out of here faster than a guy who's just stepped on a fire ant hill."

An hour later they had completed the inspection of Brenda Hart's home and were headed back to the 2nd.

"One more thing." Chris said as they drove out in Chris' sedan. "If we can refine what we've discovered here today, we can be ready for that time when we catch this creep in the act and have men stationed at the points where we think he'll have planned to escape, should he make a break for it.

Better yet, if we reach a time when we can anticipate where he's going to strike next, we can have men stationed at the points where we think he'll try to enter.

That's the real value of what I and my people try to do in helping the police. We look for ways to come to understand the perp and especially hid behavior. In so doing, we discover how to get him to help us catch him."

THIRTY-NINE

The incident room looked far different when Morgan entered it at 2 p.m. than when he had left it at 9 a.m. and he thought he knew why. Fran had been in the office when Morgan told Evan of his plans for the day and Morgan was sure it was she who was responsible for what he saw when he and Chris walked in.

A large coffeepot sat on a table to left of the entrance and six ceramic mugs, together with a small pitcher of milk, a sugar bowl, and spoons were neatly laid out.

The main conference table had been placed in the center of the room, and the two corkboards and two marker boards had been set in a semicircle around the far end of it.

Large yellow notepads and pencils were stacked neatly on the conference table.

The forensics results had arrived and Morgan, scanning them, noted, among other things, that Hart had been dead for almost 72 hours before her body had been discovered and that several of her teeth had been broken off, most likely with the chisel and hammer. It was clear her jaw had been crushed by the vise. She'd died where she'd lain.

Morgan smiled. Next to the coffeepot were a small Styrofoam cooler containing ice and several bottles of Coca-Cola and 7-Up, along with a large bag of potato chips and a box containing a dozen double chocolate donuts.

For Evan. A real mother hen when it comes to him.

"Have a seat, Chris. Fran says Sarah called ten minutes ago to say she was on her way, and if I know my partner he won't be far behind."

Evan's not about to let a chance to see Sarah get away.

"Dusty, you really didn't need to go to all that trouble. We'd have waded through the mess." Morgan said as he walked back into the office. Then he walked up to Fran, who was standing by the one window in the room, and placed a kiss gently on her temple.

"None of that now, you devil." She teased, playfully pushing him away. "I know your tricks. Butter the old girl up so she'll keep on taking care of you and your shameless partner."

"Dusty! How could you!" Morgan recoiled in mock horror. "I'm crushed. You know I'm putty in your hands. Say the word and I'll sweep you up and haul you off to some island where we can make mad love all day long."

"If you don't *haul* your sorry ashes out of here right now I'll call for the Captain and you *will* be putty in *his* hands.

But she couldn't hide the smile that told Morgan she was flattered by the attention, any more than she was by the attention Evan always seemed to shower on her.

Fran was their darling, much like the sister neither of them had. They loved her and they made no bones about it; and Fran returned that affection unhesitatingly.

"Whoa, no need to call in the cavalry." Morgan retreated to the incident room.

"But if you change your mind I'm ready and raring to go." He just managed to dodge a cardboard pencil holder that flew past him.

"Friendly group you have here." Chris noted lightly. "A truly cohesive working relationship."

Morgan laughed, grabbed a cup of coffee and a doughnut, and seated himself at the conference table next to Chris who'd taken a Seven-Up.

Moments later Sarah showed up followed shortly by Evan.

I knew he'd find a way to get here once I told him Sarah was coming.

Morgan introduced Chris to Sarah, waited for Sarah and Evan to get beverages and snacks, and then began the meeting.

"I've asked you here today in the hopes that we can begin to nail down a better picture of who we're dealing with. But rather than listen to me ramble on, I'll simply throw the meeting open to anyone who wants to jump in.

One quick point. Chris is completely up to speed on this."

"Not that *I'd* ever take advantage of it but I believe the saying is 'ladies first'."

Sarah's coy look brought a smile to the men's faces and they nodded their heads in unison.

"I'm now convinced that the letters in the codes are in fact an acronym of the words that make up messages which have been left for someone to decipher."

When no one said anything Sarah continued.

"I think he *wants* us to figure these out because he has something terrible to say about these victims and he wants *us* to know what.

Or, he's made these little puzzles simple to decipher so they'll eventually end up in the newspaper and then the whole world will know the victim's dirty little secrets.

Either way I'm confident I'll crack the code soon and when I do the picture we need to collar this guy will become clearer."

"But if he *wants* the dirt dished on these vics, why doesn't he just come out and say so in a letter or note or something?" Evan posited, looking confused. "Even if he does get a sick thrill out of branding the poor bastards, why doesn't he do so in plain English?"

"Because he needs to make sure that we know that *he's* responsible for these crimes, which I believe he sees as justice served." Chris interjected. "Our killer, like all criminals of his ilk has a need to put his personal stamp on the crimes he commits.

I call it his *signature.* It's his way of saying,

'*I* was here, *I* own this. This is who *I* am.

Essentially, these personalities *need* to tell someone why they are doing what they're doing, and why the person or persons they're doing it to deserved it.

It's also a justification inside their twisted mind that they aren't doing something bad because they're rectifying a wrong that the rest of the world is either too stupid or too indifferent to deal with.

My guess is that all or most of the things being left behind at the crime scenes will turn out to be statements of some kind.

And I agree with Sarah. Deep within his psyche, this person has a moral need to be caught; he can't help but leave clues that will lead us to him or at least help us to identify him.

Now I think our time would be best served by looking at the various pieces of evidence again.

Then we can brainstorm, bouncing ideas off of each other for the purpose of refining the profile of this guy. I've prepared some material—lists and pictures of evidence. I'd say thirty minutes should be enough for everyone to go over the lists and pictures.

Does that sound agreeable to everyone?"

Nods of assent signaled to Chris to pass out folders containing the information he'd collected on the three murders.

"One thing before we start. I believe, having reviewed the materials contained in these folders, that what we're dealing with here is a compulsive personality. I'm fairly sure this person has what we like to refer to as a messiah complex.

Messiahs believe they've been put on this earth to put right wrongs they perceive have been overlooked by the rest of society.

This particular brand of messiah resorts to murder as a means of righting the wrongs that prey on his mind.

That's bad enough. What is really alarming, however, is the method by which he carries out these *executions,* as I'm sure he sees them.

He's not content with simply eliminating these people; he is *compelled* to annihilate them in a way so vile as to completely erase their identities as human beings.

This need to demolish the physical presence of these victims and, in so doing, nullify their humanness suggests to me a *personal,* obsessively driving force at work.

If I'm right, he won't stop unless he's captured or killed because he's constantly reliving the moment in his past when a terrible wrong was visited upon him, and his desire to be vindicated for that wrong leads to the rage with which he carries out each atrocity.

Make no mistake, my friends. The killings will continue because every time he finds, or conjures up, a new miscarriage of justice, he gets to release the anger that has been building up within him for a long time, probably five or more years.

By the way, for anyone outside this room who's still wondering, the connection between the victims is as simple as it is obvious—he's picking people he believes have committed crimes for which they've never been punished and *he's* going to see to it that they are.

Well, as Morgan so aptly put it, rather than listen to me babble, your time will be better spent poring over the stuff I've given you.

He sat down and the room fell silent except for the sounds of liquid being drunk and food being chewed and swallowed.

***

"Has anyone noticed anything peculiar about some of the items found at the three murder scenes?" Sarah said when the brainstorming session began. "We found fake *Roman* coins at the Gregg murder scene, a *bone* knife and a pair of *bronze* tongs at the Carr murder scene, and a *bronze* scalpel and *iron* chisel and hammer at the Hart murder scene.

Does that suggest anything to anyone?"

"Well, they're all *old*." Chris offered. "But, the coins were plastic fakes that were relatively new."

"Wait" Evan interjected. "I see what Sarah's getting at. It's not the objects themselves, it's what they *represent*—things from the distant past; ancient or primitive. In that respect the charcoal he used to burn Carr's genitals could be considered ancient in the sense that charcoal burning dates back to 4,000 B.C and that's *really* old."

"Primeval even." Chris added. "The questions we now need to answer are why did Vindicator choose those particular items and how does this knowledge fit in with his portrait.

This is what I meant when I was talking about matching behavior to personality. He clearly was sending another message when he did this and it's a message aimed at saying something specific regarding his MO.

What we have to do is to regard all of these items of evidence as pieces in a jigsaw puzzle, and when we finally put all of the pieces together we will have a picture of this person's thought processes which will, in turn, allow us to anticipate his moves.

That will, I guarantee you, lead to his eventual capture."

"I have a theory." Morgan, who'd said nothing thus far, volunteered quietly.

"We all agree that this person is under the delusion that he is addressing wrongs that need righting.

What if he sees those wrongs as something more?

What if he sees them as sins, *age old* sins, perhaps, even, the breaking of commandments?

What if that's the message he's trying to convey by using primitive torture and murder instruments?"

The room fell silent as the other three people turned their eyes to Morgan.

"Great!" Evan exclaimed. "If you're right we got a religious nut on our hands, complete with biblical ranting and God knows what else, no pun intended."

"The films are also a means of conveying messages to us." Sarah observed. "The question is what message?"

"Maybe the nut is an archaeologist." Evan ventured. "Who else would have access to that many ancient artifacts?"

"A museum curator, for one." Sarah said. "But I think your suggestion is at least as likely, Ev."

Ev, huh. Morgan thought. *Pretty familiar.*

"The point is, this opens up another avenue in our search." Chris pointed out.

"It also adds to the number of blisters on my feet." Evan groaned. And, I've got another question that could raise that total.

We know *why* he's picking his victims. What I'd like to know is *where* he finds out *who* they are.

I mean they come from completely different backgrounds and it's highly unlikely that he randomly knew all three. So what's his source for knowing about their 'sins'?

Hello? Any comments? Suggestions?"

"Only that you don't have to worry about the blisters, partner." Morgan said. "His source, as you call it, could be in any of about a half dozen places, which means we'll have to run them all down.

Newspapers, radio, T.V., magazines, police and court records; it's gonna be a long list old buddy.

I'll get the Captain to put some uniforms on this. We can't spare the time to go rabbit chasing.

Now, anything else?"

When no one advanced any further insights, Chris summed up the meeting.

"It would seem, at least for now, that this person is desperately trying to bring to attention some very evil deeds, at least as far as he sees it.

I believe the investigation should concentrate on interpreting all of the evidence left at the crime scene in light of that.

One thing worth mentioning. Thus far Vindicator has not tried to contact anyone in the media.

That's unusual for this kind of offender. They usually have a *need* for publicity.

It's how they show the world how clever they are and, as I said before, why they're doing this.

I think this offender's way of getting that publicity is in the pieces of evidence he leaves behind, his clues so to speak, including the films.

They're his contact with us and the press, his way of talking to the world.

We interpret the meaning behind the clues; the press gets hold of that information, or at least a portion of it, and voila, instant publicity.

Plus, he gets to avoid any direct contact such as phone calls or letters, thereby eliminating a source for identifying him.

It's clever and strengthens my belief that he is unusually intelligent."

"Well, I think that's about all any of us can handle for one session." Morgan said, rising from his chair. "Sarah, Chris, thank you for coming. Your input is always invaluable.

Now, Evan and I have to get moving on the suggestions we've heard here today."

***

Morgan walked directly to the back room and seated himself in a booth facing the door. He had phoned the *Steakout* earlier to make a reservation for the back room because he wanted some privacy with Jen, and was informed by Linda that *he* didn't need to call ahead. He and his friends were always welcome.

"You and Ev are family, Morg. Dave and I wouldn't have made a go of this place if you and Bud hadn't spread the word and gotten the cops in this area to make this restaurant their go to place to eat and talk."

"Dave and you made a go of this place because you understood what cops needed and wanted, not because of anything Bud or I said. But thanks for considering Ev and I as family. It goes both ways."

"How was your day?" Jennifer asked, sliding into the booth across from Morgan.

"Pretty standard. We're learning more about the perpetrator of these murders each time he kills someone and I'm confident we'll catch him soon, but I get a bit frustrated when I realize that it will take time during which more people will almost certainly die."

"I know. My job brings people to me who are already beyond any help I could give them. The only thing I can do is to try to insure that whoever violated them will be brought to justice. But you're right, it is frustrating."

Over a meal of Reuben sandwiches, hot German potato salad, and steins of imported beer, Morgan and Jen discussed further aspects of the case. By the time dessert arrived the conversation had moved on to hiking and camping, an interest they shared.

"Have you ever seen the Valley of the Ten Peaks near the village of Lake Louise in Alberta, Canada?" Jennifer asked between mouthfuls of her raspberry lime sorbet.

"No, can't say that I have." Morgan replied. "It sounds like a mountain range, Have you seen the Tetons in Jackson Hole, Wyoming?"

"Yes, they are truly magnificent. But for my money Moraine Lake in The Valley of the Ten Peaks is more beautiful. When you come over the ridge leading down into the valley the panorama is almost overwhelming in its grandeur and spirituality. The water of the lake is a mesmerizingly beautiful iridescent green and the peaks, each soaring over 10,000 feet, stand as sentinels, magnificent and silent.

It would make a great summer fly/drive vacation destination, considering it's less than twenty kilometers from the Chateau Lake Louise, a five star hotel.

I stayed there about five years ago. Had a seventh floor suite with a wraparound view of the huge glacier that feeds Lake Louise. You have to see the morning's first light view out of the windows to believe it.

I swear, Morg, it feels as if you could reach out and touch the face of God."

"Wow. It sounds incredible and if it can outdo the Tetons then I suggest we change that Wyoming vacation with Ev and Sarah."

"I'll check out reservations for August. If we can't get into Chateau Lake Louise, there's always Jasper Park Lodge in Alberta. It's a bit further but well worth the extra driving time and we'd be right in the heart of the Queen Elizabeth Mountain range."

"Sounds good. I'll talk to Ev and he can run it by Sarah. Now, are you up for a little bowling?"

"That depends on what you mean by 'little'. I'm on early shift tomorrow."

"Tomorrow! Tomorrow's Saturday."

"Yeah, well I don't exactly have a Monday through Friday, 9 to 5 job. People have a habit of inconsiderately dying on the weekends."

"Okay, three games then. We should be done by 9:30." Morgan offered. "I'll have you home by ten and all tucked in by 10:30."

"In your dreams, buddy." Jen laughed, her eyes mirthful. "I'm quite able to tuck *myself* in, soldier."

Later that night as he drove home, Morgan realized that he had real feelings for Jennifer but that those feelings also made him feel guilty, as if he were betraying Senna's memory.

It was why he had been avoiding social settings with Jen and he knew it wasn't fair to her. Somewhere down the road he would have to commit or turn her loose and that time had to be sooner rather than later.

FORTY

Quentin Manning walked in the front door of the 2nd and moved over to where the desk sergeant was talking on the phone.

"Can I help you, sir?" He asked as he hung up the phone.

"My name is Dr. Quentin Manning. I'd like to see the detective in charge of the Martin Gregg murder case, please."

"Uh, let me see if he's in." The sergeant replied, reaching for the phone again.

"Morg, there's a doc Manning here wants to see you about the Gregg murder. Yeah, right away.

Go up the stairs by that drinking fountain, sir. Detective Jeffords will meet you at the top."

"Good morning, Dr. Manning, please take a seat." Morgan greeted the man standing at the top of the stairs, pointing to the chair beside his desk. "I understand you're here in regard to one of the cases we're working on."

"Yes, sir." Manning replied. "I've been hesitant to come forward because it would involve my revealing confidential information protected under the patient/physician relationship."

"Excuse me." Evan cut in, swinging his chair around so that it faced the small, balding, bespectacled man. "Are—*were* you Judge Gregg's doctor?"

"Not in the sense you mean detective. I have been Martin Gregg's psychiatrist for the past four years."

Morgan's mouth dropped open and Evan snapped in half the pencil he was holding.

"What the hell!" Evan exclaimed. "One of our vics has loose wrappings and we don't know about it. How'd that get by us Morg? We interviewed everyone Gregg ever knew except the family dog."

"I haven't a clue. Dr. Manning?"

"Because, except for Martin and me, nobody knew.

Remember gentlemen, Martin Gregg was an appellate court justice. It would have been devastating to his career if it had been made public that he was seeing a psychiatrist.

Remember also, he was an elected judge and, as such, could have been removed from his position which almost surely would have happened if the voters found out.

So when he first came to me he insisted on absolute secrecy.

I told him that as long as we didn't discuss any future criminal activity on his part, I would access to any conditions he might demand with regard to the manner in which we met.

Obviously, he already knew, based on the sanctity of the patient/ therapist relationship, I could not reveal *anything* that was discussed in our sessions except as I pointed out before."

"Well, if you can't reveal anything Gregg told you, why are you here." Morgan asked, noting with admiration that Manning had not reacted defensively to Evan's use of the term "loose wrappings".

"Two reasons.

First, Martin's dead now so anything I might say can't hurt him.

Second, it's clear that whoever murdered Martin is seriously disturbed, and will certainly continue killing people if he or she is not stopped.

So, I'm here to tell you what I know about why Martin came to me in the hope it will help you to catch his killer.

I do this with full knowledge that I am, in part, violating my oath of confidentiality, but I feel that I need to talk to you.

You must understand one thing, though. I will tell you what I can, but I cannot reveal anything discussed in our sessions that would jeopardize Martin's family because that would be a betrayal of Martin, which is what patient confidentiality is all about."

"Fair enough, sir" Morgan said, realizing that Dr. Manning couldn't *legally* be made to discuss anything that transpired during the time Gregg was in the psychiatrist's office.

"Now, what is it that you think might help us?"

"Four years ago Martin called my office and set up an appointment.

A week later he showed up and we began a professional relationship.

He said he was depressed, feeling suicidal, and needed to talk to someone concerning something he'd just found out.

Back in 1955 Judge Gregg presided over the trial of the especially vicious rape and beating of a young Portland girl, named Nancy Bremer.

Emlyn Morrison, the 16 year old boy accused with the offenses was convicted on all counts.

When it came time for Martin to sentence the young man, he decided everyone would be best served by sending the boy to Hadleyville, a minimum security correctional institution that focuses on rehabilitation as opposed to punishment.

The Portland press had a field day with the sentencing and for a time Martin became persona non gratis in the Portland area.

Eventually, over the period of a year, things returned to normal for Martin.

He was elected to the Oregon Fifth Circuit Court of Appeals in 1957 and had a spotless, if unspectacular, record up until he was killed."

Manning stopped here to take a drink of water from the glass Fran had brought him.

Morgan and Evan remained silent, waiting for Manning to continue. Neither had mentioned to Manning that most of what he had said was already known to them.

"Anyway, what brought Martin to me was an unexpected consequence of the Bremer decision.

Emlyn Morrison had been released from Hadleyville in 1956, after serving only six months of the year to which he'd been sentenced. The authorities had determined he was no longer a threat to the community and since his behavior had been exemplary, it was decided to release him to the custody of his parents with the understanding that he would be another year on probation.

Nine months later, Emlyn raped, beat, tortured and murdered Janet Carroll, a 13 year old girl.

When Martin learned of this he was devastated, and though I tried to convince him that the sentence he gave the boy was fair and he was not responsible for the second girl's death, he was inconsolable.

He kept saying that he'd made a horrible decision to put Emlyn in a facility that Martin knew was relatively soft on violent criminals.

He was trying to do what was best under the law for everyone—

Emlyn, the girl, her parents, and the community.

He felt at the time that justice would be best served by trying to rehabilitate Emlyn rather than to simply throw him in a punitive institution and forgetting him.

But now, he believed that he'd overlooked the obvious; Emlyn Morrison was a sadistic, unrepentant killer. No more, no less.

'It's simple' he'd said. 'I let my belief in the innate goodness of people blind me to what my common sense was telling me—Emlyn Morrison was never going to be rehabilitated and should have been locked away for as long as was legally possible in the deepest hole the prison system could find.'

That was, of course, an oversimplification of the situation but I could not budge Martin from the belief that he was directly responsible for the death of a 13 year old girl.

In the end Martin stopped coming to see me altogether.

Since I'd agreed to keep our relationship secret, there was nothing I could do.

I think it's quite possible that someone connected to the Bremer case killed Martin and that's what I've come to tell you.

"The same thought has occurred to us, Dr. Manning." Morgan said. "What makes your information so valuable is that we've had the same thought regarding several other cases and people connected to all three murders.

This may make our work a great deal easier in many ways, some we don't even know yet.

Thank you very much.

Now, if we could trouble you a bit more, I'd like for you to repeat what you just said to Miss Hull so she can transcribe it for our records.

***

"Well, what d'ya make of *that* partner." Evan asked when Manning had left.

"For openers, it clears up a one question we've had concerning things Gregg said. "The debt he was trying to repay was to Janet Carroll and her family.

And, if he was concerned that one of Nancy Bremer's family members had found out about the murder of Janet Carroll and might be looking for a little payback, he may have bought a gun to prevent that."

Evan nodded his head.

"Yeah, and the comment about being a bit too zealous for his own good in looking for the jury tamperer *could* have been a reaction to the knowledge that he might be in danger from one of Nancy's family and didn't need a confrontation with someone else who'd also wish him ill. Especially since Gregg told his brother he had a lead on the person."

"Which reminds me." Morgan said, raising a finger. "I've been wondering what possible role the mysterious jury tamperer might have played in all this.

I doubt it's a lead that will go anywhere because even if Gregg had somehow alerted the tamperer that he was on to him, the guy would only have had to bump Gregg off to make his problem go away, not go on a killing rampage.

On the other hand it *is* a lead of sorts.

I don't know. What do you think Ev?"

"I think it's a pain in the rear, go nowhere idea that we had better follow up anyway.

Wait! Gregg jumped on the D.A. about this. I'll call over tomorrow and see if he's turned up anything. Maybe we can save ourselves some legwork."

By the way, last night I went over to the apartment complex in Hillsboro where Sharon Wolff's fiancé lives and guess what?

He wasn't there and his landlady said she hadn't seen him for a week.

She then let me into his apartment.

It was clean, nothing out of place or suspicious, but the bed looked like it hadn't been slept in for awhile.

The refrigerator was empty except for a quart of milk, and it was sour.

So I called the Hillsboro Auto Detailing Shop where he works and was told he hadn't been at work for three days.

Looks like another loose end for now."

"Well, stay on top of it partner" Morgan directed. "We do *not* want anything slipping by us under the radar.

Grief can do strange and powerful things, my friend. It can cause a man to harbor a grudge for years, and it *can* completely unhinge someone."

FORTY-ONE

Sergeant 1st class Alex Lopez couldn't believe his eyes. Wedged between two large, metal filing cabinets was a thick, yellow, legal size envelope. It was further hidden by the fact that half of the envelope was lodged behind one of the cabinets.

Now how the hell did that get back there?

He moved the left cabinet enough to allow him to reach the envelope and pulled it out.

The envelope was addressed to Detective Morgan Jeffords and Sergeant Lopez felt his stomach shift uncomfortably when he noticed the postmark—May 27, 1961.

"Grab your ass and kiss it goodbye, Squint." Lopez called across the mailroom to his partner while holding the envelope up for Squint to see. "When Captain Byrd finds out we got mail for one of the detectives that's been here since May they're gonna be picking our pieces up all the way to Montana."

"What?" Sergeant Thomas Huett, whose nickname had come from Morgan and for obvious reasons, spun around on his chair, the thick lenses on his glasses reflecting light. "How the hell did we miss it in the bin for third floor?"

"That's just it my friend. It wasn't in the bin. Somehow it wound up behind one of the filing cabinets."

"Hooo boy, that's not good. Byrd will skin us alive. Maybe we should just pitch it in the garbage and play dumb."

"Play? Look, I'm going to run this upstairs. If I'm not back in ten minutes, call for an ambulance."

The Captain was livid. His eyes were bulging out so far Lopez was afraid they were going to pop out onto his cheeks. The Captain's face was beet red and the veins in his temples were mountain ranges. His hands were doubled up in rage.

"If you and the four eyed wonder spent as much time doing your job as you do sitting on your duffs drinking coffee and eating donuts, crap like this wouldn't happen."

His voice came crashing down on the frightened sergeant, each word a sledgehammer on his eardrums.

Lopez broke out in a sweat and began backing up.

Oh boy. The old man's really pissed this time. God, please let him have a heart attack before he gets to me because I think he's gonna kill me!

"Take it easy, Captain." Morgan said, stepping between Lopez and Byrd. "Killing Alex just means Squint will be in charge down there, along with some rookie they send us from God knows where.

And that will *literally* be the blind leading the blind.

I don't know about you but *I* don't want to even think about the mess the mailroom will be in then."

Byrd fussed and fumed awhile longer then threw up his hands in disgust and stormed back into his office, leaving one last comment hanging in the air like a sword waiting to fall.

"Just remember, they don't convict people in this state for killing someone while temporarily insane!"

Morgan looked to see that Byrd had closed the door to his office, and then turned to Lopez with eyes that said,

"Run while you can."

Lopez didn't need to be told twice and beat a hasty retreat.

Evan, who'd been watching the whole comic scene laughed and reached for the envelope.

"Well, let's see what we've got here."

He opened the envelope and turned it upside down.

A red velvet sack tied into a bundle and a folded piece of paper spilled out onto his desk.

The two men looked at the sack, then at each other.

"No, it can't be!" Evan said, disbelief in his voice.

Morgan slammed his fist on the desk.

"Son of a bitch!

He opened the sack, revealing a purple ceramic figure of a bird, and a pouch containing several dimes.

"Can you believe it?" Evan said disgustedly. "The guy left us this *before* he killed Gregg. Now, what's that all about?"

"Let's look at the paper, Ev. Maybe the sick freak told us at the beginning what he was doing."

Morgan opened the piece of paper. It contained one sentence.

"The future lies within your grasp. Will you?"

"Will we what?" Evan asked.

"Grasp it would be my guess." Morgan replied. "But what he means by 'future' is the real question."

"My headache is coming back again, partner. When we do catch this guy you're gonna have to pull me off of him.

Morgan nodded wearily. He knew exactly what Evan was saying because it perfectly described what was going through his mind.

In a sense, it was as if Vindicator had sent them back to square one. This new evidence would require them to reevaluate everything, and it made his head hurt just thinking about it.

Looking at the bird figure Morgan momentarily felt the tug of a thought lying at the back of his consciousness. Then, as quickly as it had come, it was gone, and he had the nagging feeling that he had seen or heard something recently that was somehow connected to what this object represented.

"Well. At least there are no new surprises from the forensic reports on Brenda Hart. Everything the same as with the other two except the letter shaved into her pubic hair was an "X". Just another example of a twisted mind sending a twisted message."

"Be nice to figure it out though." Evan suggested. "I get the feeling that if we could break one of these codes the others would fall like dominoes.

Letter groups, Single capital letters, old weapons, and films. They all mean something and I think they're connected by a common thread."

FORTY-TWO

Max Herrick dropped into the chair beside Morgan's desk, sighed, and knuckled the sweat stained pork pie hat that Morgan had never seen him without back on his head.

"I thought you'd like to know I've got Joey locked up over at the 7th."

"What's the matter, Max? Did he sprain his parole?"

"Morgan, that poor slob's been programmed for disaster. It's like there's a stupid button where his nose should be and he keeps pushing it."

"Pardon?"

"Not only has he got the Mob after him but his alibis for the Gregg and Carr murders *both* fell through. The dumb cluck got one of his dumber buddies to say Joey was playing poker with him when Gregg was killed. Only problem was, at the time Gregg was getting himself knocked off Joey's friend was sleeping it off in the county jail. To make matters worse, the jail house records prove it.

Now is that bad luck or what?"

"Or maybe it was fate, considering how many drunks we saw Joey hanging with when I was at the 7th." Morgan sagely observed.

"Anyway, his second alibi was even more laughable. He tried to claim that at the time Carr was being carved up he was *consoling* some dame in a bar. It seems she'd just been stood up at the altar and was heartbroken. Joey told her not to feel so bad; that she'd been lucky not to get trapped into a lifetime of misery. He said he went on to tell her that he'd learned at an early age that only suckers get married and was proud of the fact that *he'd* never made that mistake.

I listened patiently to him and was especially touched by his conclusion that at the time of the Carr murder he was actually doing a *good* deed."

"So, what did our resident idiot overlook?" Morgan's smile threatened to burst into open laughter.

"Only that there was a place on the third finger of his left hand that wasn't tanned because he had been wearing a ring there some time in the last few months.

When I called his attention to it he tried to bluff it out, saying it wasn't a wedding ring he'd been wearing. But when I reached for the phone to call city hall and the marriage records office, he folded like a cheap suit.

I'll grill him a little while longer, but we really don't have anything on him so I'll have to cut him loose pretty soon.

Oh, he doesn't own a light colored station wagon, not that he wouldn't borrow or steal one if it suited his purpose.

Seems like the poor dumb bastard just can't get a break."

"Sounds like you don't believe he's our killer, alibis or not."

"Well, like you said before Morg, Joey's mean enough to kill. He's also crazy enough to kill several people just to hide his real target among the others. He just doesn't strike me as being *smart* enough to have done all of that, let alone do the things that nut did to those people and not fall all over himself in the process.

Our Joey would have made so many stupid mistakes he'd have been caught within twenty-four hours of the first crime."

"I tend to agree with you, Max. All the same, I'm keeping him on my radar. This case is strange and keeps getting stranger all the time.

By the way, thanks for coming all the way over to the 2nd. You could just have called."

"Actually, I wanted to talk to about something else and I didn't want to do it on the phone."

"Oh? Something serious?"

"No, no. It's about the other night at *Frank's.*

Seeing you reminded me that the old timers haven't seen Bud in a long time.

So, I was wondering if you, Evan, and anyone else at the 2nd who was interested would like to set up a little party for him. The guys at the 7th would love to come."

"Sounds like great idea, Max. Any special occasion or just an informal get-together"

"Well, I checked, and it seems that Bud never had a real retirement send off.

You remember that was when JoAnne's mother was bad sick and they flew to San Antonio for two months.

By the time they returned the moment had passed and nothing was ever arranged."

"You know, I'd forgotten about that." Morgan said.

"You're right. We should do something special to honor him. Any suggestions?"

"I was thinking of a good old-fashioned roast. It would give us all a chance to tell our favorite stories about Bud, but wouldn't be so formal as to put him off."

"Perfect. We get to bust his chops and honor him at the same time. Let me talk to the guys here and you check with the troops at the 7th over in Portland.

How about we get together for lunch next Thursday and get the ball rolling."

"Fine." Max said, uncurling his legs and standing. "If we get enough people we can have it at *Fantisco.* There's a banquet room there that would be perfect and the tab wouldn't be too stiff.

Gotta run. There's a sale at Murphy's gun store in Portland and boxes of Remington .357 jacketed hollow points are going for three bucks apiece."

"Whoa! That's way below cost. Did Murphy pop a gasket?

Say, could you pick up ten boxes each for me and Evan?" Morgan said, reaching into his back pocket for his wallet.

"No problem." Max replied, taking the three twenty dollar bills Morgan was holding out. "Naw. He's using the ammo as a come-on to get guys into the store. If he can build up enough cop business he'll have a shot at getting the city to officially recognize him as Portland's go to guy for cop weapons.

Murphy figures if the guys come in for the ammo they might just trade up the .38 specials most of them now carry for some of those new Smith and Wesson .357's he carries. Or they can keep the .38's as backups and just buy the .357's outright.

Either way, between the new gun sales and the guys who already pack .357's buying just the ammo, he figures to rack up a pretty impressive list of cop customers.

Then when he applies to become the city's gun dealer he can say he's already handling a lot of the guys. That, plus the fact he was a street cop in Portland for twenty-five years with a chest full of ribbons by the time he retired, should put him at the front of the line with the mopes down at City Hall.

Jeez, it's a quarter to five. I'm outta here, Bulldog."

Ten minutes later Morgan also left the building, heading for home, a ham sandwich and a beer followed by an early hop into bed.

The strain of the case was beginning to tell as evidenced by the fact that Morgan was going to bed early almost every night, including weekends.

He smiled wearily as he turned off the light.

If this case doesn't break soon my social life, such as it is, will disappear altogether except for those who visit me at the silly farm over in Leesburg.

FORTY-THREE

Arlen Weiss had been Portland's District Attorney for the past eight years. His record as a district attorney during that time had been impressive. He'd personally prosecuted 27 cases and won every one, while overseeing several others to successful conclusions.

As one opposing lawyer had aptly put it, Arlen was the last person a defense attorney wanted to go up against, a description that had turned out to be literally true in more than one instance.

Arlen went for the jugular, especially in high profile cases; and he was not above using every legal dirty trick in the book to win.

It was rumored in some circles that he'd even resorted to *illegal* tactics to secure a conviction, on those few occasions when his charisma, good looks, and prodigious knowledge of the law failed him.

That Arlen would soon sit on the bench in one of Oregon's higher courts was taken for granted. The only obstacle to the attainment of that goal would rest with Arlen himself, *if* he decided that Oregon was not worthy of him and chose instead to relocate to California or possibly even New York.

It was widely known in judicial circles that Arlen fully expected one day to sit on the highest court in the land, and would do whatever was required to further that ambition.

Put bluntly, the man was powerful and ruthless and God help the person who got in his way or incurred his wrath.

Evan was well aware of this as he waited to be put through to Arlen. He had purposely chosen not to arrange a meeting in person with Weiss because he knew the man would wave off a meeting with a lowly detective sergeant from a hick town like Deliverance.

Evan's second reason for contacting Weiss by phone, which he hadn't mentioned to Morgan, was simple. He'd met and didn't like this arrogant jackass, and he was afraid if he met with him face to face and Weiss started giving him a hard time, he might say or do something that would get him in trouble or even tossed in jail.

Not that Evan was afraid of Weiss, but if he *did* get into trouble with the Portland justice system it might embarrass the Deliverance police department.

That meant Byrd would soon learn of it and Evan *was* afraid of the Captain.

Besides, he wouldn't want to cause any trouble for Morgan who had a good relationship with the Portland law enforcement system.

So, Evan decided a phone call would do just as well to get him the information he needed.

"Mr. Weiss has an open line now, Detective Flack." Weiss' secretary said sweetly. "I'll put you through."

"Detective Fleck? How may I help you?"

"That's *Flack*, Mr. Weiss." Evan said through gritted teeth, desperately trying to keep the annoyance out of his voice and only partially succeeding. "I'm calling you in reference to something you discussed with Judge Martin Gregg back in May.

It's regarding a trial that both of you were involved in at that time.

It seems that a possible case of jury tampering was brought to your attention and you relayed your concerns to Judge Martin who showed equal concern."

"Yes, yes, I'm aware of all of that detective. What's your point?"

"Well, we were wondering if the identity of the suspect was ever established and, if so, could you supply us with the name of the suspect."

"Detective, I'm assuming you're calling me with this request because it is somehow connected to the death of Judge Gregg. I can only say that my office thoroughly investigated that matter and determined that the rumor was not true.

No one was ever connected to the rumor and since the case resulted in a justly arrived at verdict of guilty, we felt the matter was closed.

Now if there is nothing else, I have a very important meeting in ten minutes with Senator Conway King."

"Actually, there is one other thing. If in fact, your office *did* run down one or more suspects, even if they were not subsequently held or charged with anything, they might still have had a reason for holding a grudge against the judge.

You see what I mean, sir. We are looking for *anyone* with reason for wanting Judge Martin to come to harm, even if it is only a small one.

If you have any names we'd really appreciate your cooperation."

"As I've already stated, I am not aware of anyone who was identified in connection with *any* jury tampering.

Now, I'm going to put you back on the line with my secretary. *She* will answer any other questions you might have or put you in someone from my office who can.

In the future, Detective Fleck, please do not disturb me with routine inquiries. There are numerous subordinates in my office who can adequately handle such concerns and whose time is not quite as precious or as valuable as that of the D.A.

I'm sure your precinct captain would agree with me on this matter and I will suggest to Mayor Raines when I dine with him tonight that he remind the captain of that the next time he sees him.

Now, good day!"

That went pretty well. Evan reflected sarcastically after being handed back to Weiss' secretary and being told that Assistant District Attorney Randall Stoddard would contact him as soon as his request could be answered.

Weiss is definitely in need of a serious ass kicking. I'd bet a week's pay there were suspects and he knows who they are.

But there he was; obnoxious as hell and blowing smoke up my backside.

Well, let the little schmuck play all the games he wants.

As long as I get the information I don't care; and I will get the information.

Evan got up from his desk and headed for Byrd's office.

I'd better give the old man a head's up on this or my life won't be worth a plugged nickel when the mayor blindsides him.

"So the pompous ass thinks he's gonna tell us how to do our job here in Deliverance, does he." Byrd chuckled as he pureed the cigar clamped between his teeth. "Evidently Weiss doesn't know that Raines thinks he's as big a blowhard as I do.

Don't worry Evan, you kept your cool and handled that jerk professionally. Neither me nor Raines is gonna jump in your chest for that.

Going through the assistant D.A. for the info you want is better anyway.

Stoddard is an old friend of mine. Let him know I'd appreciate any help he can give you."

"Will do, Captain. Thanks for the support. I'll check back with you later. Morgan's meeting me at the Hart house. We want to run the crime scene again to see if we missed anything.

This guy doesn't leave much he doesn't want to, so we can't afford to slip up on the one mistake he might make.

All of the physical evidence from the Hart scene matched what we got from the other two scenes—no fingerprints or any other possible forensic leads except for a repeat of what we found at the Gregg and Carr scenes including chloroform in the blood, indications of a cattle prod having been used, blah, blah, blah.

So we're going back over the scene hoping we find something we missed that is significantly different from what we've found before, and therefore not what he wanted to leave. If we find something like that it could be a huge break.

If you need to get hold of me with any questions the mayor has regarding the phone call I know he's going to get from Weiss, Fran has the Hart residence number."

Evan walked out of the room and Byrd leaned back in his chair.

Where do we get these men? He wondered. *Day after day they go out on those streets, risking their lives to keep a largely thankless public safe from scum.*

And, what do they get for their troubles? Whining, jackass citizens, irresponsible newspaper reporters who'd sell their own mothers into prostitution for a chance to rag the police, and television anchors and radio jocks who are no better.

*And, as if that isn't enough to cause a sane man to dump this underpaid, miserable excuse for making a living, in waltzes some moron of a D.A. who's **supposed** to be in our corner, and who proceeds to get his pantyhose in a twist because a good cop comes to him for help in nailing down the facts of a case that same D.A. will have to prosecute.*

Jesus! Doesn't Weiss realize Evan was just trying to help him? What an idiot!

Byrd got up from his chair, took his captain's jacket from the coat hook behind him and slowly made his way to the door.

"I'm going for a walk, Dusty." He said using the name Morgan had given her and which he said with affection. "If the Mayor calls tell him I'll get back to him just as soon as I figure out why I even give a damn anymore."

"You *give* a damn," she called to his back. "Because those guys need someone they *know* gives a damn about them, and you are the one man in this city they all respect and look to for approval.

You *give* a damn because you know that without you they'd have *nobody* to go to bat for them with the cretins at City Hall.

That would make what is all too often a lousy job even more unbearable.

But know this, old man. *We* give a damn too. We give a damn about a gruff, cranky, old buzzard who pretends he *doesn't* give a damn so he won't seem soft to men who need a strong leader.

Those boys *love* you Captain, and so do I.

Now you take your walk and chew on that for awhile."

Byrd made his way out of the office and down the stairs, grateful that Dusty couldn't see the tears filling his eyes.

FORTY-FOUR

Sarah pulled up to Evan's townhome at precisely 6 p.m. on Saturday. He was standing outside in front of his garage and directed her into the asphalted space directly in front of it.

"Ready for some good food and a relaxing weekend evening?" He called to her as she exited the car.

"I'm ready for good food, a couple of hours trying to crack this case, and *then* a relaxing evening. When are Morgan and Jen coming?"

"My partner, Deliverance's resident absent minded professor, just called to say he and Jen would be about fifteen minutes late because— are you ready for this?—he was almost here when he realized he'd forgotten he was supposed to pick her up first.

I swear, it's a good thing his head is attached or he'd lose it."

"I can tell you one thing." Sarah said, arching her eyebrows in surprise. "Morgan's ride over here is going to be one cold trip for the middle of July.

I'd have thought Morgan was more sensitive than to completely forget her."

"He didn't *completely* forget her." Evan said quickly, displaying a protective attitude concerning Morgan. "You have to understand, Jen usually drives herself when they meet at other people's homes.

That way she's more independent if she wants to leave early. Still, he *will* pay for this screw-up."

"Oh, please!" Sarah smiled in mock exasperation. "Jen is one of the nicest, calmest people I've ever known. She'll call Morgan to task for forgetting to pick her up but she won't crucify him. You men are such babies.

Besides, you know the Brits are slow to anger. She'll wait a couple of weeks and *then* make Morgan pay."

"Maybe so, but I'd rather chew on a razor blade than be in Morgan's shoes right now."

Ten minutes later the doorbell announced Morgan and Jennifer.

"So, who wants to start?" Evan said, setting his cup of coffee on the side table next to his leather chair.

The four friends had just finished a large sausage, mushroom, and cheese pizza and were gathered in Evan's living room with coffee and slices of Cherry pie that Jen had brought.

"Something you and Morgan alluded to the other day when you were with Chris Verble at the 2nd has been rattling around in my brain." Jennifer opened. "It has to do with the age of the weapons found at the murder scenes.

Morgan, you said that the wrongs Vindicator was trying to right might be viewed by him as *sins,* and Evan, you said something about him being a religious nut complete with *biblical ranting.*

My point is that those references *mean* something but I can't figure out what.

Damn, I'm not saying this right. I mean my brain *knows* that those words are important to this investigation, but as to how, I'm stuck.

It's like when you walk into a room and you *know* that something in that room isn't right but you can't get your mind around what it is.

God! I sound like I've gone completely bonkers. Does anybody know what I'm trying to say?"

"If by *bonkers* you mean nuts, don't worry." Morgan chuckled. "I've had that feeling on a number of cases. It goes with the territory.

Some cases have a lot of information to digest and this case has more than most.

The problem is many of the pieces of info in a case overlap and connect so that the sight of one piece triggers a memory about another.

Unfortunately your conscious mind doesn't always make the correlation between the two, but the subconscious *always* does. The result is that your subconscious keeps trying to force your conscious to make that correlation and pretty soon you're hearing yourself talking in circles in an attempt to satisfy the subconscious part of your brain.

Usually, the trick is not to try so hard. Just let go of it for a bit and it will eventually come to you.

However, since time is critical here that idea won't fly so I have a suggestion.

Why don't the four of us discuss your concerns and maybe something we say will crack the wall that separates your subconscious from the conscious.

By the way, something's been nagging at me too. It's not formed enough to discuss but I thought you'd like to know you're not the only one."

"Thanks, Morgan." Jennifer said. "It's just that *something* about sin and biblical ranting is an itch in my brain and I can't scratch it."

"Has it got anything to do with the possibility that Vindicator might be a priest or connected to the church?" Evan offered.

"I don't think so, but that is a good suggestion."

Jen was clearly trying not to downplay Evan's offer of help, which made Morgan smile.

"Maybe the guy is or was a priest or minister, or indirectly connected to the religious community in some way. Anyway, it's a possible lead." She concluded.

"What about some connection between Chris' idea of a messiah complex and the associated need by such a personality to bring his message to the world." Morgan suggested.

"Such a person would look for ways to publicly state his *holy* mission, hence the religious connection to any statements he makes.

So, maybe your itch is based on the conveyance mode of those messages and how *that* fits into what *you're* doing."

"Or, the killer's statements are couched in biblical terms." Sarah, who'd thus far been silent said, awareness spreading over her features like the sun breaking through a cloud. "What if the cryptograms are actually biblical declarations?

In fact, the cryptograms may be a series of proverbs that describe the sins the victim has committed."

"Or that Zealot Boy *thinks* are sins." Evan added. "We don't yet know that these people did anything wrong, though I suspect they probably have done *something* that most would consider unethical or immoral, if not illegal."

"These proverbs could also be divulging the consequences for those sins in terms of the punishment meted out." Jennifer pointed out.

"Wait a minute!" Sarah interjected, pulling some papers out of her briefcase. "I've got the list of cryptograms here.

Let's look at them and see what we come up with. Lord knows I could use the help, no pun intended."

For twenty minutes the room was silent.

"That's it!" Sarah exclaimed. "They're *acronyms* for proverbs! Look. AEFAE translates to *An Eye For An Eye* and ATFAT translates to *A Tooth For A Tooth.*"

"Well, I'm a monkey's uncle!" Evan uttered sharply, eliciting instant laughter from his friends. "That sure sounds like it comes from the Bible. Does it?"

"I don't know. Some proverbs are word for word from certain Bible passages. Others are just clever sayings that have been coined by pundits and famous people like Will Rogers and Samuel Clemens."

"I think this one *is* from the Bible." Jen said, walking to a nearby bookshelf. "Ah." She said moments later. "It's from the Book of Mathew, Chapter 5, Verse 38."

"Those are the letters that were branded on Brenda Hart." Morgan said. "It fits considering what was done to her."

"Say that again!" Sarah exclaimed.

"Yeah, pretty grim." Morgan replied. "He kills them then leaves a cryptogram that translates to what he's just done to them. That way he gets us running around like a chicken with its head off trying to decipher the damn thing. Nice scam to keep us off his track."

"That's not what she means, Morg." Evan said. "This creep is using the proverbs to tell us the *crime* the victim committed and the mutilation to punish the victim for committing that crime."

"If that's true then we can decipher the first two proverbs." Jennifer realized.

Fifteen minutes later the codes found on Gregg and Carr were broken.

"The one for Carr works. Evan said. "He sold cocaine, so it makes sense his nose was cut off and the white powder jammed into the hole. So, DCOYNTSYF leads to *Don't Cut Off Your Nose To Spite Your Face* makes perfect sense. But I can't figure out what Vindicator was trying to say by frying his privates."

"The connection between TLOMITROAE, *The Love Of Money Is The Root Of All Evil* and what was done to Martin Gregg is obvious from the use of the plastic coins and the rolled up currency." Jen chimed in. "But again, I wonder why Vindicator burned his victim. It would have served just as well to insert the bills sans fire."

Something about Hellfire and Damnation, maybe?" Morgan mused.

"Maybe. The other questions now are what crimes did Gregg and Hart commit to earn these particular punishments."

"The films left at the Gregg and Hart scenes might give us that, Jen." Evan replied. "That's our first order of business tomorrow."

"I'll research the other two proverb's origins." Jen said.

"And, I'll start writing a program that will make it easier to decipher future cryptograms using the data we've uncovered here today." Sarah added.

"Now, unless someone disagrees, I say we use the rest of the evening for fun." Evan declared, giving Sarah a knowing look that was lost on Morgan and Jen.

FORTY-FIVE

Randall Stoddard was a remarkable man.

In high school he'd been the captain of the debate team that had captured three state championships and was the valedictorian of his graduating class.

He'd maintained a 4.0 GPA at Harvard University while starring as a guard for the Princeton basketball team for four years; no mean feat considering he was also the editor for the University's student newspaper, *The Harvard Crimson,* for three years.

When he left Harvard in 1939, third in his class with a degree in criminal law, it was assumed by all who knew him that the 24 year old was well on his way to becoming a renowned jurist, beginning with a job at some large corporation, followed soon after by a career in politics or a seat on the bench.

It was also speculated by his friends that Randall would someday sit on an appellate court or state Supreme Court, perhaps even the United States Supreme Court.

But Randall fooled everybody.

Instead, he went to work with a small law firm in Detroit, Michigan.

These four men specialized in handling the cases of people who had run afoul of the justice system in Detroit and who were, by the nature of their economic situation, unable to afford proper legal counsel.

The next two years saw Stoddard gain a reputation as a bright, exceptionally articulate lawyer whose dedication and passion for defending his clients was matched by his success rate.

In those two years Randall won all but one of the 15 cases he tried, demonstrating an intimate knowledge of the law that grew with each case.

His presence in a courtroom was commanding, making him a favorite of juries who saw him as honest, informed and insightful.

His ability to take a straightforward matter of law breaking and twist it into a call to arms against a justice system that had become hardened and unresponsive to the average citizen earned him the respect and fear of prosecuting attorneys across the state.

By the time Stoddard had been in Detroit for a year he was known by all as a man prosecuting attorneys hated to see opposing them in a trial.

Several prestigious law firms tried to woo him away from the firm he was with but Randall was content to remain where he was. Even the D.A. attempted to bring him over to the prosecution's side, primarily because he was a veritable scythe, cutting a swath through assistant D.A.'s like a hot knife through butter, once putting even the D.A. himself to the sword.

Then, in 1941, six days after Pearl Harbor, Randall Stoddard, over the strenuous objections of friends and family, enlisted in the military.

He was immediately taken into the officer corps and spent the next four years as a fighter pilot for the Army Air Force.

For the next eighteen months he flew missions over China in his Curtis P-40 Warhawk until he was shot down in the summer of 1943.

During that time Stoddard downed 9 Japanese zeros and was awarded the Distinguished Service Cross and Purple Heart, as well as the title of "Ace".

When Stoddard finally returned to civilian life in 1946, he was a changed man.

The war, especially the three months during which he fought his way through Japanese controlled China, where he had been shot down, had forever altered his view of his fellow man.

Stoddard had gone down behind enemy lines, only to discover that he was on his own. He had no way of contacting his air group and he was in enemy territory alone. That thought was chilling enough but nothing compared to what was to come.

He began making his way through the jungle, trying to get back behind Allied lines.

During that time he suffered serious physical injuries from the Japanese soldiers who'd captured him and from whom he'd escaped. He'd lost the use of his left eye as the result of a severe beating in a P.O.W. camp in Shen Lu, and had his left hand severed from his arm by a Japanese soldier who was attempting to prevent Stoddard's escape from Shen Lu.

As a result of the inhumane treatment Stoddard received from his captors, a cynical regard for people in general replaced the benevolent and trusting mindset Stoddard had once had.

Thus, he chose not to return to the law practice he'd left in 1941.

Instead he applied for a job with the D.A.'s office and was warmly received by the same D.A. who'd vainly tried to recruit him five years previously.

Randall approached his new job with a zest bordering on obsession.

Gone was the belief that people were basically good and that criminals were born out of a culture that neither cared for nor took responsibility for the nurturing and raising of its young.

Granted, the Randall Stoddard who had been respected for an unassailable level of integrality and loyalty by all, including his staunchest adversaries, was the same Randall Stoddard who now appeared on the prosecution's side of the courtroom.

But his demeanor had noticeably altered; some said hardened.

His new belief system embraced the removal of the misfits and lawbreakers from society's midst so that law abiding citizens would be able to enjoy their constitutional rights of life, liberty, and the pursuit of happiness.

Not long after he took the job in the D.A.'s office he said:

"If a man has cancer you cut it out. You don't apply salves and ointments to it and hope it goes away."

It was at that point that the legal community of Detroit knew that the defenders of human rights in that city had lost one of their brightest lights.

In 1959 he took the job as an assistant D.A. in Portland, bringing with him an impressive record of 22 consecutive convictions and within a year, anyone who was anyone *knew* that Randall would be the next D.A. when Arlen Weiss retired in 1963.

***

"Thank you for seeing me on short notice, Mr. Stoddard." Evan said, sitting down in the chair opposite Stoddard. "Nice office. Big, but not sterile like some lawyer's offices I've been in."

"No problem, Detective Flack." Randall replied, smiling. "I consider it a privilege to do anything to help a fellow law enforcement official."

Wow! How different is this from my meeting with that jackass Weiss?

"Thank you, sir. I'll try not to take up too much of your time.

I'd have done this by phone but your secretary said you'd prefer a meeting."

"Yes, I don't trust the security of phones and some of the material we'll be discussing is highly confidential.

Now, let's get down to business. I understand you're interested in a case Mr. Weiss was trying back in May? Something about one of the jurors on that case being approached and offered a bribe?"

"Yes sir. We're looking for the person who supposedly contacted the juror because, as I'm sure you already know, Judge Martin Gregg, the judge on the case, has been murdered and we have information to suggest he may have taken a personal interest in finding that person.

We believe that because of Judge Gregg's efforts to unmask this individual, he might have put himself in harm's way.

We'd like to interview this suspect, as we've come to consider him or her, and find out if he had an alibi for the time the judge was murdered."

"But as I understand it, the person who murdered Judge Gregg has also murdered two other people and all three murders show the mark of a homicidal maniac."

"That's true Mr. Stoddard and while we doubt that this is the person we're looking for in connection with the murders, we like to cover all of our bases."

"Quite so, Detective. Well, let me see how I can help.

First, you must understand that everything we discuss here is completely confidential. Neither you nor anyone else can copy the files you see here today.

The case you're talking about was not just a simple drug raid gone badly.

The Portland branch of the F.B.I. has long been interested in mob action throughout the city and, in particular, the Dominici family.

That raid was part of a bigger sting, a sting the Feds have been hatching for over two years.

One of the defendants caught in the raid was actually an undercover agent for the Bureau.

Actually, the raid was *supposed* to fail and it was intended for the mole to be shot and wounded, but not seriously, *and* he was supposed to get away.

The idea was to solidify his stature in Godfather Rico Dominici's eyes, thereby making it easier to get closer to the old bastard—don't repeat that, and, consequently, closer to the running of the family business.

The Feds figured that sooner or later the mole would come up with enough dope on the family to put them out of business, kind of like what they did to Capone back in the '30's.

Trouble is, the mole got shot in the *leg*. I'm sure you'll understand that seriously hampered his chances of getting away.

Fact is he was caught, arrested, and indicted with all the other bad guys apprehended in the raid—not exactly as the Feds had wanted it would go.

Somewhere in Northern Alaska there's a former sharpshooter for the Feds now making sure no reindeer break any federal laws.

Anyway, what I'm about to tell you now cannot leave this room.

The mole and the other men indicted were eventually acquitted of all charges, thus accomplishing for the F.B.I. what they had hoped for.

He's now a lieutenant for the Dominici family and *very* close to the old man's bookkeeper.

We are hopeful we'll be able to shut this arm of the mob down soon.

But *any* investigation into that trial will very likely jeopardize the Fed's plan and probably put the undercover agent in great danger.

So, here's what I *can* do.

The file I'm going to give you contains a report of the investigation the D.A. conducted concerning a possible charge of jury tampering in that trial.

You may look through the report for as long as you want here in the office and take any notes that you want.

But the file stays here and no copies will be allowed, understood?"

"Yes sir. I'll need about an hour."

"One other thing, Detective Flack. I want a copy of your notes, and I am now personally swearing you and your people over in Deliverance to secrecy concerning this matter until such time as I release you from that oath.

"If what you find in that file helps you to catch your killer, and I doubt that it will, fine. But you may not use the information you take from this office to indict or to try him until I say so. If you or anyone else does it will *not* be appreciated.

Is that clear?"

"Yes sir." Evan replied. "I'm sure my people will agree to your stipulations. All we really want to do is find this nut, and if information contained in this report helps us to do that we have more than enough forensic evidence to fry him without ever divulging what I learn here today."

By the time Evan finished with the report it was going on five. He waited for Stoddard's secretary to type up a copy of his notes then headed back to the 2nd to drop them off and head for home.

His time spent at Stoddard's office had been interesting. The report contained information he believed might prove useful to the team, but he was anxious to see Morgan's reaction tomorrow.

One thing was sure. If he and Morgan collared this guy based on the information Stoddard had released to him, Evan was going to buy the guy a steak dinner.

FORTY-SIX

Morgan had arranged to meet with Evan at the Deuce on Saturday, and review the films from the first three murders over a brown bagged lunch.

"Whatcha got in the bag, partner?" Evan inquired, walking into the incident room and throwing his lunch on the table.

"Uh, that depends on whether you had time this morning to pack something you like."

"Morrrg! I'm cut to the bone!" Evan could play the hurt feelings card better than anyone Morgan knew. "Are you suggesting I'd mooch part of your lunch just because yours looks better than mine? I can't believe you think I'd stoop so low."

"Let's see. Last Tuesday I brought smoked ham and Swiss on rye, and you ate half of it while leaving your baloney sandwich on the table.

On any number of occasions you've collared my grapes and apples.

Oh, and don't forget your quaint habit of eating my éclairs and Jen's homemade chocolate chip cookies on the pretext of wanting to help me watch my weight.

Should I continue?"

"No, but I'd like to point out that a true friend shares without complaining or keeping track of what he's shared. I'd share my lunch with you anytime."

"Yeah, well, when I'm in the mood for dry peanut butter or green baloney, I'll let you know.

It *would* help, Evan, if you'd pack your lunch the night before, not ten minutes before you had to leave for work.

It would also help if you actually *looked* at what you were preparing for lunch."

"Aw, making lunches is boring. I eat in so little I don't realize how long it's been since I've been in the fridge.

Anyway, what *did* you bring? My baloney *looked* okay this morning but it didn't smell so good."

Morgan sighed, threw up his hands in resignation, and emptied the contents of his brown bag onto the table.

"On the up side, the origins of the three cryptograms have been unearthed by Jen. She called me to say that two of them came from the Bible and the other from an old dictionary dating back to 1796."

Ten minutes later the two men were sharing Morgan's lunch and studying the first of the three films left at the crime scenes.

"Well, the Carr film seems pretty obvious." Evan commented, scooting his chair back and putting his legs on the chair next to him. "It's clear that the bloodsucker is trying to cozy up to those kids for god knows what reason other than to use them.

Look at the scumbag. The oily, sleazy way he's hitting on them, especially the girls.

Damn, Morg, I can't say as I don't agree with the guy that killed him. That sick schmuck needed to be taken off the street."

"I agree partner. Too bad our guy couldn't wait for the police to do that.

Meanwhile, let's assume that Carr's 'sin' was perverting and abusing kids via drugs. Probably brought some of them into prostitution too."

"Hey, that's why our boy used Carr's privates for a marshmallow roast." Evan exclaimed. "He turns the kids into hookers, so Vindicator figures *that's* an eye for an eye too—sort of."

"I don't know as I'd put it quite so colorfully, buddy." Morgan smiled. "But if I read you right, then he put the powder in Carr's nose because he gave or sold drugs to kids, and he flambéed his genitals because Carr drew those same kids into prostitution once he had them hooked on the drugs."

"Works for me.

Question is did he have a personal stake in those kids, like a brother or sister, or just offed Carr on general principles?"

"I doubt the word *principle* applies to our boy, but we will have to check for a possible connection to any of the kids Carr recruited.

That wraps up the Carr film. Which one do you want to see next, Sherlock?"

"How about Brenda Hart?" Evan suggested, rewinding the Carr film.

After scrutinizing the film for twenty minutes it was agreed that nothing suggesting Brenda's sin was evident.

"I noticed one thing that seemed a bit out of place." Morgan said. "The setting for the film is social and in a private home.

So, I'm asking myself why Brenda was in hospital scrubs. She seemed pretty fashion conscious to me, considering the clothes in that railroad car she used as a closet."

"Yeah that caught my eye too. Maybe she just got off from work and didn't have time to go home and change clothes.

Did you notice her face? She was either on something or dead tired."

"Yeah, well I think we're gonna have to wait a bit until we come up with something on Hart that makes this sin a bit more obvious.

Cue the Gregg film and let's see if we can go two for three."

Again, after half an hour, nothing of value came forth.

"The murderer's intent with respect to the Gregg film doesn't seem clear, Morg. It just shows a man receiving honor from his peers at a formal gathering expressly convened for that purpose.

There's nothing in that film suggesting Gregg had committed any crime, or 'sin' as nut boy sees it. On the contrary, the film shows a man being recognized for the *good* deeds he's done."

"I don't think the event that's occurring is what Vindicator wants us to notice." Morgan replied. "I'm betting there's something or some*one* we're supposed to notice that will lead us to the 'sin' Gregg's supposed to have committed.

Let's get the photo boys to make some stills from the film and see if we can identify the people in the film, especially those coming in close contact with Gregg.

Come to think of it, that may also be the key to the Hart film too. Let's identify the people in her film too."

"Okay, boss. I'll set that up and then I'm heading home. I'm kinda tired."

"Makes sense to me." Morgan sighed. "I need a quiet evening alone at home."

"I'd have thought a quiet evening at home with Jen would be your choice. Any reason you haven't seen her lately? You mad at her?"

"No, I've just been tired more than usual because of this case."

"Okay. Just remember the four of us are going to Jackson Hole after this case is over."

"And it can't happen too soon." Morgan added. "Although, Jen has told me about a place in western Canada that sounds even better than the Tetons.

FORTY-SEVEN

Morgan and Evan approached the River View Suites hotel, which was located a block from Portland's Williamette River and, coincidentally, two blocks north of Images Camera Store on Burnside St.

Morgan parked directly across the street from the front entrance and the two men studied the building intently.

It only took a few moments for Evan to conclude that the hotel was the shabbiest looking thing around in a decidedly run-down area, a realization that concerned him greatly since they were about to go inside and possibly confront a truly *bad* guy.

"Well, there's no getting around it Morg. This is the address in the report Stoddard showed me. The D.A. believed the guy living here was the one who leaned on that juror to acquit the men caught in that Fed raid. Too bad the dummy didn't know the trial was rigged *by* the Feds. He could have saved himself the trouble."

"Well, before we go in there I want to be clear on just who we're dealing with here." Morgan said, pulling out a manila folder. "This guy's file is as thick as my wrist."

Morgan pulled out a sheaf of papers and began to leaf through them.

"Let's see. Louis Romano, a.k.a. Knuckles. 5'9" tall, 200 pounds, dark hair, stocky, has a two inch scar on right cheek, and an annoying habit of cracking his knuckles."

"Yeah, and he's as cute as he looks. Listen to this" Evan put in, looking at the charge sheets that accompanied Romano's mug shots. "Charged with racketeering, battery, aggravated assault, attempted murder, etc. Never convicted. A real prince of a guy."

"It's worse than that." Morgan said. "He's been muscle for the mob in Portland for fifteen years. That's a *long* time for a guy to stay alive in a business as dangerous as his.

This guy is one tough hombre. Smart too. We take no chances with him.

As far as Louie is concerned, we're here for routine questioning on a case that we believe he may have some pertinent information about— Martin Gregg's murder.

We simply want to know where he was when Gregg was murdered, and we do *not* mention jury tampering.

Louie hasn't stayed alive and out of the joint this long by acting macho and stupid. He'll play along with us as long as we don't threaten him.

Still, you never know with a wacko like him so stay alert."

"Roger. Well, let's get this over with."

The lobby of the Riverside was remarkable only in its singular absence of anything resembling a normal, functioning hotel. Everything was stained, dirty, dingy, torn or broken, or so it seemed. The air inside the hotel was oppressively damp and humid, in stark contrast to the air outside.

"Suites, huh. Only if you consider the Portland Water Treatment Plant a luxury swimming pool." Morgan observed drily.

The man behind the front desk exemplified the hotel's atmosphere perfectly. A sweaty, fat, balding, smallish man whom Evan surmised had not seen the inside of a tub or shower for six months—a grimy little toad inhabiting a swamp.

He was perched on a wooden stool, his right hand firmly attached to the cigar stub wedged between his teeth, and a partially eaten hamburger lying on a plate next to him. The fresh stains on his undershirt were a testament not only to his lack of hygiene, but also to the greasiness of the burger. The flies circling the hamburger were in mute agreement.

An open bottle of beer in his other hand completed a none too pretty picture.

"We'd like the room number for Louis Romano, please." Evan said, flashing his badge close to his body, as if he were afraid to get too close to the man for fear of contamination.

"Yeah, right." The man replied tersely. "Number 324, far end of the hall."

"We'd be *real* disappointed if somebody called Louie's room and warned him we were coming up." Morgan said meaningfully as the detectives began to climb the stairs. "The kind of disappointed that could get this pace closed down, and the guy who made the call a free vacation, compliments of the city.

I understand this place is owned by some rather nefarious people with names like Jake No Nose and Harry the Hammer. I'll bet they'd also be disappointed with that same guy if their hotel got closed down by the cops. Only, the kind of vacation plan they'd offer would be permanent. Capiche?"

"Hey, man. I got no horse in this race. You wanna screw around with Louie, knock yourself out.

I'd be careful about ticking him off though. He doesn't go in for idle chat and the fact that you guys are cops won't cut any ice with Louie."

"We'll be sure to treat Louie with kid gloves." Evan said, sarcastically.

"Yeah, well don't say I didn't tell ya."

324 was the last room in the hallway. The door was just left of a window that looked out onto a fire escape. Morgan opened the window and peered out, noticing another window, presumably an exit from Louie's room.

"Get out there and wait." Morgan instructed. "In case Louie decides to break up the party I want that exit covered."

"If he does come out that window I'll be sure to politely invite him back inside."

Evan displayed a wicked smile as he climbed out onto the fire escape.

Morgan knocked on the door to 324 and waited.

At first he could hear nothing, and then muffled sounds of movement from inside.

"Who is it?" A gravelly voice inquired.

"Police, Louie. Open up."

"Whadda ya want, copper? I already gave to the Society for the Feebleminded."

"I just need to ask you a couple of questions, Louie. Nothing to do with you personally, just information gathering."

Morgan could hear the click of the lock, signaling that Louie was opening the door.

He checked to see that the snap on the holster of his .357 was open and inhaled sharply.

Here we go. I hope this guy isn't going to be a problem.

Dealing with a pissed off Louie would be bad enough but if I have to put a cap in his head the mob is going to be very upset, and I don't need that.

"Okay, cop what's this all about? I got a meeting downtown in an hour and I ain't done my hair or nails yet."

Morgan again ignored the sarcasm and moved past Louie into the living room.

"Don't get your knickers in a twist, Romano. I just want to ask you a couple of questions about where you were on May 31st and June 1st of this year."

"And that's your business *why*?"

"We're looking into the murder of Judge Martin Gregg. He was killed around midnight on the 31st.

And, we know for a fact that certain friends of yours had a vested interest in one particular case that the judge was presiding over at the time of his death.

We also know that over the years you've assisted those friends in resolving *situations* that they wanted, shall we say, *managed*.

So, we'd just like to assure ourselves that you weren't involved in resolving the Judge Martin problem."

Louie stared hard at Morgan, his eyes smoldering.

Uh, oh. He looks really pissed. This could get very ugly fast.

"Not that it's any of your business flatfoot, but I was in Florida from May 21st through June 3rd." Louie said in a measured, calm voice. "I was attending a business seminar with some of my associates.

If necessary, I can verify that with hotel and restaurant receipts, and eye witness accounts.

Would that be satisfactory?"

Morgan blinked in surprise.

Gone was Louie's "mob" demeanor. In its place was an intelligent, well-spoken, thoughtful man.

It was as if Morgan had asked his banker where and when he'd last had lunch.

Louie was so calm and reasonable it momentarily alarmed Morgan.

Is he waiting for me to let my guard down so he can jump me or, worse, pull a gun?

"Now, if you don't mind, I'm in a bit of a rush. I've some *situations* which need *managing*.

In short, flatfoot, scram!" Louie concluded, slipping back into his alter ego.

The look in Louie's eyes told Morgan he'd gotten as much as he was going to get and it would be wise to make a hasty exit before the big lug *did* get pissed.

Morgan realized that the thing about guys like Louie was that beneath whatever veneer they chose to display was the mentality of a coldblooded killer. If, in the process of eliciting information, you pushed the wrong button, these psychopaths *would* go off in a violent way.

And it didn't matter if you were a cop or what the consequences might be.

"Fine. Give me a list of your contacts for the dates I mentioned and where you were staying, I'll be on my way."

Ten minutes later the detectives were on their way back to the

Deuce, the information Morgan had come for inserted into the jacket on Louie.

"Checking Louie's alibi should be simple, Ev.

I doubt he's our man, but you never know with a guy like Louie. He's just crazy enough to kill like that."

"Yeah. I decided to be on the spot if he tried to bolt out the window. So, I was just outside the window and could hear the two of you talking.

What's creepy about that guy is how easily he switches personalities and how convincing he is in either one.

Maybe he's got a split personality, not that I necessarily believe in that psycho babble."

"No, Ev, he's a true psychopath—ice cold, calculating, and completely devoid of any of the moral and ethical restrictions the rest of us have.

Louie can play whatever role he believes will serve his purpose at the time. And he can be incredibly convincing because he simply adopts the persona of whomever he's impersonating.

He can do so because he operates without the inherent roadblocks we'd run into if we tried to be someone antithetical to whom we really are.

However, if you're interested in seeing the *real* Louis Romano, just be around when someone gets in his way or incurs his wrath.

I warn you it won't be a pretty sight."

"No, thanks. Then I'd have to arrest him and I get the distinct feeling that would necessitate shooting the bastard.

Not that I'd really care, mind you, but I'd never be sure afterward if I'd capped him in the line of duty or simply as a way of giving myself an early birthday present."

"I hear you, partner. I think sometimes the powers that be made an error in judgment when they decided that certain men should be allowed to carry weapons in connection with their duty to protect the citizens of a community.

Under certain circumstances no one is quite sane enough to be trusted with a gun. All cops can hope for is never to be confronted with those circumstances."

FORTY-EIGHT

Carter and Sons was the largest department store in Deliverance, sitting on two square blocks in the center of downtown.

The store was solely owned by Mason Carter and his wife Jerilyn, who ran the home, leaving the day to day business dealings to Mason.

Mason was the president of the company and the chairman of the board, just as his father, grandfather, and great-grandfather had been before him. He also controlled 64% of the company's stock, the remaining shares belonging to Jerilyn.

The company had been founded in New York in 1878 and had moved to Deliverance in 1934.

In 1957, the store underwent a complete renovation in an attempt to bolster lagging sales and to woo back customers lured away by the big discount stores popping up all over Portland.

Mason had hired Victor Book, an efficiency expert out of New York, to bring about the changes needed to make Carter's competitive again.

Mr. Book assured Mason and Jerilyn that a complete restructuring of the company's operations was necessary in addition to the renovation of the physical plant. He also promised to accomplish these tasks painlessly and quickly.

Though somewhat apprehensive Mason and Jerilyn ultimately approved Book's plan which included, among other things:

Downsizing the company by one-third, including letting go a company executive with over fifteen years of experience.

Completely revamping the store's inventory to include some lesser quality items which were more interesting and, at the same time cheaper to sell.

Convincing Mason and Jerilyn that they needed to make some of their stock available to the general public in order to access the capital needed for the renovation of the building, 49% of the company was thus put on the block.

Book proved true to his word. Six months later the company was once again running smoothly and he was handsomely rewarded for his efforts.

"Sometimes I have to bring my Sword of Damocles to the table, but in the end most everyone is happy with what I've done." Book bragged, taking the generous check offered to him by Mason. "I've been called a headhunter and worse by the dead wood in the companies I'm trying to save, but that's alright. I know I'm doing good things for the majority of people involved and that's enough for me."

However, in the ensuing two years a number of problems surfaced that neither Mason nor Jerilyn had anticipated but which proved disastrous to their company.

A thoroughly disgruntled staff, reacting to the arbitrary cuts Book had made, forced through a union that created a rift between the owners and their employees and created an adversarial relationship between the two. Such a schism ultimately trickled down to the service offered at the store.

Customers, dissatisfied with the quality of many of the new items, stormed angrily into the store demanding a refund; dismayed by the lack of service and product standards they'd become accustomed to when shopping at Carter's.

The culmination of all of this was a decline in the number and frequency of people choosing to patronize Carter's which, in turn, led to the almost complete loss of the store's customer base.

Business continued to worsen and early in 1960 it became apparent that Mason's only recourse to staving off bankruptcy and financial ruin was to sell the company.

The best offer came from Synergistics, a firm whose sole purpose, though not widely known and certainly not to Mason, in acquiring a company was to buy it cheap, milk it dry of any remaining assets, and then abandon the company and declare it as a capital loss on the firm's income tax return.

Of course, that meant hundreds of people being laid off and the company being sold for pennies on the dollar of its original worth, but Synergistics could hardly be blamed for the previous owner's poor business practices.

What never came to light, however, was the fact that Victor Book *knew* that all of this would almost certainly happen when he took the job offered him by Mason Carter.

He had correctly sized up Carter's as a company he could not save and decided he might as well sample from the gravy train that an eventual takeover would create.

In fact, Book was instrumental in seeing to it that Synergistics bid for Carter's was the winning offer by looking at all of the other offers on the sly and inserting a bid from Synergistics that would be the highest but just above the next highest.

When the dust finally cleared in June of 1960, Victor Book walked away from the utter destruction of several lives, including the executive with fifteen years in at Carter's who committed suicide two weeks before the sale of the company.

And, Book never looked back.

He was much richer, had improved his standing in the eyes of companies like Synergistics, and was feeling pretty good about his most recent performance.

That ought to make the boys over at Feldman Properties sit up and take notice. I bet I'll get a call from them before the week is up.

For more than ten years Book had been thirsting for a chance to get his foot in the door of the largest land investment corporation in the Northwest. Book knew that Feldman was the big leagues, a company that dealt in *big* land deals and were respected nationwide. He was getting tired of grubbing around with the sleazy kind of people he was used to associating with and hoped to move up the ladder socially and professionally.

Truth be told, Victor Book was feeling pretty smug. Life was definitely about to get better.

Or so it seemed.

Forty-Nine

"It looks like our resident mob muscle is off the hook." Evan said, pulling his chair over by Morgan's desk. "He was where he said he was on the 30th and the 31st."

"I didn't think that lead was going to pan out." Morgan said. "Fact is I doubt Vindicator was connected to the jury tampering issue. Let's put this lead on the back burner until and if something else on it turns up.

So, where are we? We've got a psychotic individual who is killing people because he believes they're getting away with the breaking of biblical laws, commandments if you will.

We know why he picks his victims and that he mutilates and marks them in such a way as to make public the crime and to make the punishment fit that crime.

We know he's leaving clues in a red velvet sack, but we don't yet know what those clues mean.

What we don't know is *how* he chooses the victim or how he finds out that they've committed the sin he kills them for."

"*That's* what's been rolling around in my brain like a marble." Evan sat up and slammed a fist into the palm of his right hand. "You said commandments once before and it registered with me but I wasn't sure why.

Now, you just said it again along with something else and suddenly I know why I reacted the first time you said it.

What if these sins are just that—commandments from Moses' tablets that Vindicator thinks the victims are breaking.

And, how are the original Ten Commandments numbered?

In Roman numerals!"

"What are you getting at Evan?"

"You just now pointed out that he's marking each victim and you're right.

The letters cut into the victim's hair aren't letters at all. They're Roman numerals for the numbers one, five, and ten and I'll bet a week's pay they stand for the first, fifth, and tenth commandments.

"Son of a bitch!" Morgan's jaw dropped open and a look of absolute astonishment covered his face.

This means we can figure out which sins these people are supposed to have committed.

The First Commandment says not to have false gods, the Fifth says not to kill, and the Tenth says not to covet other people's goods.

Great work Ev."

"Well, *thank* you sir. While we're at it I got another flash for you.

You know the note Vindicator sent with the first set of items? The one that talked about having the *future* in our grasp?"

"Yeah, what about it?"

"I think that the message could mean that the items themselves might have something to do with murders subsequent to the one at which each items have been left. Sort of a crystal ball."

"Excuse me?" Morgan looked up from the report on Louie Romano that Evan had dropped on his desk. "Sorry Ev, I didn't catch where you're heading."

"For example, the items left at Gregg's murder scene were meant as clues concerning one or more of the other murders that were yet to take place.

So, the Gregg items might have been pointers to one or more aspects of, say, the Eddington Carr murder, since it directly followed Gregg's murder.

"Oh. Yeah, that makes sense." Morgan agreed, pulling at his moustache. "The trick now is to figure out which murder or murders each set referred to and what their significance is."

"Why don't we haul them out, spread 'em out on the conference table and take a shot at doing just that."

"Good idea. I'll pop over to the deli across the street and grab some lunch for us while you get things set up in the incident room.

Now, before I get the food, I have a flash for *you*.

You know the guy who introduced Gregg in the film left at the Gregg crime scene? Turns out he's William Morrison. Does that ring a bell?"

"My God!" Evan exclaimed, his eyes widening. "That's Emlyn Morrison's father, and Gregg gave his son a slap on the wrist for one the most heinous crimes I've ever heard of; not to mention Gregg's responsibility for the girl Emlyn killed when he got out of that resort Gregg sent him to."

"Bingo! I'll bet if we look into it we'll find out that Mr. Morrison has played a role in helping Gregg's rise to prominence in Portland.

I bet we also find that the onset of that help emanates from the date when Gregg adjudicated the Morrison case."

"So, what does that tell us about the sin Vindicator believed Gregg committed and got away with?" Evan asked.

"According to the Roman numeral carved in his hair, Gregg broke the first commandment and that commandment deals with false gods.

So, I think he sees Gregg as having pride, wealth, and power as his gods, and he believes Gregg was responsible for the death of the girl Emlyn killed because of his worship of those gods.

I think Vindicator sees Gregg as having sold his soul to the devil and it cost one girl her innocence, another her life.

Now, can we please get some lunch?"

"Afraid not, boys." Byrd interjected from the doorway to his office. "My ears on the street just called in to say there's been another murder that is almost surely your boy."

"Oh, crap. Here we go again." Morgan exclaimed. He knew that Byrd's "street ears" were as good as gold when it came to tips on what was going in Deliverance. "Let's roll partner."

"I'm calling the M.E.'s office now." The Captain called after them. "Forensics should be there soon."

FIFTY

Thornton Quarry was located four miles north of downtown Deliverance. It had been a rich source of the finest native Oregon stone for more than fifty years, one of the few blue collar industries left in the area.

Numerous Deliverance high school students had worked there during the summer, sifting, sorting, and bagging the stone chips that were a byproduct of the large stones that were quarried.

Morgan had been one of those students during his junior and senior years and those two summers had taught him a great deal about the value of hard work.

The bowl shaped crater was huge, fully two miles in diameter and over six hundred feet deep.

As he and Evan descended into the quarry, memories long faded like morning mist in the sunlight flooded back and Morgan smiled at the thought of old man Jensen, his shift boss for those two summers.

Face gleaming with sweat as he labored alongside his boys (as he called the students who worked there), Jensen would prod, cajole, and sometimes browbeat the boys into "putting in a straight eight"—Jensen's name for eight hours of nonstop work, save for two fifteen minute breaks and a thirty minute lunch.

What made the fifty year old man exceptional in the eyes of those boys was the fact that he never asked them to do anything he wouldn't do right along with them, and he never humiliated anyone, just pushed them to do their best.

Every one of the young men who worked with him came away with the best damn role model a boy could ever hope for, something some of them didn't have at home.

When Bill Jensen, a lifelong bachelor, died in 1957 at the age of 71, more than three hundred people attended his funeral, and most of those were his boys and their families.

The dry eyes could have been counted on one hand.

"What's the story?" Morgan motioned to the man approaching them. He looked like he'd seen a ghost. Morgan and Evan had reached the quarry office located on a ledge some two hundred feet down into the hole.

"Afternoon gentlemen, my name is Mark Kent. I'm the foreman here.

Well, about eleven one of the guys was moving dirt and stone with a steam shovel when all of a sudden he come flying out of his cab, yelling and pointing.

I ran over to him thinking he'd busted the scoop, but when I got to where I could see what he was pointing at, I thought he'd hit an animal.

That is until I got a little closer and saw what was really lying on the ground next to the machine.

I don't mind telling you I lost it then—puked my guts out and damn near fainted.

I'm not gonna say anymore, you need to see this for yourselves. It's right over there by that big steam shovel."

The three men made their way lower to an area that was relatively clear and somewhat set off from the rest of the digging that was going on.

A man was sitting on the big earth mover, body bent over, head in his hands.

"This is Charlie Potts." Pearson said. "He's the guy I told you about. Over here is the body."

What lay before the men hardly looked human. Rather, it reminded Morgan of the time his father took him to the slaughterhouse in Portland.

Someone had completely eviscerated the corpse, the entrails and intestines having been carefully laid on the ground next to it.

The body had been propped up into a sitting position against a large boulder and was canted slightly to the right.

"Jesus, Morg, the head is missing. And what's that sticking out of where it was?"

"It looks like some kind of sword." Morgan replied, moving closer to the body. "I want this crime scene locked down *now*. This is our guy and I don't want some quarry worker stumbling around in it.

Evan, take this roll of crime scene tape and start roping this place off. Give us a 100' radius from the body. Mr. Pearson that will put your machine inside our tape, but it's necessary."

"No problem. By the way, the head isn't missing. It's there."

Pearson pointed to a large rock sitting thirty yards from the body. Just behind it were a film canister, another red velvet sack, and a human male head.

The forensic people began arriving and making their way down to where Evan was marking off the crime scene. Jen was among them and waved as she made her way to where Morgan was standing.

"Another bad one, eh Morg?"

"Yeah, it's our boy again." Morgan said. "Be extra careful with this one Jen. I have a feeling that we've reached a new plateau in this investigation."

Morgan related Evan's revelations regarding the Roman numerals and the items in the red velvet sack, eliciting a raised eyebrow from Jen.

"If he's right, we're going to have to look at the evidence in a completely different light.

I'll tell my boys to handle this one with kid gloves and go back over the evidence from the first three murders too.

I hope you nail this bastard soon, Morg."

Evan completed his roping off of the area and rejoined Morgan who, after waiting for Jen and the physical team to complete their processing of the evidence, was taking a closer look at the head and the items.

"Well, we have a VII on the head and what looks like a model airplane, a photo of downtown in a large city, and a photo of a middle aged woman."

"The one photo is a view of Portland." Morgan added.

"So the sin is stealing, the Seventh Commandment." Evan said. "Wonder what the poor sole swiped that justified this, even to a sick creep like our guy."

"It may not *be* stealing as we know it. It just takes Vindicator to see it as stealing.

As far as I know, Eddington Carr never actually killed anyone but, thanks to you, we now know the Vindicator branded him with a V—the fifth commandment—*thou shalt not kill.*"

"The letters HWLBTSDBTS have been branded on the victim's left forearm." Jen announced, walking over to where Morgan and Evan were standing. "I'll bet we find traces of chloroform and signs he's been electrocuted too.

By the way Morg, how about you come over tonight and we grab a pizza?"

"Okay if I take a rain check on that? Evan and I are going to go over the velvet sack items when we get back to the Deuce and that will eat up most of the evening."

"Sure."

"I got an idea." Evan interjected. He'd noticed the look of disappointment on Jen's face. "Why don't the three of us meet at your place at six, I'll bring Sarah, and we'll have four brains to work on those things. I *know* Sarah would love to get her hands on a good puzzle and I bet Jen would too.

What say, partner?"

"That actually sounds like a good idea." Morgan concurred, which came as a pleasant surprise to Evan. "Do you mind if we impose on you Jen?"

"Absolutely not. I'd invite Jack the Ripper over if it meant good food and a mystery to solve.

See you at six. I'll have the food and drinks ready."

"No way." Morgan exclaimed. "The least we can do is bring the food. Evan, if you buy the beer and soft drinks I'll get a couple of pizzas from San Frantello's.

How about a large sausage, and mushrooms, and a large pepperoni?"

"Great!" were the twin replies.

Jen then collected the new pieces of evidence and left the scene.

Twenty minutes later, having made sure the scene had been thoroughly processed and sealed, Morgan and Evan left to head back to the Deuce.

"I can feel a change coming, Ev." Morgan said, as they drove away from the quarry. "The evidence is starting to pile up and this guy is behaving more erratically. He's gonna make a mistake soon and we are going to be there when he does."

"I'm with you there, partner." Evan replied. "He *will* screw up and we *will* nail his sorry behind. I just hope it's sooner rather than later."

***

By six forty-five the four friends were seated around one of the card tables in Jen's great room. The pizzas had been divided up and tray tables placed at their sides to hold the food and drinks.

Morgan quickly told the women of Evan's theories regarding the possible connection between the items and subsequent murders.

The items were then placed in sets in the chip holders that were around the table. Each set had been given a card identifying which murder it had come from.

"Let's start with the set of items from before the Gregg murder." Morgan said, placing those items in the center of the table. "Any ideas about the purple toy bird or the bag of dimes?"

After an hour prolonged silence, interspersed with several headshakes and suggestions that went nowhere, Morgan pushed the items aside and moved the items found at the Gregg murder scene to the center of the table.

"A model Corvette, a picture of Joan of arc, and some kind of cola.

Morgan said, trying again. "Any thoughts?"

Again, after several minutes, there were no responses.

"Well, this isn't going too well." Morgan sighed.

"Why don't we change our perspective on this?" Jen suggested. "Instead of trying to identify items as a group, why don't we focus on just one item in each set and attempt to figure out its meaning?

Then maybe that revelation will help us to decipher the other items in the group."

"Can't hurt to try." Evan said. "Lord knows we're not getting anywhere the way we're going.

"All right, how about the bird?" Morgan said.

"Well, it's fairly small, it's purple, and it's plastic." Sarah observed. "Those are the physical characteristic—it was probably obtained pretty cheaply too.

But what did it mean to Vindicator?"

"How about the fact that it's purple?" Jen offered. "Not too many birds are purple."

"If it's a kid's toy, like I think it is, it could be any color." Morgan pointed out.

"Wait, Sarah may be on to something." Jen offered. "Maybe the color of the bird *is* significant."

"But what could *purple* have to do with the other murders?" Evan asked, incredulously. "It's just a color."

"Think people!" Morgan urged. "Were any of the victims wearing purple clothes? Were any of the victims bruised more than the others?

Something like that."

"The coins on Gregg's eyes were plastic." Evan said. "But they weren't purple."

"Well, maybe it has to do with the item being plastic and not its color." Jen conjectured.

"I don't think it's that simple." Morgan said. "It has to be something more specific than *just* the color, or material the bird is made out of.

What we need to figure out is what this bird stands for and how that connects to one of the other murders; assuming, of course, this whole theory holds water in the first place."

Several minutes passed while the four people pondered this.

"You're right, Morgan." Sarah said suddenly. "This is about determining what the bird stands for and the answer has been staring us in the face."

"Huh? What is *that* supposed to mean?" Evan demanded, perplexedly.

"Simple. This item represents a particular bird—a purple *martin.*"

"Okay, but what is the significance of that?" Again, Evan clearly did not understand where Sarah was going.

"It means that Vindicator was referring to *Martin* Gregg when he left this clue." Jen said softly, grasping Sarah's meaning. "And *clue* is precisely what it is, as I suspect are all the other items. They're meant as identifying markers for one of the victims."

"Exactly." Sarah smiled.

Morgan and Evan looked at one another momentarily before breaking out is simultaneous grins.

"That's good." Morgan said. "Looks like the women score first.

So, ladies. What do the dimes mean?"

Several suggestions were made but it wasn't until Evan noticed that there were exactly thirty coins that the meaning of the coins became clear.

"I guess he saw Gregg as a Judas who betrayed Nancy Bremer and planted the kiss of death on Janet Carroll when he gave Emlyn Morrison a lousy year in a resort prison." Evan concluded, shaking his head.

"Makes sense to me, Ev." Morgan said. "Let's look at some of the other items."

Now that they had a perspective to work from, the four friends tackled the other objects with fervor.

By ten p.m. the significance of the model Corvette, picture of Joan of Arc, and cola beverage had been uncovered.

"Well, Vindicator's message is pretty obvious for this group." Evan declared. "The Corvette is a car and Eddington's last name is Carr; Joan of Arc was a heroine, and Carr dealt *heroin*; and the drink is Coca Cola, or Coke and Carr dealt cocaine, or coke."

"I think we can all now agree that the items left at each scene serve to identify the next victim." Morgan said. "I can't speak for the rest of you but my brain is worn out for today. Evan and I can finish this up tomorrow, starting with the items from the Hart murder scene."

"I'll process the items from the Book scene first thing in the morning and get them over to you ASAP." Jen promised, then, noticing the surprised look on Evan's and Morgan's faces, "We identified the victim from a wallet found in his clothes. His name was Victor Book.

What say we clean this up and finish the evening with some dessert and coffee?"

"If we can figure out what the Book items and are able to identify the next person on the Vindicator's list *before* messiah boy gets to him, we might be able to save a life and catch a psychopath." Morgan conjectured, setting his cup of coffee down. "At least I pray that's the way it'll go down."

"I pray everything goes just the way you said, except for one thing." Evan added, the words icicles falling from his lips. "I hope when we catch up to him the crud refuses to be taken alive."

"Evan, you're starting to let this case get to you." Morgan warned, his eyes fixed on Evan. "I can't have my partner going loopy on me just when I need him to be clearheaded.

We do our best to take this guy alive and only if our lives or the lives of others are put in danger do we use deadly force. Am I getting through to you, Ev?"

"I hear you all right, and I'm on the same page so don't worry. Just don't expect me to go into mourning if the scumbag decides to commit suicide by cop."

Ah, I'm just tired Morg, and frustrated. I think it's time I went home and got a good night's sleep. I'll be better tomorrow."

"Me too." Sarah echoed Evan's sentiments. "I have to be at work by 8 a.m. tomorrow."

"I hear you, people. Let's call it a night and hit the bricks running tomorrow."

"Well, this means I don't have to kick the three of you out." Jen needled lightly. I know it's hard to believe but I work for a living too."

The four friends stood on Jen's spacious front porch for a few minutes, drinking in the sweet warm air, chatting and laughing. It served as a relief valve from a long evening scrutinizing a decidedly unpleasant subject, a few moments to escape from the maniac to whom they were all tied.

Across the street, hidden in some bushes, Vindicator watched and smiled knowingly.

Plod on fools. Long before you find me I'll have completed my mission and melted away.

FIFTY-ONE

"Okay, the Navarre Bible stuff points to Victor Book because it is a—*book*." Evan noted, putting their findings on the marker boards next to the findings from the items left at the other crime scenes.

"Yep." Morgan nodded. "But what do the little statue, can, and the photos mean."

"Beats me. Why don't we look at what we've already got? Maybe something about the other items will help us with these."

The two men looked at the list of items recorded on the marker board.

From the items before Gregg was murdered:

A purple plastic bird—> purple *martin*

30 dimes—> 30 pieces of silver—> Judas

From the Gregg murder scene:

Toy Corvette—> car—> Carr

Picture of Joan of Arc—> heroine—> heroin

Coca Cola—> Coke—> cocaine

From the Carr murder scene:

Valentine—> heart on card—> Hart

Toy stethoscope—> doctor's instrument—> Hart was a doctor

A small, empty, coffee can—> ?

From the Hart murder scene:

A small bible—> book—> Book

A miniature human figure—> ?

A photo of what looks like a company conference room or board room—> ?

From the Book murder scene:

A model airplane—> ?

Photo of Downtown Portland—> ?

A professional photo of a plain looking woman—> ?

The two men sat at the conference table silently; looking back and forth from the list on the board to the notes they were scribbling into their notebooks. Occasionally, one would make a comment or ask a question, but for the better part of two hours there was little in the way of dialogue.

"Okay, that's it for me until I get some food." Evan declared.

"Yeah, I'm with you, partner." Morgan agreed. "What say we take ten minutes to sum up what we *have* nailed down and hit *The Steakout*."

"More like ten seconds considering what I've got."

"We didn't do so badly." Morgan argued. "We figured out the miniature doll is some kind of aborigine or pygmy. Plus, we're pretty sure the conference room photo has something to do with what Victor Book does for a living, assuming the items refer to the next victim in the sequence."

"I think the conference room photo is Vindicator trying to show us the environment in which Book committed his 'sin'." Evan deduced. "My money says that when we know more about him we'll see the connection better."

"That makes sense to me. And, don't forget you noticed that the plane was a Boeing 707, a passenger airliner. That could be important in identifying his next victim, or maybe the victim's profession."

"Maybe the specific model of airplane works something like the purple martin as a specific kind of bird did." Evan seemed serious, but then he laughed. "Does that mean we're looking for somebody named Boeing, or a girl named Seven O'Seven?"

"Keep your day job, Cochise." Morgan groaned."We can work on the coffee can and the photos when we come back from lunch."

"You know this is still all guesswork."

"I know, but it's all we've got right now and I'll take anything that gets us to the next poor sod in Captain Sadistic's sights before he does.

Anyway, let's blow this pop stand—what?" Morgan had noticed the peculiar look on Evan's face.

"It just came to me." Evan said, stopping in the doorway. "What if the city photo is a symbol of the next vic's 'sin' environment like the board room is for Book?"

"Yeah? And, what does that get us?" Morgan's face suddenly sharpened with interest.

"Well, we know from talking to Book's landlady yesterday that he worked freelance for a number of companies that bought and sold other companies.

We also know that Book was single and, according to the landlady, had no friends she knew of. And, from what she remembers, he kept to himself.

That portrait jibes with what the people he worked with and for said."

"Which means his work was the focal point of his life and, therefore, if we focus on his work we'll most likely find the 'sin' he committed."

Morgan interjected, following Evan's train of thought. "As a matter of fact, the film left at the scene showed him receiving an honor in what appeared to be the same board room depicted in the photo."

"Yep. And, the point I'm trying to make here is that the same logic may also apply to the city photo and picture of the woman found at Book's murder."

"So, we need to find out what those pictures have to do with the next victim's 'sin'." Morgan concluded. "Damn, Ev. That gives us two great leads to follow up. Good work.

I'm beginning to think your psychic."

"If I was, I'd be rich as hell and lying on a beach somewhere instead of busting my bottom here.

Now, let's get the hell out of here and get something to eat! On you of course, because I'm not psychic, not rich, and I left my wallet at home."

Morgan started to say something, thought better of it, shook his head and headed for the door.

Fifty-Two

The M.E.'s report and forensic write-ups added little to the detective's fund of knowledge regarding the motivations of the killer or the reasons he had for choosing who was to be the next victim.

Victor Book, a 47 year old, tall, thin, athletically built man, had undergone the same violations of his body as had the other victims—cattle prodded, chloroformed and branded.

Beyond that he had died, not from decapitation as the detectives had thought, but from massive quantities of lye that had been injected into his veins and forced down his throat.

"I'll bet the guy was conscious when the sick crud did this and he let the effects of the lye run their course before the head was severed from the body." Evan said, shaking his head in disgust.

The time of death was set at around one a.m. on the morning that the body was found.

In addition to the other atrocities inflicted upon him he had been eviscerated and his entrails posed next to the body.

As a final insult, the killer had inserted a medieval looking short sword into the cavity where Book's head had been and had plunged it up to the hilt into the torso.

One oddity that Jen had noted was a small piece of ceramic floor tile found near the body at the murder scene. It was the size of a dime and had been broken off from a larger piece.

"There's a note from Sarah I want to attach to these files after I tack a copy of it on the corkboard." Morgan said, laying a piece of paper on the table. "Apparently, she had no trouble deciphering the cryptogram because of the sword stuck in Book."

Evan turned the note around so he could read it.

"This one was easy." Sarah had written.

"HWLBTSDBTS translates to *He Who Lives By The Sword Dies By The Sword.*"

"How does he pick 'em and how does he know about their 'sin'?" Morgan said.

"Not a clue, partner. For right now, I say we put those questions in the drawer and check out Book's life more, and try to run down the identity of the next winner on Dr. Demento's dance card.

You check on Book and I'll troll the local photo shops and try to figure out who the woman in the photo is. You know she does look little familiar."

"Good enough."

FIFTY-THREE

When Chris Verble arrived at the quarry where Victor Book's body had been discovered, Evan, who with Morgan, was waiting at the entrance to the site, noticed with a low whistle of approval the stunning redhead who got out on the passenger side of Chris' white, 1960 Cadillac Coupe Deville convertible.

Morgan shot him a look, rolled his eyes in exasperation, then got out of the car and began walking over to her, a welcoming smile on his face.

"Morgan, Evan, this is my wife, Jessica." Chris said, coming around from the driver's side. "She's also an invaluable part of my practice—does a far better job of portraiting than I do."

"You *could* say we're partners in crime." Jessica quipped, taking Morgan's outstretched hand. "And, it's just Jes."

Evan hung back, looking a bit sheepish.

"That's okay, Ev." Chris laughed. "It's a reflex action."

"I am *truly* sorry!" Evan groaned, his face ashen. "It just slipped out—she's so beautiful, I mean, uh…"

"Really, Detective Flack, no offense taken." Jessica's demeanor was so genuine and friendly that Evan immediately relaxed, though the look of reproach from Morgan told him his partner wasn't so accepting of Evan's outburst.

"I asked Jes to come with me today because I wanted her to read this crime scene first hand." Chris said, gracefully steering the conversation back to the murders. "She has a gift of perception that is radically different from mine and is often more insightful."

"My loving husband is trying in his own sweet way to make me sound more important than I am.

The simple truth is I bring a woman's perspective to these horrible events. In that respect my input has been, on occasion, useful. My training and Chris' are virtually the same. In fact we met in a college level criminology course."

"We appreciate you lending us your expertise Jes." Morgan said. "We need all the help we can get on this one."

While Chris, Morgan, and Evan waited by the Cadillac, Jes walked the site, taking notes and occasionally stopping to scrutinize something.

Some thirty minutes later she rejoined the men.

"What do you think, babe?" Chris asked.

"Very interesting, this case. Of course, I've gone over all the evidentiary material on the previous three murders, but walking one of the scenes provided for a perspective I hadn't yet had.

I won't waste your time rehashing what you already know. However, I have a couple of thoughts I believe may be helpful.

To begin with, having seen firsthand a crime scene, I now know what I had before only suspected. This person is extremely ordered, methodical, and obsessed with the details of each crime being set up just so.

Everything he does is for a purpose and all of the facets of each crime are connected in a very organized way.

He's creating a mosaic gentlemen; a mosaic in which the individual murders are used as tiles to compose a picture."

"A picture of what?" Morgan asked.

"Don't know. But I think it has something to do with a need to legitimize what he's doing, and I believe I know the reason.

I think he was the victim of a serious crime at a distant point in his past, probably a physical assault of some kind, and it's left him with a lot of pain and rage.

Furthermore, I have a feeling the perpetrator of that crime was not brought to justice, adding frustration to what Vindicator felt.

Those emotions have been buried ever since, building and simmering.

Then something occurred which caused that pain, rage, and frustration to surface.

It probably happened some time ago and he began to plan his revenge.

Now, four bodies later, he's trying to empty an ocean of hatred and searching for the justice he was denied several years ago."

"Why do you say the crime against him happened at a distant point in his past?" Evan wanted to know. "Isn't it just as likely to have happened in the recent past?"

"The horrific brutality of these crimes makes it more likely that they were planned and carried by an immature individual, whose development was arrested at an early age by the trauma he or she suffered.

I doubt Vindicator was more than sixteen when he suffered the assault that precipitated this slaughter.

That help any?"

"If you're right it helps us a lot." Morgan replied, a look of satisfaction on his face that Evan had not seen in awhile. "If he's doing this because he was assaulted it's possible that one of the *victims* was the perpetrator of the crime committed against him."

"Which means there would be a direct link from that victim back to Vindicator." Evan picked up on the train of thought. "So, maybe we can investigate each victim's background and catch this freak."

"This is all just theory." Jes said quickly. "Even if what you say turns out to be true, the victim who assaulted this man may not have been murdered yet.

It's also possible that *none* of the victims turn out to be the person who attacked Vindicator."

"It gives us a possible lead and that's what's important." Morgan observed. "You got any other ideas, Jes?"

"Only that I noticed that the Commandments he's used so far are from the Catholic list of ten. The Catholic list is slightly different from the Protestant.

Could mean he's Catholic."

"I told you she's better than me." Chris said, noting with amusement the stunned looks on the two detective's faces.

"Damn! I should have seen that."

"Evan's Catholic." Morgan explained.

I'm beginning to see what you meant by a 'woman's perspective'. Cops, who are almost always males, tend to look at crime in terms of good guys and bad guys.

To us a killer is a killer and all we care about is catching him before he does any more damage.

You bring a new dimension to crime solving. I'm impressed.

I've got one final question, Jes. How does he know that these particular people have committed the sins he's murdering them for."

"He's most likely spent a great deal of time researching them. Remember this person is very methodical and *very* focused.

It wouldn't surprise me to find out that he's been setting this up for years.

Now, gentlemen, it's nine, I've been up since six, and I'm hungry. Since I can't think of anything else for now I suggest *somebody* buy me breakfast."

"Uh, oh guys." Chris said. "I can take a hint. It's either buy breakfast now or suck lemons for supper. Breakfast sound good to you two?"

"Not today." Morgan smiled. "Evan and I are due in court in an hour. A guy we busted a few months back is coming up for trial and we have to testify for the prosecution. Rain check?"

"Absolutely." Chris and Jes said simultaneously.

Evan, who'd been standing quietly behind Morgan during this exchange, stepped forward and extended his hand to Jes.

"Thank you Mrs. Verble. You've been a great help. We would really appreciate any further insights you might have."

"Evan, you are going to hurt my feelings if don't call me Jes and stop worrying about what was a totally natural and quite flattering gesture."

"Better do what she says, Ev." Chris interjected a wide grin on his face. "If you don't, she'll hound you to the grave trying to get you to."

"Less talk, more food, you goof." Jes said, lightly punching Chris on the shoulder.

It was a good natured signal for the two of them to go and the men laughed in assent.

"That is one bright couple." Morgan observed as he and Evan

headed toward the courthouse. "I bet when they get on a case they stick to the perp good and proper."

"Like rats on a corpse, partner." was Evan's succinct reply. "You know they remind me of William—college smarts, accomplished, and successful, yet as nice as anyone can be. Good people who see others before they ever see themselves.

Which reminds me, William and I are playing chess tonight, right after he gives blood at the clinic.

Okay, partner. Let's roast that crud down at the courthouse and earn those big bucks we make."

FIFTY-FOUR

William slid his white rook to black's queen bishop one, announced check, and softly proclaimed mate in three.

"Sorry old man." He chuckled. "Your only move is to interpose your queen whereupon I take your lady with my knight, uncovering a second check by my other rook. Then when you move your king to queen knight two, which again is your only recourse, I move the knight to your queen bishop three and regardless of what you do I mate you with the rook on your queen rook two."

"Right! That makes three straight my friend, counting the two we played last Sunday." Evan said, shaking his head. "At this rate my Chess Federation ranking should be somewhere around my hat size by Thanksgiving."

"Not true, Evan. Last week you won four out of six, two of them from me."

"Maybe so, but I'm not on top of it tonight. What say we head over to Capetti's for a late night snack?"

"Sure, it's only 8:30."

Capetti's was a pizza parlor frequented by cops and Evan had introduced William to it some weeks past.

"Got the best combo sandwich in the state." Evan had said as a way of inducing William to go there with him one evening. "*Italian* sausage, *Italian* meatballs, mozzarella cheese melted on top and peppers on the side. Hook it up with fries and a beer and you're in heaven. You can *not* find anything like it for two hundred miles."

"My brother Remy used to say the same thing." William laughed. "If it wasn't *real* Italian, it wasn't worth bothering with as far as he was concerned."

"So, how's the case going?" William asked, finishing the last of his beer. "From what I read in the papers and magazines, plus what I see on the tube you guys have a real psycho on your hands."

"Oh, yeah, he is that, my man. But we will eventually get him.

Right now we're still trying to figure out what makes him tick so it's going a little slow, but he's becoming more and more frenzied which means it's a good bet he'll screw up pretty soon."

"What makes someone go off like that?" William asked, shaking his head.

"Hard to say. Sometimes something happens that makes an otherwise normal and rational person just snap. Other times they've been a few eggs short of a dozen their whole life and one day the last eggs scramble all by themselves."

"All I know is I'm glad there are men like you and Morgan out there running these characters down, though I imagine most people take for granted the job you do.

If not for you guys and the courts, we'd all be at the mercy of people who are completely devoid of conscience or compassion *and* who aren't always held accountable."

"I'll remind you of that the next time I need a sweet car to take my date out in. "I'd love to pull up to her door in that Aston Martin DBR1 Black Beauty of yours."

"You can borrow her anytime you want Ev."

"I might just take you up on that. Right now though, this fearless crusader just wants to hit the hay. Gotta be bright eyed tomorrow so I can go catch some more bad guys."

Fifty-Five

Morgan was sitting at his desk when Captain Byrd walked into the office, a fried egg sandwich, a hash brown wedge, and a cup of coffee in his hands.

"You're not going to have to worry about retiring early, chief. The grease in all the junk food you eat and the truckloads of caffeine you inhale will kill you long before you're old enough to even consider pulling the plug."

"Yeah, yeah." Byrd acknowledged with his usual morning gruffness, walking into his office with Morgan in tow. "Let's just skip the pleasant banter, shall we?

What the hell have you got for me on these damn murders?"

"Actually, quite a bit. We now figure we're looking for a guy who was himself a victim of violence. Somewhere in his past he was assaulted and the perp was never caught, or at least that's what we think right now.

All of the clues he's leaving seem to point to someone who is trying to punish people he believes have gotten away with crimes similar to the one committed against him. Again, we're guessing but it's an educated guess.

We also think he may be Catholic based on the Roman numerals he's cut into the victim's heads which correspond to the Catholic version of the Ten Commandments.

We know that the articles left in the red velvet sacks are clues to the identity and 'sins' of the next victim and we're working hard to decipher the items left in the bag at the Victor Book murder.

Finally, if we can find the car observed at the first murder scene or match up the footprints found at the second, it might just lead us to someone we can then link to these other leads.

The only piece of the puzzle we don't yet have is how he chooses them. If we could get that, I know we'd be on him like sour on lemon."

So, I hope that gives you something to throw to the wolves other than various choice parts from your rapidly deteriorating body."

"Oh, it won't be *my* body that feeds the City Hall wolves, friend.

Seriously, Morgan, are you and Evan really closing in on this one.

Because I'm getting a lot of pressure from the mayor to bring in the Portland ViCap unit to help you on this one."

"We're on top of this S.T. Just another break or two and we'll bring it home, I guarantee. But I wouldn't mind any help I can get so don't write off ViCap right now."

"Yeah, well, if you guys don't clear the board on this one soon ViCap won't need to be asked in 'cause they'll be coming here to apprehend *you* for causing me to have a heart attack."

"Gee, S.T., you don't think maybe you'd need to *have* a heart first, do you?" Morgan was smart enough to be half way to the door of the Captain's office before he said that, thus avoiding the paperweight that sailed after him by rocketing through the door and into the detective's room.

"Slow it down Speed Racer!" Dusty yelled as Morgan shot past her.

"You're gonna kill yourself and I swear I'll disembowel you if you step on my sore feet."

"Nothing you can threaten me with trumps what Byrd will do to me if I let him catch up to me." But Morgan did stop and slide into his seat seconds ahead of a tennis ball that missed Morgan's head by inches.

"Cripes, can't ya take a joke?" Morgan called out, doubling up with laughter.

Then, realizing that the Captain had ceased his attack and gone back to his desk, he looked over at Fran, winked, and broke into a big grin.

"Works every time. Hey, whatcha reading?" Morgan asked casually, noticing the magazine on Fran's desk.

"Oh, it's one of those goofy true crime rags. I read them for laughs because they're as dumb as a box of rocks. This one's fairly good, though. Attempts to expose injustices that have escaped the notice of the law. Matter of fact that's the name of it, *Shine The Light.*"

"Dusty, you'll rot your brain with that stuff." Morgan observed.

"You'd be surprised what you can learn browsing through one of these magazines, friend. It's like panning for gold, sifting through all of the dirt and grit to find one or two nuggets.

Granted it's exactly what you'd expect, a lot of rumor and sensationalism justified by a bit of fact. But the reason I read the *Light* is because it includes the Portland region so some of the stories are about what's going on around here. A couple of the stories were actually about people in Deliverance.

Anyway, it's fun, not to mention informative."

"Whatever floats your boat Dusty, but it still smacks of gossip. Give me hunting and fishing magazines any day."

Dusty rolled her eyes and went back to what she'd been doing when

Morgan had come flying out of Byrd's office—working on the monthly duty roster for the uniforms.

"Hey out there! Tell me you two wizards have figured out the latest set of red sack items." The challenge sailed out of Byrd's office like a homing missile.

"How did he know *I* was here?" Evan asked incredulously, and a bit too loudly. "I just walked in the door and he can't possibly see me from his office."

"I see *everything* and I *hear* more! Now have you two, or have you two *not* figured out what those things mean?" The last sentence shot out of Byrd's office and hung in the air, like a hawk eager to swoop, impale, and devour its prey.

"Uh, we're on it, Captain. I just said to Morg that identifying those items should be the first thing on our list today. Yessir, we'll have that in to you pronto."

A patchwork quilt of profanity weaved its way out of Byrd's office. Fran, used to such outbursts from him, inserted earplugs at the first curse.

Morgan and Evan shook their heads helplessly, unable to decipher the undecipherable, which was unnecessary anyway. Byrd didn't require their comprehension, just immediate compliance with what he wanted.

"I still don't understand how he knew I was here." Evan whispered, not wanting to make the same mistake again and incur further ranting from an obviously upset Captain.

"His door is partially open and he could see your reflection in the glass." Morgan replied as they moved to the incident room, the items in question in hand. "All I know is we'd better get on this or Byrd will blow a gasket."

"A model airplane, a photo of part of Portland, and a picture of a woman in her fifties or so. A professional woman too, from the look of her.

Morg, I think I've seen her somewhere before."

"Yeah, me too.

Well, the answers ain't just gonna jump out at us. Fasten your seat belt partner; it going to be a bumpy ride."

"We need to identify where in Portland the picture was taken." Evan said. "But, wherever it is, I'll bet it has something to do with the next victim's sin or the environment in which the sin was committed.

Sound right to you?"

"As a starting point yes. We have to be careful to keep all options open until we can systematically and definitely eliminate the ones that don't work out. The photo of the woman is of someone who I'd bet is a celebrity of some sort. But who?

Ah, that is the sixty-four dollar question."

"Yeah, well I'd give sixty-four bucks to know who, but I've only got three dollars to my name.

Hey, maybe she's an actress registered with SAG. I'll check it out later today.

How about the model plane."

"It's a model of an American Airlines Boeing 707 which says it's *not* military or private, if that means anything. Also it's a jet as opposed to a prop job.

That's about it for what we do know."

"So, let me understand. We know the plane's use and makeup, the woman is an older, possibly well-known, and the photo of Portland may have something to with the next victim's sin or where it took place.

And that is pretty much it.

Well, that journey into deep thinking has moved us gloriously all the way to square two. I feel my backside starting to get uncomfortably warm, Morg.

Byrd is *not* gonna be happy!"

"No, but he'll take that much because nobody else will give him any more.

Don't sweat it, Ev, All Byrd wants is something he can tell the jackasses downtown until we get this guy, which he knows we will."

"I hope you're right."

"Now, you go I.D. the woman and I'll find where the city picture was taken and nose around. The model plane can wait until we do that."

FIFTY-SIX

The Screen Actors Guild, commonly referred to as SAG, was established in 1933 in response to the unfair cost cutting tactics employed by many Hollywood studios who were reacting to the hard times associated with the Great Depression.

Many actors during that period were without contracts and at the mercy of the Hollywood moguls.

Over the next 28 years SAG matured and grew powerful until, by 1961, it was universally accepted that while actors were by no means in full control of their careers, they did have a great deal of say in when and for whom they worked.

Someone had once said that the Academy Awards was in reality a thinly veiled message to the big studios that the *actors* would decide what films would be recognized and, therefore, become the most profitable.

All in all SAG had become an extremely efficient and powerful organization.

"Excuse me, where do I find someone who can identify a possible member of SAG?" Evan said to the secretary seated at a desk in the waiting area of SAG's Portland headquarters.

"Room 315, ask for Marianne, sir. The stairs are to your left and the elevator is directly in front of you."

Evan took the stairs two at a time, preferring the exercise to waiting for the elevator.

Reaching the third floor, Evan turned left down the hall, reaching room 315 three doors down on the right. He opened the door and walked into a small room that looked like a made over closet.

"Pardon me." Evan said to a small, nondescript young woman sitting behind an equally nondescript wooden desk. "Could you look and see if this woman is a member of your organization?"

The woman took the photo left at the Book murder scene from Evan and studied it for a few moments.

"Have you been living on some other planet?" She teased, and her smile made Evan look at her appraisingly.

"I don't need to look. This is a picture of Hedda Hopper, the famous Hollywood columnist. I thought everybody over the age of seven knew her picture."

"*That's* who she is! I knew I'd seen her before. Is my dunce cap on straight? I might as well be a neat idiot."

"That's alright Mr., uh, what is your name and why are you asking after Miss Hopper, if I may ask?"

"You may, and my name is Detective Evan Flack of the Deliverance P.D. Marianne.

That picture is part of an ongoing murder investigation. Identifying the person in the photo might give a lead in solving the crime."

"Oh, I see. Say, how did you know my name?"

"The lady downstairs gave it to me. Now, Marianne, how old would you say that picture is, or rather how old was Miss Hopper when that photo was taken.

"Well, the photo is probably 25 years old judging by the paper stock and the fading of the emulsion. That would have made her about 51 years old at the time."

"Thank you." Evan said, copying the information into his notebook. "That should do it. Thanks for all your help."

"Drop by anytime Detective, there's not much excitement around here."

Evan left the office and headed back to the Deuce.

"I hope Morg had it as easy as I did." He said aloud to no one. "By God, I think we're starting to get near this guy. When we do pin the bastard down, I hope he decides not to be taken, regardless of what Morg thinks."

***

Morgan was standing on the corner where the picture of Portland had been taken, presumably by Vindicator, and trying to figure out what the deranged man's reason had been for doing so.

The picture encompassed a full city block and had probably been taken with a wide angle or panoramic lens.

As Morgan scanned the 180 degrees in front of him, he methodically scrutinized the area, looking for anything that might stand out. Behind him was a large hotel that spanned the entire block.

*What the **hell** is he trying to say?*

The only things in the picture are five building fronts and he's even cropped the skyline out of the photo.

It's got to be something to do with the buildings but what?

Might as well check out what's in those buildings.

Three hours later Morgan left the last of the buildings in the photo, his notebook filled.

The first building in the block was a leather goods shop owned solely by a seventy-six year old Jewish man, Moshe Tal, who'd come to Portland from Hamburg, Germany in December of 1938. He'd seen the writing on the wall and fled his beloved land before the coming storm of World War II could envelop him and his family; or almost. Morgan had spent the better part of an hour in this shop, listening with interest and awe to the incredible stories the old man reeled off without effort; stories of sacrifice, survival, and heartbreak.

The old man, had lost both parents to Nazi thugs during the infamous *Kristall Nacht*—'The Night Of Broken Glass'. His mother and father had been in Paris when, on November 7, 1938, a Jewish teenager, whose parents and 17,000 other Jews had been expelled by the Third Reich and sent to Poland, killed a German diplomat in the German embassy.

The Nazis launched swift and lethal reprisals two days later.

The SA, SS and other party operatives ran amok, randomly killing Jews, and destroying everything in their path.

When the perpetrators of these pogroms had burned through their fury, thousands of homes, businesses, and synagogues had been damaged or destroyed and at least 91 Jews had been slaughtered.

Kristallnacht became the point at which many learned minds would later mark the beginning of the ever increasing violence by the Nazis against the Jews because for the first time Jews were arrested en masse and sent to Nazi concentration camps.

30,000 Jews were sent to Buchwald, Dachau, and other death camps as a result of *Kristallnacht,* and two of those were Moshe's parents.

All that saved Moshe was that he was with his family in Hamburg at the time, and he found out about his parents because his younger sister, who was with their parents in Paris, escaped after seeing her mother and father thrown on a train.

For weeks Moshe tried to find out where his parents were, but it became apparent that that was not to be. In fact, Moshe soon became aware that his inquiries, rather than providing him with information he wanted, brought an unwanted attention from the very people he was trying to avoid—the Gestapo.

Anticipating the imminent arrest of his family, Moshe made arrangements to flee Germany with his family and sister, torn as he was by the realization that in so doing he was forsaking his parents.

Now, years later he was still haunted by what he did.

No lead here. Morg thought as he left the shop.

Whatever else this man is he's no murderer.

But I'm coming back the first chance I get; might even bring Ev with me. This man could speak volumes about the human condition and what people are capable of doing to one another.

The next two doorways were actually different entrances to the same establishment, radio station WKXP, Portland's favorite outlet for discussion, news, and gossip.

Morgan spent a little time here, questioning Harvey Gunn, the station manager and his secretary, Mary Hennessey, the programming director; and Aaron Clinton, Wynona Barnes, and Red Wilson, the station's disk jockeys.

Nothing was gleaned from these interviews that Morgan saw as immediately useful, either in the way of information or as an avenue for identifying possible suspects.

Still, God only knew Vindicator's mindset. So he dutifully noted everything said, reserving the possibility that he might be revisiting this place.

Building three was a used and collectible book store, noted for its inventory of rare books and the reputation of the owner to be able to get his hands on almost any first edition a customer might want.

Again, Morgan failed to sense an immediate connection between this place and the murders he was investigating, but again he dutifully interviewed and recorded.

Building four housed an auto parts shop and here Morgan caught a break.

Jason Reade, one of the clerks, recalled seeing a station wagon similar to the one described as having been at the first murder scene.

"It drove by here one night and when I read in the papers about a station wagon at one of the murder scenes I was gonna call the police, but it wasn't the same color or make so I figured it couldn't be the right one."

"Mr. Reade, would you please do me a favor?" Morgan said softly. "I'd like you to take your time and think back to the day when you saw that vehicle. I'd like you to tell me everything you can remember about it. Please be as detailed as you can."

"Uh, sure." The man replied, noting the seriousness in Morgan's voice. "Let's see, it was quite a few weeks ago, sometime in June, I think.

I was working late, it was about 9:30, and I'd stepped outside for a smoke.

I was just turning to go back in when I heard a car coming down the street.

I stood in the doorway and watched as it passed by. What caught my attention was how slow it was moving, almost as if the guy was casing the area. I know he didn't see me 'cause the doorway is unlit, but then I got a real cold feeling in my gut. I could actually feel his gaze on the doorway where I was standing, and for one dizzy moment I was afraid he could see me right through the darkness.

I don't mind telling you, detective, it scared the hell out of me. Anyway that's pretty much it. I never saw the wagon again."

"Do you recall the make and model of car you saw?"

"Yep. It was a 1958 Ford Country Sedan. It looks a lot like the vehicle described in the papers so I can understand if a mistake was made. Still, the car I saw may not be connected to your case at all.

By the way, I think it was light gray in color, but I can't swear to it."

"One final question, Mr. Reade." Morgan said, writing furiously in his notebook. Could you possibly narrow down the day when you saw that station wagon?"

The young man thought for a moment.

"I'm pretty sure it was early in the month…wait! It was the 7th of June.

I'm sure now because I had to work on the night my daughter was starring in a play and my wife was hopping mad."

The final building was uninhabited and had been so for some four months.

Morgan went back to his car and sat there for 30 minutes, eating a sandwich, drinking a warm beer, and reviewing the notes he'd taken. A smile played over his face as he reread the information on the station wagon Jason Reade had seen.

Then he started back to the Deuce.

What luck! Ev will freak out. This could be the first big break in the case. If we can I.D. this vehicle as the same one that was seen at the Gregg murder scene, we'll have a direct link to Vindicator. First thing I get back to the Deuce I have to call that guy who saw the car where Gregg was found. Maybe he'll change his mind when we show him pictures of a 1958 Ford Country Sedan.

We're breathing down your neck, you sick crud and soon we'll wrap a rope around it, real soon.

FIFTY-SEVEN

"Ah! There's good news today, Cap'n." Morgan's jovial call to Byrd's office was more to test the air regarding the Captain's mood than to herald any good news about the case.

"The only thing that I might *remotely* consider to be good news is that you and that miscreant you call a partner have found and disemboweled the nut you've been chasing."

Evan rolled his eyes and shrugged.

"C'mon S.T. Evan and I have been busting our humps on this case and we've run down two new leads that could break the case.

Honest, Captain, we're on this like white on rice."

"Alright, haul your sorry butts in here and enlighten me, and it had better be good 'cause the boys downtown want results and they are looking to me to provide them ASAP."

Morgan and Evan spent the next hour in Byrd's office, filling him in on what they had discovered regarding the items discovered at Book's murder scene, the latest updates on the evidence collected at the other murder scenes, and discussing what these revelations meant in relation to capturing Vindicator.

"We are convinced that the next victim is somehow connected to radio, possibly an anchor or disc jockey. The picture of Hedda Hopper together with the picture of the WXKP radio station in Portland leads us to that assumption." Morgan pointed out. "Now, if we can get a name we might beat this bastard to his next prey."

"If we can do that we stand a good chance of getting him too." Evan broke in. "We think the model airplane is how he chose to name the next victim, and when we figure that out we'll know who it is.

By the way, before I forget it, Sarah called me last night with a brilliant thought. She reasoned that the little figure of a native we found at Brenda Hart's murder scene might be representative of a group of pagan tribes that originated in Borneo.

So she dug around a bit and sure enough, the little figure looked a lot like a Dayak, a small, fierce, warlike aborigine populating Borneo since the Stone Age. They were cannibalistic and very savage.

Now here's the good part. Sarah found out that these little monsters were also called 'headhunters'."

"What's your point?" Byrd growled.

"It just so happens, S.T., " Morgan said, sensing that the Captain was becoming impatient, "that *that* term is also used to refer to someone who goes into companies and makes them more efficient, in part, by firing a lot of people.

I got a feeling we'll find out that Book was a headhunter and that was *his* sin."

"And that theory is supported by the conference room photo found with the statue of the aborigine. Headhunters usually call employees into a conference or boardroom to let them go. Less of a scene that way." Evan added.

"So, cutting to the chase, if you two have figured out what all the velvet sack items are, and I assume you have, how long before you get this guy?"

"We can't be specific until we decipher the model airplane clue and identify the next target, but I'd say within the next day or two." Morgan replied.

"Also, we haven't figured out the coffee can clue yet but I don't think it will matter since we already know the victim associated with that set of items."

"Alright, I know you two are giving 110% on this case." Byrd said. I'll buy us some more time downtown but those guys aren't *completely* stupid. I can hold them off only so long. Now get out of here and get cracking."

Morgan and Evan thanked the Captain for backing them up and then beat a hasty retreat before Byrd thought of something else to dump on their plates.

The two detectives spent the rest of the afternoon poring over all of the physical evidence one more time, hoping to make some connection between the meaning of one of the deciphered clues and the model airplane.

By five-thirty they were no closer to an answer and decided to get a good night's rest and go at it again the next day.

"We're gonna crack this one soon. Ev, I can feel it. The guy's been giving us too much info all along and now that we've begun to figure him out it's just a matter of time."

"Yeah, I feel it too. I don't think he knows it but we're breathing down his neck and when we come up beside him he'll be the most surprised person on the planet."

The two detectives packed up and headed out of the Deuce, noting as they went the Captain's light still burning.

"He drives himself too hard, Morg." Evan said, concern in his voice.

"Sometimes I wish he *would* retire, before the damn job kills him."

"The old man's a lot tougher than you think, Ev. Remember when his eight year old niece was kidnapped two years ago. He went without sleep for 50 hours because he wouldn't go homee for fear he'd miss something.

Then, when she was found beaten and dead in a cornfield, he dragged himself to the site to identify her so his sister wouldn't have to go through that hell.

I went with him and I could see the fatigue in his face but he seemed alert and strong.

When we got there, the lead detective took us to where she was lying and uncovered her little body.

The sight of that child, torn and battered as she was, took my breath away and my legs almost buckled.

Then I looked at Byrd. He was death white, his face frozen in shock and grief. I knew right then he was gonna have a heart attack.

But he didn't. He just straightened up, started giving orders to secure the area, and then left to go to his sister.

He never left her side for the next three days until the child had been laid to rest and all of the friends and relatives had gone.

Then he crashed for two straight days after which he resumed his duties as if nothing had ever happened, though he was eerily quiet for a couple of weeks.

I think he was working though the grief he couldn't express while he was being strong for his sister, but trust me, a silent Byrd is worse than what we're used to.

The point I'm trying to make is that he was 61 at the time and he came through the whole tragic mess better than guys half his age."

"I know. It's just that I'd like this place a hell of a lot less if anything happened to that grouchy old buzzard."

FIFTY-EIGHT

Morgan hadn't seen Bud and JoAnne for over a month, primarily because of the case he was working on. So when JoAnne called to invite him for supper he quickly agreed.

"And bring Jen, Morg. We haven't seen her in awhile. Bud and I look forward to seeing you two at seven tomorrow night."

JoAnne had taking to calling her husband by Morgan's nickname since the first time she'd heard the reason why Morgan had chosen it. It had touched and pleased her to use a nickname for her husband that reminded her of how much he loved her and she loved Morgan for thinking of the name.

"Thanks Jo. This is just what I need right now. We'll both be there unless Jen can't make it. Either way wild horses couldn't keep me away. You want me to bring anything?"

"Just yourself and Jen.

Fair warning though. Bud is like a kid with a new toy anticipating talking with you about the case. The evidentiary information you've sent him since the first murder have kept him engrossed. I tried to tell him you'd want to get away from it for one night but he said partners never tire of chewing over cases together.

I swear, Morg he's never really left the force. He's always listening to his police radio and dragging me into theories about the latest crimes committed in Portland and Deliverance, which means he theorizes and I'm just the sounding board.

Don't ever tell him this but I too get a kick out of trying to figure out the who, what, and why of criminal investigation. It's a puzzle waiting to be solved and you know how I love puzzles, even if Bud does most of the talking."

"Actually, I wouldn't mind getting Bud's take on this case; it's partly why I agreed to send him the particulars of each case. I knew it would let him keep his hand in and have some fun in the process.

To be honest, I'd have talked to him about it before but I wasn't sure you'd approve.

Sounds like there's no worry on that front though."

"Count on it." JoAnne laughed. "So, we'll see you tomorrow night; have some good food and lively conversation, as Irv Kupcinet always says."

Morgan smiled. He recognized Irv Kupcinet as a late night television talk show host that on occasion he'd watched because he considered Kupcinet and his guests to be intelligent and the topics interesting.

"Okay, Jo. See you tomorrow night."

***

Morgan and Jennifer pulled into Bud and JoAnne's drive at 6:30, feeling as if a heavy weight had been lifted from his shoulders. The last several weeks had been pressure filled and the thought of chucking it all for one evening was delicious.

Assuming nothing else cropped up, like another murder, the closest this evening would come to the case was batting it around with Jen, Bud, and JoAnne.

Bud answered the door and enveloped Morgan in a crushing bear hug.

"Uh!" Morgan groaned. "I love you too, old man."

"You getting soft in your declining years, *old* man?" Bud shot back. "I'll have to learn to go a bit softer, and I know who to practice on."

He gently hugged Jen and kissed her on the cheek, and she responded in kind.

"Jeez, first you fracture my spine then try to steal my date. Some friend."

"If Bud wasn't married to Jo I'd have dumped you for him long ago." Jen teased.

Dinner consisted of meat loaf, cut green beans, and baked potatoes; with coffee, vanilla ice cream, and blackberry cobbler for dessert.

The conversation matched the full but relaxed character of the meal.

"If you weren't the wife of my former partner, I'd get down on my knees and beg you to run away with me." Morgan said, an impish grin on his face.

"Yes, well I'd be hard pressed not to be swept off my feet, *if* I thought it was my body you were after, not my blackberry cobbler." JoAnne replied, her arched eyebrow pointing like an accusing finger at Morgan's duplicity. "Watch out for him, Jen. He's a devil."

Only when the group moved into the den did the conversation turned to the case.

"We're riding pretty high right now." Morgan began. "I think this guy's made a mistake and Ev and I are going to use it to bring him down. He's given us too much information this time and we believe we have a good chance to identify the next victim before he gets to him."

"How do figure that?" JoAnne asked.

"By comparing evidence at one crime scene to the identity of the victim at the next scene, and with a little good old fashion nose-to-the-grindstone brainstorming, we figured out that the clues left in the red velvet sacks were Vindicator's way of telling us who he was going to kill next."

"Are you saying you know the name of the next victim?" Bud broke in.

"Not exactly. We know he or she is connected to the radio news profession. It's only a matter time until we figure out what the last item means, which should give us the name.

Now, Bud, what do you think?"

"Heh, heh. I'm no Merlin and I've no magic wand with which to conjure up your killer. But there *are* one or two points that piqued my interest.

First, having gone through everything you sent me, I've concluded that this person is bent on righting a wrong that was done to him at some time in the past.

Further, he wants the righting of these wrongs made public. It's as if he can't get closure until he publically humiliates these people as he was humiliated those years ago, thus the graphic and completely abasing way in which he's extinguished their lives."

"That's pretty much how Evan and I figured it too." Morgan concurred. "Although the idea of mutilating the bodies as a way of humiliating the person *hadn't* occurred to either of us. Thanks."

"There's something else. Now, this is off the top of my head and I can't say why other than it just feels right, but I think one of the victims may actually be the person who inflicted an injury on this madman.

I can't say if it's someone already dead or someone to come, but I believe you'll be able to distinguish that murder from all the others if you compare them close enough. There will be something more *personal* about that murder. The trick is to spot the difference."

"That had occurred to us too. Thanks for the vote of confidence."

"And, if you know which victim has a personal link to Vindicator you might be able to track that link back to him." Jen finished Bud's thought. "Very clever."

"Yes, well it remains to see just how clever I am." Bud observed. "One final thing that's been nagging at me. All the physical clues seem to fit into one category or another. First, the items in the red velvet sacks. Then the weapons and other items used to carry out the murders—using age to indicate that Old Testament Commandments were broken.

You get the idea.

But there was one item in the list that I couldn't seem to categorize. The brass disk with a horse's head on it didn't seem to fit anywhere in the pattern."

"We think that may have been dropped accidently by Vindicator." Morgan said. "It looks like a part of a cufflink and we're trying to trace it, without much success I might add.

Of course, it may have been dropped by someone else and is totally unrelated to the case."

"Looks like a chess piece to me." JoAnne interjected. "You know, from those training sets. But who carries around one chess piece in their pocket?"

"We'll keep trying to identify what it is and to whom it belongs, but for now our main focus has to be identifying the next victim before he or she *becomes* a victim."

"Well, that's it." Bud said. "You've picked my brain clean. What say we depart the world of crime and play some pinochle for awhile?"

Morgan and Jen left at midnight, promising to come back soon.

"You can't work all the time and stay on top of your game, Morg." Bud cautioned as he walked them to Morgan's car. "All work and no play *does* make Jack a dull boy.

The mind needs rest and diversion to operate efficiently. Make sure you and Evan take some time out for both.

My first captain told me that and I never forgot it.

Of course, I never took that prudent advice when I was working on a tough case and I doubt you will either, but it's worth saying."

"Is it me or did Bud seem a bit more sage than usual tonight?" Jen said, breaking the silence of the ride home.

"He gets that way sometimes. He's a great deal more intelligent than most people think. He just doesn't show it publicly very often.

Bud is a simple man. He knows who he is and he's comfortable with that. He doesn't need to show others how wise he is.

Bud was the best cop I've ever known for three simple reasons. He knows what he knows, he does what he does better than anyone I've ever met, and he just keeps on doing it."

"I don't know if you understand, old bean, but Jo is like that too." Jen said. "She does what *she* does so well, and it gives him what he needs to help him be who he is."

"I understand, all too well."

A vision of Senna filled Morgan's eyes and he turned away so Jen would not see the pain etched on his face.

FIFTY-NINE

Evan parked his Impala in Sarah's drive and walked around to the back yard.

Sarah was kneeling next to a garden border, weeding.

"I thought you were going to be ready when I got here." Evan said. "If we take off right away we can just make Good Samaritan Hospital in Portland, complete our investigation and have lunch before heading over to Feldman Properties Inc. for the afternoon."

"Holy crime stopper, Batman; don't dismay. I'm ready to go and eager to follow my fearless leader into battle. Before the day is done we'll bring the evildoers to justice."

Sarah's light sarcasm brought Evan up short.

He looked at her perplexedly, then with an expression that bespoke his sudden comprehension of the meaning of her words, burst into laughter.

"Okay, okay, I get the message. But we are on a bit of a schedule if I'm to check out Brenda Hart's and Victor Book's backgrounds and be done by six this evening. The movie starts at 7:30 and I need time to clean up leave time for us to grab dinner somewhere before that."

"I've thought of that. Why don't we get a pizza and watch *The Maltese Falcon* on the tube in the comfort of your living room tonight.

We can always go to the movies next week."

"Ah, dazzlingly beautiful *and* brilliant. You're on. That takes the pressure off of the rest of the day."

Legacy Good Samaritan Medical Center was a large, sprawling medical complex. It was an all encompassing hospital with comprehensive care programs in the areas of cancer, stroke, coronary disease, and neurological disorders. That this was a five star medical center was obvious to anyone visiting the site.

"It's a good thing I called patient and visitor information yesterday and found out what building houses staff records. We're looking for 203."

"There will be a map and directory over here." Sarah said, pointing to a glass and metal visitor information kiosk standing just to the right of the main entrance. "That lady inside should be able to direct us to building 203."

"Excuse me miss, where is building 203?" Evan asked, flashing his detective's badge. "We're looking for the staff records department."

Sarah noted the effect Evan's voice and presence had on the young woman manning the kiosk and smiled at Evan's unawareness of the change that came over her.

"Just follow the brick walkway to your left here and take a right at the intersection." She replied brightly, eyeing Evan appreciatively."When you reach the large circular building you're at 203. Enter through the left door, take the elevator right in front of you to the third floor and it's the third office on the left as you step out of the elevator."

"Thank you." Evan said.

"I can show you if you want officer. I'm going off duty now and I have to go to building 203 myself." There was a note of hopefulness in her voice that Evan apparently didn't pick up on, which triggered another smile from Sarah.

"That's alright, Miss." Sarah said. "I'm sure we can find it ourselves with the excellent directions you've given us."

The look that crossed the woman's face said Sarah's reply was not what she had wanted to hear.

"There it is." Evan exclaimed, pointing to a wooden door.

"It's amazing to me what a badge and a court order can do to cut through the red tape of privacy laws." Evan said. "Now let's see who Brenda Hart is."

Evan and Sarah divided the thick file on Brenda Hart and spent an hour sifting through the various records.

"Well, it appears Hart has had a rather unremarkable career as a cosmetic neurosurgeon at Good Samaritan." Evan concluded after reviewing the notes he and Sarah had taken. "Nothing in these files indicates anything that would be grounds for our charmer to want to harm her." On the contrary, she's had a spotless record here at Good Samaritan.

"As a matter of fact she was never even on the radar, either in terms of accolades *or* controversy." Sarah pointed out. "If there's anything it must have happened before she came to Portland."

"This means I'm going to have to make a call to New York because that's where she practiced before she came here." Evan groused. "According to her records she transferred from Geneva General Hospital in Geneva, NY.

I hope I don't have any problems getting access to her records; otherwise I may have to fly out there and I don't relish that."

Sarah knew why. Evan hated flying.

"Well, that's as far as we can take that young lady. Let's get some lunch and head over to Feldman Properties, Book's last employers."

Lunch consisted of egg salad sandwiches, potato chips, pickles and lemonade, courtesy of Sarah who'd suggested a picnic lunch in Greystone Park. It was only a few blocks from Feldman Properties and the day was perfect for a picnic.

Sarah had prepared the lunch, and put it in a cooler packed with ice, while Evan had provided the eating utensils and blanket.

"Any luck with the last clue from the Book murder scene." Sarah asked.

"Not yet. Morgan's interviewing the employees at WXKP again to see if he can shake something out."

"I still think finding a victim that is personally tied to Vindicator is your best chance of tracking him down, if that theory is, in fact, true. Time will tell.

Evan, what's your read on Morgan and Jen."

Evan blinked and tipped over his glass of lemonade, which, fortunately, emptied into the grass.

"Whoa! That came out of left field. What are you talking about?"

"Well, I used to think they were a couple but lately I don't know."

"Yeah, it's Morgan. I'm pretty sure Jen would like to take it to the next level but Morgan's not getting the message."

"So why not? He seems really taken with her. Maybe he's leery of making a long term commitment."

"Sarah, how much do you know about Morgan's past?"

"I know he was married before and that his wife died. Other than that I'm clueless."

"I came to Deliverance a year after Senna died.

I never knew her and Morgan never talks about her, but from what I've heard from the people who knew her, she was an angel.

Bud says Morgan fell head over heels in love with her the first minute he saw her and Senna reciprocated that love tenfold.

They were married soon after and it was clear to anyone who knew them that this was a marriage made in heaven.

Then Senna got pregnant and their joy sky rocketed.

JoAnne recalled that Morgan, normally a very quiet person, sang constantly, couldn't stop smiling, and drove Senna and everybody at the Deuce crazy, calling her at least five times a day to see if she was okay.

No two people were ever happier and it seemed that the birth of the baby was going to achieve the impossible by increasing that joy.

Then the unthinkable happened; a stupid and senseless tragedy.

In December of 1955, just days before Christmas, Senna was out shopping for, as it turned out, Morgan's gift.

She was entering a bank to get some cash when some sick degenerate burst through the door firing a revolver wildly. A slug hit Senna in the stomach, killing her and the unborn child.

As she lay on the ground bleeding to death, one of the cops who'd arrived on the scene heard her say…"

Evan's face clouded over and Sarah was astonished to see the mix of hatred and pain that was choking him.

"Evan? It's okay. You don't have to say anymore."

"No, I want you to know so you can understand where he's coming from now. What she said with her last few breaths was,

'Oh, God! Morgan, poor Morgan.'

The world ended that day for Morgan. According to Bud he went somewhere inside of himself and no one could reach him, not even the mother he adored.

Bud and JoAnne were terrified he'd kill himself."

"Sweet Jesus!" Sarah whispered, overcome by the enormity of Morgan's loss.

"Over the next several months he returned to a semblance of the person he'd been but he wasn't healing right inside and all of us were afraid that he'd never be whole again.

Then he met Jen and the old Morgan began to resurface. He seemed truly happy and appeared to be moving on, letting go of Senna and the child he never knew.

And that's pretty much where he is now, only I know him. In the depths of his soul he still grieves, and I think he's putting on a show to comfort his friends.

I don't think he's let go of Senna, even though he's trying to for Jen. I think she was the love of his life and I'm still worried for his state of mind."

"My God! That is so sad. It must have been devastating to his friends and family too, to see someone they loved in so much pain."

"You know Bud, Morgan's first partner. He and JoAnne love Morgan as if he was their son and Senna was like a daughter to them.

Well, if you ask anyone who knew Bud back then they'd have told you he was the kindest, most thoughtfully intelligent person they'd ever met who believed all people were inherently good or at least worth saving.

When Captain Byrd got the news, he called Bud and told him to find Morgan and stay with him. Bud went to the hospital where Senna had been taken and found Morgan. What he saw in the eyes of the young man he loved so much transformed him. He got Morgan back to Morgan's mother's house, and called JoAnne to come over and stay with both of them.

When JoAnne reached the house she didn't recognize her husband.

His lips were pressed thin, his face was white, his eyes pinpoints of ice and he was loading his police revolver.

'Help Agnes with Morgan, Jo. He's in a bad way. I'll be back later.' Was all he said.

'Do what you have to.' Was her reply.

Bud walked off of the front porch, got into his car and drove off.

Later, Bud showed up at the bank. He collared the first patrolman he ran across and growled through clenched teeth,

'Where did the sonofabitch run to?' This from a man who seldom raised his voice, let alone used profanity.

Bud wasn't aware that the creep, who'd been trying to rob the bank at the time he'd shot Senna, had been arrested and was in a cell down at the Deuce.

The patrolman, who saw the look in Bud's eyes, lied and said he didn't know. He swore later that he believed if he'd told Bud where the guy was, Bud would have gone down there and made the crud eat his .38.

Bud eventually cooled down but he was never the same after that day. Like Morgan, he'd changed forever. He became more cynical when it came to criminals, especially violent criminals, and the trust that had always been in his eyes was gone. He was still a wonderful person and excellent cop but his belief in the innate goodness of people was gone.

That bastard killed three people that day, one who was to become my best friend.

Morgan wouldn't like it, but I think somebody should have capped the guy instead of taking him in. It would have been justice served and it would have saved the state the expense of feeding and housing the subhuman low life."

"No, Evan, you wouldn't really have wanted that." Sarah said softly. "You're reacting to the injustice of what happened to someone you love deeply, and you want retribution against the criminal commensurate with the heinousness of the crime he committed. You also want that retribution to be delivered immediately."

"Yeah. The saying 'justice delayed is justice denied' happens to be a truism."

"But it should be justice, not revenge. And it should be carried out lawfully, not in vigilante fashion.

I know you, Evan. You believe in the law. Taking it into your own hands or advocating that someone else should goes against everything you believe in.

You might talk about wishing someone would *cap* a bad guy, but you'd never really want them to do it, and you'd sure never do something like this yourself."

"Maybe so, but don't be too sure. More than once I've seen the look in Morg's face when Senna's name or what happened that day was mentioned by some rookie who wasn't aware that he was talking about Morg's wife.

And, you're right. I love that old bear and I hate anyone who'd cause him that much pain.

I don't know. This job gets more frustrating each day. The bad guys get all the breaks and the crazy juries and judges turn them loose faster than we can put 'em away.

Anyway, let's finish up here and get over to Feldman. Maybe we'll have a bit more luck there."

Sixty

Morgan began the interviews with radio station employee Aaron Clinton, while Wynona Barnes and Red Wilson waited outside of the sound room.

"Any reason someone might wish you harm, Mr. Clinton?" Morgan asked, noting Clinton's job at the station consisted of doing the news and weather along with commentary on some of the more interesting news items.

"No, except for my ex-wife, but I doubt she would waste her time on a loser like me. At least I bet that's what she'd say.

I don't have enemies, officer." Clinton said caressing his lower lip with his thumbnail. "I'm pretty much of a loner. Get up real early on Monday through Friday, inhale my breakfast 'cause I'm usually late, go to work from 7 a.m. to noon, spend an hour or two at the station working up the next day's program, go back home, watch T.V. or read until ten or so, and back to bed.

Pretty boring but I like it."

"What about weekends?"

"Well, I moonlight as a piano player at the *Udder Cup* coffeehouse over on Belmont Drive from 9 p.m. to 1 a.m. Saturday nights. I only do that a couple of times a month though. Other than that I pretty much hang around my apartment, playing piano, watching the tube, or reading."

"Girl friend, wife?"

"Nope. Burn me once, shame on you. Burn me twice, shame on me. I take a woman out once in awhile but I make it clear I'm not interested in a relationship.

Of *any* kind?"

"Of any kind!

Look officer, I got lucky. My wife cheated on me and I got pictures. I told her I'd have my lawyer introduce those pictures at our divorce proceedings if she asked for alimony. No judge on earth would have awarded her a dime after seeing those photos.

Since we were childless, I didn't have child support to think about.

So, I got away free and I'm not about to get caught in that trap again."

*This guy is pretty bitter. The saying is **Fool** me once shame on you. Too bad he never met someone like Senna.*

Then again maybe he was the jerk in the marriage. Either way, adultery is not the answer to marital problems.

"Okay, Mr. Clinton. But if you think of anything, call me." Morgan said handing the man his card. "The guy we're looking for is a full blown psychopath."

"Yeah, I read the papers. But I doubt seriously I'm in his sights. I'm just too boring to have ruffled anyone's feathers, primarily because I have almost no contact with the public and the stuff I report and comment on is pretty generic."

"Have you recently flown on a Boeing 707 airliner?"

"I don't fly period. There are no fender benders in those things. You get into trouble and three things can happen. You burn to death, you slam into something hard, or you somehow get out of it alive. I don't like those odds.

Plus, getting out of it alive isn't necessarily a good thing if you wind up maimed or in a vegetative state.

Are you checking out a particular airline or will any 707 do?"

"Just a lead we're following." Morgan replied, but he entered a reminder in his notebook to find out which airlines used 707's.

"That should do it for the time being, Mr. Clinton. Thank you for your cooperation. Would you please ask Miss Barnes to come in as you leave?"

"Sure thing. Just don't call her Miss to her face. She's a bit testy about men since her divorce a year ago. She doesn't like people referring to her femininity in a condescending way and she considers that term to be condescending. She prefers *Dr*. Barnes."

Lovely! Here I am trying to protect these people from a crazed killer and this woman's gonna get here knickers in a twist if I don't address her properly. Come to think of it, she'd probably really get offended if she heard me talking about her knickers.

What a world!

"Thank you for taking time to see me Dr. Barnes."

Morgan was trying to get the interview off on the right foot but not holding out too much hope. This lady looked like she ate people for a snack; most of them being men would have been Morgan's guess.

"*Taking* being the operative term, Detective, because it's for sure I'm not giving it to you.

Why is it that the police never seem to do things efficiently? I can assure you that when *I* interview someone I make sure I've got *all* of the questions I'm going to ask them in mind *before* I contact them. Of course, I have an incentive. If I don't get all the dirt the first time around, I might miss something and leave myself open to a law suit for slander."

"Uh, yes I understand. It's just that some new information has come into our possession and we need to ask you some more questions.

I promise to make this short. It really is for your protection, Dr."

For the briefest of moments Morgan considered that the world might be better off if this woman *was* the next victim.

The interview with Barnes and, subsequently, Red Wilson went pretty much the same as it had gone with Aaron Clinton.

Barnes admitted that her show, which investigated people for the purpose of exposing wrongdoing, sometimes led to people being angry with her. On three occasions since she'd come to the station in 1958, she'd received death threats. But all of those threats had been followed up and had been satisfactorily resolved.

Red Wilson seemed the most likely of the three to be the target.

"About ten years ago, I was involved in an automobile accident. A woman was killed in the accident and I was given a ticket at the scene and later charged with running a red light and vehicular manslaughter.

During the trial, however, my lawyer pointed out that the woman, who lived long enough to accuse me of running the light, was being treated for depression and paranoia.

I had claimed all along that the light I'd gone through was green for me and that she'd was the one who'd run a red light.

But since it was late at night and there were no witnesses, and since my car had struck hers broadside, the cop who arrived at the scene ten minutes after the accident decided to issue me the ticket. Though he wouldn't admit it at the trial I think he did so because when he ran my plates he found that I had a previous moving violation in the past year. That, and a dying woman's assertion that I was at fault.

Well, the upshot of all of that was that I was acquitted of all charges because there was no proof who'd run the red light.

I think the jury let me off because my lawyer proved to them that the one eyewitness to the accident was unbalanced.

After the trial, the woman's husband was furious.

Not only had the murderer of his wife been acquitted, his wife had been drug through the mud so a celebrity with a lot of money could escape justice.

He swore he'd get me if it was the last thing he ever did and it didn't help to assure him that I was neither a rich celebrity nor at fault.

Over the next two years the man hounded me relentlessly. My phone would ring at 2 or 3 in the morning and when I'd answer it the person on the other end would hang up. I found feces smeared on my car three different times, and all four tires slashed.

On one occasion, my brakes went out and the garage mechanic said the brake line had been cut.

The cops tried to catch him but never did.

Finally, I learned he'd started drinking and lost his job. He moved out of state and the harassment stopped. I hoped it was over.

But about nine months after he moved I got a letter made with words cut out of magazines which said I'd pay for my sins and in kind.

I can tell you *that* scared the hell out of me, especially when it went missing two days later.

Somehow he got into my house and stole it back.

I haven't heard anything more now for almost seven years but you never know. Maybe this guy you're looking for is the same one, maybe not.

I'll say one thing. Before his wife was killed, John Santorum was known around town as one of the nicest, most level headed persons in Portland. I found that out from the police who investigated the possibility that he was after me."

Morgan left WXKP and headed back to the Deuce, stopping long enough to pick up a sandwich, chips, and coffee at the restaurant across from the precinct house.

As he sat in the incident room, chewing thoughtfully and reviewing his notes from the morning's interviews, he wondered if what he was recording on the marker board was really going to be all that helpful.

Any of these people could be the next target. Trouble is, they could also wind up as false leads. The last thing we need now is to waste time running up our own backsides chasing ghosts while Vindicator calmly goes about slaughtering his next victim.

Damn! This case keeps getting more complicated when it should be getting simpler.

Sixty-One

Evan boarded Northeast Airlines Flight 673 to Waterloo, N.Y. and found an aisle seat in first class. Morgan, knowing how much his friend hated flying, had called in a favor from a friend at Northeast to get Evan upgraded from tourist to first class so he would at least be as comfortable as possible.

Listening to Evan doing his best to get the records department at Geneva General Hospital to give him the information he wanted on Brenda Hart over the phone, or at least to mail her personnel records to the Deuce had brought a smile to Morgan's face.

After what seemed like an hour during which Evan pleaded, cajoled, threatened, and finally begged, he gave up and resigned himself to having to fly to New York.

Now, thirty thousand feet over the lovely state of Colorado, he was trying to relax and concentrate on something other than the fact that he was 30,000 feet over *anything*.

The stewardess offered him a meal but he deferred, asking only for a 7-Up.

To pass the time and, hopefully, take his mind off of the flight, Evan reviewed the notes he'd taken when he and Sarah had visited Feldman Properties.

Background information showed Victor Book had been an efficiency expert, a.k.a. headhunter, and had revamped several companies before coming to Feldman properties.

He would be retained by a company, ostensibly to modify and streamline its operational structure for the purpose of increasing productivity and competitiveness.

Book assured the owners and administrators that he would do this in a fashion geared towards a minimum of disruption with regard to personnel and operations while "cutting out the fat" that was bogging the company down.

Unfortunately, this usually involved in the firing, laying off of, or involuntary relocation of a number of employees.

While Book's methods were rather ruthless, the ends usually justified the means.

True, a number of those companies failed within five years and had to be sold on the chopping block for a fraction of their true worth, but Book was never accused of purposely causing that to happen, though it had been rumored that on more than one occasion that his fingerprints were all over the strategy that led to a company's downfall.

Then, looking for a change and better position, he came to Feldman Properties as their new merger strategies executive, and seemed to fit in perfectly with a company that specialized in hostile takeovers.

His new responsibilities were similar to what he had done before but without the wet work. There was now an insulating layer between him and the people who actually did the firing, and as such he no longer had to get his hands dirty.

Victor Book was a happy man who saw his future as being very bright.

But only six months after taking a position at Feldman he was himself summarily fired.

The reason was simple. An employee at Carter and Sons, one of the businesses Book had been hired to streamline previous to his employment at Feldman's, committed suicide by drinking lye when Book fired him. If that fact were to be made public it would prove deleterious to Feldman's's image.

Hence Book had to go.

By the time Evan had finished interviewing Feldman and talking on the phone with Mason Carter, the patriarch of Carter and Sons, regarding the suicide, he knew two things. Victor Book had been made to drink lye because of the suicide and, based on a statement made by Mason Carter Evan knew that the sword used to decapitate Book was chosen because of a statement Book had made to Mason referring to the "sword of Damocles" Book sometimes used to streamline a company.

***

The automobile Evan had rented in advance of the trip was ready when he arrived at the reservation desk after picking up his suitcase from the airport's baggage section.

The drive to Geneva, N.Y. took a little over an hour; including the time it took for Evan to grab a quick lunch at Waterloo's only steakhouse.

Reaching the hospital he parked in the visitor's lot and walked through the large double doors that marked the front entrance.

"Could you please tell me where your personnel records department is located?" Evan asked the lady sitting at the reception desk.

"Take the elevator over there to the second floor. It's the first door on your right as you get off."

The meeting with Adrian Eastman, the Records Department supervisor, was strained. The man simply did not want to give Evan any information.

"These are highly personal files and as such are carefully guarded. I realize that Dr. Hart has passed away but she was a fine doctor who exemplified everything that is best in the physicians that practice at Geneva General. You would have to provide a truly imperative reason for me to now violate this woman's privacy, not to mention risking the chance that some of the information contained in her files might become public.

It would be like stealing some of her humanity to have her personal records dissected and analyzed as if she were the subject of some sterile clinical study."

"I've got the best reason possible, Mr. Eastman." Evan retorted, his green eyes fixed on Eastman; twin glaciers that lowered the temperature in the room by several degrees. "Dr. Hart was *brutally* murdered by a blood lusting psychopath. No, she was *slaughtered* in the most grisly fashion you can imagine, and then laid out for us to find.

Now if that isn't *really* stealing her humanity, I don't know what is, and you can bet Brenda would want everything possible to be done to find and punish the subhuman slime that did that to her."

Eastman fidgeted nervously as beads of sweat glistened on his forehead and began a mad race towards his nose.

"I do understand Detective Flack. Look, some of the information in these records could be misinterpreted, especially by people ignorant of the entire situation surrounding them.

I just don't want this woman to be violated a second time, that's all.

Why don't you fill me in as to what you're looking for to further your investigation and I'll try to give you as much help as I possibly can, but please understand that I will only release what is essential to helping you find Brenda's killer."

"That's not quite the way it works Mr. Eastman. Dr. Hart's records need to be professionally scrutinized to determine if anything in them might be of use in bringing us closer to her attacker.

You are not qualified to do that, just as I am not qualified to do your job.

Now, if you would please allow me to see her files."

When Eastman began to protest further Evan reminded him that he could obtain a court order for the release of the records.

"I'd hate to have to force you into compliance, especially since the more paperwork involved the more likely it is that newspaper reporters will smell the prospects of a scandal, and the hospital would be right in the middle."

The implication was not lost on Eastman; the negative publicity surrounding anything as sensational as the murders committed in Deliverance would not sit well with the administrators at the hospital, Eastman's superiors.

That would be especially true if the murders were somehow connected to one of Geneva General's top surgeons.

"Very well, but I wash my hands of the entire affair.

You will, of course, sign for any of the records you take with you. Also, I insist you put in writing your request for these records, and please note my strenuous objection to such a request. Please sign and date it."

Evan's smile was polite to a fault, an ever so slight smugness framing his lips.

"Of course, Mr. Eastman. Now, if we could proceed I won't take up any more of your valuable time than is necessary."

Brenda Hart's time at Geneva General was far different than her tenure at Good Samaritan in Portland had been.

She had been an energetic, outstanding surgeon, skillfully performing several operations each week.

Other doctors noted her tireless dedication, bedside manner, and sincere concern for her patients.

Additionally, Brenda had received several commendations and awards for her innovative and masterful surgical skills.

The only comment in her file that wasn't a glowing testament to her was that she worked too hard and sometimes stretched herself too thin. The result was that she often seemed tired.

One memo caught Evan's eye. It referred to an "incident" that had occurred during her third year at Geneva General. A staff report identified only as SR15 was mentioned but Evan couldn't find it anywhere in her file.

When Evan asked Adrian Eastman where the report was, Eastman shrugged and said,

"That was before my time. I can check with archives to see what they know but that's as much as I can do."

"I'd appreciate you're doing so now, Mr. Eastman. This may be the very thing I'm looking for.

If necessary, we can enlist the help of the local police department to help search for the report."

"That won't be necessary, detective." Eastman replied crisply.

Twenty minutes later he reentered room and tossed a folder on the table next to Evan.

"I think this is what you're looking for, detective, and you *will* need a court order to take it out of here." Eastman's voice was as flat as a straight line, the words struggling to get through clenched teeth.

"Yes, well I'll get back to you on that."

Eastman threw a baleful look at Evan as he left the room but he had already opened the folder and was beginning to read through it.

The incident referred to in the memo involved the facial reconstructive surgery she had done on a nine year old boy.

He'd been involved in an automobile accident and had sustained significant injuries to his face. The fact that his fifteen year old brother had been driving the car when it ran into a tree only made the accident more tragic.

Unfortunately, the tragedy was compounded when the post operative period went badly. The boy, Rembrandt Fallon, developed a virulent infection which resulted in the flesh on his face sloughing off in several places and several teeth had to be removed.

Further surgery was required and the boy was left blind and seriously disfigured.

Four months after the operation Rembrandt, suffering from deep depression over his looks committed suicide.

His brother blamed himself for the whole nightmare, needing several years of therapy to come to terms with the guilt he felt.

As is often the case Brenda, as the lead surgeon, was sued, along with the Geneva General.

It was claimed by the Fallon's attorney that she had performed several other relatively complicated surgeries that day and was too fatigued too have competently operated on Rembrandt. Her incompetence caused the infection. It was also claimed that the hospital was negligent for allowing a surgeon to operate that often in one day.

Attorneys for Brenda and the hospital refuted that saying that Dr. Hart had performed three or more surgeries in one day on several occasions with no adverse results.

Furthermore, three hospital staff members agreed to testify that they had seen Dr. Hart at the seventh floor nursing station an hour after the operation, laughing and joking.

She most certainly did *not* look tired, according to their account.

Finally, Brenda's attorneys landed a broadside when they pointed out that the infection came *after* and separate from the operation, an unfortunate but not uncommon occurrence in the best of hospitals, the responsibility of which could not be laid at the feet of the surgeon.

That took the wind out of the sails of the prosecution's attorneys, and an out of court settlement was quickly reached; the Fallon family receiving 1.5 million dollars for pain and suffering, while Brenda and the hospital were legally absolved of any culpability.

Also, as part of the settlement, all of the court proceedings were sealed and the Fallons had to agree to refrain from any discussion of the case.

It was not what the family had wanted, the father in particular. He had been very vocal in insisting that his attorneys demand that Dr. Hart at least lose her license to practice. What he really wanted was for her to go to jail because, as he put it, she had murdered his son as sure as if she had slit his *throat* with her scalpel instead of merely slicing up his face.

But his attorneys assured him that no jury would ever convict the doctor of any criminal charges and the settlement was agreed upon.

It was not long after that Brenda Hart left Geneva General. The official reason given was that she wanted to move west to be near her mother and father but rumors said otherwise.

The plain truth was that Brenda Hart had become a liability to Geneva General and had, therefore, worn out her welcome. Inside sources claimed that board members from the hospital and Brenda reached an agreement. Brenda would quietly leave and Geneva would provide her with a glowing recommendation.

Makes sense. That's why the difference in her manner at Good Samaritan.

Dr. Hart was no fool. She wasn't gonna make the same mistake twice. She did her job conscientiously but without calling attention to herself.

She found the ideal solution—take the money, be satisfied with a life filled with material gains, and forego the fame and attention route.

Worked too, by the look of her home and the things in it.

Only she didn't count on her past following her to Oregon and abruptly terminating her plans.

Evan, realizing the significance of this information, packed up all of materials relevant to Brenda Hart's murder and left the room.

He then found Eastman, discussed what he'd found in the report, and got Eastman to make several photocopies; at which point he exchanged the photocopies for the written request Eastman had demanded, complete with Eastman's objections, and Evan's signature. Then Evan headed out for the city's courthouse.

If I can get the transcripts of that trial, I'll have the names and, hopefully, addresses of the Fallon family. If ever someone had a reason for wanting Brenda Hart dead, it's that family.

I'd put my money on the father but I'm going to cover all the bases here.

One thing's for sure, some of what was done to her makes perfect sense in light of what happened to little Rembrandt.

He was blinded and her eyes were put out.

His face was disfigured and hers was also.

He had lost some teeth and hers had been pried from her mouth.

Driving back to the airport to drop off the rental and board a flight home, Evan felt elated. This was a solid lead, one that could lead them straight to Vindicator.

Morg would be pleased. More to the point, Byrd would be too.

SIXTY-TWO

The fan in the incident room did little more than move the air about two feet in front of it which was sad because the window air conditioner didn't work at all.

In addition to failing to cool the room the fan clanged occasionally due to a bent blade, adding insult to injury.

"Aw, crap, not again!" Evan groused. "Can't those clowns from maintenance *ever* fix anything right? How long's the A/C gonna be down *this* time?"

"You want the good news or the bad news?" Morgan offered.

"Is the bad news going to make me forget all about the good news?"

"Of course not. That wouldn't make any sense."

"Okay, then tell me the good news first. Maybe that will make me forget for a minute how hot I am and how much I hate this job."

"The good news is the guys are coming today to fix the A/C."

"That *is* pretty good. And the bad news?"

"The A/C they're fixing isn't ours, and that fan is being taken out of here because Byrd's broke."

"What? You said the bad news *wasn't* gonna make me forget about the bad news."

"I'm hot too, and seeing your face after I've just yanked your chain makes *me* forget the heat for a minute."

Evan glowered at Morgan for a moment. Then, in a voice that could have kept ice solid,

"Keep it up wise guy, and your corpse won't need to worry about the heat."

Morgan laughed and indicated for Evan to sit down.

"So, give me all the gory details from your trip to WXKP. Spare me nothing."

"I've got a gut feeling the next poor slob that gets killed is going to be one of the three disk jockeys working at that station, but I don't have enough concrete proof to order police protection for them. It's all just supposition."

"If we could tie that model airplane to one of the jock's names we'd have that proof." Evan observed.

"Yeah, well I've been trying to make that connection and I'm not getting anywhere. How does Aaron Clinton, Wynona Barnes, or Red Wilson link to a model airplane?"

"Do any of them fly a lot? Maybe the connection isn't with the names."

"Negative." Morgan replied. "I thought of that too, but nothing I've tried works.

I even considered Harvey Gunn, the station manager, and his secretary, Mary Hennessey. But they don't work either.

I still believe that toy plane represents the name of Vindicator's next victim. Maybe it's somebody else; some star crossed soul that we don't yet know who, *because* we don't know their identity, is probably going to suffer an ugly death. Damn!

Enough of my troubles. How'd you do?"

"Pretty good since, unlike you, I wasn't pressured to find the next victim before he or she *becomes* a victim.

Book was an efficiency expert and as such fired a lot of people. So there were plenty of people who would have liked to see him dead.

Points of interest. One of the people he fired committed suicide by drinking, guess what?"

"Not lye? We couldn't be that lucky."

"Say the magic word, win a hundred bucks.

And, he used to talk about using his 'sword of Damocles' to trim the fat out of a company."

"Good work, Ev!' Morgan exclaimed. "That supports our theory that the way Vindicator kills these people *and* the weapons he uses are tied directly to his perception of the sin they've committed to deserve condemnation."

"Wait; there are more rabbits in my hat."

Morgan smiled, seeing that Evan so excited. He'd been worried that his friend was becoming cynical and disenchanted lately. The detective in front of him now was excited and eager, a pleasant change.

"Okay, Houdini, impress me."

"When I checked Brenda Hart's past in Oregon, I drew a blank as you know.

But, her history at Geneva General Hospital in Geneva, New York was juicy.

It seems the good doctor was involved in an operation during her third year at Geneva Gen that went south in a bad way. Some nine year old kid came to the hospital as the result of an auto accident and Hart was the surgeon who operated on him.

The surgery went well, but the kid developed a staph infection that resulted in his going blind and winding up looking like Phantom of the Opera. He lost several teeth, and his face was horribly disfigured because the infection literally *ate* the flesh off of it."

"My God, Hart's eyes were gouged out, her teeth were ripped from her mouth, and the guy took a vise to her jaw.

It's the Book scenario revisited. Destroy the victim as the victim destroyed someone else."

"Yep." Evan concurred."The family was outraged, blaming Hart for botching the operation and not monitoring her patient properly."

"Do I detect more prime suspects on our radar?" Morgan interjected.

"Better. The father filed a civil lawsuit against Hart, trying to break her and the hospital financially.

Then, the mother of all nightmares happened. The boy became severely depressed and committed suicide.

Now, the father *and* the mother wanted her *criminally* prosecuted and when their own attorneys told them that Hart would never be convicted in a criminal trial, they went ballistic."

"Whoa!" Morgan said. "That is about as prime as it gets. We need to get on this pronto—find out where the mother and father live, bring them in for questioning, check alibis for our murders, etc."

"I'm ahead of you, buddy. Two years after Hart left New York Roland and Nancy Fallon, together with their other son, packed up and split too. Guess where?"

"Oregon."

"Another C note. At this rate you'll be able to retire in no time. As a matter of fact, they moved to Hillsboro, a small town 20 miles north of Portland.

Furthermore, they live there now.

One final note before you put me up for Deliverance's detective of the year.

Rembrandt's 15 year old brother was driving the car when the accident happened and he blamed himself for everything that happened. He also tried to commit suicide and was in therapy for years afterward. Think how *that* went down with the father."

Morgan sat there, stunned. His mouth opened and closed but no words came out.

"You look like a fish out of water, buddy." Evan teased. "But I'm with you. *This* may be the victim Bud was talking about, Morg.

In terms of the father, and possibly the mother, though I doubt she's Vindicator, Hart being responsible for the death of their son doesn't *get* any more personal.

I know it's possible that any of the other vics *could* have been killed because of what they did to someone that directly affected Vindicator.

But my gut feeling, and I'll bet yours too, is that we have a winner here."

"So, job number one now is to run these people down and either eliminate them as suspects or…"

"Right. We're in the home stretch, I can feel it."

"Alright, Ev, let's play it that way for now. We're going to call Hillsboro and see if the Fallons are home. You get our lunches and a couple of sodas. We'll eat in the car.

The sooner we see these people the sooner we find out if one or both of them is responsible for these murders."

Morgan went to Byrd's office to update him on the new evidence and phone the Fallon home, while Evan picked up the food and a new notebook and pen.

Fifteen minutes later, having spoken to Roland Fallon and arranged to meet him in an hour, the two detectives were on their way to Hillsboro.

"We play this close to the vest, Ev." Morgan said between bites of his sandwich. "If Roland Fallon is Vindicator, I don't want to tip him off before we're ready to take him and maybe wind up with a mess on our hands."

"Is that your subtle way of telling me you want the bastard alive." Evan said, his voice stone. Cold anger and disbelief battled for control of his features, age old adversaries warring on a scarred battlefield.

"If it is him, Morg, and he makes any wrong moves, I'll drop him in a heartbeat.

Barring that, I know my duties as a cop and I'll do them to the letter *and* the spirit of the law."

"Enough said, partner." Morgan dropped the subject. He trusted Evan to do his job regardless of personal feelings; something Morgan knew wasn't always easy to do.

The next few hours might bring about an end to this nightmare or it might just be another dead-end in a labyrinth of what so far had been all dead-ends.

Either way Morgan could sense that something was about to break, like the smell of the air and how still it became just before a storm.

Five minutes out from the Deuce Evan was fast asleep, his head resting against the window. Morgan looked at him and smiled.

Evan's such a good detective; I forget how young he really is. It's not unnatural to feel things as strongly as he does or to blow off steam on occasion.

What I have to remember is that he hates injustice and sees it as his personal responsibility to bring the bad guys to account.

It frustrates him when the punishment for a particularly heinous crime doesn't seem to be enough, but I have to remember that venting is his way of accepting that.

Truth be told I feel the same way myself about some of the cruds we've collared.

SIXTY-THREE

Turning on to the I405 Morgan noticed a red pickup truck weaving erratically ahead of him.

A deep sigh escaped a Morgan's lips, rousing Evan from his nap.

"Hmm, what's up?" Evan asked groggily.

"Looks like we got a drunk ahead of us."

"You take him, I'll back you up."

"Check." Morgan said.

Morgan flipped the switch on the siren, rolled down his window, and placed a flashing red light on the roof.

The vehicle slowed down and pulled over onto the shoulder.

Evan straightened up in his seat while Morgan pulled in behind the truck and stopped.

"I hope this clown isn't gonna be difficult. I'm not in the mood."

Morgan stepped out of the car and walked towards the truck, noticing how beat up and dirty it was.

Suddenly, without any warning, two men burst from the vehicle and began running towards a wooded section several feet off of the road.

"Stop! Police! Stop dammit!" Morgan ejaculated.

One of the men was about 40, six foot tall, tanned, and scruffy looking; with matted dishwater blonde hair and a ragged beard. He was wearing a polo shirt, faded, torn Levis, and tennis shoes, all of which were filthy.

Morgan thought he looked rather anemic.

The other man was about 50 and no more than 5'6". He was completely bald, chubby, and pale skinned. He was wearing a butterscotch sport coat, hunter green turtleneck, tan dress slacks, and oxblood wingtip shoes. Unlike his companion, he was very neat in appearance.

Neither man slowed though the skinny one did look back momentarily. Clearly, they were not going to comply with Morgan's command.

"Evan!" Morgan yelled, trying to alert him to the situation, but Evan had seen the men bolt and was already out of the car in hot pursuit.

Morgan speculated, with some alarm, that this was no simple drunk driving incident they'd stumbled onto. These men were fleeing as if their very lives depended on it.

His cop sense told him they were not easily going to be put under arrest.

"I got the dwarf, you take Pigpen!" Evan yelled, bearing down on the smaller man.

Leave it to Evan. Short and to the point.

Morgan shot into the woods seconds behind Pigpen, shouting again for him to stop. The man veered left trying to shake off his pursuer, but Morgan followed doggedly.

As the pair moved deeper into the dense cover, Morgan found it harder to keep up with the man. Pigpen was stronger than Morgan had first thought, and he was faster and had more stamina than Morgan had counted on. Furthermore, Morgan was at a disadvantage in that Pigpen *knew* when he was going to make a sharp turn, and Morgan didn't. That gave the fugitive a few precious seconds during which time he was out of Morgan's sight, which was all he needed to make it harder for Morgan to follow him as he darted back and forth.

I'm going to lose him if I don't run him down soon. I can't see through the foliage and these damn branches are turning my face to hamburger.

Morgan began to fall behind as he was forced to hack his way through the brush and small saplings that choked the path through the larger trees.

He tripped and was about to go down when suddenly he crashed through into a small clearing, righted himself—and froze.

Twenty feet in front of him stood Pigpen, rooted to the spot, eyes wild and menacing. He was breathing hard, like his heart was about to explode through his chest. Morgan guessed it was a combination of fear and adrenalin.

What was almost certainly a .44 magnum revolver filled his right hand, and it was leveled at Morgan's chest.

"Back off, cop!

"Easy, man." Morgan said, raising his hands palms upward. "No need for either of us to do anything stupid."

"That's right, cop: you just stand there *not* being stupid while I figure out what to do with you. Where's that punk partner of yours? He run out of steam? Young people just can't go the distance nowadays, can they?

Whoa! I told you to stay put. You move again and I'm gonna introduce ya to a brand new *personal* ventilation system." Pigpen shouted, looking around nervously. "Now, where in the hell is your partner?"

"Put the gun down, man." Morgan urged, playing for time and hoping Evan would show up. "This doesn't have to go down bad if you just keep your cool.

But if you kill a cop, there isn't a hole deep enough you can crawl into.

And, when they *do* find your sorry ass one of three things is gonna happen."

Just keep talking. Evan's out there somewhere. Keep this head case neutralized until he gets here.

"One, cops don't like cop *killers* so you may never even make it to trial.

Second, you *do* make it to trial? Killing a cop is a mandatory death sentence in this state. Trust me; you will *not* look good extra crispy.

Third, you somehow beat the death rap and they send you to Q or some other maximum security prison. A lot of ex-cops wind up as prison guards at those joints and *they* don't like cop killers either, which means you *accidentally* take a header off the third tier one day, or something similar.

Trust me, man you…"

An explosion in Morgan's right ear cut him off, and he reflexively dove for the ground, reaching for his .357 as he did.

As he hit the ground, rolling to his left a second shot rang out.

His body was pumping adrenalin through his system in what felt like gallons, and he knew if he'd been hit he wouldn't be aware of it.

In one fluid motion he came to a kneeling position and swung his now leveled revolver in an arc, trying to find Pigpen.

But Pigpen was nowhere to be seen.

What the hell! Where is he?

Morgan, fearing he was about to be shot again, rolled once more, trying to buy time until he could get the man in his sights.

Center mass. Center mass. Where is he?

And then, coming up to a kneeling position for the second time, Morgan saw him.

Pigpen was dead ahead, not ten feet away.

Morgan put his front sight on the man's chest and was about to squeeze off a shot when his brain told him something was wrong.

Pigpen was standing there and the .44 was still in his hand, but something was wrong. The revolver was unsteady in his hand and there was a large red blotch on his shirt, right where Morgan's weapon was aimed. Red foam was running down his chin and a scarlet bubble burst on his lips.

As if Morgan were seeing a film in slow motion, the hand began to lower, the .44 dropped from it and Pigpen pitched forward, slamming into the ground as only the dead do.

"It's over, partner."

Evan, still in a shooting stance, blinked and lowered his weapon.

Morgan, shaken from the adrenalin rush and the ferocity of the moment, nodded his head in mute gratitude.

"I thought it was lights out for a moment there, Ev. Thanks."

"Yeah, well, remember that the next time I ask you to share your lunch." Evan's smile was fixed, betraying the tightness in his gut.

"Where's the dwarf." Morgan asked as he re-holstered his revolver and dusted himself off.

"Oh, we've come to an understanding.

I caught him just as he hit the woods and, after some gentle persuasion, he was no trouble."

"Leaving aside the 'gentle persuasion' part, exactly what understanding did you come to?"

"He understands that if he manages to find himself free from the door handle of our car, where I cuffed him, he will remain at the car until we return."

"And what do *you* understand?"

"That if we get back to the car and Mr. Redfield *isn't* there, I have his permission to find him and relieve him of certain portions of his anatomy."

"Evan! Uhh, what am I going to do with you? You simply can't threaten prisoners like that."

"What I *really* told him was that if he escaped my partner would probably shoot him on sight.

Don't worry so much, partner. This guy is smart. He knows we're not gonna hurt him.

Plus, I ran the handcuffs through the door handle and then cuffed his ankles. He ain't goin' anywhere."

Morgan shook his head and walked over to Pigpen. He checked the man's pulse but he knew there was nothing that could be done to help him now.

"Alright, you wait by the perp's car; I'll make the ten minute ride back to Portland, drop Redfield off at the 7th and get Max or one of the other boys to take this off of our hands. It's their jurisdiction anyway."

Back at the car, they found Redfield, still securely shackled to the car and mad as a hornet.

"This is *unbelievable*! You have absolutely no right to treat me this way.

When my lawyer gets through with you two you'll be lucky to be assigned to crosswalk duty at an elementary school."

"Yeah, yeah." Evan said. "You got an awfully big mouth for such a little guy.

Course your hotshot mouthpiece *might* just have a hard time explaining why you took off running like a jackrabbit and then failed to stop when Officer Jeffords ordered you to.

And, when I caught up with you and flashed my badge so you'd know I was a cop, you tried to decorate my skull with a tree limb.

Whatta ya think, sport? You wanna go for double jeopardy?"

"You don't scare me, cop. I ran because Jerry and I thought we were going to be robbed and murdered, and we didn't stop for the same reason.

As far as the tree limb is concerned I was merely defending myself from a crazy man who was bent on chasing me down and killing me."

"The badge." Morgan interrupted. "What about the fact that Officer Flack showed you his badge."

"All *I* saw was a flash of metal. I thought it was a gun. You can't prove different and you've nothing on me or my friend that you can arrest either of us for."

"You're right about one thing, stud." Evan smirked, derision naked in his voice. His eyes seemed to penetrate all the way to Redfield's soul.

"We are *not* going to arrest your bathed in a dust cloud friend. Because right about now he's lying back there in those woods going cold and stiff, his chest a bowl of blood, bone, and lung tissue.

Redfield blinked and sucked in deeply, his eyes wide and frightened.

"You sonofabitch!" He shrieked, lunging at Evan with his hands.

"Why'd you kill him? We didn't do *anything*! You hear me, damn your soul, nothing!"

"Yeah, Jerry was a real sweetheart." Morgan said. "He was cooperative, friendly, and downright docile—right up until the time he pulled a .44 magnum and targeted *my* chest.

If it hadn't been for my partner here, I'd be the one lying on the ground back there.

I'll tell you honestly, Redfield. You'd better start cooperating with us or you are going to go down for a serious felony, including some *really* hard time for involvement in a crime committed with a weapon."

"I'm not saying jack until I see my lawyer."

With that, Redfield folded his arms and refused to say anything more.

"Evan, handcuff this guy's hands behind his back and put him in the front seat. I'll be back in about forty-five minutes."

As Morgan drove away from the scene, he noticed Evan in the rear view mirror, walking towards the suspect's car.

That's my partner. Checking the vehicle. Cross all the t's and dot all the i's.

An hour later, Morgan returned with two detectives from the seventh, including Max Herrick, a forensic team, and an M.E., complete with ambulance.

"What's up, Ev? Morgan asked noticing the smile on Evan's face.

"Oh, I got bored, and you *know* how curious I get when I'm bored. Sooooo, I just sort of poked around a bit in that little old car over there."

"Skip the chatter, partner. What did you find?"

"Look in the trunk and see for yourself."

Morgan walked over to the car and raised the trunk.

"Well, well, well. Looks like our friend Redfield had better hire Perry Mason."

"I got news for you, Morg. Not even Perry is gonna get Redfield off the hook on this one. There's gotta be at least 30 kilos of marijuana in there, not to mention all the weapons on Omaha Beach *after* the landing."

"No wonder they bolted. Well, Max, I think you've got a slam dunk case here. Time for Evan and me to move on."

"Thanks, Morg. We'll do you guys proud,

Next time you see Redfield, he'll be registered at the hotel Quentin."

Morgan and Evan gave their statements, then left the crime scene and headed on toward Hillsboro.

"I called the Fallons while I was at the 7th. We're going to meet them at their home at 2 p.m."

"That gives us twenty minutes, plenty of time.

I hope this is going to be quick and simple, Morg. I've had enough excitement for one day."

"I hear you, Ev. Trust me, I hear you.

By the way, don't forget to write up a report of what happened as soon as we get back to the Deuce. There will have to be a hearing on today's shooting and I don't want any loose ends when we go into IA's review board."

"Think there will be any trouble?"

"Not a chance. But I want us locked down tight on this. Nothing slipping through the cracks.

So we write it down as soon as we get back. Capiche?"

"Roger."

The rest of the trip was spent in silence, each man running what had happened over and over in his mind; Morgan searching for anything that might become a problem for Evan, Evan trying to justify what he'd done, even though he knew it was a righteous shooting.

By the time they reached the Fallon home both men knew they'd earned their day's wages, and they still had the Fallons to interview.

I'll sleep well tonight. Morgan thought as he pulled into the gravel drive that snaked up to the home. *Maybe Byrd is right when he tells us to pull our twenty and bail out. Lord knows nobody in the community gives a damn if we go or stay and it's getting too flipping hard to do this job the way it's supposed to be done.*

The bad guys get all the breaks their lawyers can fabricate for them. Cops don't have lawyers to help them.

So, we just keep grabbing the crooks and hope we don't do something or forget to do something that will let them get off on a technicality.

It's not fair and it wears me out to the point I just want to chuck it all.

But if I do chuck it, what will I do with all the hours to keep me from thinking about the .357 on my hip and how easy it would be to..."

Sixty-Four

The Fallon home lay nestled in a copse of Oregon ash trees. It was moderate, both in style and quality—an average sized Cape Cod with attached two car garage.

"You'd have thought they'd own something a bit more lavish." Evan observed. "Considering they got almost 2 million green in that lawsuit against Geneva Gen and Hart."

"I doubt the money has brought them any joy. Or peace of mind for that matter.

You know, Ev, the more I think about this the harder it is to picture Roland Fallon killing all those people. Hart yes, but not the others"

"Unless his grief drove him mad and he sees the others as having escaped justice just as his son's murderer did."

"Pretty much what we figure Vindicator is like. Still, he…I don't know."

A tight lipped, middle aged woman answered the door. It was apparent from her manner that this interview was not welcome.

"I hope this isn't going to take very long, Mr. Jeffords." Nancy Fallon said resignedly, brushing a gray-streaked wisp of hair away from her forehead." My husband is not a well man and he tires easily."

"We'll be as brief as possible, Mrs. Fallon." Morgan noted the reference to himself as Mr. as opposed to Detective. "We only have a few questions to ask and they really are important or we wouldn't be bothering you."

"Very well, follow me."

Nancy led Evan and Morgan to the rear of the house and outside to an enclosed patio overlooking a spacious back yard.

As they walked along, Morgan noticed how incredibly plain looking the Fallon woman was. Her hair was pulled back on her head, adding to the severity of her countenance, while her olive green house dress looked like a prison uniform.

She wore absolutely no makeup and her stooped walk suggested a burden she was struggling to bear up under.

Morgan glanced at Evan, who was also studying Mrs. Fallon.

He shrugged his shoulders, raised his eyes, and made it clear that felt sorry for the woman.

Evan's thinking what I am. This family has gone through the trials of Job. They lose one son and the other has a nervous breakdown. I wonder if a parent ever completely recovers from the death of a child, especially when that child commits suicide.

Well, I doubt this lead will take us anywhere, but we have to follow it through anyway.

Reclining on a wicker chaise lounge was a thin man. Morgan guessed him to be approximately seventy years old. He would later be surprised to find that the man was, in fact, forty-nine.

Morgan's misjudgment could have been laid to the man's appearance. The weathered face, sallow complexion, gaunt features, and lack of any visible signs of vitality would have fooled anyone.

"Good afternoon, Mr. Fallon." Morgan said, offering Fallon his hand.

"Yes, Detective." Fallon replied, rising slowly until he was sitting upright."Please excuse me for not greeting you at the door but I've been a bit under the weather lately."

"Not at all, sir." Morgan said. He shook the man's hand gently, fearful that he might injure him if he squeezed too hard. "We merely want to ask you and Mrs. Fallon a few questions regarding Doctor Brenda Hart. As you may already know, she was recently murdered and we are investigating her death, along with several other similar murders."

"Yes, we were aware of Dr. Hart's death." Nancy Fallon answered, her voice emotionless. Then, noticing the look on Evan's face, she continued.

"You'll understand if I'm not particularly moved. She was responsible for our son's death."

"Nancy, it's been 14 years. Time to forgive."

"I've forgiven her, Roland. I just haven't forgotten."

"If we could please get on with the interview, Mr. and Mrs. Fallon." Evan broke in. "We really feel bad having to bother you at all."

The next hour ran routinely. Morgan asked the questions and Evan took notes. At the end of that time Morgan felt everything that was worth probing had been covered.

"We'd like to thank you for your time and cooperation, Mr. and Mrs. Fallon." Morgan said, concluding the interview. "If you think of anything else please contact us at the phone number I've given you."

""We do hope you catch whoever is committing these horrible murders, Detective Jeffords." Nancy Fallon said at the front door. "We really do. But it will be a long time before we can be objective when it comes to Brenda Hart."

"We understand, ma'am. Thank you again for your help."

"So, what do you think, Morg?"

"I don't know, Ev. They both *seem* to be benign but you never know when it comes to the kind of grief and anger they've gone through."

"Yeah, I can't begin to imagine what they've had to endure. I mean it was bad enough about Rembrandt's suicide without having to see Liam, the other son, going through the torment he suffered; not to mention Liam's leaving home and going to England when he was 20."

"I'm bushed. Let's get back to the Deuce, sign out, and go home. We can take this up tomorrow."

"That and the name of the next victim. It's somewhere in that pile of stuff we've collected, I can feel it."

Sixty-Five

"What do you want for supper?" Sarah called out from Evan's kitchen.

"Whatever's quick and no work. I've had a full day, what with spending 6 hours with Internal Affair's shooting board. And, since I know you had a full day too, I think we deserve a break from shouldjas. How about a pizza?"

"Fine, as long as we don't get onions." Sarah answered, walking into the living room where Evan was sprawled on the sofa.

"What the heck is 'shood juice'?" The look on her face was priceless.

"No, no. It's *shouldjas*. Bud said it one time when we were playing poker. It means those annoying little jobs people *should* do in the course of getting through their day, like I *should* do my laundry tonight, but I'd rather crash here with you."

"Yes, well, I *should* know better than to expect anything logical from you, but I keep forgetting you're just a bit off center.

So, don't keep me in suspense. How'd the board's assessment of the shooting go?"

"Pretty standard. They called it justified and set me up with the department shrink for three sessions. I'm to talk it over with him to see if I'm okay to carry a gun.

It's strictly routine, Sarah. I had no choice. That crud would have shot Morg if I hadn't shot him first."

"I know, Evan. It just seems it's always the good guys who have to get down in the mud with the crazies in order to protect the community."

"That's what they give me the big bucks for.

Now, what do you want on your pizza, and what movie would you like to see?"

"Cheese, sausage, and pepperoni. As far as a movie, *North by Northwest* with Cary Grant and Eva Marie Saint is on at eight tonight."

"Sounds like a date. I'll call in the pizza order and it should be delivered within an hour."

"And I'll set up a pot of coffee and make some fudge brownies for later."

"God, woman, I'm gonna get fat and lazy if I hang around you too much."

By seven-thirty the pizza had been eaten and Sarah and Evan had settled in to watch the movie.

Sarah was curled up on the couch and Evan was sitting at her feet.

"While we're waiting, I was going to ask you a question before, but it slipped my mind. Wait. Did you or Morgan ever ask Wynona if Barnes was her married or maiden name?"

"Why?"

"Because, silly, if she's divorced, she will most likely have taken back her maiden name. It might be useful to know her married name."

"Say, that's a good idea. I'll call the radio station. She might be there, and if she isn't they might know where she is.

Good thinking Sarah. Thanks."

"That's why *I* get the big bucks."

"Could I speak with Wynona Barnes? This is Detective Evan Flack." Evan rolled his eyes as he waited for the person on the other end of the line to see if Wynona could be tracked down.

"She isn't? Well would you know where I can reach her? It's police business and it's important.

Yes, thank you." Evan motioned to Sarah for a pen and paper. "324 Shenandoah Drive in Fallwood…Wyandotte 6-3327. Thank you.

Say, would you happen to know what her married name was?"

"Okay, that does it. Her married name was Jett and they don't know where she is right now."

"Evan!" Sarah sat bolt upright. "Do you realize what you just said?"

"I know. The model airplane is a jet. Wynona Jett is going to be Vindicator's next victim.

I'm calling her house now. She's in terrible danger and she needs to know."

When no one answered at Wynona's home Evan acted immediately.

"I'm calling Morgan. Sorry about the evening and movie but we need to find her as soon as possible and warn her."

"Right. Anything I can do?"

"Just cross your fingers, old girl. This could be it."

"Get down to the Deuce and start going through the Barnes info for anyone who might know where she could be." Morgan said when Evan told him what he'd discovered. "I'll meet you there as soon as I get cleaned up a bit."

Forty minutes later Morgan walked into the squad room.

"Any luck?"

"Not so far. Her sister says she hasn't seen her in a week and none of her friends or coworkers know where she is. I'm calling the station manager now.

The station manager said he'd seen Wynona that morning, but since she wasn't due to host her regular show until the following afternoon he hadn't expected to see her again until then.

Morgan decided that it was time to go over to Wynona's house.

"Maybe we'll find some indication of where she went and when."

***

The drive to Wynona Barnes' home wound through the west side of Deliverance.

"How do you want to play this partner?" Evan's face was tight and Morgan knew why. They were heading into a precarious and possibly dangerous situation.

"We check the home to be sure she *isn't* there. After that we sit on this until tomorrow morning and do it all again.

When we get to the house we go on full alert. I don't know what we're gonna find there and I don't want any surprises, especially like the one I got the other day with Pigpen."

"Check, partner. How about I take the front door and you go in the back, *if* we don't get an answer."

Morgan nodded and pointed to a huge French Colonial home situated just ahead on the right.

"Jeez, Morg. That home is big enough to get lost in. Maybe that's why she isn't answering her phone—can't find it."

"Evan, sometimes your sense of humor borders on the unbelievably asinine."

"I'm guessing I've been insulted. What's asinine?"

Morgan parked at the end of the drive and the two men walked up it to the front door.

"No answer, damn!

We don't have probable cause to suspect that she's in there and needs help so I guess we go home and start again tomorrow."

"I'm for breaking in now." Evan objected. "We can always come up with probable cause later. C'mon Bulldog, this woman is in real danger."

"I understand, Ev". Morgan replied, smiling at the mention of Bulldog. Evan was playing on Morgan's sense of determination. "Here's how it's going to go down. We'll ring the bell again, then walk around the house looking in windows on the off chance we might see something. That's the best we can do and you know it. Okay?"

"Yeah, it's just a shame to drive all the way out here and then turn…"

"Did you hear that?" Morgan whispered, holding his hand up palm outward to silence Evan.

"Hear what?"

"Sounded like a window sliding up somewhere around the side of the house."

"Very clever, partner." Evan said, a sly grin on his face. "Oh *dear*, Oh dear, we *must* hurry now that we have probable cause for entering."

"No, you goof. I'm serious. You go right, I'll go left. Call out if you see or hear *anything.*"

Evan's face went serious instantly and he nodded in understanding.

Both men drew their weapons and cautiously began moving forward.

As Evan rounded the corner of the house he sensed, then saw movement a few feet ahead and near the house.

"Back of the house, Morg. Suspect running."

Evan bolted after the figure, impossible to identify in the dark. The fugitive disappeared around the corner and Evan accelerated to catch up.

He took the corner at full speed and ran headlong into a huge fist, taking the blow full in the face.

He dropped as if he'd been pole axed which, in fact, he had been.

As consciousness left him, Evan had the fading image of the figure running back the way the two of them had just come. Something about that blurred image was wrong.

"Stop! Now or I'll shoot!"

Evan faintly heard someone shouting followed by gunfire, then he surrendered to the enveloping darkness. His last thought was,

Something's wrong! It's not right!

Sixty-Six

"How are you feeling, old man?"

"Crap, Morg, I'm barely alive. Sonofabitch blindsided me. Hit me with a two by four."

"If he did, he also made it disappear because there's no two by four here now.

No, my friend, I think he hit you with his fist."

"He probably took it with him. I tell you he hit me with something big." Evan insisted, but Morgan knew his protestations were halfhearted.

"Anyway, he's gone. I can see you're going to be alright except for a bruise under your eye and some swelling around your cheek.

You okay enough to search the house now?"

"Yeah considering we now have *real* probable cause."

"I'd say what just happened, *and* the fact that the window on the side of the house where you first saw our phantom is open, *definitely* gives us probable cause."

The window where Evan had first seen the intruder was still open, but Morgan wanted to go through the front door anyway.

"I don't know what we're going to find in there but I figure there's a light switch near the front door and I want as much light as soon as possible."

"I hear you brother."

The front door proved easy for Morgan to pick. Evan wondered where he had become so skilled at it but chose not to ask.

"You take the living room, Ev. I'll go through the dining room to the kitchen."

As they made their way through the first floor of the house, they turned on lights where they found them.

Finding nothing on the first floor, Morgan and Evan moved up the stairs to the second floor.

Again a search yielded nothing.

"That leaves the basement, chief." Evan pointed out.

"Well, that's it, partner. A blank." Morgan said after completing a search of the basement.

"What about the garage and the grounds?"

Yeah, we'll hit that when we get back outside, but I doubt we'll find anything."

"Ah, she probably went to a show. Double feature or something."

Evan's tone told Morgan he didn't quite believe that.

Morgan opened the front door and was about to pass through when he stopped short.

"What's wrong?" Evan asked. "You forget something?"

Morgan pulled a sheet of paper off of the door.

"If you're clever enough this will lead you to where that viper's tongue is being kept before it's too late." Morgan read. "A journey west so long ago, passed by here and is marked so. An Indian maid fair she be, helped two men to reach the sea."

"Morg? Is that from…?"

"Yep, our mysterious figure tonight was none other than Vindicator. Sonofabitch had the nerve to come back and stick this under the door knocker."

"I don't believe it!" Evan slammed his fist against the wall.

"Get mad later, partner. Unless I miss my guess, Wynona Barnes is the 'viper's tongue' and will soon join our other cold, quiet companions unless we move it."

"Yeah, well, then the boys down at the morgue better put a *reservation pending* sign on one of their meat lockers 'cause the rest of that thing makes no sense at all."

"Yes it does, old man, yes it does."

"You mean you *know* what that says?"

"So do you, Ev. You just don't realize it. You had history in high school, didn't you?"

"And?"

"Ever hear of the Lewis and Clark Expedition?"

"Of course, but what would that have to do with Wynona Barnes?"

"Lewis and Clark stopped in Portland on their way to the Pacific Ocean. There's a park named after them right downtown. Built in 1949."

"I'll be damned! And, the Indian maid refers to Sacagawea, the Shoshone woman who served as their guide and translator."

"Precisely, now let's roll."

SIXTY-SEVEN

The Lewis and Clark Memorial Park was a good thirty minutes from Wynona Barnes' home. It was situated on a little over an acre and was situated just off the east side of the Steel Bridge a mile from the Willamette River.

Life-size statues of the three principal figures responsible for the success of the venture had been erected in the middle of the park.

Meriweather Lewis, William Clark, and Sacagawea, the Indian maiden who served as their guide and interpreter, had been meticulously sculpted using alabaster and red sandstone. They had been posed in front of a replica of one of the keelboats they'd used to make the journey.

The memorial was surrounded by several gardens, interlaced with cobblestone paths.

The only buildings on the grounds were a visitor's center that housed a souvenir shop, restrooms, and an administrator's office; and a groundskeeper's shed.

The park was fenced off and as Morgan and Evan drove up to the gate, Evan grunted.

"What?" Morgan said looking over at him.

"Nothing. Just thinking it's late at night, this place looks like it's

371

lighted with fireflies, and I've already had my ambush for the year."

"Yeah, my antennae are way up too. I don't know what we're going to find here but we're not gonna do Wynona *any* good if we wind up injured or dead, so we go in attached at the hip on this one. You cover my back and I'll cover yours."

Evan nodded in agreement as the two men exited the car and headed for the gate.

"Where did you learn to do that?" Evan asked, his eyes wide with surprise.

"Just a little something I picked up during my misspent youth." Morgan replied.

He was manipulating two lock picking tools in an attempt to open the gate they had found. Moments later a smooth click signaled his efforts had been successful.

As they entered the park both men drew their weapons and assumed the standard ready position; weapon level at chest height, finger just outside the trigger guard, left hand holding a flashlight shoulder high and slightly left of the torso. Their knees were slightly bent as they moved slowly forward, allowing them to instantaneously react to any situation.

"Let's check the buildings, visitor's center first." Morgan said.

Morgan tried the front door while Evan stood guard.

"It's locked electronically." He informed Evan. "No chance to pick *this* lock."

"Seems like an awfully expensive lock for a relatively unimportant building."

"Just what you'd expect from a government official, Ev. They don't mind spending taxpayer money."

"Hey, Morg, look over there." Evan whispered, interrupting Morgan's efforts to see if there was any other way to open the door.

"What?"

"The door to that shed is ajar."

Morgan looked to where Evan was pointing and whistled softly.

"Why do I get the feeling that it isn't an oversight on the part on the groundskeeper? Be alert partner."

Morgan went through the door first with Evan right behind covering his back.

Morgan found the wall switch with his flashlight and flipped it.

Nothing happened.

"Damn!" Evan exclaimed in a low whisper.

Nudging Evan away from him Morgan moved to his left, sweeping a ninety degree arc with a flashlight.

Evan mirrored Morgan's movements and between the two men the room was methodically cleared.

A small desk lamp in one corner was turned on that dimly illuminated the room.

"What's that smell?"

"Well, if it isn't a dead body, it should be." Evan replied, edging toward a heavy khaki colored tarpaulin covering what was clearly the entrance to a back room.

"Careful, Ev, pop the curtain from the top while I cover you."

Evan reached up took hold of the top right corner of the tarp, looked at Morgan who nodded, and pulled down hard. The tarp came away from the doorway and Morgan's flashlight bathed the rear of the room in an eerie, harsh light.

A cursory check revealed the source of the odor they'd detected; a mouse caught in a trap that had been dead for some time.

"There's nothing here, Morg. Maybe this creep's jerking us around."

"I don't think so, Ev. Let's try the visitor's center again."

Morgan and Evan moved around the building looking for a means of entrance.

"We're gonna have to break a window, Morg."

"Yeah, time's critical. Let's do it."

A sharp tap from the butt end of a flashlight took out the glass in the front door.

Morgan reached through and opened the door.

"Well, at least the wall switch in here works." Evan said.

"Let's check the restrooms, then the souvenir shop, and finish with the office."

It took twenty minutes to discover that the visitor's center, like the groundskeeper's shed, was devoid of anything that would lead them to Wynona Barnes.

"I'm telling you Morg this ain't goin' anywhere. Vindicator is running smoke and mirrors at us. Let's get outta here."

"I don't understand, Ev. Vindicator isn't the sort to blow smoke. The note said she would be in a building here. I was sure she'd be here, or at least a clue to her whereabouts would be."

"Why don't we check out the grounds, just to be sure?" Evan suggested, trying to be helpful. "Maybe there's a building somewhere that we don't know about."

"Alright. It shouldn't take too long."

"Morg, back at the Barnes home, just before I passed out, I got a flash of Vindicator running away." Evan said as they walked along. "It was blurred and I *was* about to blackout, but something was wrong about that figure. I just can't make it out though."

"You said it Ev, you were bonkers. Anything you saw *would* have been distorted. Let it go for now. Later, if there's anything to it, you'll figure it out."

The grounds surrounding the memorial yielded nothing of further interest. There were no other buildings anywhere on the grounds, and there was no sign of Wynona Barnes.

"I guess you're right, partner. Vindicator is apparently jerking us around. But…"

"Yeah, I know." Evan interrupted. "It's not his M.O. Vindicator snuffs people and lets the crime scene and the state of the victim do his talking.

Still, it could be as simple as a variation on his pattern, a variation we just haven't figured out yet.

Anyway, I say it's time we blew this pop stand.

Let's go back to Barnes' home. Maybe we missed something the first time through.

I'd hate to miss the boat on this one just because the jerk's note distracted us."

"Makes sense partner. It's ten-thirty now. Let's give it another hour and call it a night."

On the way back to the Barnes home the detectives discussed what they were going to do the next day should they fail to locate Wynona Barnes tonight.

"First we try to locate Miss Barnes by phone." Morgan said. "If that doesn't work, then you go to her home and I'll go to the radio station.

Her absence tonight may be quite innocent, spending it with a friend or something like that. But we have to find her soon. Her life depends on it."

"Don't I know it." Evan agreed. "Why don't we call the radio station when we get to her house? Maybe they've heard from her or know where she is."

"Good idea.

Let's go over the grounds a bit more carefully this time, then the garage.

Time is critical now so we'll leave the house for last since we already made a cursory check of it."

"You start looking around the back yard while I call the radio station." Evan suggested. "I'll catch up with you as soon as I finish."

Evan let himself in the front door, switched on a light and went to the wall phone in the kitchen.

"Excuse me, could I please speak to the station Manager. I'm Detective Evan Flack of the Deliverance Police Department.

Well, then, let me talk to whoever is in charge on the nightshift.

Hello. Would you or anyone at the station happen to know the whereabouts of Wynona Barnes? It's extremely important.

Yes, thank you. If you *do* learn where she is please call the Deliverance Police Station at WY 6-7112."

Evan hung up the phone and headed for the back door to the house.

"Evan! Come out here. Hurry!"

Evan bolted through the door and down the back steps, aware of the urgency in Morgan's voice and drawing his weapon in response to that note of alarm.

"Head for the car." Morgan shouted motioning Evan towards the front of the house. "We've screwed up big time!"

"I can't believe I missed it!" Morgan exclaimed pulling out of the drive and heading back towards Portland.

"Missed what?"

"We were both right, old man. Vindicator is jerking us around like you thought. But he wasn't lying either. That note said she was *being kept* and we both jumped to the conclusion he meant in a building."

"But we searched every place possible in the park." Evan argued. "She wasn't in *any* kind of structure, nor were there any clues where she was either."

"I'm afraid we missed something Evan.

Think. There was another structure staring us right in the face. We just didn't recognize it as such.

You even mentioned it earlier. You just didn't realize it and neither did I until I recalled what you'd said earlier."

"But we didn't miss anything. We searched every place around that memorial that could hold a human being."

"That's the catch, *around*."

"Whaaat? That makes no sense. The area around the memorial *is* the park. There's no place else to sea...

Bloody hell! The memorial itself—the keelboat!"

"Cover me, Ev." Morgan instructed, walking toward the three statues, gun drawn.

The young detective scanned the area around the memorial, his weapon a compass point as he turned.

Morgan approached the boat cautiously, aware of what he might find there. The replica was approximately 30 feet long, slightly more than half the length of the original ship, and had a beam of six feet.

The ship was outfitted with a 20 foot mast and, unlike the statues, was constructed completely of wood. A rear cabin provided for shelter from the elements.

Lewis and Clark chose this ship primarily because of its versatility. It could be rowed, sailed, poled like a raft, or towed from the riverbank, and was capable of carrying large quantities of goods and men.

"Nothing so far." Morgan called out for the bow of the ship.

"Avast ye swab!" Evan growled, attempting to sound like a sailor and failing miserably. "Look sharp now, or I'll keelhaul ye."

"If I get shot because you're playing Long John Silver instead of covering my backside, I'll haul *your* keel to the top of that mast and leave it there.

Alright, I'm going to check the cabin. Be ready."

Morgan moved toward the cabin door which stood closed. Placing his hand on the door handle and steeling himself, he slowly turned the handle and stepped inside, stooping as he did so.

"Oh, dear God. Evan! Get up here."

Hearing the crack in Morgan's voice Evan bolted for the ship.

Son of a bitch! The bastard's done it again.

"Hold on Morg."

Evan reached the cabin to find Morgan standing just outside, leaning against the wall and shaking his head. Evan could see that his face looked drawn.

"Don't go in there Ev, unless you want to lose your lunch."

Evan stepped through the doorway and shone his light around the interior.

The cabin was small, approximately 10' by 6' by 5' high. It was dusty and the windows which owned the starboard and port walls were dusty.

It at first appeared to be empty. Then Evan's flashlight captured a bundle of rumpled clothes tossed carelessly into a far corner. At least that was what Evan first thought.

On closer inspection it became obvious that the shapeless mass was *not* a carelessly thrown bundle of clothes. It was the body of a woman.

Evan moved closer.

Something was terribly wrong, but his mind was unable to comprehend what his eyes were silently screaming to his brain.

Suddenly he froze, as the realization of what he was seeing slammed into him like a freight train.

He reeled back and stumbled out of the cabin, unable to digest the horror that lay before him.

What the hell!

"My God, Morgan, it looks like every bone in her body has been broken."

"I think we'll find you're pretty close to being right Ev. Did you see the other?"

"There's more?"

"Her mouth is wide apart and her cheeks are bulging. I think the sicko stuffed something in her mouth.

It's him Ev and I bet we find this crime scene's identical to all the others."

"Except for the note. Why did he leave a note this time?"

"I don't know. It's a deviation from his M.O. that's for sure."

"Maybe the smug s.o.b. thinks we need help catching him."

"Uh, I don't think so. Vindicator's sole driving force is revenge. I doubt he'd distract himself with anything as unimportant as heckling.

No, I think he left that note because he wanted Wynona found quickly and took advantage of the fact that he'd accidently run into us at her house,"

"Why the hurry? He wasn't concerned with when we found the others."

"Not sure. Could be he thought she might not be found for a long time, her being *inside* the memorial where it was unlikely anyone would enter."

"But then why put her there in the first place. Besides, she would have announced her presence in a few days, if you get what I mean."

"I'm not an oracle, Ev." Morgan smiled. "I don't have all the answers.

He might not have thought of these things until after he'd put her in the cabin, too late to do anything without taking needless risk.

Look, we'll sort that out later. Right now I want to get forensics and Jen down here.

Oh, we need to contact Portland PD and the Portland coroner. Don't want to step on any toes, especially considering how cooperative they been so far with the cases they could have claimed jurisdiction over."

"That's what I like about the Portland P.D. We caught the case first and they're letting us run with it. Some other P.D.'s would have gotten all territorial."

An hour later Morgan and Evan exited, Morgan having satisfied himself that they'd done all they could for the time being.

"Go home and get a good night's sleep partner. Tomorrow we're gonna go through every murder again, just as soon as we get the medical and forensics reports."

Sixty-Eight

Evan walked into the Deuce at nine. Morgan was in the incident room setting up.

"What's the game plan, old man?"

"The game plan, as you put it, is to once again go through each of the murders in detail." Morgan replied, setting the coffeepot and donuts on the table. "Maybe we'll notice something we missed before."

"Jeez, Morg. That'll take all morning."

"Most of the afternoon too if we have to interview witnesses again. Sit down. The sooner we start the sooner we'll finish."

Evan pulled up a chair and poured a cup of coffee.

"Evan, we're up against it. We've got five murders and no real leads. If we don't come up with something soon Byrd will take us off of the case, bring in the Portland detectives and set up a task team with detectives from both cities."

Morgan walked over to a new marker board he'd had brought in and wrote VINDICATOR MURDERS in the top center.

"Okay partner, dazzle me with your brilliance. How should we start?"

"List those points common to most or all of the murders? If we can see connecting links between the murders, it might reveal a link back to Vindicator."

"Good a start as any, but we also look for inconsistencies as well as commonalities. Any deviations from the killer's pattern could be significant."

Morgan wrote the word LINKS centered just below VINDICATOR MURDERS. On the third line Morgan wrote a 1 off to the left.

"Well since you mentioned it, I noticed that all of the bodies except one were left in public places. Brenda Hart was murdered and left in her home."

"That *is* interesting." Morgan said, writing the point on the board.

Over the next three hours Morgan filled the board as he and Evan sifted through the evidence collected during their investigation of the five murders.

"Okay Ev, let's see what we have before we go to lunch. Then we can decide over lunch whether or not we'll have to go back and interview people again or revisit crime scenes."

"Nine points of similarity. Doesn't look like much for three hours work.

First, the bodies that were left in public places suggest the killer *wanted* the victims to be displayed and found.

Actually, Brenda's body *was* displayed too, just not publicly."

"What interests me about that is why *didn't* Vindicator want Brenda Hart found right away?"

"Yeah." Evan said. "That bothered me too. Any ideas?"

"Not right this minute. Let's finish the list and go to lunch. Maybe we'll pop a few more ideas over some good food."

"Okay. Second point, each of the vics could be said to have *actually* done something wrong.

The judge let that kid go for political reasons. Eddie Carrington was a drug dealer. Brenda Hart screwed up that operation."

"She wasn't held liable for that, Ev."

"No, but an out of court settlement doesn't mean innocent. All it means is that Geneva Hospital had the money to make the whole thing go away.

Anyway, it's a possibility. As for Victor Book, he caused a man to kill himself as a result of Book's firing him for no good reason."

"Evan, that doesn't mean Victor Book committed a crime."

"Morgan, there are *legal* crimes and then there are *moral* crimes. To my way of thinking the moral crimes can be just as bad as the legal.

Finally, we have Wynona Barnes. I suspect her crime is gossiping considering Vindicator beat a Roman numeral eight across her *lips*."

"Alright." Morgan conceded. "Each of the victims did something that can be *construed* to have been a crime. What does that mean?"

"I'm not sure."

"I am. It means Vindicator had to have read or seen something concrete on each of these people." Morgan said. "Either that or he had to have known each of them fairly well, which is doubtful. That means if we find his information source maybe we'll find him."

"He could have gotten the information from several different sources, but I don't think so."

"Why not?" Morgan asked.

"Because I think he knew who the next victim was going to be long before he killed them. I think he has one source and he began the selection process months ago."

"I'll go you one better, partner. I think he chose them all from that source before he ever committed the first murder."

"Except for the one that *caused* all of this." Evan noted. "*That* one he chose a long time ago. Whoever he or she is, is the driving force behind his madness. If we can identify that person we find Vindicator.

Third point, each of the murders took a *lot* of time to commit and in light of the extremely violent way in which they were committed required a place where the sounds of that violence could not be heard."

"Good point Ev. Somewhere Vindicator has a kill room that he brings the victim to.

He subdues them with electricity and chloroform, secures them in such a way that they can't even move their heads, and then spends what must be hours, possibly days, torturing them before finally putting the poor bastards out of their misery.

Now to do this he has to have a soundproofed room in an out of the way area so he can bring them in and carry them out without being seen. And, he has to have a boatload of equipment—tables, instruments, possibly a cell to hold them until he's ready to start his sick ritual, etc.

All of this takes money so I'm betting the guy is pretty well off."

Let's finish up."

"Fourth, the videos. Nothing clicks for me on this one."

"How about this. I'd bet most if not all of those films were made by someone other than Vindicator. They show the victims in social or public situations that he wouldn't have been in a position to film unless he knew them intimately."

"And, we agree that that's not likely." Evan pointed out.

So what was his source for those films?"

"No idea there. Another lead to follow."

"Roger. The fifth similarity is my favorite. I think the old tools, some of which aren't easy to come by may mean he has a hobby or profession that either uses them or collects them."

"That's good too, Ev. You're on a roll."

"On and off. I don't have a clue as to how the bags of items help us catch him."

"Well,…" Morgan thought for a moment, ideas forming and fading as he digested the information on the red velvet bags and the items found in them.

"One thing. The fact that those items identified the next victim means that none of these people was a random choice. That supports our contention that they were all selected for a reason, and that means Vindicator has the intellect to select, plan, and carry out very complex murders,

I'll bet his I.Q. is well above average, maybe close to genius."

"That makes sense, If we're lucky we'll both be 'on' today and catch this scum.

Moving right along, the seventh similarity is the cryptograms. Their significance lies in the fact that the ones we've researched so far have come from sources the average person doesn't read—the Bible and some 1796 obsolete dictionary.

That jibes with your I.Q. theory and my contention that the guy is highly educated and well read."

"The Bible is read by a lot of people, Ev, and a lot of them are *not* highly educated, nor are they highly intelligent."

"No, but the average guy doesn't usually choose to quote the Bible chapter and verse. Besides, the old dictionary is one *I've* never heard of and I'm not exactly brain dead."

"Point made. Let's come back to that one later."

"The eighth point is the commandments. The only thing I get out of that is the guy may be Catholic which is hard to swallow considering what he's done."

"That's the point, Ev. A religious fanatic might behave just like Vindicator if he thought he was on a mission from God. No, that *is* the significance of the commandments."

"The final point is a culmination of the others. Almost all of the physical evidence has been given to us as a series of puzzles to solve."

"How does that help us?"

"Morg, I'm a game player and I know this guy is too; I can sense it. He is a big time game player, trust me on this one."

"I trust you on a lot of things partner, not the least of which is my life. Okay, I buy it.

Well that's the list. Now, Let's get out of here, I'm hungry and it'll be good to get away from this for awhile then come back to it with fresh minds, and summarize everything we've done here today."

"Check. Off to *Steakout.*"

The phone rang on Morgan's desk. It was Jen saying she was on her way to the Deuce with the forensic and autopsy reports on Wynona Barnes.

"I'll be there in five minutes and I'm expecting someone to take me to lunch for rushing this over to you."

"Looks like we got company for lunch, Morg." Evan said hanging up the phone.

"Hmm. I smell blackmail. On the other hand, I can't think of anyone nicer to be blackmailed by."

Five minutes later Jen arrived, walked into the incident room and handed the files to Morgan who placed them on the table.

"Now, who is taking me to lunch?"

"Your chariot awaits m'lady." Evan said bowing deeply and pointing to the door.

Well, I'm deeply flattered Sir Lancelot, but what about Old King Cole there.

"Old King Cole is your carriage driver.

Probably be shelling out for the cost of the meal too, since I'd bet Evan forgot his wallet again."

"You're deductive powers are outstanding partner, I'll give you that."

Morgan smiled, shook his head and walked out of the room, his friends close behind.

***

"I hope you don't mind if we combine work with pleasure, Jen. Evan and I are up against it." Morgan said as the food arrived at the table.

"Of course. Maybe I can be of some help."

"You can start by giving a thumbnail sketch of what those reports on Wynona say." Evan suggested.

"Well, Vindicator certainly lived up to his reputation. Wynona Barnes suffered an incredible amount of pain before she died, from repeated blows to the temple by the way.

I can't be completely sure but I think he secured her face up to something like a table and then proceeded to methodically beat on her for a long time."

"Why do you say that?" Evan asked.

"First the abrasions and contusions were regularly spaced and formed a pattern. He couldn't have done that if she weren't completely immobilized. Plus, there were two small wood splinters imbedded in her back which makes me think she was on her back."

"I'm almost afraid to ask." Morgan broke in. "What was the pattern?"

"I'm almost afraid to tell you. Starting with her right arm, going up across her breasts, and down her left arm he raised welts on her body in the form of Roman numerals from one to seven."

"Aw hell!" Evan exclaimed. "This creep just gets sicker and sicker."

"Where did he put eight through ten?" Morgan asked, anticipating Jen's next comment.

"Nine was on her left leg, ten was on her right leg, and eight was centered on her lips and chin."

"So if you spread her out face up on a table the commandments read left to right and top to bottom like the page of a book." Evan observed.

"Wait, that doesn't make sense. He stuck the eight at the top of the 'page'."

"Because the eighth commandment is *Thou shalt not bear false witness against thy neighbor*." Morgan replied. So he put the eight on her mouth.

What else?"

"Pretty much the same as all the others. Duct tape, cattle prod, a Roman numeral eight carved into the hair on the back of her head, and the letters SASMBMBBNWNHM branded on her back.

Vindicator didn't leave any forensic evidence behind of course. The guy is eerie.

One deviation from his pattern though. He didn't leave a film, but he did leave a reel to reel audio tape.

One other thing. Her mouth was crammed full of little pebbles."

"Well, that explains the cipher." Evan offered.

"Pardon? How do you figure?" Jen asked.

"Sticks And Stones May Break My Bones But Names Will Never Hurt Me."

"What about the velvet bag items?" Morgan asked.

"My tech reviewed those. There were two photos and a letter in an envelope.

He said one photo appears to be a statue of a woman whose arms have been severed, the other is the interior of a horse barn complete with four horses in their stalls.

The envelope is charcoal colored and the letter inside has words pasted to it made from letters cut out of a magazine—*der frau ist kaput.*"

"What did the guy use to beat her up with?" Morgan asked. "We didn't see anything at the scene."

"We found a fifteen inch long, quarter inch diameter copper doweling rod wedged under a bench seat in the cabin. He obviously chose it to make marking her up easier."

"I can tell you one thing; it took time to mark her up that way." Evan said. He did her somewhere else; some place where he could take his time and where nobody would hear her scream, just like we figured."

"Anything else Jen?"

"Morgan, I think he's self destructing. His attacks are becoming more and more frenzied and personal. To *beat* someone the way he did implies a ferocious energy and hatred.

I think this started as a quest, or mission if you attach a religious component to it. But over the course of the first three murders something's snapped in Vindicator's mind.

If you don't find him before he kills again I'm afraid we won't recognize the next victim as even being human."

"That's creepy Jen." Evan cut in. "I thought Wynona Barnes was a just pile of clothes when I first saw her lying there in that cabin."

"I hear you Jen." Morgan sighed. "We're piecing this together as fast as we can.

I do think we're now getting a clearer picture of this man and I think for the first time that the case is going to crack soon, maybe in a few days."

"By the way, I located the origin of the cryptogram found on Book." Jen said. "It's from the Bible too; Book of Revelations, Chapter 13, Verse 10. It wasn't verbatim but close enough."

When the detectives returned to the 2nd they reviewed their notes and drew up a composite of Vindicator.

A religious fanatic, probably Catholic or who at least had been raised as one.

Someone who likes to play games, solve and create puzzles.

His hatred is likely focused on one person, probably one of the victims.

May be connected to archaeology or some profession involving the unearthing and retrieval of ancient artifacts.

Has a single source of background information from which he selects his victims.

Has access and opportunity to a place to commit the murders in secret and the wherewithal to purchase numerous pieces of equipment and supplies.

Is financially independent as evidenced by point 6.

Has the time to do all that he's done (See point 7).

Has had access to films taken by several people.

Is highly intelligent, well-read, and highly educated.

"Well, that's a mouthful!" Evan exclaimed.

"Yeah, makes for a nice picture though."

"A *portrait* maybe. What do you think Morg?"

"I think we're going to go see Chris Verble and get *his* take. Nice call, Ev."

SIXTY-NINE

When Dave Ways heard about the roast for Bud he immediately offered *The Steakout* as the place to hold the festivities.

"Bud's one of the good guys; I'd be honored to host this." He told Morgan. "If you get the people I'll set up the food and drink."

"Thanks Dave. I was hoping we could get your place. I'll take up a collection from the people who knew Bud personally to help pay for the bash."

"That won't be necessary." Frank said. "You guys collect money for a gift and Linda and I will pick up the tab for the food and drink.

I'll close the place for an evening and we'll have a private party."

"Won't losing a night's business cost a bundle?'

"Nah. We'll do it on any Saturday. We usually close at five and the party can start around seven."

"It's a plan. Thanks again and I'll call when I know the earliest we can do it.

Oh, we're gonna tell Bud it's a roast for Max Herrick. That way it'll be a surprise and we can be sure Bud will come because he can't resist taking a few shots at his old partner from the 7th."

The list for the party was easy to compile. Morgan called Max Herrick over at the 7th. Max said he'd take care of notifying the Portland guys who'd known Bud in the old days.

"Give me until tomorrow to get back to you." Max said. "How does this Saturday sound as a target date?"

"That should be plenty of time. Most people don't fill up their weekends five days out so the turnout should be good.

Thanks Max, I'll be talking to you."

"Before you hang up something crossed my mind about that mess you found at Lewis and Clark and I went over to the memorial to have a look for myself.

The way I see it the guy had to be pretty tall and *damn* strong to have gotten a body up on the deck of that ship. I went over to the site and checked the ship for marks indicating he'd used a ladder. Morg, you know that ship is all wood. If he *had* used a ladder there would have been *some* fresh scrapes or nicks. There weren't any.

That boat is over six feet high meaning he would've had to *pitch* her up there.

Scary stuff my friend. Straight out of King Kong land.

Morg? You watch your ass. This guy ain't human."

"Jesus! That *is* scary. Thanks for the heads up. We thought he used a ladder too. Never considered checking for marks where it had been placed.

I'll let Chris and Jen know about this. It may change the physical profile on the guy.

Again, thanks for backing us up."

"Well, I wouldn't want the next generation of cops telling the *new* version of the dog that ate the I.V. story."

Morgan's colorful response told Max he'd ever so skillfully slipped the needle into his friend.

"Okay, gotta go. Say hi to Evan and tell him we're looking forward to seeing you guys at *The Steakout* for Bud's party."

SEVENTY

"Jen's changed the physical profile on Vindicator." Morgan said as Evan slid behind his desk. "Based on the info Max gave me, and the fact that after hearing that she went back and looked at the casts of the footprints left at the Carr murder scene, she now places his height at around 6'6" and weight at maybe 240.

"She found something else too. When she looked at the casts again she noticed something she'd missed earlier. One of the prints had made a deeper impression, indicating the man walked with a limp."

"That's what was wrong!" Evan slammed his fist on the desk. "I told you that something was wrong about the guy running away from me that night at Wynona's.

He was running with a hitch in his giddy up!"

"So, add point number eleven to our portrait." Morgan said. "By the way Chris thinks our portrait is pretty good."

"What do you think the cufflink, broken floor tile and the ticket to a classical music concert mean?"

"It's only a guess, but considering the surroundings we found Book in, it's unlikely the tile was already there. It may have come from Book, but my gut says no.

I think Vindicator left that piece of tile at the scene and that it came off of his clothes or shoes. We can try to trace it, but I doubt we get anything.

The cufflink, if it's his, most likely means he dresses formally which fits with the concert ticket.

Bottom line though, I don't think any of those items mean jack. We've tried to trace the ticket and the cufflink, no luck. If by some miracle one or more of them turn out to be game breakers it will be just that, a miracle."

"Well, gee, Morg. Tell me how you really feel."

Actually, I agree. It's the other stuff that's going to catch this guy, and the sooner we start acting on our portrait the sooner we get him.

So, which of our points do we start with?"

Morgan looked at the list of eleven points for a few moments.

"I think point 5 is where we should start. We can go through back issues of all of the rags sold in a radius of 50 miles around Portland. We'll be looking for articles on the victims, and one magazine or tabloid paper that reported on *all* of them."

"How do you want to divide the work up?"

"Simple. You take the newspapers, me the magazines. Let's start by making a list of each and then hitting the bricks."

After calling several grocery stores, and news agencies that dealt in underground publications, Morgan and Evan had their respective lists.

"See you later this afternoon." Evan said as he and Morgan walked to their cars. "Good luck."

"Right, partner. Same to you."

SEVENTY-ONE

Evan glanced down at the folded out list of newspapers. There were only five but they were scattered around the area and he groaned at the thought of the time it would take to run them all down.

Two in Portland, two in Haverstock, and one in Deliverance. Might as well start in Deliverance.

The World Voice was housed in a small, red brick building only three blocks from the 2nd. It was a modest establishment, housing all of the facets of a news publication; copy room with reporters, composing room editorial and management offices, and the printing presses. Circulation was approximately ten thousand copies on a weekly basis. The *Voice* was relatively benign as tabloids went, focusing primarily on preposterous claims regarding Hollywood celebrities and public officials.

On occasion stories involving beings from outer space and the supernatural found their way into the publication, making all the more obvious how ridiculous and implausible the reporting really was.

"Excuse me, could I see the managing editor?" Evan asked a man sitting at a desk.

"Who are you? This is the copy room. Only reporters allowed in here."

"Sorry." Evan said pulling out his shield. "The name is detective Flack and I'm here on police business."

Five minutes later Evan was sitting in the editor's office requesting to look at the paper's archives.

"No problem detective. I'll have one of the copy boys take you to the basement. That's where we keep the back copies of all of the issues of the *Voice* dating back to 1951."

It took Evan and David, the copy boy, the rest of the morning to go through all of the newspapers back to 1958, which is when Wynona Barnes had come to Portland.

"If we can't find a story on *her*, it's a good bet there won't be a story on the others." He explained to David.

Well, that was a wasted three hours. Evan thought, pulling away from the curb. *However, one down, four to go. Next up, Haverstock.*

The first stop for Evan once he reached Haverstock was a small local paper called *The Haverstock Companion,* which turned out to be one of those folksy little journals that specialized in informing the community of upcoming events and local news.

Granted, there *had* been a couple of articles over the five issues Evan read through that dealt with minor scandals but Evan quickly realized that there was nothing in any of the copies to suggest Vindicator had read the paper.

"Has this paper always had this format?"

"Yessir, Detective. We've been a family oriented paper since we started in 1944."

"Any really sensational stories ever make it in? You know, sex or murder."

"Naw. This has always been a pretty boring little town.

You want gossip? Go over to Hamilton and 6th. That's where *The Oregon Reporter* is. They print all the *crap* that's unfit to print, little of which is true and none of which is about Haverstock."

"They've *never* written something dirty about Haverstock?"

"Most of those reporters live in this town. There's an old saying; you don't crap where you live. Besides, they get more than enough material from Portland and the surrounding area to fill that rag they call a paper."

It took Evan less than a minute of reading to realize that the *Reporter* was exactly the kind of paper he was looking for, a true gossip rag. Plus there were several stories about people in the Portland area public eye, many of which were unflattering at best.

But after spending another 21/2 hours rummaging around in the trash bin the *Reporter* was, Evan still had not found an article on any of the victims.

It was now five o'clock, he was tired, and Morg had said to meet him back at the 2nd at five-thirty. So, Evan decided to save the two remaining papers for the following day.

"Any luck?' Morgan called out as Evan walked through the door to the squad room.

"Nope. How about you?"

"Zero. Some promising possibilities, but nothing panned out."

"This could be us running up our own backsides, Morg. Maybe Vindicator doesn't read trash like this."

Maybe. How many you got left?"

"Two papers. And you?"

"None. All three of my mags ended up duds."

"Then how about going with me tomorrow. It gets lonely by myself."

"On one condition. Either you bring your own lunch or, if you forget, you pay at *Frank's*. We'll clear up the papers and break for lunch.

"I'll glue my wallet to my chest. That way I can't forget it."

"Yeah. And put some money in it. If I have to pay double for one more lunch you're gonna being eating yours up your butt 'cause that's where your head will be."

"Jeez, Morg. You never trust me. I'm not cheap you know."

"Not cheap, just conveniently forgetful. Now, what's next on our list?"

"I was thinking one of us could check out the films again next week. Maybe we can scare up a lead. Also, one of us should look at the victims again and see if we can figure which one Vindicator was really after."

"You take the films, I'll check up on the vics first thing Monday. Okay?"

"Sounds good to me, Morg.

I'm outta here."

"Before you take off, we're thinking Bud's party on Saturday; so keep your calendar free for that day."

"Check. I wouldn't miss it for anything. Who're the roasters gonna be?"

"So far it's me, Max Herrick, Byrd, and Jack Shaw, the former chief of the 7th in Portland. I imagine we'll find plenty of cops who are *more* than willing to nail Bud to the wall."

SEVENTY-TWO

It was a testament to Bud's reputation that *The Steakout* was literally packed. Better than seventy people were in attendance and the mood was definitely festive.

"Ladies and Gentlemen, I want to thank you all for coming tonight." Morgan greeted the audience. He was clearly uncomfortable as a host, but all the oldest of Bud's cop friends had agreed that Morgan was the one Bud would like to see directing the honors.

"You're the son he never had Morg." Max Herrick had said. "He loves and respects you; nothing would please him more."

"Now, Bud would be the first one to say keep the chatter down to a minimum and get on with food and drink.

Normally I'd agree with that but we are here tonight to honor the finest policeman and friend I've ever known and we are *not* gonna shortchange that process.

I know everybody up here at the speaker's table wants to be able to share *all* of their *loving* and *respectful* experiences with Bud over the thirty years he was a cop.

So, without further ado I'd like to introduce Max Herrick, a veteran homicide detective and Bud's first partner."

"Good evening, which is more than I used to say when I pulled the night shift with Bud. I won't say he didn't pull his weight; in fact that's about all he pulled, from the passenger seat to the donut shop and back again."

The laughter was loud and genuine, including Bud who patted his ample midsection and threw up his hands.

"I won't bore you with a lot of longwinded cop stories about Bud and me." Max continued. "I'm sure *Bud's* already done that to most of you and…"

Max paused while the audience roared and Bud blushed, smiled, and slowly shook his head. JoAnne actually stood up and applauded, which brought another round of laughter.

"Bud Oslen spent 30 years doing what he does best to keep the bad guys off of the street.

Fortunately, for the public, we were able to overcome his efforts and, as a result, the crime rate *has* dropped."

When the laughter died down Max's demeanor changed and he leaned close to the microphone.

"I can say these things because Bud and everyone here know that, in reality, I worship this man.

I learned more about law enforcement from Bud in the six years I was his partner than I've learned in the fifteen years since."

"That's because that whack you took to the head the year you moved over to vice left you brain dead."

A slow smile enveloped Bud's face as the words fell quietly from his mouth. There was a moment of dead silence.

Then, gradually, laughter began to fill the room, spreading in waves.

"Sorry, old man. I couldn't resist."

"As I was saying, I worship this man, or at least I did until a few minutes ago.

Seriously, Bud, it's been a helluva ride. Thank you for making me a better cop and for making all of us better people.

If there was ever a role model for how a human being should conduct himself on this tired old planet, it's you.

You're a prize."

Max sat down to vigorous applause, his eyes moist.

The rest of the evening was spent poking fun at Bud, and praising him.

"What I remember most about Bud was his patience with the rookies." Ray Banks said.

Captain Byrd, the last speaker, told of the time a seventeen year old heroine junkie was waiting in the squad room until he could be transferred to a holding cell.

"The guy was pretty strung out and jumpy. Suddenly, he lunged for the weapon of one of the detectives sitting at his desk.

The cop tried to stop him but the junkie, crazed from the withdrawal symptoms, managed to get his gun anyway.

He stood there in the middle of the squad room, waving the gun around and screaming he'd kill anyone who tried to stop him from leaving the station.

I could see the thing was going to get ugly fast, but we were all so surprised by what the man had done we sort of froze for a moment.

Then, out of the corner of the room Bud started walking toward the guy. He was speaking softly and moving very slowly."

"You don't want to do this, son. You're here on a drug beef and we can handle that by getting you help at a hospital. No need to do time, or die in the chair, which is what you'll do if you kill a cop."

The junkie looked at Bud for a moment, blinked, and licked his lips.

"You serious man? You ain't jiving me are you? I'm not going to jail and you'll give me somethin' so's I can get straight?"

"That's right, son. No jail time and we'll get you help.

I know you Tommie. You've had that monkey riding your back for a long time. We can help you to get it off, maybe get you straight and get you back to that little three year old daughter you love so much. I've seen the picture of her in your wallet. She's beautiful, son. I know you want to get back with her. Give me the gun."

"The whole time Bud is talking, he's moving ever so slowly towards the guy, a calmness in his voice that could not have been less threatening. The rest of us were paralyzed, as much from Bud's voice as from the surprise of the guy grabbing the gun.

By the time he finished talking he was face to face with the man. He just reached out ever so gently and Tommie dropped the gun into Bud's hand.

Bud laid the weapon on the desk, put his arm around the man's shoulder and escorted him back to his chair."

Byrd paused for a moment and looked at Bud with a look of respect Morgan had rarely seen in the Captain's eyes.

"I learned something that day that I will never forget.

All of the poor sods that come through our precinct doors are human beings, and as such deserve to be treated as such.

I believe that the reason Bud didn't get shot that day was because he touched a chord in that man. Bud gave him a way out of what must have to seemed to the boy to be an impossible situation. More importantly, by treating him as a fellow human being, he gained his trust to believe what Bud was telling him.

When I thought back on it later I remembered Bud saying 'son' a lot and calling Tommie by his name. I realized some time later that was Bud's way of identifying with the young man and letting Tommie *know* that.

I'm here to tell all of you tonight that from that point forward I began to look at the people who come through our doors differently.

And, when a young tough gets hauled in, I look at him, I see Bud, and I pause just a minute to remember how Bud handled a frightened boy that day.

Thank you, old friend. You truly are a hero."

As the solemnity of the moment passed, Harold Byrd, the gruff, cranky old leader of the Deuce quietly took his seat, his head bowed.

What he could not see was the effort his men took not to let their feelings at that moment overcome them.

You're our hero, old man. Morgan thought. *And you're right up there on that pedestal alongside Bud as role models to us all.*

Bud approached the dais and stood there silently for a minute. It was clear that he was having a hard time composing himself.

"Thank you all so much for being my colleagues, friends and loved ones. Whatever I have become in this life is due to the love of those around me.

Thank you and God bless you."

Simple, succinct, and noble, like Bud.

SEVENTY-THREE

The last two newspapers had proved to be of no help so Morgan and Evan were back to the Deuce having lunch and looking elsewhere for leads to Vindicator.

It was agreed that the list of eleven points of similarity would wait for a day.

"I don't know if deciphering the red bag clues is really of any use, Morg. By the time we finally figure a set out the crud has already offed the vic."

"Maybe so, but we still have to do it, so let's get to work. The sooner we get this done, the sooner we can go back to our 'list of eleven'."

"Roger. Let's see. We have a photo of a statue of a Greek lady with no arms. How sick is *that?*"

Evan! That's the Venus De…" The look on Evan's face said it all.

"Gotcha. Some cop you are. If I knew about the Vitruvian Man doesn't it make sense I'd know about the *Venus De Milo* too, one of the most renowned works in the world of art.

Really, Morg. I'll lay you 3 to 1 the name of the next vic is a woman named Venus."

"Yeah, yeah. What else we got?"

"Uh, a photo of a barn with some horses in it, and a black envelope with a cancelled stamp on it and a piece of paper inside that says 'der frau ist kaput'. *Marvelous*."

"Look at the bright side, Ev. We already know one of the clues. We only need to figure out the other two.

The words in the letter are German. *Frau* means woman and I think *kaput* means dead. So, Vindicator is telling us he's killed some woman."

"What's with the other photo?"

"Just a barn with horses. Doesn't make much sense at this point, but we'll work it out."

"I say we use the rest of the afternoon to start checking out points 3 and 9 on our lists."

"Okay, you take the victims. I'll take the films. I think I'll start with Book."

"Me, too. I'll come back here at five in case one of us comes up with something. Then I'm off to finish that date I had with Sarah the other night."

"You're seeing quite a lot of her aren't you?"

"Yeah, we click, primarily because we like a lot of the same things.

Just between the two of us, and I *mean* that, she's like a guy friend only a lot prettier and softer.

Honestly, Morg. If you think about it women are just like us, they just smell better."

"Not if they've been stuffed in a ship's cabin for a few hours, they don't."

Seventy-Four

The film left at the Victor Book murder scene had come from an award ceremony given in the fall of 1960 by Synergistics, a company known for taking over failing businesses. In the film Book is being recognized for his part in the takeover of Carter's and Sons, a large department store that had been popular in Deliverance for years.

It had been shot by a Synergistics employee to be used by a reporter covering the event for the society section of the Portland times.

The reporter had also interviewed Book after the event was over.

"That's funny, my partner and I have been searching through all of the local newspapers and magazines, looking for mention of Victor Book and the other victims of the recent murders in the Portland area.

How come we didn't see the article on Book that would have gone with this film?"

"It turned out that the paper decided not to run the article in favor of one on Jackie Kennedy." Giles Manners, an executive with Synergistics said.

Morgan had phoned him to schedule an interview regarding the film.

"The article was supposed to be in the next issue, but for some reason it never ran."

"What happened to the film? Does the paper still have it or was it returned to the company?"

"After you called I checked and discovered that the film *was* returned, according to the reporter who covered the event and, in fact, there is a receipt for it in our records department.

But, nobody can find it. If I had to guess, I'd say the film got appropriated by someone working here and sold to one of the local scandal rags."

"Why do you say that?"

"Victor Book, to put it bluntly, was a bastard who reveled in bringing misery to people.

The fact is it's the reason he was so good at his job. He enjoyed going into companies and 'cutting the fat out with his sword of Damocles", as he was fond of saying; by which he meant giving the ax to as many as employees as he could without completely gutting the company."

"Yes, we've heard reference to his sword." Morgan interjected. "We think Book was disemboweled as the killer's way of cutting the fat out of *him.*"

Manners blanched and licked his lips nervously.

"Yes, well, getting back to the film, there are some magazines that specialize in exposés. That film concerned the takeover of Carter and Sons. In the course of that undertaking one of the employees who'd been let go committed suicide in a particularly grisly and sensational way;

The man had a wife and two children.

That story should have made the papers but for some reason it didn't.

Now, I think a paper of less than reputable status would be pretty interested in a film that showed so many people celebrating an event that caused the horrible death of an innocent husband and father. It would be grist for their mill, so to speak.

Anyway, that's my guess for what happened to the film."

"Thank you for your time, Mr. Manners. You've been a help, really."

Morgan thanked the man and quickly left a broad smile owning his face.

*That's the key! These films are all about **publicly** exposing despicable behavior. Even the film honoring Book is an exposé once you know about the poor guy who sucked on a lye Popsicle because of what Book did to get that honor. I'll bet each of the films and the one audio tape contains material a scandal rag would love to get their hands on.*

Time to go back to the Deuce and examine those films again.

On the way back to the Deuce Morgan called the station and told Fran to hold Evan if he came in.

"He's here now Morgan."

"Good. Tell him I want to talk to him and I'm ten minutes away. Oh and tell him to get the films from the murders out and to set up the projector in the incidence room."

"What's up, partner? It's six and I'm supposed to meet Sarah in an hour." Evan complained when Morgan walked into the incident room.

"I think we've got the link that connects the films and we need to go through them again."

"Morg! Can't this wait? If I break off another date with Sarah, I might as well join a monastery as far as she'll be concerned."

"I thought of that. Tell you what, you call her and tell her you have to work but that I'll treat you both to dinner and tickets to the Johnny Mathis concert in Portland next month."

Evan made the call and talked with Sarah a few minutes before hanging up.

"She says yes and suggested you and Jen come too."

"Sure. I'll check out availability and get back to you.

Now let's start on the films and that audio tape. We're looking for something in each recording that a tabloid would likely view as newsworthy."

"I thought we covered that angle."

"I think we missed something Ev. We pretty much know that Vindicator has been harboring a grudge against one of these victims for years and his anger has been simmering all that time. Then something caused that rage to surface, resulting in five deaths, so far.

I think the trigger was he saw several articles in a magazine or newspaper, and I think those articles were about our victims."

"So, if we identify what about each film would be newsworthy to a scumbag newspaper or magazine, we might actually be able to *portrait* the print source we're looking for. That's ingenious Morg."

"Yup. Then maybe we can ask around at news agencies and the like. Somebody might just know of a mag or rag that we haven't scoped out yet.

I already know what it is in the Book film that we're looking for."

"We know Gregg's film too. Letting that stone cold kid killer off in return for power, position, and wealth. And, like the Book film, Gregg is shown being rewarded for doing something that caused tragedy to others."

"That leaves us Carr, Hart, and the audio tape from Barnes. Shall we?"

"The Carr film shows a drug dealer and pimp rustling up business but Carr was such a lowlife I don't figure he was worth telling the public about. So why Carr?"

"I don't know, Ev. But I'd bet a week's pay the film shows *something* a paper would find valuable. We need to find what that something is."

Two hours of running films and the audio tape forward and backward, slowing the playback down to hear more critically what was being said and to see more clearly what was being shown left the detectives with a list of revelations.

"Ev, it's seven. You take off. I'm going to type this list up and leave it on S.T.'s desk. Maybe it will get him off our backs for a few days.

I'm going to tell him this list will help us track down the publication that used those films and that that will lead us to the killer."

"Isn't that stretching it a little?"

"Yeah, but not by much. We *are* gonna track this rag down and I think it *will* eventually lead us to Vindicator."

"Okay, Morg. See you tomorrow."

***

Before compiling the list Morgan decided to make a few calls, hoping to obtain the answers to questions that would flesh out the information he was preparing for Byrd.

One of the board members of the Big Brothers organization, who happened to be working late, confirmed something Morgan and Evan had guessed. William Morrison had contributed $10,000 to the Big Brothers following the trial of his son. Further, Morrison had put the word in the ears of several influential Portland citizens that Martin Gregg was a brilliant jurist. It was just what Gregg needed to catapult him into a seat on the 5th Circuit appellate court in 1958.

So, it could be argued that Gregg got where he did because of the man whose child he let go on a beef the kid should have gone away for twenty-five years for.

Morgan and Evan had *not* known that.

His second call was just as successful. On a hunch, Morg called Max Herrick and asked him if Eddington Carr had ever done anything notorious enough to rate press coverage.

"Well, one of the kids he got on dope turned out to be some state senator's daughter. It never made the newspapers because the senator had it hushed up."

Round two to the good guys.

A final call to WXKP led to the revelation that one of Wynona Barne's shows caused the beating death of a man whom Wynona wrongly claimed had molested another man's ten year old son. The victim was beaten to death with a baseball bat.

Three for three. Mickey would be proud of me.

By ten o'clock Morgan had finished his list. He looked over what he'd just spent an hour typing.

Murder Film Highlights Newsworthy to a Tabloid

Martin Gregg—Greg seen being honored at ceremonies for a charitable group. A man named Morrison is at the party. He is the father of a boy who savagely raped and beat a young girl. Gregg was the judge on the subsequent trial and let the boy off with a light sentence. Shortly after his release he raped and murdered another girl. The father is shown at the ceremony. It has been established that he gave money to the charitable group Gregg chaired *and* his considerable influence in the Portland community helped Gregg rise to prominence as an appellate court judge.

Eddington Carr—This film shows Carr talking to a number of what appear to be young street waifs. Since he is a known drug dealer and pimp, it is assumed that he was "recruiting". The part that makes the film newsworthy is that one of the waifs Carr recruited just happened to be the daughter of Morris Withers, a state senator in Portland and the girl is shown talking to Carr.

Brenda Hart—The film shows Brenda at a party, dressed in scrubs, drinking what appears to be a cup of coffee and looking tired. Brenda was part of a malpractice lawsuit in Geneva, N.Y. She was accused of performing an operation in which the patient, Rembrandt Fallon, was terribly disfigured. Later the boy committed suicide. The attorneys for Rembrandt claimed Hart had performed several surgeries that day and was therefore impaired when she operated on Rembrandt. Therefore, the infection Rembrandt got subsequent to the operation was due to Dr. Hart's negligence. The case never came to trial thanks to a generous settlement on the part of the hospital, but Rembrandt's parents always contended that Dr. Hart was criminally responsible for their son's disfigurement and death.

Victor Book—Book's film shows him being recognized for doing his job so well; going into a failing company, firing a number of people and making changes that would eventually send the company into bankruptcy. Unfortunately, one of the men fired in a particular takeover killed himself, leaving a wife and two children behind. The company,

Synergistics, quietly got rid of Book afterwards, diffusing to an extent the scandal that followed. No criminal charges were ever filed but more than a few people thought there should have been.

Wynona Barnes—Her audio tape is a recording of segments of several of her shows. The intent is clear. Each segment consists of Wynona spreading her form of gossip which is largely based on innuendo. One of the vicious rumors led to a man killing the person Barnes wrongly claimed molested his son. The man beat the victim to death with a baseball bat.

That should please the old man. Now if I can just locate the magazine those stories came out of, this thing might be over before the next death occurs.

Seventy-Five

"The Captain get the paper I left on his desk last night, Dusty?" Morgan said,

"He hasn't been in yet today, Morg. He's over at City Hall talking to the big boys, getting his marching orders and planning strategy.

John F. Kennedy is going to be here in two weeks speaking at the Multnomah Hotel in Portland. Portland's mayor is asking several mayors in the area for manpower help in securing the motorcade route to the hotel and within the hotel itself.

The old man is gonna be the *supreme* commander of the six uniformed units that will assist the secret service inside the hotel; at least that's what I thought I heard the mayor tell him."

"Oh, boy. You know S.T. He'd rather chew on a razor blade than get stuck in the middle of some politician's publicity event, especially one involving the President of the United States." Morgan said.

"No matter how it shakes out you wind up with egg on your face because *somebody* under your command *always* screws something up and the guy in charge ultimately gets the blame.

Plus, Byrd will most likely be coordinating things from some remote command center, which means he won't have direct control over his men.

And, with six units that means a *lot* of men to potentially ruin your day. So, I'm gonna make a point of being out of the office as much as possible the week after Kennedy's in Portland.

Say, Dusty, can you read that paper over? I probably made a million grammar and spelling errors."

"Sure. Give me a half hour. I've got the uniform's duty roster to type up first."

Morgan wandered into the incident room, waiting for Evan to show up. When he did Morgan motioned for him to come into the incidence room.

"I meant to ask you, anything with the list of victims, other than the connection with the films?"

"Not much. All of them were professional people, if you can call what Carr did professional.

Then there's the method of death. All of the victims were, of course, horribly mutilated and suffered great pain. But there were a couple of oddities peculiar to just one victim. In Brenda Hart's case there were *two* cryptograms branded on her. Also, she was the only victim where Vindicator used part of her body to form the Roman numeral he put on all the victims.

Victor Book is the only victim who was decapitated.

Wynona Barnes is the only victim where an audio tape was left instead of a film.

I went over each vic's private and professional life too; zero."

"Okay, Ev. We'll keep on digging."

"Morgan?" Fran stepped into the incident room, Morgan's list in her hand.

"I fouled up the list didn't I? Well, just retype it for me and I owe you a dinner."

"No, Morgan. I was reading over the list like you asked me to and I suddenly realized I'd seen some of these names in print before. I can't remember where but I know I have."

"In the paper after their deaths?" Evan asked.

"No, somewhere else too. I'll remember it soon; I just wanted you two to know."

"Well, try hard, Dusty." Morgan said. "The sooner you do the sooner we may find the magazine we've been looking for."

"That's it! I *knew* I'd seen those names in print before. It's that magazine you were teasing me about—*Shine the Light.*"

"Have you got that issue?"

"I think so. I keep all the back copies in my desk drawer."

There were actually three issues that contained names. September and November of 1960 and January of 1961.

"Well, they're all there, partner." Evan said. "All the dirt that was fit to print on each vic. Looks like we've got our magazine, partner.

Funny thing, I get the feeling I've seen this magazine before."

"Grab your hat, Ev. We are off to see the editor at *Shine the Light.* By the way, how come this magazine didn't make our list?"

"Probably because it isn't your run-of-the-mill, grocery store tabloid." Fran answered. "*Shine the Light* can't be purchased in stores or news agencies. It's a subscription only magazine.

They don't advertise either. The only way you find out about it is through word of mouth."

"Sounds like an underground source for dirt on people." Evan said.

"It didn't used to be. When I first started reading it six years ago the

Light focused on environmental and social issues, not people. It's only been in the last couple of years that it's changed."

"Ironic, isn't it?" Evan said. "If the magazine had stayed as it was Vindicator never would have seen those stories and five people would still be alive."

"Unfortunately, we can't change the past, partner. Our job now is to prevent a future that includes *more* dead people."

Using one of Fran's copies Morgan found a phone number and called the *Light's* office. The editor, Ben Thomas agreed to meet with them in an hour at the Deuce, but only when Morgan pointed out to him that the interview had to take place at the police station.

"Your choice Mr. Thomas." Morgan said tersely. "You can choose to cooperate or we can do this down here anyway, *after* escorting you personally and *publicly* from your office."

Thomas quickly got the message and agreed to the meeting.

SEVENTY-SIX

"As I'm sure you're aware, we are working on a series of murders in the Portland area." Morgan began after ushering Thomas into the incidence room. "We're here today because your magazine has published, shall we say, unfavorable articles on all five victims. Furthermore, the information in those articles pretty much mirrors what the killer believes is the motivation for him to murder them.

What we'd like to know is where you got your information."

"I'm well aware of what's been going on in Deliverance and Portland, Detective Jeffords." Thomas said, leaning forward and placing both arms on the desk. "But you need to understand that I cannot and *will* not reveal our sources. Neither will any of my employees.

You should also understand that I'm not only the editor of this publication, I also own the magazine. As such I will see this paper go down, go to jail, or anything else you can think of."

"It may come to that, sir." Evan said. "But we're hoping we can come to a meeting of the minds. All we're asking is that you work with us to the extent you can. If that gets us what we need to catch this maniac, then any problem goes away.

On the other hand *you* need to understand that if we think you're stonewalling us, we *will* clap the cuffs on you and put you in the box where, as far as I'm concerned, you can stay until you either cooperate or the second coming happens. Capiche?"

Morgan sat through Evan's pointed effort to intimidate Thomas and said nothing. Maybe the attempt would work, maybe it wouldn't. Either way it was worth a shot.

"Well, let's see what we can work out, Detective Flack. But I'll tell you right now your threats won't alter my decision on confidentiality of news sources. I've been in worse places than your jail cells, on several occasions.

Now, what do you want?"

"First, we'd like you to look at some films and listen to an audio tape. What we are interested in is which, if any, of these films and audio tape you've seen or had in your possession.

Second, if you *haven't* seen any of these recordings and you can ascertain that none of your people have seen them either, then we'd like to know where you got the information in your articles that match parts of these recordings."

"That sounds workable, within reason. Let's go through the recordings and see where we are."

At the end of two hours of viewing and talking, with a half hour break in the middle, a picture began to take form.

"So, you're saying the information for the article on Judge Gregg came from having access to that film and an investigation into his background." Morgan asked.

"That is correct, officer." Thomas concurred. "We had heard a rumor about Gregg some time back and decided to check it out.

When we found out about the Morrison kid and that dead girl, Janet

Carroll, we knew we'd struck gold, uh, so to speak." Thomas had noticed the look of disdain on Evan's face and tried to soften what he'd said.

"Anyway, we also checked out Morrison's father, discovered the money he'd contributed to the Big Brother organization on behalf of Gregg and bingo, the film turned up. We used the fact that Morrison actually honored Gregg on that film to question Gregg's light sentencing of the Morrison kid back in '55; that and the help, both financially and otherwise, that Morrison provided Gregg.

Funny thing, though. The word in the right ear and the contributions to Gregg's career were never *proven* to be connected to what Gregg did for Morrison's kid."

"Yeah, we know." Evan said. "Problem is our killer didn't see it that way."

"As for the Eddington Carr story, he was a worthless lowlife that would never have made as much as the last page of the *Light* until it came to light, no pun intended, that one of the kids ruined by his dope was a senator's daughter." Thomas continued. The film came from the Portland Police files. They had been surveilling him for months because they'd had a tip he was connected to a particular drug they wanted to take down."

"Police files?" Morgan interjected. "How did you get access to confidential narcotics division films?"

"And don't say it's public record because surveillance films in the narcotics division *remain* confidential." Evan added.

"Ah, well. Here we may have our first roadblock. All I'm willing to say is that the source was one of your own, or should I say one of Portland's own.

Don't be too upset, though. It would have been a rare cop indeed who didn't want to see that bastard hung by his short hairs. This one figured it wouldn't hurt to give the prosecution a slight advantage by putting the public against Carr; at least the part of the public that reads the *Light.*"

"You're not shed of us on this matter Mr. Thomas." Morgan said evenly but not menacingly. "We're a bit preoccupied with a killer right now, but when the case is finished we'll be back to your office to have a discussion on constitutional rights and the press."

"What about Brenda Hart?" Evan inquired, directing the interview back to the films.

Well, *I've* never seen the film. I'll check with my people, but I seriously doubt any of them have either.

"We tumbled to the Brenda Hart thing by sheer luck." Thomas looked at Morgan and realized he'd put his foot in his mouth again. "What I mean is one of our reporters was doing a story on a Portland physician who'd practiced previously at Geneva General Hospital in New York. Turns out the guy was one of the doctors sitting on the board that reviewed the Brenda Hart debacle. Our guy got the records on the lawsuit filed against her and Geneva Gen, took one look at *that* case, remembered she now practiced at Good Samaritan in Portland, and decided her story was more newsworthy than the one he was working on. We printed it, minus the more graphic details of what happened to the boy.

And don't even *think* of asking how he got the records."

"That leaves Book and Barnes." Morgan said ignoring Thomas' remark.

"Barnes is simple. We didn't have to hear her audio tape, which I bet was taped by the killer himself. She was well known in Portland for smearing people. We all knew that sooner or later she'd demonize someone and it would blow up in her face. We kept track of her radio rantings and when the explosion came we had a story already written, except for the last paragraph.

As for Book, again we were aware of the things he'd done as a headhunter.

When Carter's went under, it was big news, including the suicide by one of their execs. We didn't need a film to write our story, just the man's record."

Thomas shifted in his chair, leaning back and stretching. It was clear he was done sharing and was merely waiting to be dismissed.

"Alright, Mr. Thomas." Morgan said. "That wraps it up—for now. We'll get back to you if we need to."

Thomas got up walked out of the room and the building without a word.

"Real piece of work."

"I know, Ev. He's not exactly the guy I'd like dating my sister, if I had a sister.

So, what did we gain from going through all of that?"

"To begin with *Shine the Light* didn't use the films *or* the audio tape to do their stories on Book, Hart, or Barnes. That means Vindicator himself acquired or recorded them himself."

"Right." Morgan agreed. "The Book film doesn't look like something our boy would have been invited to take, so I'm betting he got a copy of it somehow. It's possible Vindicator *could* have run in the same circles as Book, but I doubt it. I don't see him the heartless mercenary Book and most of his associates likely are—were in Book's case.

True, he's a homicidal maniac and completely without mercy where his victims are concerned. But Book and the rest of that rat pack he ran with had just one emotion, greed. Vindicator's emotions are instinctive and visceral. He hates passionately and I suspect he does so now because someone he loved *as* passionately in the past was harmed by one of the victims.

No, Vindicator would have found men like Book to be disgusting at best."

"Well, the Barnes audio tape is obvious. Anyone could have copied those segments from her broadcasts. Again, I'm betting Vindicator *did* record that tape.

As for the Hart film, I'm not sure. Vindicator could have run in the same *social* circles as Hart so he might have been at the party recorded on the film.

Then again, maybe not."

"Bottom line?" Morgan looked at Evan hopefully. It was something he did occasionally to get Evan to be an active part of the deduction process, even when Morgan already knew what he was pushing for Evan to say.

It was all part of the training process the senior partner put the junior through. Bud had done it for him and Morgan was passing it on.

"Bottom line, huh. I got a bottom line for you. When this case is over, we both quit this stinking job and buy a bar in the Bahamas. All the free booze we wanna drink 'cause we own the bar. And those gorgeous beautifully browned native girls.

Honest Morg, it's the closest thing to heaven I'm ever gonna get to.

Now, all you have to do is ditch Jen and I'll dump Sarah and we'll be set."

"Evan." Morgan said quietly with just a touch of reproach. "If you could just land the starship for a moment we have a maniac to catch."

"Yeah, yeah. Well, my bottom line is that the odds are Vindicator's *personal* axe has been buried in Book's, Hart's, or Barnes skull.

So, we find out which one, we got a direct line to Vindicator.

That's my bottom line."

Morgan smiled. Evan was a fine detective. He would only get better with time.

SEVENTY-SEVEN

The final clue left at the Barnes murder scene proved difficult to decipher.

"What the hell does a barn full of horses have to do with the *Venus de Milo* and some weird German phrase?" Evan was not happy. He and Sarah had met at *Frank's.* She had invited him for lunch in Portland and a tour of the F.B.I. complex.

"Let me see the photo, Ev."

Sarah studied the photo for a full minute before handing it back to Evan.

"Those aren't just horses Evan, their *riding* horses, maybe thoroughbreds."

"And, that helps me how? What does it matter what kind of horse…oh, now *that's* brilliant! It's not a barn, it's a stable."

"I know it doesn't connect the three clues from the red sack but it may help to lead to one later on."

"I'll run it by Morg tomorrow. Meanwhile if you come up with any more ideas call me anytime, and I *do* mean anytime.

Look, why don't we go back to your office. You finish up any work you have left for today and I'll nose around the Bureau firing range. I could use a little practice.

When you're done, come get me, we'll swing by your place if you want to freshen up and then hit the bowling alley."

"What makes you think they'll let you loose on the range?"

"You're not the only Feebie I know. Your director, Jim Herrick, is the brother of Max Herrick, a detective with the Portland P.D. and Morg is good friends with Max. So, Max has set it up with the Bureau here in Portland to let the detectives from Deliverance use the range."

"I don't know. Seems like the Bureau is giving a loaded gun to the Beaver.

Okay, sounds like fun. Tell you what though, why don't go back to your house after you shoot, and then come to my place about 6:30. I'll grill a couple of steaks complete with baked potatoes and a salad, and we can go bowling afterwards."

"Like I said, brilliant. You stuff me full, then sit back and watch me barely break 100 at the alley because I can't bend over.

Let's see now. Choice A, decline to eat at your house and bowl 200. Choice B, accept your generous invitation and *bowl* like Beaver Cleaver.

Hmm. From the look on your face I conclude choice B to be the wisest."

"Apparently I'm not the only brilliant one. Good choice.

Would you like me to come over to the range after I finish my office work? That way you'd have a chance to beat me at *something* today."

"No thanks. I happen to know you shot a perfect 450 at last year's competition?"

***

The *Starlight Bowl* was a brand new 36 lane bowling alley, the largest in Portland. The owners had been smart enough to set aside a room with two pool tables, a shuffleboard game, and a dart board. That way people who didn't care for bowling would still find the *Starlight* a fun place to be.

"So much for bowling like the Beaver. Evan, a 223 and a 196! I want a fifty point handicap for the third game."

"Madam, you can have a hundred points for all I care. This is the best I've ever bowled. Must be your home cooking."

"I'm not *that* old Evan. Madams are older and usually married. Sometimes I wonder about you. "

"Oops. I didn't think. Actually, I should quit using the term altogether. It can also refer to a woman who, uh, shall we say procures certain ladies for men."

Sarah gave Evan one of those "I can't believe you said that", shook her head and rolled her eyes.

"For a man with a bright mind you can be *such* a dufus. Only you would connect the word madam to prostitution. Tell the truth, I hold stock in Dufus Inc. too. Looks like we're two of a kind.

Evan?"

Evan was staring at Sarah, his mouth open and a perplexed look on his face.

"Say that again."

"Say what again?'

"You said something about my using the word madam.

Sorry, I was setting up the score sheet for the next game and I didn't catch all you said."

"I *said,* only you would connect the word madam to prostitution. Why?"

"Because you may have found the answer Morg and I've been looking for.

Stay with me now. Frau is German for a married woman. Fraulein is German for an unmarried woman. I wondered if Vindicator was telling us he's going to kill a married woman next. But I forgot that one English word for a married woman is *madam.*

Now I think he was trying to tell us that he is going to kill a woman who employs prostitute and who has a *stable* of girls. And, I think her first name is Venus.

Make sense?"

"Yes it does. That's good, Ev. Morgan will be impressed."

"*If* I'm right. Say, enough shop talk. One more game?"

"Sure. Don't forget to add a hundred points to my first frame score. How about a friendly bet on this one, say five dollars?"

"Well, I shoot like the Beaver and I bowl like the Beaver. I might as well make bets like the Beaver would. You're on."

As Evan predicted, Sarah won the last game 235 to 217. She promptly took Evan's five dollars.

"I suppose you want me to pay for the bowling too."

"I seem to remember you asking me out."

"Whoever said it's a man's world is an idiot."

"You *did* get a nice meal, Ev."

"A great meal and I know when to quit when I'm only a little behind."

SEVENTY-EIGHT

Morgan pulled up to Evan's house at eight a.m. Evan's Impala had blown a lifter and would be in the shop for three days. Morgan had agreed to pick him up during that time if he promised faithfully to be ready when Morgan pulled into his drive.

"Morning, partner. How'd your date with Sarah go yesterday?"

"Good for both of us, Morg."

"Excuse me?"

"We broke the code on the Barnes clues. We're looking for a madam named Venus."

"Well, *now* you have my attention. How did you two geniuses figure it out?"

"Sarah gets the kudos, Morg. She figured out that the barn in the one photo wasn't a barn. It was a stable. If she hadn't glommed onto that I'd have never realized that frau was another name for madam, and madams run stables of prostitutes."

"Great work. Let's get started. I'll call Max over in Portland from your house phone. He can check with his vice boys and start running through names. "

"It's weird, Bull Dog." Todd Hinton, head of vice in Portland said. We have hundreds of files with thousands of names, but No Venus. Are you sure that's the name?"

"We're relying on a data source that has so far been reliable." Morgan replied. "However, it *is* possible we've misinterpreted the information."

"Okay. We'll continue to nose around on this end, you guys reassess your information and see if you can come up with a different name."

"Back to the drawing board, Ev." Morgan said as they pulled out of the parking lot of the 7th.

"I don't get it Morg. That *was* a picture of the *Venus de Milo*, wasn't it?"

"I thought it was. We need to look at it again, now."

The 2nd was deserted when Morgan and Evan walked in.

"Where is everyone, Dusty?"

"The whole force went fishing down at Shamsky's hole. Byrd's trying to get closer to the men.

Whatta ya think, Morg. Today is the day everybody was supposed to be in Portland running through the drill for the Kennedy visit. And I do mean *everybody.*"

"Oh, shit! I forgot, Ev. We're dead. Byrd will have our heads spitted and roasted."

"Wait a minute. Dusty, I thought this dog and pony show was only for Byrd and fifteen of our best uniforms."

"That's correct *Detective* Flack. But Byrd wanted all his men there today. He thought his detectives might spot any flaws in the plan.

"Didn't you two clowns get the memo?"

"I got it. Sorry Ev. We been so busy I completely forgot."

"You forgot! Morg, how could you. Why didn't you just take a razor and cut my throat. We'll be lucky if the Captain *only* roasts our heads on a spit. At least that way it'd be quicker than a lot of ways he could pick."

"Now, now boys, things aren't as bad as they look."

"No? Why, has World War Three started?"

"No, Evan, it hasn't. But when Byrd asked why you two weren't here this morning I told him that you were out of the office when I passed them out and I forgot to give them to you later. He wasn't happy, but then he never *really* gets mad at *me*."

"Dusty, I love you!" Evan walked over to her desk, lifted her out of her chair and threw his arms around her, planting a kiss on her cheek as he did so.

"Evan!" Dusty, face red, pushed Evan away and pretended to straighten her hair.

"I'm old enough to be your mother...*almost*."

"No you're not, you sly wench."

"It's a picture of a statue of a Greek woman with no arms; that's the *Venus de Milo* or I'm the Mad Hatter." Evan was clearly agitated. He and Morgan were sitting in the incident room looking at the photograph left at the Wynona Barnes crime scene.

"It is and you're not, old man. It is clearly a photograph of the sculpture that was found in an underground cavern on the Aegean island of Melos early in the 19th century.

The anonymous Greek sculptor was thought to have been paying tribute to the Roman goddess Venus. Supposedly, the missing right arm held the drapery around her hips in place and the other a mirror so that she could admire herself."

"Then what have we missed?"

"That's the 64 dollar question, Ev. Vindicator wanted this picture to mean something. We just haven't figured out what yet."

"Maybe it doesn't represent a name." Evan reasoned. "As I recall, Venus represented love, beauty, and fertility. Men could not resist her."

"That's right. But if the picture doesn't represent a name, it may represent a characteristic of the victim or the sin that person committed, at least if these clues follow the pattern of all the previous ones."

"Meanwhile, we've got the leads produced by visiting with the guy at the *Light*. My favorite is Barnes. Vindicator, or someone close to him, would have had to have been somehow connected to Book and what he did for a living.

We've already decided Vindicator wouldn't have run in the same circles as Book. That means Book would be less likely to have run into Vindicator than the other two.

As for Hart, we've already been down that street, and it was pretty much a dead end. That leaves Barnes."

"She is the most likely, Ev. God knows how many people from all walks of life she damaged. Vindicator could have been connected to any one of them."

"Or been one of them."

I think we should pay the station manager another visit. Radio stations keep audio logs of their programs for up to a year. We'll listen to those logs. Then starting with the guy over at Carter's that croaked himself we'll check out anyone that Vindicator might have had reason to feel close to.

Cross your fingers, partner. This could be the break we're looking for."

"Ya know, Morg, I keep thinking there's something we've overlooked; something we should have seen but didn't. This is crazy but I keep thinking...it's like not being able to see the forest for the trees, only the other way around. Something's right in front of us, close, but I can't make it out because of all the other clues and leads blocking my view."

"Let it go, Ev. What you're after is buried under a lot of other thoughts. Don't think about it and it'll come out on its own.

Time to see Mr. Gunn again. We'll call him from here, explain what we want and why, and set up a time."

SEVENTY-NINE

Harvey Gunn was waiting at the door to station WXKP when Morgan and Evan pulled up.

"If you'll please follow me, I've had the logs for the last year sent to my office."

"I'm sure you'll understand my hesitance to give you access to these officers." Gunn said when the men were seated in his office. "The station doesn't want to get mixed up in this affair, if possible. Bad publicity and all that.

We had a devil of a time when that man killed the supposed child molester. Lawyers crawling all over the place. The lawsuit that came out of *that* fiasco was a nightmare. We had to settle for a pile of money.

I wanted to fire Wynona right then and there, but the station owners nixed that; said she made too much money for them."

"We understand, Mr. Gunn, but those logs may be material to finding the man who killed Wynona."

"Speaking of which, who did the suing?" Evan asked.

"The murderer, of all things. We would have been tapped for a lot more but the dead man was a bachelor who had no family and the murderer, Finlay Brooks, was a widower."

"What about the boy and Brooks' family." Morgan inquired.

"Funny you should ask. The guy was a Korean War vet who'd adopted the boy while in Korea. The kid had apparently saved his life somehow and Brooks had taken to him. When he was convicted of manslaughter, the child was returned to Korea. That was in 1956.

Brooks is still in jail, serving a 15 year sentence."

"Yes, well thank you Mr. Gunn." Morgan said. "We'll let you know when we've finished listening to these. Thank you for providing us with a tape player."

"Dead end number one, Morg." Evan sighed, cueing up the first tape. "Unless the kid came back from Korea to ice Wynona."

"Not likely. He'd be fifteen now which would hardly qualify him to fit Jen's physical description."

Over the next two hours Morgan and Evan listened to the tapes, taking notes and discussing what they heard.

"*That* doesn't seem too promising." Evan concluded. "Just a lot of inane gossip over trivial matters."

"Yeah. I would have expected at least a couple of darker revelations from our cold friend, something that would have *seriously* damaged someone.

Still, let's ask Gunn if any of these slurs led to any legal action. Maybe we'll find a pearl in this basket of oysters yet."

Gunn, however, said that the only legal action ever brought against the station and Wynona was the one they'd already discussed.

At the end of the day, Morgan and Evan were no further than where they'd been that morning. Plus, they'd have to face Byrd when they got back to the Deuce, and they both knew he would not let Dusty take the blame for their absence this morning.

EIGHTY

Jen closed the door to her office and headed for the parking lot. She had called Morgan twenty minutes ago to say she'd have to meet him at *Fantastico* instead of waiting for him to pick her up at home at 6:30.

"I have to go over to Old Towne first. Some poor fool did a swan dive off the roof of the Hemmen building and the police want me to see if I can determine if he had a little help. How does meeting you at Fantastico's at seven sound?"

"Fine. I'll get there a little early and grab a window table. Lake Edward is beautiful at night."

"That's great, Morgan. Thanks for understanding."

Morgan was already seated when Jen walked in. The maitre d' approached her and escorted her to the table.

"How did he know who I was?" Jen asked, a bit taken aback.

"It was easy. I just told him when I came in to keep watching the door and when the most beautiful woman he'd ever seen walked through it, he should bring her to my table."

"Funny. No, how did he know?"

"I just told you, Jen. Honest."

"Well, how kind of him. I think I'll go over and thank him now."

"You're cold, Dr. Lime, real cold. Alright, I showed him your picture and asked him to escort you over here when you arrived."

"Morgan, you are the *most* exasperating man some times."

"Maybe so, but I'll bet if I *had* asked him to bring the most beautiful woman he'd ever seen to my table it would have been you anyway."

Jennifer grimaced in mock disgust, faint lines fanning the edges of her eyes.

"Against my better nature I'll take that as a genuine compliment, and now to supper." Jen opened her menu and handed one to Morgan, smiling slyly as she did.

"Right. I've already decided. This place has the best homemade Fettuccine Alfredo I've ever tasted. That and the shrimp cocktail as an appetizer make for a great meal.

That's *my* contribution to tonight's dining recommendations. You're the wine expert. What do you suggest?"

"Well, with the lasagna I'd recommend the *Vino Nobile,* 1955.

It's from Tuscany and very full, ripe, and fruity."

"*Vino Nobile* it is. And, for dessert?"

"I'll pass on dessert until I finish my entrée."

"How's the case going? Have you and Evan come up with any suspects yet?'

"No known suspects yet, but it's funny you asked.

Evan said something this morning that struck a chord with me. He said we were missing something that was close, like not being able to see a particular tree because the forest surrounding it engulfed it.

I didn't say anything at the time but when he said it I got a funny feeling; as if he'd read my mind.

Trouble is it's *just* a feeling, nothing substantial. But that feeling of missing something obvious keeps gnawing at me.

Hell, maybe this case just has me spooked."

"For what it's worth, Morgan if this is bothering you that much I'd say that it *is* substantial, and significant. If there's one thing I've learned in the time I've known you it's that you don't spook.

Quite the contrary, you are the most grounded individual I've ever met. You're methodical and thoughtful, and I've never seen you rattled.

No, you've got hold of something. Just don't try to force it. Let it alone and your mind will work through the barriers.

Why are you laughing?"

"I'm sorry. It's just that that's the advice I gave Evan this morning."

"Yes, well, great minds and all that.

Hey, did you guys figure out the red sack clues from Wynona's site yet?"

"We thought we had, but we've missed something somewhere. We thought we were looking for a prostitution madam named Venus, but there isn't one with that name anywhere in the Portland."

"How did you come up with that?" Jennifer asked with growing interest.

"Well, we figured out that the photo of the horse barn was really a stable, thanks to Sarah, and from that Evan figured out that the German word *frau* meant *madam*.

Then, of course, the photo of the statue was obviously of the *Venus de Milo*.

So, we figured we were looking for a madam named Venus.

Say, maybe it's a hooker who works for a madam. I'll have to check it out."

Jen looked at Morgan, a look of sympathy mixed with amusement written across her face.

"What? What's wrong?"

"I don't know how to say this you dear man, without risking hurting yours and Evan's feelings.

Actually, it's quite logical that you wouldn't necessarily know."

"Wouldn't know what?

Uh, oh. I have a sinking feeling I'm about to look stupid."

"No, you're not. It'd just that the *Venus de Milo* is a *Greek* statue."

"Yeah, I know. What does that have to do with it?"

"Well, Venus was the *Roman* name for the goddess of love and beauty. But it was sculpted by a Greek and is more appropriately titled *The Aphrodite de Milo* or *Aphrodite of Milo,* since it was discovered around 1820 beneath the Aegean island of Melos, sometimes called Milo.

I think your madam's name is Aphrodite."

"Oh, great! That's a substandard education for you. Should've concentrated more on the arts and less on crime.

Would you excuse me a moment? I've got to call Max at home. He needs to get back to his vice boys."

"Did you get hold of him?" Jen asked when Morgan returned to the table.

"Yes, he said he'd head into the 7th early in the morning and start going through the files again."

"Good. Now, what say we go back to my house for some homemade éclairs and blackcurrant tea?"

"Sounds good to me. I'll catch the check and meet you at the front door.

***

"We found her, Morg. Her name is Aphrodite Pleasureman, a.k.a. Matilda Gromyck." Max Herrick said next morning in a phone call to the 2nd. "Originally from Gdansk, Poland, she now lives at 233 W Filmore St. I'm on my way over there now."

"Great. Thanks Max. Ev and I will meet you there."

Morgan hung up, collared Ev in the dayroom and the two headed out.

"Nobody's seen her since yesterday morning." Max explained when Morgan and Evan showed up at Aphrodite's home.

"Since this is obviously her place of work as well as her residence, I guess we'll have pretty much covered all her *social* contacts when we finish interviewing everyone here." Morgan said.

"Okay, Max, we'll take it from here." Evan said. "Thanks for locating her."

"Right. I hope we found her in time."

"You and me both." Morgan agreed. "One more murder is about the last thing I need. My hold on sanity is tenuous enough already."

None of the people in the house had any idea where Aphrodite was.

"She pretty much comes and goes as she pleases." A skinny, pasty faced girl said.

Evan figured she was no more than 17.

When Morgan was satisfied they'd gotten as much information as they could he suggested to Evan that they go back to the Deuce, start working over the other leads for the thousandth time, and wait to see if Aphrodite showed up.

"I was thinking, Morg. How many six and a half foot tall, 230 plus pound archaeologists do you think there are in the Portland area?"

"Not many I should think. Why?"

"Well, number four of that composite of Vindicator we drew up says he's either an archaeologist or someone with a profession that involves digging up ancient artifacts.

So, how about us looking for a tall, heavy, rich archaeologist who is now, or was, a Catholic."

"Sounds better than any idea I've got. Where do you suggest we start?"

"The Universities and Museums in the area. Maybe one of those hundred year old professors or dust ridden curators can remember someone who fits our portrait."

"At least it's a lead. We can use a break and this has as good a chance as anything.

Okay. Let's head back to the Deuce and get started on your brainchild."

EIGHTY-ONE

The search for Aphrodite Pleasureman was into its second day when a call came into the 2nd and Morgan took it.

"You and the Boy Wonder are gonna want to get over to the Marx Hotel, Bull Dog." Jim Peavey, a uniform who Morgan had worked with in the past sounded shaken.

"What's up, Jim?"

"We got a ripe one Morg and I think she's a *personal* friend of yours; at least she *looks* like one of the stiffs, pardon the expression, you've been hanging with lately."

"You I.D. her yet?"

"Nope. Just got here.

The manager of this dump went into room 302 about 30 minutes ago and found her.

Seems one of his tenants complained about the smell coming from the room.

She's about 45, blonde, 5'8", maybe 175 lbs., although it's hard to tell 'cause she's so bloated. Sound like anyone you know or were looking to date?"

"Yeah." Morgan sighed. "Secure the scene, Jim. I'll phone Jen.

Ev and I will be there in ten minutes."

"Okay. I already called Jen, though. She should arrive about the same time you and Evan do."

The scene that greeted Morgan and Evan when they walked into room 302 at the Marx Hotel was straight out of a horror show. The woman on her back lying on the bed appeared to be morbidly obese…until Morgan and Evan looked closer.

"What the hell are all those dead spiders covering her body?"

"More specifically black widow spiders, boys. There must be over fifty of 'em, and from the looks of it they bit the hell out of her.

All I know is that somebody hated this woman a *lot* to do that to her."

"Thanks, Jim. We'll take it from here. Keep the press out of here and nobody up those stairs unless I give the okay."

Morgan and Evan surveyed the scene, waiting for Jen and her people to show up.

"There's the red sack and there's a Roman numeral VI shaved into the hair above her forehead." Evan noted. "Plus, there's a film over on the desk.

"You know, Ev, aside from the obvious reaction to the spider bites I don't see any other insults to her."

"How many more do you need?"

"No, I mean the other victims had multiple traumas. It's just curious, that's all."

"Maybe Jen will find other signs of attack when she does the post." Evan offered.

"Maybe."

Jen arrived five minutes later.

"Give us what you get ASAP. Ev and I are heading back to the Deuce. We'll be there until five or so."

"Will do. Don't know if you'd noticed it but that many spiders would *not* have been remained connected to the body unless they were somehow contained until they died."

"Yeah, we noticed." Evan said. "Jacko the Wacko probably put her in a box and then somehow poured the spiders in on top of her and slammed the lid shut."

"I think you're pretty close to right on that, Ev." Jen concurred. "From the number of bites that are visible, and most likely an equal amount that aren't, I'd say she went crazy and started flailing about. Then, when she *and* the spiders couldn't get away from one another the spiders went mad with fear and rage.

That would only have happened if she and the spiders were contained in very close proximity to one another."

"Unless the spiders were dumped on her, killed her, and then later when he had her in this room he spread the dead spiders, which he'd killed prior to coming here, all over her body." Morgan calmly observed.

"Possible, but I don't think so." Evan said. "I think Jen's right.

How's this for a scenario? Vindicator has a clear plastic container big enough to hold a body. He puts Aphrodite in it, she's probably unconscious at the time, waits for her to wake up, somehow puts the spiders in with her, and then the sick puke watches her die from fear and the massive amount of venom injected into her by the spiders.

How does that sound so far?"

"A bit scary, Ev." Morgan smiled and shook his head in amused disbelief. "Are you psychically wired to Vindicator or what? How did you come up with that based on what we've seen so far?"

"I'm starting to get into the creep's head, Morg. If it didn't go down that way it went down pretty close to it.

Only two things I can't figure. How did he get the spiders in with her? How did he kill the spiders in that box, because it's certain he wouldn't let them back out alive…not as p.o.'d as they would have been being locked up with Mama Berserk."

"I have an idea." Jen interjected. "What if the box had two chambers separated by a sliding panel and the spiders were allowed to crawl through a tube into one of the chambers. Then Aphrodite's unconscious body was placed in the other chamber."

"Now you're *both* starting to scare me." Morgan exclaimed. "Why a tube for the spiders?"

"Yeah, why?" Evan echoed.

"Because that's how he could kill the spiders without opening the box. He'd just pump poison into the tube and bingo, no more spider problem.

Besides, if Deliverance's finest were paying attention to the crime scene, they'd have smelled a faint trace of DDT on the clothing of the victim.

Oh, and I think Evan is right. Vindicator arranged it so that Aphrodite was conscious when the sliding panel was raised."

"Jen, could you run prints on the red sack and the items in it. I'd like to take them to the station and look at them right away."

"The film too, please." Evan said.

Jen nodded, saying she'd do the autopsy and blood work as soon as she got back to her office.

"What do you think, partner." Morgan asked. He and Evan had returned to the 2nd and were sitting in the incident room, the items from the red sack on the table."

"The film is self explanatory. She's seen being booked three times at the Deuce, for prostitution I'd guess.

The Roman numeral corresponds to *Thou shalt not commit adultery,* though I don't see where that ties in with Aphrodite right now.

"I imagine some of her clients were married men." Morgan offered.

"And, Vindicator blamed her for their committing adultery. Great!"

As to the picture of the infield at Yankee Stadium, the little toy hatchet, and the photo of the woman; I haven't a clue."

"The picture is a reproduction of an old photo." Morgan pointed out. "Looks to have been taken in the late 1800's or early 1900's."

"The woman in the picture appears to be rather young, slightly plump, and well dressed for the time. Not pretty, but not ugly either."

The phone rang out in the office and Fran called out that Jen was on the phone.

"Discounting the cattle prod burns, traces of duct tape, and some chloroform in her blood, the only other insults to her body were significant amounts of DDT in her blood and lungs, and the cryptogram branded on her abdomen."

"Thanks for getting back to us so soon, Jen." Morgan said. "What were the letters of the cryptogram?"

"TFOTSIDTTM. I called Sarah over at The Bureau and told her so she could start working on it."

"Again, thanks. It's always a pleasure to work with true professionals.

I'll call you later tonight to get any ideas you have."

"Right, Morgan. Talk to you later."

"The spiders were it, Ev." Morgan said back in the incident room.

"Maybe he's losing the stomach for gore."

"No, I think you and Jen were right. He got all the kicks he needed for now just watching her die. That had to be one gruesome scene, Ev.

No, I don't think he's running out of steam, maybe just refining the way he gets off on these killings.

"What say we call it a day and go back at it fresh tomorrow? I want to go over all the evidence again and visit the crime scenes again."

"I don't think three days straight of sleep would get me fresh enough to go back over our tracks *again.* But you're right. Somewhere there's a lead that will crack this case Sifting through the evidence again and again will be our best bet for finding that lead.

You want to interview witnesses and other people connected to the case again too?"

"Let's start with the physical evidence first, then the crime scenes. If nothing shakes out from that then we can start interviewing people."

"Okay, partner. I'm gone. See you tomorrow."

"Nine o'clock, Ev. I want to get an early start.

I'm going to call Chris and Jess, along with Jen and Sarah. We can use all the help we can get."

Eighty-Two

By nine-thirty Chris, Sarah, Jen, Morgan, and Evan were seated around the table in the incident room.

"I've asked you here this morning to help Evan and I brainstorm everything we know from the six murders and hopefully find a way to identify the maniac who's doing this." Morgan began.

"Chris, I'd appreciate it if you would lead the group. Your expertise in portraiting makes the two of you ideal choices."

Chris nodded and stood next to two marker boards on which all of the physical pieces of evidence had been recorded.

"To begin with, Jess sends her apologies. She's tied up with a murder case in Sacramento.

Second, I took the liberty, with Morgan's help, to come here early this morning to set up the boards you see next to me.

Now, I think we should look at the pieces of evidence left by Vindicator at each crime scene from the perspective of what they meant to *him*. Each of these items has a special significance to Vindicator. He left them to *instruct* us *and* the world on things he believes have been unjustly hidden from public view and judgment.

Vindicator knew the media would get hold of most of these *revelations,* as I'm sure he saw them, thus guaranteeing that the victims would be publicly exposed for the terrible crimes they've committed.

But, and it is here that I hope we will find a way to him, he also left pieces of himself when he chose those items.

As we look at the evidence we should realize that Vindicators personal environment will impact on those choices."

"Pardon?" Evan interrupted. "I don't quite follow you."

"I'm sorry Evan." Chris replied. "Jess keeps telling me to talk like a normal person instead of a computer program.

I have a tendency to say what my mind is processing and wind up being to be too clinical.

Some of the items Vindicator chose came from his physical surroundings."

"How do you know that?" Morgan asked.

"To put it simply, because they were handy. When you have a series of crimes as complex as these have been, the sheer number of clues left purposely by the perpetrator limits his ability to find them from outside his immediate environment.

Granted, Vindicator is meticulous. He is also exceedingly intelligent, resourceful, and methodical. He would therefore be careful to avoid leaving evidence that would be traceable to him.

But, we must remember that the driving force behind these murders is rage and the perverted need to find justice; rather I should say mete out justice.

And, that single-minded focus works to our advantage because it means that it opens wider the chance that Vindicator will slip up and miss noticing something he would otherwise see and avoid."

"You're saying that one or more of the red sack clues might have been a personal possession?"

"Yes, Sarah. Or, belonging to someone Vindicator came in contact with."

"But we would first hope to find something *he* owned because that would take us right to him."

"Right again, Evan. And, it doesn't necessarily have to be a *physical* piece of evidence.

All people tend to reveal facets of their personalities in the course of their day-to-day communication with others. They do this without being aware that they are.

Things like religious, political, and sexual preferences. Bias with respect to race and ethnicity are all areas where most people expose themselves, often without realizing that they have done so.

Disturbed personalities are no different. In fact they are *more* likely to reveal themselves because they are driven and can't help themselves.

To sum up, we need to look for pieces of Vindicator in this evidence. They *are* there; we just need to look hard enough and with the right pair of eyes, Vindicator's eyes."

Chris sat down and Morgan stood up.

"Let's start by looking at the red sack items first. Study the list and shout out if anything seems important."

"There are quite a few toys in the group." Jen said after thirty minutes. "The automobile, toy bird, stethoscope, the toy aborigine, model airplane, and the axe."

"Maybe he's a toy salesman, or works in a toy store." Morgan suggested.

"Good. That's what I was talking about." Chris said. "Who Vindicator is includes what he does, when he's not slaughtering people, that is."

"What about the picture of Joan of Arc, the thirty pieces of silver, and the bible?" Sarah said. "They seem to imply a religious connection."

"A *Catholic* religious connection." Evan declared. "That is a Navarre Bible, a Catholic bible. Plus the commandments Vindicator references in the Roman numerals he carves into the victim's hair are Catholic Commandments."

"And, some of the proverbs came from a bible." Sarah pointed out. "It could have been a Catholic bible.

By the way, the cryptogram on Aphrodite is *The Female Of The Species Is Deadlier Than The Male.* I figured it out when I realized that female black widows kill and eat their mates after sex."

The brainstorming discussion that Morgan favored when his people were trying to make sense out of diverse data went on for another hour.

"Okay, folks, that seems to be it." Morgan said. "Any other ideas or questions?

Then let's see what we have."

Morgan went to a third marker board which Fran had brought in when he called for her to do so.

Writing as he talked, Morgan transferred the notes he'd been taking during the discussion to the board.

"First, Vindicator is likely to be directly connected to the game and toy industry in some fashion, perhaps as a manufacturer, salesman, or owner.

Secondly, Vindicator is probably a Catholic; though how seriously he practices his faith is unknown.

Third, Vindicator is likely to be connected to the field of archaeology in some fashion, possibly as an amateur.

Fourth, Vindicator's physical description thus far is that he's about 6'5" tall, 230 to 240 lbs., blood type most likely B negative, and he limps.

Fifth, we can assume this man to be highly intelligent and well read. Also, he has most likely had some university training, possibly earned a degree. The complexity with which this entire affair has been carried out together with the various reference sources he's cited in his cryptograms testifies to all of that.

I would like to add a sixth observation to the list. Though I can't be sure, I believe Vindicator to be fairly wealthy, possibly independently so. The question is how does that knowledge help us?"

"If what you say *is* true his affluence will stick out like a sore thumb once you garner a list of suspects from the first five characteristics of our killer." Chris replied. "It may well isolate a solitary subject for you to pursue."

"Ladies and gentlemen, unless someone has something to add, I believe we'll call this meeting to a close." Morgan said, effectively ending the session.

***

"Well, that pretty much verifies the portrait we drew up for Byrd." Evan observed once he and Morgan were alone. "You know, I didn't think of it before but the fact that we discovered that Aphrodite was blackmailing her clients might be significant too."

"You mean how did Vindicator know that?" Morgan said, anticipating where Evan was going. "We know he did from that black envelope he left.

"Yeah. I suppose he could have read it in *Shine The Light,* which means we need to check that out. But what if he *was* one of those clients at one time?"

"Could be. Could also mean she was the victim that wronged him, the one that takes us right to his door."

"That's something else we didn't cover in today's meeting, Ev. Which of these victims is most likely to be the one that Vindicator *really* hated?"

"Well, the only other victim that didn't shake out was Brenda Hart. Vindicator made that one more personal with the teeth in the pubic hair, teeth freaking *bashed* out of her head. Not to mention the fact that she was the only one to rate two cryptograms."

"That's true. What about Gregg's relatives? For that matter, what about Nancy Bremer's or Janet Carroll's relatives?"

"It doesn't calculate for me, Morg. Those people might have resented Gregg, but before they would have gone after Gregg they would have iced Emlyn Morrison or his father. Since neither of those two Princes of Darkness have been murdered, I figure Gregg wasn't Vindicator's prime target."

"How do you know neither has been killed?"

Because I did a little checking on my own." The smile on Evans face broadened as he talked. "Emlyn is still in prison and he ain't ever gonna get out, unless fortune smiles on the world and one of his cell mates does him in for killing a thirteen year old girl. The father has since moved to Cincinnati and is retired to farm in a rural suburb."

"Very good, partner. I can't see any connection to Carr and we've already determined he most likely had no direct connection to Book.

That leaves Wynona Barnes.

"Again, she doesn't feel right to me. Her gossip is, for the most part, harmless, except for the guy who killed the other guy and we've already checked that avenue out.

"Alright, Ev. Your gut feelings have panned out more than once before.

Now, anything else before we go to lunch?'

"Well, the cufflink, play money, the broken piece of tile, and the concert ticket still haven't been accounted for."

"Hey, you two." Fran stuck her head in the room. "If either of you star sleuths is going out to buy and bring back lunch I'd like to make an order.

Oh, Ev. Your chess playing friend, Bill, called while you were guys were in conference to say he had to beg off tomorrow's chess game. Something about helping the priest over at your church."

"Father Stone; and it's William."

"Pardon?"

"William, Dusty. My friend's name is William."

"William, Bill, Billy, Liam. A rose by any other name, etcetera."

Fran walked back to her desk, content she'd dutifully relayed the message.

"Let's go get some lunch, Morg. My brain's feels like a fried egg sandwich that's been stepped on."

"Okay." Morgan couldn't hold back a chuckle. It was always comical when Evan went into his "Oh I'm so put upon!" routine.

"Since I bet I'll be paying for this how about you going over to the deli and grab three sandwiches and potato salad. Stop by Dusty's desk on your way out."

"I'll have you know I *have* money today and will be paying for the refreshments."

Evan left the room in a huff that Morgan didn't buy for a minute. Again he laughed and shook his head.

"Evan, what was the name of the Fallon's older son?" Morgan asked when Evan returned.

"Uh, I don't remember. Lenny or Lindsey. Something like that.

"Could it have been Liam?"

"Yeah, now that I think back on it that *is* what Roland Fallon said. Why?"

Morgan walked over to Evan and took the deli bag from his hands and put it on Dusty's desk.

"Take what you ordered and put the rest in the fridge. Evan and I will get to ours later. Evan, come into the incident room for a minute."

"Sit down a minute." The tone in Morgan's voice alarmed Evan.

"Morg? What's wrong?"

"Evan I want you to wait until I'm through talking before you react."

"Sure, Morg, but you're starting to freak me out."

For some time now I've had a thought in the back of my mind, but I didn't want to say anything until I was pretty certain I was right.

Something Dusty said a few minutes ago gave me that certainty. Again, I ask you to hold your tongue until I've finished.

Liam is one nickname for William, as Dusty pointed out.

Liam was the Fallon's older son's name, and he would have had a great reason to hate Brenda Hart. He already felt bad enough that his brother Rembrandt got injured in an automobile he was driving. When the operation to repair those injuries went bad and eventually led to his brother's suicide, Liam would have been inconsolable. I can see where he would have harbored a grudge against her for years.

Then, when he got hold of a copy of *Shine The Light* and began reading about other people who weren't being held responsible for their crimes, it wouldn't be a great leap for him to decide *he* should personally hold them accountable.

And, that is when this nightmare began."

Morgan paused, waiting to see what Evan might say.

"Morgan, I know you're getting at something but I don't know what."

This is going to be harder than I hoped it would be. Morgan thought sadly. *His loyalty won't let him see even the **possibility** of where I'm headed.*

"I'm afraid you will, all too soon partner, and for that I'm truly sorry.

We know, among other things, that Vindicator limps, is probably Catholic, wealthy, educated, has an interest in digging for ancient artifacts, and probably has a secluded place to carry out his atrocities."

Again Morgan paused, hoping Evan would say something, but Evan merely greeted him with a quizzical look.

"You asked about the cufflink, play money, and broken piece of tile. I can't yet say about the tile, but the cufflink *could* be a chess piece from a training set like JoAnne suggested. The play money *could* come from a game, say.

What I'm going to say now is going to shock you, Ev, but I want you to understand that I wouldn't say it unless I was pretty sure.

Your friend, William Kane, fits everything I've just said to a T.

Plus, if I'm right he's changed his name from Fallon to Kane. You remember the old bible story about Cain and Abel? Cain slew Abel just as Liam Fallon believes he was responsible for the death of his brother Rembrandt."

"William sometimes talks about his brother." Evan said suddenly and quietly, and Morgan held his breath, concerned for what his friend was about to have to face.

"When he does, he calls him Remy. I know where this is going now, Morg.

To tell the truth the thought crossed my mind too, but I just can't see William as a murderer."

"If we *are* right then in *his* mind he isn't." Morgan said sympathetically. "*Vindicator* sees what he does as a holy quest. That's why we've gotten the commandments and proverbs, as well as the bible and the picture of Joan of Arc.

It's *Vindicator* who's killing these people, not the William you know.

Chris was right. I'll lay odds those two articles belong to William."

"Jeez, Morg, remember when we played that game at Jen's house? William's *Murder Weekend* mystery game? One of the props was a packet of play money."

"That's right! And, I have a feeling Mr. Kane has a small chess set with a piece missing."

"Well, we have enough to bring him in for questioning. He lives in Burning Oaks."

"Did you say Burning Oaks? That's where Brenda Hart lived.

Maybe our boy wanted to be near the woman who he thinks helped to kill his brother."

"I slipped up there." Evan said. "I should've made that connection a long time ago."

"Don't beat up on yourself, Ev. It's like you said. Sometimes you don't see a tree because the forest gets in the way.

And, you had a friend's blinders on, which made it harder to see William as a killer.

One thing, though. We go into this assuming William is innocent until we get something conclusive."

"Thanks, partner. If somehow William *is* innocent and we've dropped the other leads to focus on him, we'll look pretty stupid if the real killer gets away.

I say we take our sandwiches and sodas, drive over to his house and stake it out. It's Friday which means wherever he's at he'll show up at home around five because tonight he's hosting a party of business muckity mucks; something about a charity bazaar.

He was talking about it the other night when we were at a Sam Cooke concert."

"That's another possible link. Remember, we found a ticket stub to a concert for the Portland Symphony Orchestra? Does William like classical music?"

"Afraid so. It doesn't look good, Morg."

"No, but if it is William, the sooner we get him the quicker we can get him some help and the sooner these deaths will stop.

Look, you grab the lunches from Fran while I phone Judge Harper to get a warrant to search William's house. We got enough to justify one, plus Allen Harper is a friend of mine. We'll pick it up on the way and eat lunch in the car."

After talking to Judge Harper, Morgan met Evan outside and the detectives began the twenty minute drive to William Kane's home.

EIGHTY-THREE

William Kane's home sat back about 200 feet from the road. It was only two blocks from Brenda Hart's house and was substantially more modest than her home.

"Seems kinda small for this subdivision." Morgan noted as they drove up.

"Wait until you get closer and you'll see why it belongs here. It's the Cape Cod to end all Cape Cods. Everything is top drawer and he's got that place packed full of all the latest gadgets. A year ago William had a realtor appraise it. The guy said William could easily get $600,000 for the place."

"Let's park across the street and two doors down."

"When he gets here, let me knock on the door." Evan said. "It'll make getting in the house easier."

Five o'clock came and went and William did not show up. At 6:30 Evan suggested they give him another half hour and then check the house.

"Unless I've got the day wrong, his party is supposed to start in thirty minutes. I don't know what's happened but I got a feeling he's not gonna show."

"Agreed. Thirty minutes and we take a can opener to the box."

At seven-fifteen the two detectives left their vehicle and walked up the drive.

"Hey, Morg." Evan called out, drawing his revolver. "The front door is ajar."

"Careful, now Ev." Morgan said, following suit. "We don't know what's going on here and I do *not* want to walk into a trap."

Cautiously, Morgan approached the front door visually sweeping the 180 degrees in front of him, while Evan backpedaled beside him covering the 180 degrees to their rear.

Morgan used the barrel of his weapon to inch open the front door, signaling Evan to cover him as he went through first. Then he moved quickly through and to the left, crouching and raising his .357 as he did. Evan followed, moving to his right and crouching while Morgan covered *him*.

There was still enough sunlight to be able to make out the living room and the doorway to the kitchen off to the left, and the dining room to the right with a hallway leading off of it.

Stairs leading to the second floor were straight ahead.

"Doesn't look like anyone's home, Morg. I say we toss the place. Maybe we'll find something that will clinch the case."

"Check. You take the second floor; I'll button up the first. If you find anything holler, otherwise meet me back here in five.

And, Evan; be damn careful. If William is our man we're dealing with a person who will kill without batting an eyelash."

"I read you, old man. Same to you."

Morgan walked into the living room while eyeing the dining room.

Don't want someone taking me from behind.

The kitchen was larger than Morgan would have thought

considering how small the home looked from the driveway. There was a large island in the center, a huge Sub-zero refrigerator on one side of its long side and a built-in Bosch double oven on the other.

Everything was the best of what was available and *very* expensive.

Morgan had noticed that the same was true of the furnishings in the living room and suspected the rest of the house was similarly furnished.

Evan was right. This home is deceptive looking from the outside. It must run deeper than I thought.

There was a small pantry off the back corner of the kitchen with a rear entrance opening out to a wooded yard.

As with the living room, nothing of interest was discovered in the kitchen or the pantry. Morgan looked out the rear entrance window, but there was nothing to be seen.

He was retracing his steps toward the dining room when Evan called out from the second floor.

"You'd better come up here Morg."

"What've you got, Ev?"

"The silver bullet or bullets I should say. Take a look."

Spread out on the bed were several items.

"It's all here, Morg. Duct tape, a bottle of chloroform, the cattle prod. He had it in a cardboard box in the back of that closet over there.

I guess that changes everything. Now we find him, arrest him and get the D.A. to indict him."

"Let's clear the rest of the house, including the garage and basement. Then, if he hasn't shown up by then we'll get the lab rats out here to sweep the place clean, and set up an around the clock stakeout van in case he shows up while the lab rats are here."

"Or any time after. We should impound his vehicles too, and get the forensic team over to his office building in Portland."

William still had not arrived by 9:30 so Morgan made the call to the coroner's office and asked Evan to remain at the house until the forensics team showed up.

"I'll go back to the Deuce, set up the stakeout, and get William's vehicles impounded. Be sure to tell the lab guys to sweep William's office too."

"Right, and if he shows while I'm here I'll bring him in for questioning."

"I'm truly sorry about this, Ev. Maybe somehow this is all a big mistake."

"It isn't and you know it, Morg.

Don't worry, William Kane, or whatever his name is, is the guy who's done all of this and regardless of why he did it or what our relationship was, he's going down and I won't hesitate to be the one to do it."

EIGHTY-FOUR

William Kane could not be found. Everywhere that he might have been turned up blank. It had been three days and Morgan was becoming more and more agitated.

"We better to find this guy *soon* or we're gonna have another body on our hands."

"Cool your jets, partner. We'll get him."

"Ev, you know William better than anyone else. What do you think happened to him?"

"Well, we know from talking to his people that he hasn't taken any vacation time or gone on a business trip. He hasn't been playing chess at the church either.

My best guess? He felt we were getting to close to him and he closed up shop. He's gone, Morg and he's rich enough to pull up stakes here and put them down anywhere else in the world. Or maybe Aphrodite was the last name on his guest list and his mission is completed, although that's about as likely as the Pope being Protestant. That's *my* take anyway."

"There's another possibility. He's not through killing, just moving to a new location."

Morgan and Evan spent the day calling everyone who might know where William could be.

Evan checked the airports and train stations, but no one answering to William's description had booked a reservation.

"Well, that's it. We've gone as far as we can. Nobody knows anything.

Damn, Evan, he can't just drop off the face of the earth."

"He doesn't need to if he can find a safe place where he can go to ground for awhile.

Hell, he's rich enough, maybe he bought The Fortress of Solitude from Superman.

Nah, I still think he's bolted.

Unless…Morg, I just remembered. William once told me of a cabin he owns somewhere southwest of Portland. I've never been there but it's just off of Henry Hagg Lake."

"Tell me it's in the woods." Morgan said hopefully.

"As I recall, William said you have to take a dirt road a couple of miles into the woods to reach the cabin."

"That's only a few miles away from Forest Grove.

Alright. You look up a realtor in Forest Grove and see if William's property is registered. If it is, get the address. I'll call Judge Harper and get another warrant to search the cabin."

"Check. Before we leave remind me to check a 12 gauge out of the weapons department, along with some double aught buck."

Morgan nodded knowingly.

That's my boy.

EIGHTY-FIVE

Henry Hagg Lake is located 20 miles west of Deliverance. Most of the surrounding 60 acres is pristine wilderness, but there a few home sites scattered throughout the area.

William's cabin was 3 miles from a small agricultural research center aptly named Earth Friendly One. The cabin sat back from the lake about 100 feet and was completely hidden by the dense Douglas-fir trees.

Evan had remembered correctly. The cabin was accessed via a one lane dirt and clay road.

Morgan pulled over as soon as Evan spotted the cabin through the trees.

"I don't want to alert him that we're coming…if he's in there. We'll go on foot from here."

The two men exited the vehicle and began slowly moving toward the cabin.

Evan jacked four rounds into the Remington pump as they walked, a look on his face that made Morgan glad he wasn't the object of his partner's focus.

Moving in from the left side Morgan drew his .357 and signaled Evan to hold his position and cover him while he approached a window to the left of the front door.

Evan dropped to one knee, switched the shotgun for his .357 and leveled the weapon on the door, while alternating his gaze between the window and the door.

Morgan crouched under the window and slowly rose up at the left corner.

Peering in he saw what appeared to be a living room adjacent to a small kitchen. The cabin was spartanly furnished and the rooms looked to be empty.

Pivoting 180 degrees as he reached the right corner of the window, Morgan could see a doorway leading off from the kitchen. He signaled for Evan to join him and covered his partner until Evan was beside him under the window.

"This cabin is a lot smaller than I would have thought William would own." Evan remarked.

"I don't think he bought it for comfort, Ev. I don't think he bought it to live in at all.

Unless I'm mistaken, this is his home base. He immobilizes and sedates his victims then brings them here to finish them off.

I'm betting there's a basement and that's where he takes them."

"This could get really bad, Morg. You got your backup?"

"No, we rushed out and I forgot it. I'll be okay."

"Take this." Evan said handing his revolver to Morgan. "I've got the widow maker here and a .38 with jacketed hollow points strapped to my ankle."

Morgan took the .357 and placed it in his shoulder holster, nodding his head in agreement.

"We don't knock on this one, Ev. I'll go in first and flank left, you go in to the right. If we come on him and he threatens either of us in any way we take him out."

"I'm with you there, partner. Let's go."

Morgan moved to the door handle while Evan positioned himself just behind him.

The door was unlocked and Morgan glanced back at Evan with raised eyebrows. Evan merely shrugged his shoulders. Morgan pushed the door open and slid left, his weapon pointed towards the kitchen. Evan moved in quickly and slid right, the shotgun leveled at the living room. The two detectives stood motionless, listening intently for a full minute. Then Morgan signaled Evan to follow him through the small kitchen and down the hallway where, it turned out, there were two small bedrooms. Both were empty.

The men retraced their steps and searched the kitchen and living room. Again, nothing of interest was found.

"That leaves the basement. I'll go down first." Evan said.

"Damn! Light switch doesn't work and it's a black hole down there." Evan turned on the flashlight he'd taped to the barrel of the shotgun and started down the stairs to the basement.

Morgan followed closely behind, his own flashlight illuminating areas Evan's didn't.

The basement was large, fanning out under the entire cabin. A door on one end promised yet another room. Morgan thought it strange because most cabins didn't have a basement at all.

The better to mutilate you without interruption my dears. This is one sick puppy.

"Hey there's a fluorescent light here." Evan said and a cool glow filled the room. Then, looking where Morgan was staring and seeing the door, he added.

"You thinking what I'm thing?'

"If you're thinking that we may have found Vindicator's killing room, then yes."

Morgan stood on one side of the door, Evan on the other. Evan nudged the door open with the barrel of the shotgun and the two men flashed their lights in.

Morgan tripped a switch, illuminating the room.

It was relatively small but it took only a glance to see that it was indeed a place that had seen unspeakable horror.

In the center was a large metal autopsy table outfitted with an array of metal clamps. Over it was a bank of fluorescent lights.

Against one wall was a large desk, made of rough wood. On top were various instruments; knives, chisels, hammers, pliers, and a set of heavy charcoal tongs. A chain saw hung from a large hook and an 18 inch threaded hollow steel pipe with a bolt screwed into one end.

Evan found rolls of duct tape and a bottle of chloroform in one of the drawers, along with several strips of cloth. In two other drawers he found several cast iron letters with holes drilled into them. In the lower right drawer he found a sheet of paper that caused his eyes to widen.

"Look at this, Morg. It's his list of victims. Seven names in all and the last is a Rachel Diamond."

"Then he *did* plan to end this. Question is *could* he have stopped."

Finally, in a far corner was a large coal burning stove vented to the outside.

"Now we know how the bastard brands them." Morgan remarked stonily.

"Jesus, Morg this place is straight out Madam Tussauds' chamber of horrors."

"After we catch this guy and news gets out to the world what he did, Madam Tussauds' Wax Museum in London will probably put him in it."

"The table is where he immobilizes them. Look at the number of restraints connected to it. He could shut the poor souls down so they could only move their eyeballs."

"I'll bet we find a method for shutting that down too, somewhere around here."

"What now, Morg, aside from getting forensics out here to roll this place."

"A second stakeout, this time you and me. If he comes back here I want us to be the ones he runs into.

Forget about phys ev for now. We go back to the car, pull it further into the underbrush and wait."

"Whoa! What about food? This could take awhile, if ever."

"Not to worry. I've got two bags of beef jerky and a big can of cashews in the trunk for just such an occasion. Plus, I noticed sodas, lunchmeat and bread in the fridge. I'm sure William won't mind. Now, hit the head and get ready to hunker down."

Morgan and Evan quickly used the bathroom, scooped up some food from the refrigerator and, after checking to see that they left everything as they had found it, walked back to the car and settled in for a possibly long surveillance.

***

"I'm glad we brought our jackets. It's gonna get down to 45 by tonight."

Evan was munching on a piece of beef jerky and drinking a 7-UP.

Morgan, putting down the binoculars, looked at his partner and smiled.

"Evan, it's only August and it's two hours to sunset."

"August *23rd* and that's almost September, and *that's* fall. In case you hadn't noticed it gets pretty cold up here in the fall. Deliverance ain't exactly located in the tropical zone you know."

"Which reminds me. Roger hit number 50 yesterday."

"Yeah, yeah. Mickey's a strong finisher. In September he'll pull away from that imposter and beat the Babe's record too."

Morgan laughed and went back to the binoculars.

By five p.m. Evan was starting to get restless.

"I don't think he's coming, Morg."

"30 minutes more, Ev. My gut says he'll be here.

Hold it. Here comes a vehicle."

Evan tensed, craning his neck to see the road through the foliage.

Sure enough, a car was slowly moving toward the cabin.

"I'll be damned!" Morgan exclaimed. "It's a station wagon, light colored too."

The wagon passed their position and, as it did, Morgan and Evan eased out of their vehicle and began paralleling it, staying out of sight, and noting the two people in the front seat.

"Easy now, Ev. Let them get stopped and out of the vehicle before we move in. I don't know who's in that wagon, but if it's William and Rachel Diamond I want him separated from her. The last thing we need is a hostage situation.

"Check. I'll take the driver's side, Morg; you cover the passenger." Evan whispered, bringing the shotgun to bear on the driver's side as he moved obliquely to the left of the wagon.

Meanwhile, Morgan angled right until he was slightly behind and opposite the passenger's door.

The vehicle stopped in the clearing just in front of the cabin. No movement was detected from inside.

Evan was now kneeling ten feet behind and 30 degrees off the left rear fender.

Morgan was in a similar position on the right side of the vehicle.

Both men were positioned so they could see the rear door as well as the side doors.

Come on man, ***do*** *something.* Evan's finger slipped inside the trigger guard. He *knew* who was sitting in the driver's seat; *felt* it.

As if in response to Evan's mental urging the driver's side door opened slowly and a foot emerged.

Evan signaled Morgan with an upraised index finger that swiveled downward to point at the driver's door. Then he came to a standing crouch and leveled the shotgun at the point the person inside the car was exiting.

Morgan froze at the sight of Evan's finger pointing, then instantly copied his partner's movements and approached the passenger side.

William stepped out of the car, his back to Evan and his view of Morgan blocked by the station wagon.

On Morgan's side there was no movement. The figure inside the vehicle remained motionless.

Suddenly, Morgan noticed it tilt slightly toward the door and he readied himself for whoever came out of that door. But instead of opening the door, the figure slumped against it and in a blinding flash of comprehension hit Morgan realized why.

Unconscious! Whoever's in there is unconscious.

"Freeze, Kane!" Morgan cried out, raising up and centering his pistol on the big man's back.

Instantly reacting to Morgan's voice, Evan straightened up and slid to his left, the shotgun also leveled at William's back.

"He means it William. You're in both of our sights and at this range double aught buck makes a nasty mess."

William slowly turned, raising his hands as he did.

"Well, the ace detective and his faithful lap dog have *finally* tracked me down. I must say you were certainly plodding in your efforts. Still, it's been a good run and I can't complain. There are six maggots that will never hurt anyone again."

"Shut up, William. You make me sick." Evan was trembling, he was so angry. "Morg, what about the other person…go ahead, William, make my day."

"Steady, Ev. He isn't going anywhere. I think it's Rachel Diamond and she appears to be unconscious. I'll check on her; you keep an eye on William."

Morgan moved to the door and carefully opened it, allowing the limp body of a girl to fall over into his arms. He lifted her and headed for the cabin.

"So you figured out the riddle of the baseball diamond already. Clever."

Then noticing the look on Evan's face,

"Oh, I see. Been having a walk around my cabin, have you?"

"Now, William, I want you to move away from the car verrry slowly. I'm gonna pat you down and if you even hiccup my partner there will be happy to put six in your miserable carcass after which I will *personally* finish you with this."

Morgan eased Rachel back up onto the seat and pointed his .357 at William's chest. The look on his face said movement would bring swift and certain death.

"Now, we're going to walk over to the cabin and when we get inside you are going to sit down in the leather chair in the living room and be absolutely still. Otherwise Mr. Remington is going to become extremely upset and we all know what Mr. Remington is capable of when he loses it."

"Sarcasm doesn't really suit you, Evan. You have neither the temperament nor the intellect for it. However, I'll accede to your demands. For now."

William entered the cabin and sat where Evan had instructed him to, folding his hands and closing his eyes when he was seated.

"How's she doing, Morg?"

"Looks like he just tapped her on the head with something." Morgan replied from the kitchen where he was standing next to Rachel Diamond, whom he'd gotten seated in a chair, her head on the table. "She's coming around. She'll be alright as soon as we get her to a hospital and notify her parents.

Damn you to hell, Kane. She can't be more than seventeen. What the hell could a child like this have to done to warrant your insanity?"

"Sixteen actually, and that child, as you call her, has no parents because she took an axe to them. Trouble is, the law took one look at that baby face and decided her story that an intruder had killed them had to be true because an angel like her couldn't *possibly* have murdered her parents, especially in such a grisly fashion. Didn't really even try to check her story out."

As William was talking, neither Morgan nor Evan noticed his left hand was no longer in his lap but was instead draped over the outside of the chair arm.

In one swift motion he dropped his arm down, and then brought it up again, a small gun in his hand, which he fired while simultaneously erupting from the chair.

"Sonofabitch!" Evan roared, turning the shotgun towards William, but before he could pull the trigger William brought a huge forearm against the side of his head and Evan went down, stunned and struggling to maintain consciousness.

When he had regained his senses, Evan staggered to his feet and looked around.

William was gone. He glanced over to where Morgan was still tending to Rachel Diamond.

"Sorry, Morg. I wasn't paying attention. That damn…what the hell!"

Morgan was sitting in a kitchen chair, his left hand on the table, his right hand on his chest. Blood was seeping out from around and through his fingers."

"Oh, shit!" Evan ran to his side, fear and shock etched into his face.

"Whoa, partner." Morgan said with difficulty, his voice strangely distant. "Bastard got off a lucky shot. I forgot to duck."

He slid from the chair to a sitting position on the floor of the cabin.

"Let me see, Morg. Oh, boy. I got to get you to a hospital."

"I think he used hollow points, Ev. Feels like somebody took a can opener to me. You're gonna have to take the lead on this one, partner. I think I'm going to pass out.

Get Rachel out of here *now*. We'll worry about Kane later."

"No, Morg. You stay with me now. I'm gonna get you out of here. Stay with me, Morg."

"Careful as you go, partner. He may be outside waiting for…"

"Morg? Godammit, don't you leave me!

Morgan? ***Morgan!***"

Morgan could hear Evan's voice and wondered why he was so upset. They had caught Vindicator and everything was going to be alright. It was so peaceful now that he knew it was going to be alright.

Oh, my! Is that you Senna? God, I've missed you honey.

Morgan Jeffords, his eyes closed and his body slumping into the arms of his friend, sighed deeply and surrendered to the blackness.

I'm almost home Senna. Almost home.

Eighty-Six

Rachel Diamond made a complete recovery, the lone survivor of the nightmare that had been visited upon so many people.

William Kane was never caught. It seemed he'd disappeared into thin air. Six months later all leads dried up.

The theory that he'd fled into Canada was supported by the discovery of his gray 1958 Ford Country Sedan abandoned just north of the border in a town called Surrey.

For over ten years an active investigation into his whereabouts was conducted by the Portland F.B.I., but he was never seen again.

As it turned out William had a two shot .38 caliber derringer concealed in a pop open chamber on the side of his chair. Neither Morgan nor Evan had discovered it when they had searched the cabin because the outline the compartment's cover blended into the brads and seams of the chair.

Morgan had been right about one thing. The bullets *were* hollow points.

Morgan's funeral found people from all over the area attending in great number.

As Morgan had requested, the service was simple and he was laid to rest in the same plot as Senna and Lauren had been. Morgan was beneath them at his request.

"Senna always was clearly the better person, she should get top billing." He'd said on a number of occasions.

Bud and JoAnne were crushed. Morgan had been a son to them and when a child precedes his parents in death it shakes their faith in he order of things.

"He was the best partner a man could have asked for—the best of what's good in all of us."Bud said at the service. Later he remarked that he'd wanted to say more but the words had stuck in his throat.

"Morgan would have wanted to know why I was just standing there looking silly and I wouldn't have been able to tell him why. So I just left the pulpit and sat down."

Evan had the hardest job. He had been asked by Captain Byrd to give the eulogy.

"Coming here today I tried to think what I could say that would do justice to the honor that Morg deserved. I wracked my brain but I soon realized that none of the words in the English language could adequately describe how great he was.

I walked up to the pulpit just now still not knowing what to say and terrified I wouldn't honor this man the way he should be.

Then I looked out at all of you and suddenly God showed me the way.

Words aren't the answer, you are. The people who loved Morg and who have come here today to celebrate the wonderful friend he was are the only true testament to how fantastic he was. I look out at this gathering and I see scores of people that *I* know to be respected and admired for their values, ethics caring ways, and morals.

People like Jennifer Lime who is considered to be one of the best M.E.s in the state and who helped Morg dull the terrible pain he suffered when his wife and child were killed.

People like Captain Harold Byrd, whose men would go through fire for him and who is the role model we all need to keep us on track to be the best cops we can be, though he'd deny that he's anything more than an old man doing his job until he can retire.

People like Fran Hull, I mean *Dusty* as Morg affectionately tagged her, who makes the guys feel good because she's drop-dead gorgeous *and* understanding, especially with the younger men. I can personally attest to the multitude of times her good humor and sweet but firm ways have pulled me out of a bad mood.

People like Bud and JoAnne Oslen.

I don't have to tell anyone here about Bud's qualifications as a cop *or* as a man; he's a legend in Deliverance and in Portland.

Morgan saw JoAnne as the mother he needed after he lost his mother and several of the cops at the Deuce feel the same.

I could name several others like Dave and Linda Ways or Max Herrick, people whose credentials are well known, but I can already feel Morgan telling me I need to hurry this along and blushing in embarrassment.

So, let me end by making a simple observation.

If people who are greatly admired and respected by all of *us* have come here today because *they* greatly respect, admire, and love Morgan, then *that* is the best possible testament to Morgan's worth as a human being."

Evan slowly made his way back to his pew and sat down, his lip quivering as he fought back the tears.

The church was dead silent for a full minute. Evan's moving eulogy had touched his friends deeply and they were momentarily frozen as they reflected on what he'd said.

The trip to the cemetery was duly solemn but the sun was out and shining and the sounds of the birds and small animals along the tree lined road to the grave site reminded the mourners that Morgan had loved animals and the thought gave them reason to smile.

The pastor's words were brief but poignant.

"Morgan is anxious to be on his way to everlasting life with Senna and Lauren so I'll say simply:

Thank you Lord for having allowed us to know this good man. Thank you for giving us the opportunity to rejoice in being part of his exemplary life.

We ask that you remind us of him when we are in need of guidance in our own lives.

Morgan, you have been a good friend and comrade. We will think of you often and your memory will never leave our hearts.

EIGHTY-SEVEN

Two weeks after Morgan's funeral, Jennifer Lime turned in her resignation. She had decided to return to her native England, where familiar surroundings and the comfort of her parents would help her to grieve and to start life anew.

Harold Byrd finally retired six months later.

"I stayed too long." He would often say, sadly. "I just grew tired of seeing good men taken from me and not be able to do a damn thing about it."

Dave and Linda Ways put a picture of Morgan above the bar in *The Steakout* similar to the one they had put above the bar in *Frank's Pub*. A small plaque below it said:

Morgan Jeffords

Friend and Brother

The sparkle so often seen in the eyes of Bud and JoAnne dimmed noticeably.

Frances Hull married a man she met in Portland and they moved to Batavia, IL when his company relocated him eight months after the funeral. She stopped using Frances as her name and asked people to please call her Dusty.

Morgan's death hit Evan the hardest. He stayed to himself, refused to take a new partner and, in general, was just going through the motions. A year after Morgan died he left the force and Deliverance for good.

No one knew where he went, not even Sarah who remained his only contact until he left town.

"You can't take life for granted." Morgan had once told Evan. "Each day brings the possibility of forces that will irrevocably change who you are and what your future will be.

So, cherish the day you're in and the people who are in it with you because in a flash it can all be gone."

Evan knew all too well how prophetic his words had turned out to be.

Epilogue

The weathered looking man sat in his five year old black 1968 Ford Mustang, humming a familiar tune and reading a sports magazine. He was rather scraggly with a three day old beard, unkempt blond hair, and rumpled clothes.

Someone guessing his age would have said he looked every minute of 60. In reality he was just a week shy of his 41st birthday, mute testimony to years of hard living punctuated by bouts of excessive drinking.

Occasionally he glanced up at the small, plain looking house across and 40 feet down the street from where he had parked.

It was going on seven p.m. and the cloudless sky foretold a starlit wonderment when the sun finally bowed out for the day.

The man had come far to find this house in Leduc, a small town south of Edmonton, Canada, the last leg in a journey that had begun what seemed like a thousand years ago.

Every half hour or so the man would glance at his watch and stare blankly into space, as if gauging how much time he had until some future event would take place.

At nine he glanced once again at his watch, set his mouth, by which it seemed he had conclusively decided a course of action, and exited the vehicle.

He walked slowly across the road, scanning his surroundings quickly while making his way to the rear of the house where he let himself inside via the kitchen.

The man had already known the house would be accessible through this particular window because he had jimmied the lock three days before so that while it would appear locked to someone inside the house, the latch could be slipped from the outside with a pen knife.

He moved through the kitchen and headed for the basement, sure of his movements because he had been in the house before when he'd come to pry open the window lock.

Once down in the basement he secreted himself behind a large cupboard and settled in to wait.

If I've scoped this guy out right, he should be home soon. Then it's just a matter of being patient until he comes down here.

Some twenty minutes passed before the man heard movement coming from upstairs. He steeled himself and waited for the shaft of light that would signal the arrival of the object of his journey.

The owner of the house took a full hour before descending into the basement. He walked over to a cabinet, opened it and took out a small surgical scalpel. Fingering it, almost lovingly, he turned.

The intruder stepped out of the shadows and blocked the other man's way.

A very large bore pistol was in his right hand and it was leveled at the man's midsection.

"Did you think I'd forget, William?" He said his voice a black hole that sucked the air out of the room.

"No, but I'd heard you'd fallen on hard times." William replied calmly, noticing with interest the silencer on the .45. "From the description I received of your physical and mental condition I thought it unlikely you'd ever track me down.

How *did* you find me, Evan?"

"Dumb luck and *need*. I'd tell you the particulars but we really don't have the time."

"Ah, well, it's been a good run anyway. The only question now is where do we go from here?"

"Go? *We* don't *go* anywhere. I've spent the better part of twelve years thinking of nothing but this day. It all ends here William. I don't give a damn about what's right according to the law. I don't care if you did what you did because of something terrible that happened to you as a kid. All I've been able to see for twelve years is me holding my best friend and partner while his life poured out onto the floor."

"Yes, well I know *you'll* believe me if I say I understand completely why you would harbor a grudge against me.

Then you're not here to arrest me."

"No. I'm here to kill you."

Evan's face was a granite block as he pulled the trigger.

William flew backward and went down instantly. He was clearly dead but Evan approached him, stood over the lifeless body and calmly emptied the clip into it.

Evan stood still for several moments staring down at the man who'd torn his life apart, then turned and climbed the stairs.

He left the house and returned to his car, placing the empty .45 next to him on the passenger seat. As he pulled away and drove down the street, a faint smile flitted across his face.

William was right about one thing. Some people just flat out needed killing, and who better to take that responsibility than a homicide cop.

It's fortunate that Manhattan needed a detective five years ago, and I needed a job.

***

Six months after the incident in the basement of that house in Canada, Detective Evan Flack was killed in the line of duty. The official report was that Flack had cornered and killed a known drug lord in the back room of the man's nightclub on West 59th street. The man supposedly resisted arrest and in the ensuing struggle Detective Flack was stabbed several times. He later died from his wounds.

As far as it went the report was accurate. What was left out of the report was the fact that Internal Affairs had been investigating Detective Flack for several weeks in connection with a series of seemingly unrelated murders in lower Manhattan.

The Manhattan police department was convinced the murders were the work of a serial killer that had been operating in the borough for over a year and they suspected Flack was involved. Each of the victims had been suspected of committing a serious crime for which they had never been charged or convicted.

Internal Affairs was close to pulling Detective Flack in for questioning when he was killed. The investigation was quietly dropped by order of the police commissioner, and never came to light. Evan, who had been a loner with few friends and no known family, was quickly buried and forgotten.

A small gravestone bearing his name and dates of birth and death marks Evan Flack's resting place in Park West Cemetery in Manhattan.

William Kane's madness had claimed its final victim.